The more elaborate his labyrinths, the further from the sun his face.

The Book of Mirdad, Mikhail Naimy

Chapters

1 | Dom

I

Dom Tolen was at his desk, pretending to be a claims assessor for Subiaco Insurance. His shoulders hunched as he took in the details of the client file. If he looked immersed in his case notes, colleagues usually left him alone. So he had been parked like that for some time.

He lifted his head, exhaled noisily and wheeled himself backwards to the window.

A low sun struggled to light the city sky and bunches of dark clouds lingered as though waiting for him to step outside to catch him for a drenching.

The Subiaco building where he worked was a clean, glass tower helping modernise one of the drearier parts of Sydney's business district. Through the thickest of glass, he looked down to Clarence Street sixteen floors below, its muffled goings-on of traffic flowing, people wrapped in jackets hurrying, and litter and leaves skipping.

Dom noticed the tops of people's heads. There were no umbrellas up yet.

He looked over at his lunchtime purchase, slipped under his desk, and decided it was a good time to leave. He could miss the worst of the crowds.

'I'm off', he said to nobody. Throwing on his suit jacket, he surveyed his desk for what to take for the trip home. Not the thick novel and not his earplugs—he didn't feel like reading or listening to music. A quiet journey—just him and the puzzle. He promised to get back into the boxer's autobiography later in the week, snatched the jigsaw from under his desk and left.

His mobile beeped. Dom's lips stiffened. He'd bet money it was Donald with another maddening text about his ludicrous idea.

Dom's certainty about this came less from some inexplicable bond he shared with his identical twin, and more from Donald having bugged him with his request, with increasing frequency, for a couple of weeks. Dom confirmed only that the message was from Donald, and rammed the phone back into his pocket.

'I'll kill him,' he mumbled.

He slipped away to the reception area but slowed his pace at the unexpected swarm of people congregating for the lifts. Wayne, a regional director, was seeing some clients out, his trademark seriousness plastered on his drawn face. The three women he was accompanying shook his hand and filed through the lift doors.

And there was Maggie talking to Ian, another regional director. She was dressed to leave, her brown coat buttoned over her tall frame, a huge cherry-leather bag on one shoulder and a tartan umbrella in her hand. Ian stood between her and the lifts, oblivious to her signals of wanting to go. He didn't register the umbrella twirling in her hands and he missed her glimpse at the lift buttons. For sure, Ian believed he was in the middle of an important point.

When Dom saw Ian's head turn his way, he hurled himself towards the reception desk, hoping to appear busy.

Dom smiled at the young woman sitting at one end of the long front desk. He leaned in. 'Don't forget to go home.'

Belinda flashed white teeth and rosy lips. She brandished a letter opener. 'No chance. Bring in that documentary you promised me. I've been waiting ages'—the letter opener brushed at his neck—'or you won't see your fortieth.'

The lift bell chimed and Dom ran towards it, keeping his head down and slinking his way to the back of the lift. The doors started gliding together and he heard his name being called. A hand stopped the lift doors closing. Then a head of curly grey hair appeared. Ian. The intruder propped a foot against the door.

'Can we chat with you, Dom? It won't take long.' Looming in the narrow entrance, Ian appeared even taller than his one metre ninety centimetres. He stared down on the lift occupants like a prison guard inspecting cells.

With a smirk, Dom shuffled against the back wall. 'Jump in—there's plenty of room.'

Ian didn't move an inch, his open right hand directing Dom out of the mirrored box, into the deluxe offices.

Dom reasoned the quicker he got out, the quicker he would get back in. He joined Ian in reception.

Maggie was already heading into a meeting room and a school leaver overloaded with folders hovered awkwardly near them. His arms full, he swivelled nervously on the spot waiting for Ian's next command.

'Follow her, Jamie.' Ian pointed after Maggie.

Eager to please, Jamie twisted around quickly but clumsily. This sent him off-balance and the stack of folders toppling. Instinctively, Dom dived forward to catch something, dancing with the scattering folders, with Jamie trying to keep hold of the rest. Dom's bag whacked the ground as he dipped to save the folders and the puzzle pieces rattled like maracas.

It was when he stood upright that his bag split and the plastic-wrapped cardboard box landed on the floor.

'Oh dear,' said Ian swooping for it and herding Dom and Jamie into the meeting room, where Maggie was waiting stony-faced.

Dom half-said, 'Hello,' while watching Ian retrace his steps to Belinda and leave the jigsaw with her. Their conversation floated to the meeting room.

'Find Dom a bag for this please. And see that this goes out today.' Ian tossed a letter to her and returned to the meeting room before the envelope had stopped skating along the front desk.

Through the glass wall adorned with the company logo of two silver interlocking rings, Belinda caught Dom watching and she returned a conspiratorial glance.

'Yes, Mr Read.'

Ian joined the small gathering in the compact meeting room, space large enough for a round table and four chairs. Maggie hadn't unbuttoned her jacket or removed her bag from her shoulder, which Dom took as a good sign—she wasn't expecting the meeting to last long.

Ian apologised for delaying them.

'There's so much going on and time's running out.' He massaged his temples. 'Let's talk about the restructure and how the Parramatta office will operate. Maggie's agreed to reconsider some of her stats, and she suggested you could help too. How will you be next month with case workload?'

Maggie spoke to Dom. 'You're ok with that?'

Dom creased his forehead. 'Not fully. The green accounts are in good shape.' He looked from Maggie to Ian. 'But if more come in, we won't easily cope.'

Ian stared at Dom and nodded seriously. He turned to Maggie. 'What the Parramatta team really needs is more ...'

Dom looked outside where his puzzle sat elevated, unattended on the counter. Belinda was gone. He spotted her edging up to the glass partition, a bushy plant and the company logo keeping her well hidden. She looked in, grinning, her body angled so that only Dom could see her. One by one, she mouthed the words.

'Don't. Forget. To. Go. Home.' She bounded towards the lifts.

Stifling his laugh, Dom brought his focus back to his colleagues, hoping a neutral expression would match whatever point Ian and Maggie were discussing.

'I see you want to get out, Dominic. We can chat some more tomorrow. But I agree with Maggie. I think you can handle the extra load and the best solution is for the two of you to work on this as a team.' Ian paused as though for effect, intensifying the bitterness in his tone. 'Everyone knows you work well together.'

Dom and Maggie exchanged glances. Ian stood up. 'I'll leave that with you both. It's all in the planning.' He clicked his fingers at Jamie. 'Up.'

Out in reception, Dom scooped his puzzle, giving his back to Ian, who had loitered for chitchat. 'Doing anything tonight, people?'

Maggie pressed the lift button and shook her head.

Dom said, 'Jogging with my niece.'

'Lovely time of year for it. Be careful in the dark though. I—'

'Mr Read, urgent call for you. It's Ms Arthur.'

Ian tutted and shook his head, which sent greying unkempt locks jiggling on his forehead. With Jamie shadowing, he marched off insisting on an update from them in two days.

In the lift, Maggie belted the ground floor button three times. 'Aargh. Get me out of here.'

'He can be a bit of an arse. What was all that about?'

Maggie's shoulders came up a tad. 'Did you notice his dig at us?' She deepened her voice as she mimicked Ian. 'Everyone knows you work well together.'

Her own voice returned with a shrill. 'How dare he comment on my private life—on *our* private lives.' She turned to Dom. 'Is he on drugs?'

He threw her a look. 'I doubt it.'

'Well, something's going on.' Maggie went through her list of complaints. 'He's picky. He's checking everything. He's …' She searched for the words but gave up just as quickly. Simply talking about Ian irritated her. With the flick of a hand, she waved away her whinge and cocked her head to peek inside Dom's bag.

'What's in there?' She leaned on Dom, who clutched the plastic bag to his chest, as though it were a child needing protection. The corners of his mouth rose but he stayed looking straight ahead. Maggie smiled too through plump lips and dark goading eyes. 'Oh. One of your precious jigsaws,' she said. 'Still doing those, are you?'

'Can't get enough of them. I've got a great one on the go at home.'

'It's time you created a fan page for those jigsaws, mister.'

'And it's time you stopped shitting me.'

'You love it.'

The lift stopped. As people piled in, Maggie edged closer to Dom, examining his profile. Keeping her voice low, she mumbled, 'You were the best puzzle I ever did.'

Dom avoided her eye for fear of laughing, wanting instead to keep their game a secret for their ride down.

She added, 'The one conundrum I never quite worked out.'

Dom turned to her a tad, the scent of fresh make-up penetrating his nostrils.

'Found yourself another woman yet?'

Dom shook his head.

'Want my help?' She smiled at him.

'Sure. You know my type—independent, sporty pensioners.'

'You prick.' Her wild, bushy locks tickled his neck as she looked away. She turned back with a change in topic. 'Running with your niece? How is she? Laura, isn't it?'

'Lorna. She's good. Teenager issues, you know how it is.'

'How old was she when we …'

'Fifteen.'

'Crikey.'

'She's seventeen now. Causing her parents a fair amount of grief.'

'And stirred up by the meddlesome uncle, no doubt.' She nudged him with a playful elbow.

'I think you mean tidied up—not stirred up.'

'Yes'—she flicked her chestnut hair in jest—'that's what I meant.'

Dom's eyes did an arc to meet her stare. 'Was that all your doing just then? Ian suggesting I take on extra? And us working together?'

Maggie flinched. 'Of course not. Someone's paranoid. That's Ian slinging his weight around.' She lifted her head. 'How's your brother? Is he still living with you?'

'You're not looking for a room mate, are you?' he said as they exited the lift.

Outside, the wind intensified the winter chill. Maggie pulled on her jacket collar and parted from Dom. 'I look forward to working with you again, Mr Tolen.' Elegantly, she descended the steps.

Dom hovered at the top step, allowing the playfulness in Maggie's words to wash over him, to warm him. He watched her walk off to catch her ferry, a route they had for a time shared.

Their six-month affair had played out for the most part in her cosy Balmain unit and the short ferry ride had become fixed in Dom's mind as the romantic preamble to those exciting evenings. There, at the base of the building, at the crest of the steps, where no one ever stops, a part of him wanted to follow her and ask to stay the night. But his more rational side held him back. After all, he was the same old Dom. He admitted he had done no work on the traits that had driven her away. And with a shameful heart, Dom realised that Maggie probably thought the same.

Now, down among the buildings and the city recesses where the fading light of June sunsets failed to reach, Clarence Street had darkened. The whiff and crescendo of dirty engines enveloped him and he felt gusts of cool air against his face, bringing with them the perfume of expectant rain. The wind had come from nowhere. It was as though the city was exfoliating after the toil of the day, blowing away the hordes, clearing the roads, preparing for a respite.

Dom stopped at an intersection and joined the other impatient people restrained at the edge of the pavement. Bendy buses and passenger-less cars zipped through the junction to the distributor, aided by the sharp decline of the road. Engines roared and the wind rushed by. To shield himself from the grimy wind, Dom used the man beside him, who grimaced as a truck rolled past.

The lights changed. The traffic stopped. Feeling protected by the small group, Dom's feet were in the road before the green figure lit up. A few minutes later he was on a bus heading home.

He remembered his unread text message. It was sure to aggravate him because Donald wasn't taking no for an answer. He read the blunt request, written in Donald's typical unpunctuated style.

```
Please dom for me
```

For Donald? Dom snorted with aggravation. He didn't want any part of his brother's prank. Donald needed cheering up, for sure. But Dom couldn't believe what he was being asked to do. Swapping lives for a day, going to each other's workplace, risking the careful equilibrium Dom had worked so hard to entrench—all to help lift Donald out of a low? His reply was short.

```
No way. Not worth
the risk.
```

Eyes closed, he rubbed his temples. The bus was filling and the jerking motion was niggling at him. Donald would, without a doubt, persist once Dom got home.

He stepped off the bus on to pumping Oxford Street. He ducked into a small yet dazzlingly bright grocery store, which was brimming with every item locals needed, and which was run by the most hardworking family Dom had ever known.

He did a quick lap for what he wanted, and stabilising the items in his arms, joined the queue to pay. He stepped to the counter and unpacked his arms. The owner, in shabby clothes and purple lipstick, smiled at him and started scanning his purchases. Each time she reached for a product to wave around, her eyes scanned his face. Dom recognised that familiar inspection.

His mobile rang. He guessed it was Donald. He scraped his throat and ignored the ringing.

She scanned the last item. 'Which one are you?'

He stared at her. 'This one.'

'I mean which twin.'

'The chubby one.'

Her eyes went to his middle. 'You're both chubby.' She lunged for his credit card and thumped her way through the transaction on a battered machine while Dom looked down waiting for the grinding sound. 'One of you speaks more than the other. You're the quiet one.' Her voice rose sharply over the trill of Dom's phone, her accented words out of sequence. 'Even, you don't answer the phone.'

Dom whipped the receipt and card from her rough fingers.

'Tell your brother I say hi.' Her echoing giggles tailed him outside and his phone went quiet.

He was normally good at not letting these experiences get to him. People often stared and commented on the obvious when he was out with Donald.

Being reminded they were twins was part of daily life. These days, now that they were living together, he kept his social time with Donald to a minimum. Yes, he was a twin. But he was different from Donald, he believed. He was the responsible one, the one with a career. The happier one? Almost certainly. Dom hadn't been on medication. Nor had his marriage broken down. Nor had he spent months at a time out of work.

Dom valued his simple life. It was ideal for him. He went to work and went home and went jogging and did puzzles—and he didn't fancy risking it all for Donald's amusement. Still bewildered by Donald's idea and its timing, he shook himself from his thoughts.

He was almost home.

Placer Avenue was quiet.

He walked under the bare branches of trees he couldn't name. Their leaves he had stepped on as he headed to work that morning. The sad calls of nearby magpies and the distant screeching of cockatoos reminded Dom how close Centennial Parklands lay. In its sprawling green, Dom would frequently seek refuge from the claustrophobic attention his life exacted.

The unit block was up ahead. He lived in an unpretentious building with unobtrusive features, patches of red brick and chunks of concrete. His top-floor home overlooked the street and a light in the front room signalled Donald was indoors.

Dom shifted the bags to ease the heat in his palms and snorted cool air deep into his lungs. His working day wasn't quite over—stubborn, pushy, carefree Donald would present him with one more challenge.

With the bags in one hand, he opened the security screen, turned the key in the door and pushed. The solid wood swung away and Dom braced his upper body for the familiar swing back.

II

Donald had moved in to the spare bedroom the previous July. When he separated from Robin, coming to stay with Dom seemed the obvious choice. Dom had the space and they had always got on, and Robin and the girls were in nearby Randwick. She had kept the home to minimise disruption for the children, Lorna and Niamh, and Dom had offered his place instantly to

Donald, who hadn't protested, but had been candidly hopeful that he would end up where he did.

Like magic, a few weeks last July had turned into a few weeks short of a year. Dom's pressing goal was to get Donald out of his place.

Dom dumped his bags on the kitchen counter. His eyes were drawn to a tower of software products on the floor by the cabinet—a stack that seemed to grow each week—an immediate reminder that Donald was staying there. He had lost count how many times he'd told Donald to move those boxes. One time, Dom had chucked them in Donald's room to get them out of his sight, but they re-appeared not long after.

Dom drifted effortlessly into a daydream …

He unpacks his groceries and flattens the plastic bags. Donald appears and asks to stay for another year. Dom lets out a primeval cry and, armed with a plastic bag, rushes towards Donald to quieten him, his brother's head swallowed up in a grocery bag. Their bodies lock in battle, head to head, with only a sheer film of plastic separating the identical, distorted faces. '*You've* …'—struggle—'*got to be* …'—scuffle—*fucking kidding.*'

'What are you smiling at?' Donald stood with a beer in his hand looking around him for something that might make him laugh too.

Dom came back to reality. 'Nothing.'

'Weirdo,' Donald said and shuffled back to the lounge.

Dom put his groceries away and carried the bag with the jigsaw to the back of the unit, hurrying past where Donald was lazing, seemingly absorbed in the television.

In his bedroom, Dom shook the jigsaw. The familiar shuffle brought a smile to his face. To avoid looking at the picture on the box, he averted his eyes and fixed on the small seascape oil painting hanging next to his bed. He stared at it thoughtfully as he opened the box and moments later the bag of pieces was lying on his bed, the cellophane ripped off, the box flattened.

He looked about him. The sports clothes lay where he had left them that morning. Perched on the enormous rust-coloured armchair were a thick t-shirt, shorts and socks.

The lack of chitchat coming from Donald caught Dom's attention. He changed into his running kit with the door ajar, pausing each time to cock his head and listen for any talk from Donald. The soft sounds of the television floated in.

After a short while, Donald called out. 'The university rang. I said you'd be there later in the week.'

'Why did you say that? Are you fixing my diary now?'

'Because I've been sticking to the schedule and you need to catch up. You're way behind.'

'Who gives a shit? It's boring me.' Dom stopped dressing to shout at full volume. 'Of course you've had time to go.' He paused. 'Until recently, you weren't working.'

If Dom's comment hurt, Donald didn't let on.

Holding his socks and trapping the squashed box under his arm, Dom stomped barefoot into the hall. 'I'm tired of being prodded and quizzed all for research.'

Donald turned around. 'Hey, don't go out. Lorna's on her way over.'

'Here? Is she still coming for a jog?'

'Yeah, but I asked her to drop off my tennis racquet. So you can both leave from here rather than meeting in your usual spot.'

Dom did a double take and shrieked his reaction at the image of Donald playing sport. 'Drop off your what?'

'You heard.' Donald turned back to the television. 'Josh asked me to play a game. Why wouldn't I?'

'Great idea. It's been ages though, hasn't it? Maybe you've forgotten how to play.' Dom stared at the back of Donald's angled head and shook his own. 'You can always surprise me.'

He marched to the kitchen, the slap of feet on the polished floorboards bouncing around the unit.

Donald shouted to Dom. 'Did you get my text?'

'Did you get mine? No way. Forget it.' Dom put on his socks and drank some water. He rested against the work surface waiting for Donald to appear.

In came Donald to the combined dining room and kitchen area seeming to ignore Dom's snub. 'It'll be fun. You'll love it and it's about time we did it again.'

'We're a bit old to be playing practical jokes— unlawful, unethical practical jokes.'

'Don't be a knob. The unlawful part's the best bit. Think of the thrill.' Donald moved closer and flashed wide, quizzical eyes at him. 'When was the last time you did anything remotely exciting?'

Dom spluttered. 'I know what you're trying to do. Stop it.'

'You live in that stuffy office with that safe job. You come home to the state's quietest, largest unit and you do jigsaws.' Using both hands, Donald pointed at the crushed lid near Dom and the puzzle in progress behind him at the far end of the dining table. He continued his assault. 'You think butter chicken is exotic and you're idea of a thrill is playing two-up with boozy strangers on Anzac Day.'

Dom's eyes fell to the left. They came up along with his chest. 'I've smoked pot.'

Donald hooted. '*Camille's* smoked pot.'

Dom looked astounded at that bit of news about their older sister, his mouth opening.

Donald stepped back. 'How do you *not know* that about her? Face it—you're a—'

Dom's cheeks were flushing. He stood a metre from Donald ripping at the cardboard box, destroying the image of snowy mountains that had graced the lid. The ripping continued and he spat his words.

'If you don't like this house, go.' He tore and tore. 'You wouldn't have a home if it wasn't for this uneventful existence of mine.' He stopped speaking and looked down at his hands, which were full of pieces of cardboard, now their own jigsaw.

Donald took cautious steps towards Dom. 'Don't get like that, buddy. I'm just saying you can afford to live a little.'

Dom's eyes warmed and Donald rested a hand on his shoulder.

'I don't see the big deal. Our bosses won't find out. And it's always such a buzz. We haven't done it for years.' Donald relished the nostalgia. The brothers looked at each other, their symmetry stark—the round faces, dark blue eyes, bulbous noses and cropped dark brown hair conceding no obvious points of difference. The tiniest hint of Donald's delight reflected on Dom's face.

When Dom finally spoke, the calm returned to his voice. 'There's a reason for that. We've got jobs now. The consequences are ten times worse. I know you want some joy in your life, but this is not the way.' Dom rubbed the tiredness from his face. 'Let's do it one weekend.' He binned the torn-up lid and fetched his running shoes.

'Where's the fun in tricking family?' Donald was intent on coming at it from every angle. 'I've just started at Prestons so it's perfect timing. There's no way you'll be found out—they won't suspect a thing.' The glow in Donald's eyes was building with each persuasive comment. He put on an accent to deliver his joke. 'The fun lies in the con, Dom.'

'That joke was funny when we were teenagers,' Dom said, tersely. His eyes reeled away, then back. 'And my work?' What about Subiaco? They'll know it's not me straight away. I've been there for years.' His head shook vigorously. 'Look at me.' He stopped tying his laces. 'I can't believe I'm discussing this.' His eyes darted around the room as he searched for the final reason that would kill Donald's idea. He walked over to his twin. 'I don't want to invite problems in my life. Complications do not appeal to me. I cherish the risk-free life I have here and you need to respect that.'

The doorbell rang. Donald made a move to speak but Dom growled the end of the conversation. 'Forget it. It's a no.'

Donald headed to the front door. 'You overanalyse.'

Lorna's high-pitched voice ricocheting along the hall ensured their conversation was over—for now. She appeared in the kitchen area in a green tracksuit topped with a black jacket, her brown ponytail waving over her shoulders. She skipped to Dom and kissed his cheek.

The partly completed jigsaw took her attention and she squeezed into a dining chair for a closer look at the emerging picture. 'Can I?'

Dom stood guard over her. 'This one's a birthday present from your dad.'

Donald headed to the back of the unit, tennis racquet in hand, and spoke over his shoulder. 'I had to buy him one I liked. I'm sick of looking at snowy bloody mountains all the time.'

Lorna searched around. 'Where's the lid? How many pieces is it?'

'A thousand, I think. I never look at the photo. It's meant to be a puzzle. The box goes straight in the bin. And so do the pieces when I'm done.'

Gawking up at her uncle, hazel eyes twinkling, she said, 'Liar!' She spun back to the puzzle. 'What's it going to be?'

'Here's the garden and this will be the trunk of the tree. And that bit is a mosaic at the base of the tree.' Glittering stones formed an intricate series of circles and mandorlas.

'It's beautiful. What's that in the shadow? A child?'

'Yes, he's crouching in the shade of the tree. He looks lonely, doesn't he? But the parents are close by. About here.' He wiggled a finger above the table surface. Two sets of shoes, a man's and a woman's, were almost finished, their bodies yet to appear.

Lorna snatched a piece from a pile. She assessed it while Dom watched intently. 'This is part of a branch,' she said. 'What kind of tree is it?'

'Dunno. The photo was taken in a garden in the Blue Mountains somewhere—I remember that much from the box.'

Donald joined them and saw Lorna twiddling the piece in her thin fingers. 'Good god. Is your uncle letting you touch his puzzle?' He laughed. 'Honey, consider yourself ultra-special. If I did that, there'd be trouble.'

Dom said, 'That's because if you did that, it would be to cause trouble.' He spoke to his niece. 'I find doing them relaxing.' He reached for the piece in her grasp.

'Not me.' She let it fall to the table, where, face down and undetectable, it joined a new pile.

Dom nudged her on the back. 'Let's go.'

Lorna stood up and addressed her father. 'Mum said you'd have fifty dollars for me.' Her palm went up.

Donald took out his wallet—a little too quickly, Dom thought—and went for some money. 'Oh.' His tongue clicked on his teeth. He slipped the wallet, thin and empty, back where it came from. 'Sorry, love. You'll have to get it from mummy. I spent the last of it on—'

'But she told me you had it for me.' The sparkle left Lorna's face.

'I'm sorry, love.'

'No, you're not.'

Donald waved his hands around hunting for an excuse, speechless. From the corner of his eye, he saw Dom coming to the rescue.

Dom reached up into a kitchen cupboard and pulled out two fifties. 'Here's that money I owe you for last week's shopping. Thanks again.'

'Yeah, right. A—anytime Dom.' Donald seemed unsure what to do. His arms locked rigid, by his sides.

Dom walked to him, smiling. 'Thanks Donald.'

Lorna watched the identical crisp notes pass from one twin to the other. A second later, she was clutching one of the fifties in her hand, its sharp edges pinching into her soft skin.

III

Their trot along Placer Avenue led them to a right turn on to Cook Road, a sprint across Lang Road against the lights and a snaking of the perimeter of the park, where streetlights flooded their footsteps. They must have jogged hundred of kilometres together and their sessions had found patterns. Dom would always see Lorna back home safely, they didn't stop running and they kept any chats brief.

'How's Drew?' Dom asked, eyes in front.

'Fine,' Lorna puffed on the out breath. 'Mum still doesn't'—she breathed—'approve.'

Dom's words half formed through his panting. 'And school?'

'Fine. All over soon.'

'You're staying on, right?'

She tutted. 'Drew doesn't see the point in—'

Dom stopped running. 'You have got to go to uni, Lorna. Promise me you'll stick to our plan. Your plan.'

Ahead, the teenager jogged on the spot under a low branch, which cast a shadow on her face. 'It's all so predictable. *You're* so predictable.' She waited for him to continue running.

He walked in circles, his knuckles buried in his sides, his head sagging.

Her frustrated voice sang out from the dark. 'Are we jogging?' She took off.

Dom caught up to her and they ran the rest of the lap in silence, taking the winding decline towards Queens Park.

'I want the best for you,' he said, spluttering and smiling.

IV

Dom swallowed the last gulp of beer, placed the glass down and leaned back in the stool for a better view. Harry was somewhere nearby taking a call. It was Monday evening and the two friends were in a King Street bar that was quickly filling. The interior terrace where they were sitting, next to a heater and a little too close to the DJ, had no free tables.

Dom had managed to avoid Donald over the last few days. The project with Maggie was picking up and he had found some time to meet Harry. He spotted his friend approaching, slipping through the throng of people. Carrying two dripping schooners, Harry had made the most of his time away from the table.

'Lovely.' Dom continued his chat. 'So yeah, he's getting to me. He needs to move on.' He raised his glass to his lips, but not before giving a subtle shrug of the shoulders.

'And?' Harry wiped his hands on his jeans. In one continuous action, he finished off his beer, moved his second in to place, sipped it and set it down as if to declare it current. He smacked his lips and waited.

Harry looked young for his age. He was two years Dom's junior, but the head of mousy ringlets took years off him. He seemed more mid-twenties than mid-thirties. Even his customary beard couldn't age him, so illusory was his general appearance.

'Just—just—it's Donald being himself. That's all.'

'What's he doing?'

'One or two irritating things.' Dom didn't intend on sharing with anyone Donald's proposal.

'We have such a great relationship. Well—we used to. We are incredibly close and I love him and all. But he's always criticising my boring life. And yet, he seems incredibly fragile, at the point of tipping over. So I need to be careful. I know him. I know what he's like.'

'You're worried that if he unravels, you're next. Genetics and all.' Harry said it as a fact, not a question.

'I wasn't worried.' Dom put down his drink, making out the comment bothered him. 'But I am now. Thanks, doctor.'

'Sorry Dom. I was just—' The music drowned out whatever softener Harry added. As though searching for sympathy, he held up his phone. 'That was Jackie. She can't get me the stuff for Saturday night after all. How many times has she let me down?' He tossed his phone on to the table, swapping it for the icy beer.

Dom slapped him on the back. 'Dealers. Wait til they legalise cocaine. Then standards will lift. You'll be able to give feedback online.' Dom's fingers wiggled in front of him as though typing. 'Unreliable—one star.'

They chuckled. Harry chipped in, 'Would definitely use again. It arrived quicker than the pizza.'

'I lost the entire weekend. Five stars.' They laughed and drank their beers and chatted, but Dom noticed Harry's eyes returning to his discarded mobile and the conversation waned.

Dom recalled Harry's plans for the weekend. 'You've got a dinner on, haven't you?'

Harry nodded and slouched in his seat. His thumb moved the condensation over his glass idly.

Dom hadn't been invited—Harry knew not to bother. A while ago, Dom had made it clear that he wasn't interested in turning up to Harry's evenings if they were doing drugs. Dom didn't take them, nor did he enjoy mixing with people who were high. So Harry had given up telling him when these parties came up, as infrequently as they did.

Dom looked around him and brought his hands up to cover his lips. 'There's someone at work who's always talking about it.' He ended his contribution there.

Harry said blandly, 'Right.' Unsure what Dom was getting at, his forehead creased. 'And?'

'Would you like me to ask for you?'

'Yo-ou?' Harry sang the word in two syllables, his astonishment palpable. 'You pass me a contact?' He pointed at both of them in turn as he spoke, his finger clarifying the suggestion.

'Keep your voice down.'

'Would you do that? Could you do that?'

The sarcasm pierced Dom, who crossed his arms.

Harry sat tall in the chair, his eyes big, white circles. He brought both hands down to his muscled thighs with a theatrical whack.

Dom inched back from the table. He flashed a palm to shield against the intensity of Harry's vigour. 'Don't get your hopes up—I don't want you thinking bad of me if it falls through.'

'No chance, Dom.' Harry was beaming, even as he tilted his head to guzzle his beer. 'Wait a second. Is this to do with Donald and proving you're not boring?'

Dom became exasperated. 'I don't know. Maybe. Who knows? Who cares? Do you want me to ask or not?'

'Sure. Great.'

'All I'll do is see if I can get you a contact.'

Harry punched the air. 'If you can pull that one off—'

The glint in Harry's eyes made the edges of Dom's lips curl up. He felt a pang of excitement too, the sort of animation Donald didn't think he was capable of. Dom's mind raced. Would it be too risky? Too complicated? And Donald—what would he have to say?

V

The next day, Dom had again succeeded in leaving work at a decent time and he ran around the park alone in the wet. A drizzle had been falling. The cold spray helped him push himself. He ran faster, which helped build his appetite. Back home, he showered and cooked dinner, which he ate on the sofa swigging beer from the can, eating spicy pasta and hurling answers at a game show.

The front door rattled to signal Donald returning from his tennis game. Dom heard Donald's kit and racquet clatter to the floor and Donald came in to the room and plonked down next to him. 'Josh is a good player. It'll take me a while to get back in shape.' His words were clear but his tone sounded forced. He stretched his arms along the thick rests of the armchair and his fingers drummed a short rap.

Dom turned to him and although Donald's cheeks lacked the colour of recent exertion, the smell of sweat came through. He nodded his interest and returned to his program. 'The exercise will do you good. It will lift your spirits.' He shouted at the screen. 'The nineteen hundreds.'

'I could do with that.' Donald whirled his head to make the point. 'I've been feeling really down lately.' His chin landed on his chest. 'That's why this trick would be so good for me. It would perk me up.'

Dom's fingers tensed around his fork and with deliberate chews, he mashed his pasta. He roared at the television. 'Mussolini, you fuckwit.'

'A trick like this would be such a thrill,' Donald repeated for the third time in as many days.

Dom's blood pulsed with fury. He yanked the fork out of his mouth and thrust it into the armchair, millimetres from Donald's hand, which jolted. Donald pulled his arm away.

'Stop calling it a fucking trick.' Donald froze and Dom went on. 'You're not a bloody magician. You work in IT and you've just started a new job. Grow up.'

They stared at the fork, its prongs embedded in the fabric. They watched it lower and settle on the armrest.

Dom turned back to the television. For a second, he thought the volume had risen, the buzzers and claps from the quiz show booming around the charged room.

Donald stood and moved to the safety of the doorway. 'It's ok for you—Dominic with the steady job.' He touched his chest. 'I've been out of work for ages and my marriage broke up.' He paused. 'I was on pills.'

Dom retrieved his fork and stormed towards Donald, who stepped aside. 'If you think a practical joke at work is the answer, maybe you need some more.' He passed along the hall to the front of the unit. In the kitchen, he cleaned up, banging cupboards and cracking utensils.

Donald appeared and began preparing his dinner. Dom edged past him and moved to the dining table, where he sifted jigsaw pieces, and with a careful palm, pressed the parts he had already done. The garden's complex web of tiled circles stretched invitingly before him. He sneaked a look at Donald from time to time. Neither spoke.

In his hand was a piece with an arm and jacket on it, and a dark patch. The shadow. He slotted it into place.

Without looking up, he spoke. 'I'm going to ask you calmly. Please do not raise this again—I can't handle it.' He doubted Donald sensed his exhaustion. His voice deepened. 'You have to drop this. I know where this is heading.'

Donald froze.

Dom said, 'You will rig something—you will make me. I know where this is heading.' The desperation muffled his words. 'Please don't force me.'

Donald scooped up his plate of food. 'What are you talking about?' He left the room without waiting for a reply.

VI

It was the morning of Donald's twelfth day at the job. The project manager of the fit-out he was working on was showing him around empty office space. Lisa spoke and moved fast.

'We're looking at about six workstations here for the online division.' Donald held up a tablet to where she had pointed and photographed the area. He named the file and waited for her to detail the next shot. She stepped over plastic strips and cables and he followed. She stopped, gave her brief plan for the area they were standing in and let Donald photograph it. She paused for him to catch up, running her hand over silky black hair, smoothing what didn't need smoothing. 'How are you settling in? You've started at a critical stage.'

'Events are moving rapidly. I'm getting my head around it all quite well and everyone is helpful.'

She smiled at him and looked at the finger he was using to prod the tablet. 'You'll be quite capable of everything we bombard you with. Where I come from, left-handed people are seen as highly intelligent.' She walked away.

Donald trailed her. 'If I confess I don't know which country you're talking about, does that make me an exception?'

'I hope not.' She snapped her diary shut. 'That's all for now.'

Donald heard this as *you can go home now*. He headed to Sydney University's twin research centre, a short bus trip away. Even though this stage of the twins study wasn't overly interesting to either Tolen brother, it afforded Donald a short break from his new desk job.

Pretty soon, the researchers would only need to see them around twice a year for the next five. For now, they had agreed to show up once a month. Donald and

Dom had donated a lot of time to many studies over the years. Dympna, a close friend of their dead mother, had encouraged them to take part and although Dom had started off keen, these days it was Donald who made sure they found time for the researchers.

Their parents had died young, when the twins were young themselves—only sixteen. Perhaps if their parents had lived longer and had been able to pass on to the boys more information about themselves, the twins would have been less inclined to help experts learn about them.

Donald stepped along the grey deserted wing, where scientists quizzed and tested and pushed and observed, to an astonishing array of limits, as many multiple birth children and adults as would let them. On the third floor, the researcher came to collect him from reception.

About five years younger than her research subject, Karen was as casually dressed as Donald. The only item distinguishing her as a member of staff was the security card she flashed to open the solid double doors. She shouldered her way through them thanking him for coming in.

At her desk, they began with the initial checks and paperwork. Karen flipped the pages in her folder. 'According to your notes, you've been taking an anti-depressant since last April.'

'I had a rough patch a while back. I don't take them now. Occasionally—you know.'

'How long has your GP told you to stay on them?'

Donald shrugged his shoulders to show his ignorance.

'I'm asking because a colleague is looking for people for a study about prescription medicines and you meet the criteria.' She presented a clipboard. 'Your email is all we need now and she'll be in touch, if you're keen.'

Donald went to add his name but a twinge of fear stopped him. The sheet contained only two email addresses with space for many more. 'There aren't many sick twins then? Is everyone else doing well? Am I—'

'You're not alone, Donald.' Her warm voice soothed him. 'We have about twenty of these sheets in this building alone. Lots of people are going through the same thing.'

There was a pause.

'That's wonderful news', he said, perking up. He talked and jotted down his details. 'I'm all for supporting your work. Good luck getting Dom to sign up for anything else. He's going through a funny stage. Everything's annoying him and he's sick of the research. If it wasn't for me, he'd go off the rails.'

'We understand people lose interest. That happens. I'll make a note to call him.' Karen took the clipboard and stood up. 'Come through.'

With an air of courteous duty, Donald chugged through the physical and written tests, which he was sure included repeat questions. Whenever he asked about the tests, she was reluctant to give anything away. She would smile and say vaguely, 'Yes, some parts go over familiar ground,' or 'I can't say—you might share it with Dom.'

About forty minutes later, they were finishing up at her desk. Donald was biting his lip and staring at the clipboard, which now contained his email address.

'How long is each research session? A day?'

'No, sir.' She smiled, accentuating her soft eyes. 'An hour at most. Like this one.'

Donald looked out the window. 'Do you ever have any research that goes for longer?'

'Rarely. No.' She scribbled notes and swivelled the folder around to him, holding the pen in place for him to sign.

'What about outside Sydney? In Queensland or Darwin? How would I find out about studies there?'

'Warm places.' A bigger smile creased her dimpled cheeks. 'Research and a holiday? I see where you're taking this.'

Donald smiled back. 'It would be nice.'

She said, 'You aren't in luck there. If twin research was going on in this country, we'd know about it.'

VII

Dom was at the far end of his floor away from his desk. Only he and Amy were in the small bright kitchen, talking softly and lowering their voices when people walked in.

Quiet common space was hard to come by at Subiaco. Dom had got what he needed and he was waiting for a good break in the conversation to end the informal meeting.

'Great. That sounds like it will work. I can rely on you then for this Friday?'

Amy gathered her things. 'Done. I'm happy to pass you the details. Best you're there in person.'

'Thanks.' Dom walked into the nearest men's, which was empty. He checked his mobile and found no texts from Donald, which surprised him, and another text from Harry, who was becoming increasingly frantic over his weekend dinner plans.

It was time to put an end to Harry's worries, Dom thought. Now seemed as good a moment as any. He dialled his number and spoke in a low voice. 'It's all set up, but you aren't allowed to go. It has to be me.'

Harry swore with joy.

A tightness formed in Dom's stomach.

VIII

Friday afternoon arrived more quickly than usual. Dom's nerves grew steadily when he thought about the favour for his friend. He wasn't looking forward to visiting the dealer, but he supposed he ought to go through with it.

At first, Dom had been expecting Harry to call the whole thing off—not because he didn't need the cocaine for his party—to save Dom the ordeal of having to buy drugs.

That text message never came. Harry had instead checked every day that Dom would still get him a contact, such was his desire to have a cracker of a dinner party.

Dom entered the Carhartt Hotel on Oxford Street at four-twenty and stood at the bar. The sports channel blared and the smell of stale beer hung in the air. A young muscly man appeared before Dom had decided what to order.

'I don't want alcohol yet, so a black coffee please.' He paid and sat not too far away. He had nine minutes to wait. Recounting the money by fanning the notes bulging in his wallet passed mere seconds and he was soon sitting there again with nothing to do.

The coffee arrived, its aroma drowning out the pub smells, and the strong liquid quenched his nervous thirst.

Dom's thoughts turned to Donald's persistent request. He couldn't see a way to make Donald understand how much he had to lose—how much they both had to lose—if it went wrong.

Right on half past four, Dom finished off his coffee and dialled the number he had been given, which rang out with no option to leave a message. He placed his mobile on the table in a deliberate act of casualness and it rang before he had settled back in the seat.

A voice said, 'You just dialled this number.'

'Phil? This is Dom. I'm in the Carhartt.'

'Alone?'

'Yes'—Dom decided over-nice was best—'like you said.'

'Come over now, Dom. It's number seventeen.'

Phil's place was a clean, well-tended terrace. A row of yew bushes added to the mystery of what went on inside the fortress. A light push made the iron gate groan open. Dom took the short angled path of paving stones to the black front door that appeared newly painted.

He hunted for a doorknocker or bell, suspecting the dark paint was camouflaging it. But he couldn't see anything that would allow him to signal he was there. Perhaps the house was so well monitored that knocking was unnecessary. He listened for footsteps. None came to join in the drumming of his heart and the ticking of suburbia.

A trio of strong raps on the door conveyed more confidence than he was feeling. His hand hurt. He rubbed his knuckles but lowered his hands when the door began to open.

Phil was short, middle-aged and bald, and what Dom first saw as a green collar on a blue t-shirt was a brash shapeless tattoo coating Phil's muscled neck.

They eyed each other for a split second before Phil greeted him as if they were old friends. At full volume, in a wilting New Zealand accent, he said, 'Dom! How are you, mate?'

Dom knew this exaggerated reception was for the benefit of those living either side. Neighbour Phil couldn't have strangers turning up all the time, like a corner store—way too suspicious. Dom replied in an equally friendly tone and stepped inside.

Phil locked the door behind him. He led the way to the back of the house and spoke over his shoulder. 'Thanks for coming over early. Fridays evenings are always busy.' He vanished into a room and Dom, who had been admiring the art decorating the dim hall, turned abruptly to avoid missing the entrance to the room. 'So Adrian passed you my number. Diet coke? Beer? You have to stay for a drink.'

'Coke would be good.' Dom sunk into a curved, slate sofa that took up a good portion of floor space, while his host ducked out of sight behind the bar, an oversized, bare counter of gleaming oak that robbed most of the remaining floor space. Phil popped up with their drinks and settled at the other end of the sofa.

Dom couldn't help thinking he was visiting a friend who was trying to impress with shows of wealth. But he recognised Phil's hospitality for what it was—another act for the neighbours. Dom was sure all Phil's customers got a free drink, so the huge bar came in handy. He took some of his fizzy drink and wondered why Phil had bothered adding ice.

'Take your cap off if you want.' Phil's head tilted back as he drank, revealing more of his dirty tattoo.

Dom glimpsed at it, took a swig of drink and pretended to appreciate the décor.

'I said take your cap off—I wanna see your face.'

Dom whipped the cap from his head and found fiddling with it helped dry his damp palms. Why was he here? He reminded himself—it was a favour for a mate. He marvelled at what Donald would have to say, whether this would count as exciting enough for him. He looked around for signs of the order he had placed and matched Phil's friendliness, speaking in a chirpy tone. 'This is looking lovely.'

'I had a designer do the entire ground floor. I'm really happy with it.'

Phil's ease with an unknown visitor surprised Dom. He was troubled by it. 'You're here on your own or with a partner?'

Phil didn't answer. 'Are you out for a big one, then?'

Dom hadn't planned for this question. What was the simplest way to respond? Should he tell the truth and say that he never takes drugs and that he was here buying for a friend who had been let down? Too complicated. Too honest. Plus, Dom felt Phil knew way too much about him already—his name, the mobile number. Surely a dealer would rather hear a standard reply. Dom sipped at his drink through his teeth and lied. 'Oh yes indeed. A mate's birthday.'

'So you work with Adrian?'

'Yeah.' Another lie. Adrian—the name he'd been told to mention.

'Remind me what you do.' Phil swished the ice cubes in his glass.

'Insurance.' There was no way Dom would be telling him where he really worked.

Dom repeated the word to himself. *Insurance*. Sitting in this lavish terrace waiting to buy cocaine, Dom was struck by how extraordinarily mundane his office life sounded. Donald could almost be forgiven for his comments about Dom's lifestyle.

Phil stared at Dom. 'I thought Adrian worked for a bank.'

'It's a huge place. We've got an investment arm. That's where Adrian is—I believe.'

'You believe?' Phil's face went stern. He banged his drink down. 'Tell Adrian to call me. He shouldn't be giving out my number. You tell him I'm not taking walk-ins anymore.'

Dom's head instantly bobbed his obedience, even though there wasn't a chance in hell he'd be telling Adrian to do anything. Phil left the room shouting behind him.

'Four, was it?'

'Yes,' said Dom hesitating. Was Phil expecting a *please*?

Dom wolfed down the soft drink, letting the fizz moisten his dry lips. The house went silent. Yet Dom's heartbeat was still marking time. He had the uneasy feeling Phil was staring at him through the gap in the door's hinges, but he didn't look. It wasn't something Dom wanted to confirm. Catching Phil's eye through the frame would make him panic. Eyes down, he busied himself digging out his wallet.

Phil reappeared, handed him a quartet of thumb-sized wraps, and fixed on counting the money Dom handed over. He stayed standing while Dom stuffed the drugs into his pocket, stumbled to his feet and closed their deal with a pleasantry.

'And you, Phil? Plans for the weekend?'

'Don't forget your cap.' Phil pointed to where Dom had been sitting.

Dom pounced on it and locked it on his head.

Phil said, 'A quiet one for me. In a few hours, I'll be turning off the mobiles.'

Dom wondered how many he owned.

IX

'Pass me the cream.' The woman rested her hand on Dom's shoulder and gave it a short rub. He reached for the jug near Harry, who sat to his right. As he moved it to her, the white ring of spilled cream left behind caught his eye. She picked up the jug and he checked for a second ring of cream on the maroon tablecloth. There it was—thinner—but still a complete loop.

Four hours earlier, Dom had arrived at Harry's with the drugs. Harry had opened the door in his apron and Dom had stepped inside and paused, afraid to go in further, as though the house was unknown.

Like a flash, he had handed Harry an envelope with the four small parcels and Harry had motioned for him to go through, ignoring Dom's protests about a poorly parked car in the street. Harry had run to the kitchen to turn down the stove. Reluctantly, Dom had followed.

While he was stressing to Harry that he was not to tell anyone he had been involved with the deal, Harry had shoved a beer in his hand saying, 'They won't be here for hours—you're safe.'

The second, third and fourth beers had quickly arrived, each one punctuated with Dom declaring, 'You didn't get that stuff from me.'

And now Dom was sitting around a packed dining table with dinner almost over. They had started with potato soup, had lasagne for the main, and dessert was warm apple pie with cream, which most people were skipping. Dom was on his second helping and he was the one who had started the rings of spilled cream, his coordination suffering under the effects of the alcohol.

Nobody seemed to notice when one of the guests dimmed the lights. At that point, Dom was complimenting Harry on his cooking skills. When he looked up, he saw something being passed around. He thought it was a cheese platter and he told himself he was too full for that.

He turned back to Harry, who was propping himself upright, readying himself. Dom looked over at the platter and realised what was coming his way. People were passing around a mirror the size of a novel that displayed twinkling rows of cocaine. One by one, the guests relayed the mirror and the short black straw. When his neighbour took her line, Dom passed the mirror—with enormous care—to Harry. Dom looked away as Harry's baby curls fell over his face.

One minute later, from the other end of the table, someone called out.

'Who didn't have theirs?'

A solitary line sat on the dust-speckled mirror.

The group, who had been engrossed in conversations, turned inwards to eye the unwanted present and spot the ungrateful guest. Dom shifted in his chair. Harry vacated his and began clearing plates.

Dom confessed, raising a palm to keep the drug away, but someone jumped up and served him from the left, plonking the mirror before him.

'I don't fancy any—me and drugs don't mix.'

'Rubbish.' The straw was thrust into his hand.

'Go on.'

'It's good stuff.'

Dom said, 'I—er. I'm not—'

'Don't pressure him.'

'Just one line.'

The deciding jab came from behind. He felt a hand propelling his head down to the glass. Was that Harry?

His face stopped over the mirror. He tried focusing beyond the particles and the fat line of cocaine and saw his mirrored self, his drunk face. One line then, he told his reflection. He positioned the straw and the familiar smell of washing powder emerged. An uncoordinated breath fanned some of the particles, disturbing the neat formation, drawing tuts and giggles.

With the straw close to the powder and expecting nothing more than a side-excursion of unwanted euphoria, Dom watched the coke vanish into the tube.

X

Around six hours after getting into bed, Dom stirred from a disrupted sleep, where it felt like he had been merely dozing or constantly chattering. His nose was blocked and his mouth had a foreign dryness and taste to it. He tried to bring moisture to his lips and tongue, but none came. His joints felt stiff. He had drunk loads, but he didn't have a headache.

Dance music was playing nearby. He lay still working out where it was coming from. It was in his unit—the reverberation and the thumps on the floor were strong. That wasn't Donald dancing to house music, was it? He recognised his voice over the tune. Dom cursed him for choosing that morning to perk up. Head under the covers, eyes unopened, he replayed the previous night's events—those he could remember. Lots of talking and drinking. Oh and the snorting. Damn. What time had he got in? What time was it now? His hand went hunting for the phone and brought it under the covers. It was midday. Shit. And there was a message from Donald.

> Fantastic thanks a
> million

Thanks for what? The dryness in his body magnified as memories of texting Donald stirred in his fuzzy mind. He tapped the screen. Dom let out a shout when he saw a chain of texts on the practical joke. His last message went at four that morning.

> Why wait? Let's do
> it next week. Let
> the fun begin!

Dom dropped the phone and rolled into the middle of the bed, face down. 'Ho-ly shit.'

2 | Donald

I

Donald slid the chocolate biscuits across the table. An adept swoop from Dom sent them back. 'Another cup of tea?' asked Donald.

Dom shook his head.

'You sure? I'm more than happy to make it for you.'

Without moving his elbows from the table, Dom rubbed his eyes with his open palms. Each hand moved to the side of his face forming a cup for his stubbled chin to rest in. 'Forget it. I'm asking you again. Think carefully, in case you've let it slip your mind.' There followed a slow, noisy release of air. 'Have you told anyone about this?'

It was the Wednesday evening of a week of hammering gales and noisy rain. Powerful radiators were warming the unit and the twins were lazing in shorts and t-shirts. After avoiding Donald for most of the previous weekend, after recovering from his late night, and after venturing no further than the corner shop to buy groceries, Dom had given in and agreed to sit with Donald and plan the swap.

Euphoric, Donald had managed to make Dom set a date. Donald didn't mind which day, but Dom preferred a Monday, when his office was normally quietest. After agreeing on the coming Monday, Dom was giving Donald one more chance to own up to sharing their plans, unconvinced that Donald had kept it a secret.

'No. Not a soul.'

'It has to stay secret, Donald. This is such a bad idea. Not even fam—'

'Family can find out', cut in Donald. 'It's just a practical joke. We're not robbing a bank.'

'Camille? You said Camille came by the other day— did you mention it to her?'

'Nooo. Are you right in the head? As if.'

'Why was she here?'

'She was dropping over some food she'd cooked for me.'

'She's my sister, too. Where's my meal?'

'You don't like her casseroles.'

'Who says?'

'Look, I never mentioned anything to her. Back to this.' Donald took a biscuit and turned Dom's pad towards him. He looked at the list of points Dom had drawn up. 'We'll need to swap clothes. And I'll take your leather work bag that you sometimes carry.'

He quizzed the next item in the list. 'Phones? We're not swapping phones. We've got the same model, Dom. Are your colleagues going to ask why you've changed the ring tone? I don't think so. Relax.'

'I'm thinking of everything. Stop with the sarcasm.'

Donald rolled his eyes. 'Jot down socks and underpants. Just in case someone spots me in the loos. Gees.'

'All right. Calm yourself. You cannot be this cocky on the day or you'll make a mistake.'

Donald's face fell.

Dom crossed out *phones*. He continued reading. 'Swipe cards and logons.'

'Essential,' said Donald. 'And a simple map to your desk please.'

Dom added maps to the list and tapped out the next items. 'Colleagues and routines.' He put down the pen. 'I have lunch at midday every day. You go to lunch then and you'll have to take one hour. Around ten am, a tall guy called Eugene will come by my desk and ask if you want a coffee. Tell him you'll have the usual and give him four dollars in coins—I always give coins. A large flat white with no sugar.'

Donald winced at the idea of unsweetened coffee.

'No sugar. Apart from that, it's just the occasional hello—on Mondays anyway. Midweek is busier.'

Donald finished chewing, then outlined a more laidback environment for Dom's swap day. 'At my job, you can take lunch whenever you like and you'll make your own sweet, milky tea in the kitchen, which is at the other end of the floor, and you can say hello to whoever you like, whenever you want. Get there for nine. Leave at five.' Donald couldn't resist a smug spin of his shoulders and haul of his lips.

'If it's such a great place to work, why come to mine?' Dom's eyebrows lifted, but Donald looked away and helped himself to another biscuit. 'And why aren't you taking notes? You won't remember all this.'

'Yes, I will.'

'We'll go over it again next Sunday. So we have this week'—he stopped talking over the rustle from the packet of biscuits Donald was ploughing through—'to think of everything.'

The loud chewing and swallowing stopped. 'If we need to call one another, where's safe to speak?'

'Good point.' Dom added it to the list while Donald attacked the biscuits once more. He cast his eye over Donald's middle. 'I wonder if you'll fit comfortably into my shirt.'

'I can wear my own. I have a stripy yellow one that will go with your suits.' Donald slurped his tea.

Dom knew which shirt he meant and he was quite sure Donald had honeymooned in it. 'Not your clothes.' Dom placed the pen down. 'You might as well wear a sign that says *I am not Dom.*'

'What do you mean by that?'

There was a pause. 'I mean people will realise—may realise—that the stripy yellow shirt is not mine. It's a bit old and I wear new ones.'

'It's an office shirt.'

'I don't wear yellow to work.'

'You don't what?' Donald's face contorted.

Dom leaned back in the chair, balancing on the rear legs. 'You're telling me you've lived in my home for a year and you haven't noticed my shirts?' He brought the front legs of the chair down to the floor, propelling himself forward. 'How unobservant of you.'

Donald looked into his mug of tea to hide the smirk on his face. 'Anything else I should know about your wardrobe?'

Dom gripped his brother's arm. His face hardened, but his words were calm. 'Know this, smartarse. If anything screws up, you're on the street.' He hurled his forearm away.

'It will go off fine,' Donald said, sounding like a child promising to behave.

II

Dom spent Thursday evening at home wrapped in the tranquillity of the jigsaw puzzle. Donald had texted to say he would be out for most of the night playing tennis with Josh, so Dom settled in with the television off and a new album on repeat. He tucked into a bottle of red wine and Camille's sumptuous beef casserole, which he had spotted hidden in the freezer.

Dom was finding Donald's gift—the puzzle—tricky and the many dark pieces were slowing him down. He still had his recently collected jigsaw to begin and his next puzzle would arrive at Brain Food for pick-up in a matter of weeks.

He sipped on his wine and pulled back to refocus on his handiwork. The shadow from the tree was larger than he had guessed and the child squatting in the shade was no longer alone because Dom had added an adult and a sibling to the scene.

The phone rang, jolting him from his contemplation. It was Robin. Donald's ex-wife seldom rang and Dom had an inkling what she was calling about. He swiped the screen to take the call by loudspeaker, leaving his hands free to work.

'Major dramas, Dominic. I'll be there in five.'

Dom told her she couldn't know where he was as she had called his mobile. 'What's up?'

'Where else would you be at this time?' She tutted. 'It's Lorna—who else?' There was a pause. 'Is Donnie with you?'

Dom told her he was alone for the time being.

A few minutes later, Robin arrived. Dom heard the security door being ripped open and the front door handle being rattled. She wouldn't get in. He gulped some wine and stood to let in frenetic, needy Robin.

With the bolt unlocked, he felt her barging towards him.

'Dominic!'

He kept his place and held the door longer than maturity allowed. As he gave way, his voice took on a tone of exaggerated puzzlement. 'Who is it?'

Robin gushed in. 'I can't cope with this. I just can't.' With sunglasses on top of her head, bags over both shoulders, and a cloud of pricey fragrance travelling with her, she rushed along the narrow hall like a celebrity with an entourage. Even when turning up alone, she managed to look escorted.

Dom drew a long breath and closed the front door. Robin was still speaking and he realised she hadn't been talking to him. She was on a call.

He followed her in and watched her unload her bags, her one-word answers indicating that the call was about to finish. She propped herself up on the table with one hand, shaking her head, eyes closed. The call ended but Robin didn't speak. Dom moved closer. When she looked up at him, the sadness—or possibly hopelessness—that clouded her bird-like eyes told Dom she was a short distance beyond her usual point.

'Is Lorna okay?' He moved past her to sit at the table, but not before giving her a consoling shoulder rub, coughing lightly from the scented air. The jigsaw piece he had been working with, now in his fingertips, would soon be in its place.

'That girl.' Robin brought hands crippled with tension to her head. Her fingers hit her sunglasses, which she hurled into a bag. 'The grief she causes me.' She huffed. 'This all started with that Drew. Now she tells me the family's moving to Melbourne and she wants to go with them. How am I going to stop her? I can't control her. And her father's useless.'

'Do you want me to do something?'

'Well, you're not helping any.'

The shrillness in her voice caused Dom to look over. Soft, controlled words came out. 'You guys are the parents. But I'm happy to help if I can.'

'You can start by not encouraging her, Dominic. She's only seventeen.'

He tapped in another piece. 'What?'

'She spends time with you and she mimics you. She wants to leave this and start that'—Robin's hands swung high, eager to convey the enormity of the drama she was grappling with—'and move here and sleep there.' She collapsed into a chair and squeezed her chest. 'She's too young to go off with this Drew, who, by the way, I *refuse* to allow in the house.' She pressed her temples. 'She's too young to—to—to experiment. I want her to get a good education first.' She banged a fist on the table, the vibration nudging Dom's tidy mounds of pieces.

He glared at her, steadying the table. 'We all want her to do well.'

'But she looks up to you, Dominic. She sees you here with no kids, no ties, and she gets ideas in her head.' Her arms flailed again. 'Big ideas. Huge ideas.'

'Hardly my fault. That's unfair.' He pressed home another bit of puzzle.

'She sees you travelling here and there, and she wants that too. Hong Kong one month, Japan the next. I know she looks to you instead of Donnie. Or me. Now she thinks she can go off like her uncle Dominic. I'm going to lose her—I know it.'

Dom responded cautiously. 'That's my work travel. They're business trips loaded with responsibility, Robin. They're not just *here and there*.' He shrugged without lifting his eyes from his task. 'How is that a bad influence?'

'Please tell her not to go to Melbourne. She has to go to university and it has to be here in Sydney. You can help me keep her here—that's what you can do.'

'I've already told her that. On a run last week.' Dom repeated their conversation from the jog around the park.

'Oh no.' Robin started crying into the table, her face buried in her arms. Her face lifted enough for Dom to hear her clearly. 'If you can't talk sense into the cow, what hope do I have?' She pulled a tissue from her bag and dabbed her eyes. 'She's just too wrapped up in this g—this—this *interest* of hers.'

She whimpered to herself while Dom, at the other end of the table, pottered away at the puzzle. He positioned another three pieces—a face, an arm and a hat—in quick succession, tapping each into place twice. His two-dimensional family was coming along nicely.

With each jigsaw piece correctly housed, Dom took a step towards control and understanding, the chaotic becoming ordered, the murky clear. Completing parts of the jigsaw with Robin close by helped him view her differently. The circles under her eyes were darker, the soft lines in her face more pronounced—she was clearly doing it tough. Yet she had come over to blame someone just as much as to reach out. And her capacity to trample over people's feelings was as evident as always.

Sensing Dom's wariness, Robin turned to him, as if to show off her tears. She wiped her eyes and pulled out a small mirror to neaten her face. Crying only magnified the flush in her rubescent skin. 'I can't tell if I'm coming or going.' She picked at her strawberry blonde bob until the blunt cut was at its tidiest.

'I can—you're going.' The chair scraped as he got to his feet, gesturing to the front door with a flick of his head. Robin stretched her swanlike neck and opened her mouth to let out a scream of frustration, but a disarming grin from Dom silenced her. He marched to the front door to watch her go.

Robin picked up her bags and checked to see Dom had gone into the hall. She pilfered a jigsaw piece from the nearest pile and popped it into her pocket. Running past Dom, who was guarding the front door, she whacked him with her handbag.

'You're mean to me.'

III

It had just gone seven thirty on Friday evening and the moon was tinging the brisk clouds with a silver glow. Dom was sitting on the sofa in Dympna's warm suite and with each minute that passed, he relaxed further, sinking into the black leather cushions. She had asked Dom if he wanted to discuss anything that evening. He had paused before he answered. 'Donald.' They chatted for a few minutes before he exploded.

'The freeloader thinks I'm too dull. His ex blames me for being too free and liberated'—his hands wiggled above his head—'and adventurous, and a bad influence on Lorna. How does that work?' He shook his head. 'All because they can't control their child the way they'd like to. And I feel like I have to justify the life I lead.'

'That's tough.' Dympna's soothing voice and comforting tones massaged Dom's frustrations.

'I want life to tick over. I like that. But Donald craves excitement and complications and I'm sick of catering to him and being drawn into stupid shit.' He exhaled dramatically.

Dympna brought an ear round towards him waiting for more. Not one hair covered her face. The wavy bouffant swept auburn tresses from her velvet brown eyes. An uninterrupted view of them—at once inviting, yet penetrating—was important for her therapy work.

'He's convinced me to go along with a crazy thought of his.'

'That's Donald for you, always coming up with wild ideas. How long did it take him to use up his inheritance on schemes and things?' She raised an eyebrow, waiting for Dom to disclose. A wobble in the sofa seat told her he was getting himself comfy. She nudged the conversation along. 'He convinced you—how?'

'I don't know. I—I got really drunk. *Really* drunk. I agreed. And he pretends to be so fragile. He puts it on.' He stared at Dympna. 'And yet, he *is* fragile and this guilt comes over me if I know he's losing out, and I want to help him—I really do.'

He lowered his gaze and picked at his nails. A tear loitered in his eye as he sat still. As his face muscles softened, it trickled, ignored and unaccompanied, to the side. 'It comes back to losing mum and dad, and to Camille marrying Tommie early too.'

'So going along with it is an attempt to look after him?' Dom gave a slow nod. Dympna re-worded the position Dom was in. 'Your brother has had some ups and downs recently, you're there to lend a hand, and he feels this small gesture will cheer him up and you can help.'

'But it's so pathetic. Two men playing a prank only they know about. I have no need to share a secret joke like this. I have no need to bond further like this. I despise him.' He caught Dympna's lightning frown and added, 'Sometimes.' To the room he posed the question, 'Why go through with a secret prank?' To Dympna, he said, 'It's insane.'

'Yet as you say those words, you're smiling. Why is that?' She smiled to mirror him.

Dom laughed and massaged his head into the sofa cushioning, amused by her revelation. He thought for a moment, imagining a swap.

'They are fun. It's a thrill I can't begin to describe. The thought that someone may come up and shout *you're not Donald!* is intoxicating, immense.'

Dympna moved in her chair, studying Dom from many angles. She considered the twins her nephews. Although these sessions weren't appointments, she would let Dom come to her suite in the evenings, mostly after her paid sessions ended, where the talking cure was on hand.

Their mother had been her best friend and Dympna was glad for the time with Dom—Donald and Camille didn't visit—happy to help in any way she could. 'You've been so protective of your identity, Dominic, whenever you come here. Your brother moving in with you affected that potent sense of identity you treasure.' She made a fist and shook it in front of him.

'I value that, yes. It's as important to me as a simple life.'

'Yet you're willing to play with it for Donald's sake.'

Dom stopped. 'Does that make me a hypocrite?'

'No—it shows how protective you are of him. You care for him deeply.'

Dom's head came down to shield his face from her piercing observation. The searing pain in his throat that came from nowhere stopped his words. Staying silent, he could only nod the emotion away. He finally took in enough cool air to speak. 'But why did I agree to this? It'll end in tears.'

'Do you feel you can change your mind? Donald is stronger than you think. He'll cope. I'm sure of it.'

Dom wiped his eyes. 'It's not that. If I pull out now, he'll go behind my back and do something crazy.'

'Why do you say that?'

Dom shrugged and lunged for a handful of almonds from a bag on Dympna's desk. He fell back into the sofa, happy to let the food distract him. Dympna took some too and they munched without interruption.

After a few moments, he asked, 'Is it dangerous? You know, psychologically?'

'You'll know who you are throughout your prank.'

They carried on chewing in unison.

She asked, 'Do *you* think it will be?'

IV

Donald's alarm was the first sound inside the unit on Monday, the day of the swap. Already awake, with his eyes still closed, he picked up his mobile on the bedside table, and held it up high. A few more irritating trills were sure to wake Dom, whose bedroom was down the hall.

From where he lay, he propped himself up and looked outside to get a glimpse of the day ahead. It wasn't raining now, but the ground was glistening from the steady light fall during the night and the clouds sat full and low, promising more.

Donald had slept well. He got out of bed, stretched and showered. Presently, he heard Dom moving around and getting ready, noises Donald found reassuring. The swift dance of joy in the isolation of his bedroom was a brief indulgence. Even as late as this morning, he had been fretting that Dom would change his mind about going through with it. The typical morning sounds of Dom—the splash of taps, the pull of drawers—put Donald at ease.

It was time to dress up. Donald opened the wardrobe where his costume was hanging. Dom had selected a blue shirt, which he eased into, enjoying the smooth material running over his damp arms. It looked expensive, as did the charcoal suit. Next came the tie, which Dom had thoughtfully pre-knotted. All Donald had to do was tighten the mottled navy silk and tuck it under the double-stitch collar. Dom had even insisted Donald wear his expensive Italian shoes, which his feet would obviously slip into.

He put on the suit jacket and examined himself in the mirror, gift-wrapped and outlandish. Every inch of him gleamed and he couldn't remember the last time he'd worn a tie. He went to the kitchen where Dom was having breakfast of fruit and tea.

'Suit plus twin equals Dom. How do I look?'

'Like me. Superb.' Dom lobbed some pips into the bin saying, 'There's still time to change your mind. You don't have to go through with it.'

Donald hummed a song as he made breakfast. He passed by Dom and shook him by the shoulders. 'Aren't you excited?'

Dom stared into his teacup. 'All this adrenalin is making me high.' He changed the subject. 'Have you sorted things out with Lorna?'

'Still working on that one. We've got more pressing priorities—get dressed. You've got the easier day, but don't take it all for granted. I'm new in that role, so if you don't look confident, that's fine. But you still need to pay attention.'

'Believe me, I'll be on the ball.' Dom went to walk out. 'This confident exterior is just that. I'm looking forward to seeing what goes wrong.'

Donald was going to remind Dom of his leaving time, but the door slammed shut. He had ages before he needed to leave and he sat with the Sunday paper taking in the headlines and photos, unable to focus on much else. The door opened and Dom's head popped round.

'Remember to tear off Friday's date from my desk calendar. Catch.' A packet of cough sweets flew over to Donald, who looked lost. 'If anyone asks why your voice sounds strange, tell them you're getting a cold.' Dom was smiling as he slammed the door.

Donald sipped his tea. 'Whatever.'

Dom entered a second later. 'What did you say?'

'Nothing.'

Dom pointed to the resident pile of boxes on the side. 'And get that software out of here. I'm not having stolen goods in my house.'

'I keep telling you they're not stolen. You're paranoid.'

'It even *looks* stolen. Get rid of it.'

V

The bus crawled past the Subiaco Insurance tower in the peak hour traffic with Donald sitting on the left for the best view of the building. Nothing looked out of the ordinary—not that he really knew what ordinary was for this end of town. He reminded himself all he had to do was walk in and get the lift to the sixteenth floor.

Off the bus, a chilly wind nipped at his face as he moved with the crowds along Clarence Street back towards Dom's office. Dom's bag hanging off his shoulder, as awkward as it felt, was a necessary part of his disguise. The earlier excitement at home had been replaced with a churning in his belly that had started when he got on the bus.

His costume added to the anxiety for he felt exposed and vulnerable, convinced that the swarms of commuters bubbling around him could see he was an imposter, that he didn't usually dress that way. The suit was making him walk differently. His shoulders couldn't sit properly in the jacket and so his arms felt alien.

Looking around, he was struck by how many other people were wearing suits—navy blues, light and dark greys, browns—and how similar they made everyone look, and how confident everyone seemed. That's what he needed to harness for the day. Confidence. He lifted his chest and marched on towards the building.

People walked faster than him, zipping ahead, ignoring the pedestrian lights that turned red. He gladly heeded the traffic lights, welcoming the chance to pause and develop his mental buoyancy, and he stopped at the edge of the kerb. A cyclist whizzed past and narrowly missed dragging Donald along with her. He retreated from the edge and caught someone's shoe. He turned and apologised to the man, whose smile showed he didn't care. Seconds later, he was across the road and he could see the steps inviting him up to the elevated foyer of the Subiaco tower.

'Good morning.' A female voice sang out from behind him.

Donald's stomach took flight. He turned and greeted the woman as casually as he could and repeated her greeting. 'Good morning.'

With a flick of her head, she knocked dark curly hair away from her face, revealing more of her pale complexion.

'I saw what just happened. You should give them more room.'

Her voice was educated and soft without a hint of accent. She had both arms full carrying bags. Had she not been weighed down, Donald was sure she would have shaken a disapproving finger at him.

'You mean the cyclist?'

'Yes. You were too close to the kerb.'

'I stepped on a guy's foot too. Did you see that?'

'I saw it all.'

Donald was smiling. His pilot conversation with one of Dom's colleagues had gone well and the ping of confidence drew him taller. They arrived at the tower, where the huge rings of the Subiaco logo looked impressive on the clean glass. They climbed the steps and walked through the enormous revolving door.

'How are things upstairs, Dom?' the woman asked blandly.

Donald noticed how fake it felt being called by his brother's name. This wasn't the first time it had happened, but this morning, in Dom's clothes, chatting with Dom's colleague, made the feeling so new, so heightened, so deceptive. He casually brought a hand to his thundery stomach. 'Really well, thanks. Busy—just as I like it.' He lied. 'And you?'

'Snowed under at the moment. We're trying to …'

They were at the lift and Donald had too much to think about to listen to her reply. He avoided eye contact so he could recall the floor number. Meanwhile, his companion kept talking. He lost track of what she was saying and said, 'Right, right', but he sensed she had picked up that he hadn't been listening. She went quiet.

A lift arrived, they got in with four others, and Donald made a show of pressing the metallic plate for the sixteenth floor. The doors soon opened and Donald and Dom's colleague stepped into the marbled foyer of Subiaco Insurance.

The receptionist greeted them without using names, to Donald's annoyance. From Dom's description, he guessed she was Belinda, but he had no idea who he had travelled up with.

He swiped the card and when the glass doors parted, he let his companion pass through, walking behind her. Dom's pencilled map of the office was crumpled deep in a pocket and he knew to turn left at the end of the corridor keeping the fish tank on his right. The woman spun around causing Donald to almost run into her. She held out her bag.

'Do me a favour, please. Leave this on my desk? I need to collect something from Wayne.'

'Ok,' said Donald. 'Where do you sit?'

She chuckled and walked off.

Holding two bags that didn't belong to him, he had only seconds to think.

Dom's desk was easy to find. He plonked Dom's bag on it while he went over his options. If Dom got a call this early from him, he'd be furious. Maybe he could leave the bag undelivered at Dom's desk. Or maybe there was a photo on a desk somewhere. There was no time.

He raced back to reception and started whispering.

'Belinda, where does she sit?'

'Who?'

'The woman I came in with. Bushy black hair.'

'Eva? She sits behind you.' She recoiled. 'What's going on?'

'I thought she'd moved and I was too embarrassed to ask her.'

He charged back to Dom's area. Seconds later, he arrived at her spot, which was separated from Dom's space by a square column and a tall evergreen.

Eva stood there, one arm out, unimpressed, waiting for her bag.

Donald coughed.

'You beat me to it.'

VI

Dom felt like vomiting. As planned, Donald had left a photo of the girls on the desk and Dom had found his spot without a hitch. But Donald had neglected to tell him that everyone could see his computer screen. He had no privacy at all—no partitions, no plants, no walls. Great, Dom thought. What was he meant to do for the rest of the day if he couldn't surf the net unnoticed?

He logged into Donald's computer using his slip of notes and looked around waiting for the screen to boot. He sat surrounded by strangers in a well-lit, open plan office on the second floor of a small block just off Elizabeth Street in Surry Hills. Donald had been right when he said the place was relaxed. People were smartly dressed, but none of the men wore suits or ties.

In his own jeans and casual shirt, Dom fitted in. He greeted Donald's colleagues who looked over at him as he scanned the whole floor. He pulled out Donald's work files, ready to start working as Donald.

With his head in his notes, his workspace darkened. Dom looked up. Two men greeted him—one had to be Donald's regional manager, Paul. Donald had described him well, his coal black muttonchops giving him away. Dom stood, shook hands with him and waited to be introduced to the younger man, who, in a pin-stripe suit and scarlet braces, seemed overdressed. The man's cufflinks made Dom smile. Jigsaw pieces.

'Donald, I want you to meet Richard Yaldsworthy, your counterpart in Melbourne.' They shook hands. 'You'll be working closely together, so I'd like to get things started.' Paul checked his watch. 'How are you placed for eleven?'

'Fine by me,' said Dom. 'We can step outside if you like.'

'Better to get everyone else up to speed at the same time. We'll use the boardroom. See you then.'

Paul and Richard strolled away and Dom plunged into a panic. His face reddened at the thought of what he could be called on to say, although he had time to speak to Donald. He thought about logging into the chat service they had agreed to use, but decided texting was less conspicuous.

> I've been called
> into a meeting
> with Paul and
> others. Where are
> you?

Two minutes later, Donald replied in his usual bare bones style.

> Youll need the
> notes sitting on
> the desktop print
> them off and bring
> them with u hes
> gonna ask u to
> comment on the
> state figures and
> a timeline for
> rectifying the
> lags which u didnt
> cause obviously
> neither did i
> thats a joke

Dom wasn't laughing. He messaged back.

> You've got to come
> here now. I can't
> do this. It's not
> funny.

Donald replied instantly.

```
Course u can look
over the notes it
might not even
happen he always
cancels gotta go
downloading the
software i
promised u nice
place u got here
btw and the
boardroom is on
other side of
building that
belinda what a
cracker no wonder
u work so much
```

Dom printed off Donald's notes and took comfort in knowing Donald was at least putting his expertise to superb use while at Subiaco. At work the next day, Dom would find a swag of software and sites bookmarked for review.

VII

'G'day Dom.' The man stood uncomfortably close to Donald rattling a handful of coins.

Donald looked up from the screen at the giant coffee buyer. 'Morning Eugene. I'll have my usual thanks. But there's something different today.' Donald grinned.

'What is different today?' came the rigid question.

'I don't have coins with me—I have a note.' Donald held it out for him. Eugene didn't move, looking as though he was about to refuse it. Donald flapped it closer. 'And, you know what else? I fancy sugar today. God knows why. Ask for two sugars, please.'

With a steely stare, Eugene teased the bank note from Donald's clasp. 'You realise there will be change?'

'There'd better be.' Curbing a laugh, Donald watched Eugene head off, delighted to throw tiny spanners in Dom's works.

VIII

Dom looked up from his reading spell bringing him up to speed with Donald's reports. It was almost time for the meeting. He cursed for having put himself in the situation he was in, scooped up the notes, which made little sense, and walked to the other end of the building.

He found the boardroom easily enough and it was empty. 'Great,' he muttered. 'Impress with my punctuality.' He sat in a black swivel chair, the cool leather making him shiver. As he looked out of the room to the goings-on, he could make out heads seated in the next room. His mobile phone had the time as three minutes past the half hour. Where was everyone? Then Dom remembered Donald's advice about Paul sometimes cancelling. Perhaps he hadn't been told.

Dom had another look at Donald's file. He breathed out gradually, trying to slow the thud of his heart. He shook his head lightly, pondering once more why Donald would go to all this trouble. Where was the fun in this, really? He heard the glass door open and looked around expecting to see the two men who had organised the meeting. But it was a woman, who kept her body outside and poked her head through the door.

'There you are'. We've been looking for you—we're all in Wattle. Didn't you get the email?'

'Paul said the boardroom.'

'It changed. Hurry.' She moved aside to let Dom pass. 'This way.'

Dom followed her along a short, open corridor of desks and into a larger room with about twenty people sitting around a table. He recognised Richard, who didn't look up, and Paul.

Paul was addressing the room and writing figures on a whiteboard. 'We started without you, Donald. You'll find your way around this place soon enough.' Dom did his best to squeeze between two people who hardly budged for him and he settled himself at an awkward angle and distance from the table—not close enough to be part of the group, not far enough to warrant more attention.

'And so the drivers of this project are strengthening'—said Paul—'and we needed to position an IT project manager here as well as in Victoria, and that person is Donald.' His open hand signalled Dom. 'Introduce yourself, Donald.' Paul turned his back to clean the whiteboard.

Dom's heart thumped harder as he tried to exude calmness. He launched into a short biography, adding, 'Thank you everyone. I'm still getting to know the place but you've been very kind.' People smiled as Dom scanned the room. 'For the project, it seems I'm coming in at a critical stage and over the next few weeks, my role will be to assess what the six divisions have done. We're also fitting out the extra space for the new teams.' He shot a glance at Paul, who looked content. The tension Dom held in his back eased.

Paul scanned the room. 'Is everyone clear on what relay, package and server each division will be using?' Some heads shook. Some nodded. Paul swiftly wrote numbers one to six across the top of the whiteboard.

He turned and offered the black marker to Dom. 'You may as well explain this.'

As people corrected their posture, eager to hear from the new guy, Dom went to the front wondering what the hell to write. He accepted the marker from Paul and battled in getting the lid to stay on the back end of the pen. He transferred the pen to his left hand, his control weak.

The room was silent.

He drew a square under the number one and inside it scrawled the division name *Newcastle* and in a box below it, he tried to write *Carpenter-5432305*. The *a* and *e* were illegible and the numbers sank to the right.

The laughing started when Dom filled in the box for the third division. Trying hard to make it look like he could quickly write on a whiteboard with his left hand meant the legibility was a mess. He turned to face the group, deliberately avoiding Paul's eye. Most people were well composed. Some were looking away embarrassed and others locked eyes with him smiling at his predicament. He smiled back. 'That's why I hide behind a keyboard all day.'

Laughter travelled around and in the back of Dom's mind, he felt comforted that Donald had stumbled across Prestons. It would provide a good fit for him.

'Ok. That's enough,' said Paul at the remaining giggles. He stared at Dom. 'Just an overview is fine, Donald.'

IX

'What's going on, Dominic?'

Wayne Thompson looked from Donald to Maggie. Donald had just repeated for the third time that he was ill and would need to check the reports before committing. Wayne slapped his pad on the table.

Maggie jumped in. 'We'll get those to you today.'

'I don't bloody care about getting them today. I want confidence I can rely on the accuracy—that's what's important. I'm not around for part of next month, which leaves us very little time for this.' He pointed to the files. 'We don't have time to be double checking items.' He frowned at them and left.

Donald asked, 'Is he coming back?'

'You know what he's like. It's time for lunch.'

X

In Surry Hills at Prestons, the caller was having a hard time keeping his voice down. In the stairwell, through a violent murmur, he spat into his mobile. 'He's a fucking liability. The moron hasn't got a clue who he's dealing with. You can't do business like that.'

While the person on the other end asked a question, he looked around to make sure he was still alone in the echoing corridor. 'You watch him—that's what you do. Keep me updated.' He crept back to the work floor.

XI

Ten minutes later, Donald and Maggie were cradling Thai food on their knees in a poky grassed area a short stroll from the office. The half dozen benches were taken and having asked another diner to share her bench with them, Maggie sat in the middle, hiding from the wind.

The cool gusts were starting to build, with the roar nearly drowning out Donald's ring tone.

Dom was phoning. Donald excused himself and stepped away to talk.

'Where the hell have you been?' asked Dom.

'I'm with Maggie. We were in a meeting together and she invited me—'

'You had me worried. We said we'd talk at lunch, remember? That meeting I was in was a bloody nightmare.' Dom recounted the events in the Wattle room and Donald laughed along, lapping up his brother's gaffes.

Still chuckling aloud, Donald said, 'Gotta go.'

'You're having lunch with Maggie? Shit. Watch what you say and don't look at her too much. She'll know it's not me.'

Donald went back to the bench in time to catch Maggie, who was now alone, wrestling from her lips a strand of hair the wind was tossing around. She pulled her collar up further and spoke flatly.

'I've been let down by a girlfriend on a trip we had planned. Do you fancy coming away for a weekend?'

'Sure. When? Where?' He tried sounding detached, but he wasn't sure his words came out that way.

Dom had spoken about Maggie often and Donald had met her a long time ago. He found her confidence and poise attractive, even as she sat huddled cowering from the wind.

'We were thinking of somewhere down south. Last weekend in August.'

He shoved a mouthful of curry into his mouth, pretending to chew over the idea, all along ready to sing out that he could make it. 'Will there be sex?' His eyebrows were stretched back as far as they would go and he nodded as if Maggie needed help saying *yes*.

'Not with me, there won't.' Her eyes closed longer than a blink and she crossed one leg over the other.

They ate their lunch in silence with Donald adjusting his posture to be able to look at her as he ate. She was beautiful.

'What are you looking at?' she asked.

'Nothing.' He turned away and shovelled food in.

Pings of excitement coursed through his body when he thought back to what he was doing at Subiaco. He was keen to get back to Dom's desk.

Maggie leaned forward to get a better glimpse. 'Look at me,' she ordered.

'What?' said Donald, avoiding her eyes.

'Look this way.' She rested a hand on his arm.

He couldn't meet her eyes. This was it—she had worked out he wasn't Dominic.

'Here. You've got some food on your chin.'

'Thanks.' He wiped his face, and lifted his head back and eyes up to the quickly changing sky. It was a compact film of blue-grey cloud. They were in for some rain.

Maggie tidied up her lunch packaging. 'Let's head back,' she said.

Jostled by the crowds, buffeted by a fresh wind, they began a quickstep to the office. Maggie spoke about the recent bundle of changes in her team, which Donald fought to comprehend. 'It seems every week they tamper with a process and tighten the way we operate. I'm seriously thinking about moving on.'

With his face lowered, Donald was reading a message from Lorna asking him to call her. Distracted, he said, 'Dom won't like that.'

The second he said it, he knew it was wrong. His jaw closed so tightly he was sure Maggie heard his teeth bashing. He looked straight ahead, focusing on nothing, petrified she had detected his slip up. From the corner of his eye, her double-take was easily picked up.

She was switching her vision between him and the road ahead. 'Come again?'

'We'd all miss you,' he added gently. Desperate to look at her to check it was safe, he waited until he felt the guilt lifting from his face. If his sloppy third person mention of Dom had truly registered with Maggie, she didn't let on.

For the rest of the walk, Donald worked to keep the conversation away from Subiaco, the stress of it alleviating only once they parted ways on level sixteen.

At Dom's desk, he vowed never to share that blunder with him.

The area Dom usually sat in was still. Eva wasn't in her chair and the office had fallen eerily quiet.

Donald logged on so that it looked like he was working. Reports and folders positioned for the right effect surrounded the keyboard and mouse. He called Lorna.

'What time will you be home today? I need some money for a concert tonight. Everyone's going.'

'It's late notice, honey. I'll be home at about six.' Keeping his voice down, he listened out for any of Dom's colleagues.

'Please dad. I can pass by your work and collect it. We're leaving from Central at about half past five and it'll be too late if I wait for you to get home.'

Donald swore to himself. 'I'm working offsite today, sweetheart, so you can't come here. I don't know when I'll get to the office. How much is the ticket?'

'Eighty.'

'I can't, petal.' He had no way of meeting up with Lorna and he didn't have that kind of money.

'This means so much to me, dad. Please.' Her desperate wails struck at his heart, causing him to lean forward into his lap, eyes squinting, convinced this simple act would lower the volume of the call.

'If mummy pays tonight, I can pay her back. Did you ask your mum?' He knew full well she had. When it came to money, Donald was the unreliable last resort.

'She said no.'

He was about to let her down once more. 'I've got an idea. Let's catch up at the weekend. We can chat about university, and you and your sister can come over for a film night—'

The phone went dead.

Donald winced and cupped his head in his hand.

XII

In the late afternoon, Dom looked at the time of Donald's last text message. That had been over an hour before. He wondered if the lack of contact meant Donald was in a spot of bother, but he wasn't overly concerned. Last week, he had counselled Donald plenty of times—if the situation turned bad, he was to act sick, go to the toilet and call him. Dom continued with some work that Donald had left him and twenty minutes later sent him a message.

How are you? Is
everything ok? How
is it there?

Donald's reply came through soon after.

Been checking out
yr system u know
me i read varied
cypress accounts
whats going on
there

Dom had resigned himself to Donald doing some snooping while at his desk, what with his computer skills. But he didn't want him prying too much.

Not much. Reading
the papers you
left me. Stay out
of those accounts.
I mean it.

Dom didn't have to wait too long for a reply.

I checked yr figures
and maggies u r one
of the top
performers but she
is best in the state

Dom typed a final message.

Leave those files
alone. Maggie's
got years more
experience than
me, you turd. Has
anyone said
anything? No one
here suspects a
thing.

XIII

It was a quarter to five. Donald was leaving the office with Dom's leather bag over his shoulder and his final task was to bid Belinda good night.

'See you real soon, Belinda.' He flashed her a big grin. Done.

The lift crawled its way to Clarence Street and Donald stepped out, his face a drab mask. He walked quickly with the crowd and he spotted a brief text message.

How did it go?

Responding now would slow him down and he was in a rush to get away. He dashed to the intersection but the lights changed too quickly for him. He ran into the road, hoping to make it across, too excited to stand still and hang around for traffic lights. But cars were already moving and he judiciously stepped in reverse to the kerb. He found a small patch of footpath to perch on, toes over the edge and hands in trouser pockets, unfazed at squashing into the pedestrians behind. They were so close he could feel them shuffling against Dom's bag. That's when the first fat blobs of rain landed on his shoulders and he felt the cold spots on his head.

Trucks and taxis whizzed across the intersection. Donald eyed the lights directly ahead of him. 'Come on,' he muttered.

Someone came behind him, shifting and nudging against the bag, someone even more impatient than him. The lights changed and a truck picked up speed as it entered the intersection to make it through the lights. Donald waited for the green figure.

He felt the force behind him and tried turning to say something, at the same time, trying to remove his hands from his pockets. The pushing continued and he fell forward, one foot momentarily propping him up, but not long enough to keep him upright.

He screamed as he tumbled into the truck's path. He breathed in to produce a shout, and his head pulled back instinctively to stop his face from hitting the ground. His hands were just out of his pockets, but not close enough to his face to save him. Falling further, his head took the full impact of the bull bar as the truck slammed into his body. His trunk cracked back, the snapping of bones drawing shrieks from onlookers, and the screech of brakes filled the intersection.

Donald disappeared under the truck, which skidded to the far kerb. He lay face up on the bitumen, legs splayed, with Dom's bag underneath him, propping him up awkwardly, as if he was lazing on a blanket in a park. Blood covered his face streaming from the gashes on his head, ears and nose. Once all the traffic had stopped, people joined him on the road, huddling around.

3 | Robin

|

The string of texts, missed calls and voice messages came through as soon as Dom turned on his mobile. A hundred metres from home, with the rush hour noise dying down, the rat-tat-tat of the notifications echoed in chorus with the rain hitting his umbrella. Camille's note contained the news.

```
Come quickly. It's
Donald. We're at
Saint Vincent's.
```

Dom leapt into a taxi, read and listened to the remaining messages and minutes later, he was at the hospital following signs to the head trauma ward, his frantic footsteps announcing his urgency and people ahead of him moving to the sides. The corridor opened onto an extended seating area and his eyes darted around. Camille, Robin and Lorna were over by a window.

'How is he?' said Dom, hugging his sister. He bent down to kiss Lorna and Robin.

'Where the hell have you been?' Robin looked up from her crumpled tissues.

Camille touched her sister-in-law's shoulder and repeated what the medical staff had told them. 'He's being operated on now. He went in to surgery about half an hour ago.'

'What happened?' Dom gripped Camille's arm.

Robin spoke from her tissues. 'He was hit by a car near Town Hall.' When she raised her head, fresh tears were crowding in her puffy eyes. 'The police have told us what little they know. They'll be speaking to Donnie the minute he wakes up.' Her voice weakened.

'Of course.' Dom stared ahead.

Camille said, 'It happened near your work.'

Dom let out a cry. He crumpled into a chair and buried his face in his hands. 'Where?'

Robin spoke. 'On Clarence Street, right near you. We told the police officer Donnie must have been meeting you.' She tilted her head, giving Dom a chance to confirm her assumption. 'She's very helpful. If only you'd been around when she was here. But you took ages to show up.'

Lorna and Camille exchanged cautious glances.

'I was at the gym and no, I wasn't meeting Donald. Why would you tell the police that?' His voice trailed off into a whisper. Camille held his stare as he directed his next question to her with a rising voice. 'Why would she tell them that? We don't need to meet in the city—we live together.'

'Ok. Ok. Let's all stay calm.' Camille sat next to Dom and rubbed big circles on his back. 'We're in shock and we need to wait for news. Let's not fight.'

Dom's questions flowed. 'When did it happen? How did you find out?'

'The police called Robin. They got his driver licence from his wallet, and Robin called me just as I was getting home.'

Dom looked to his sister-in-law, whose head sat angled as if a magnet was drawing it to the carpet. 'Lorna, where's your sister?'

Robin answered. 'I left her with a neighbour. She has a young girl too, so she's fine there.'

Dom leant over to pat Lorna's knee. 'You're doing ok, aren't you?' She smiled at him. 'When do we get more information?' he asked.

'When he gets out of surgery,' said Robin. 'I'm down as next of kin.'

'You?' Dom turned to Camille. 'Is that right?' His head shook. 'We'll change that. I'm next of kin.'

'Donnie has me as the next of kin. It's appropriate.'

'He told me last week—now that he's got work, he's getting the divorce.'

'Don't be so wicked, Dominic.'

'Mum, uncle Dom. Stop, please.' Lorna rammed her feet against an empty chair and Robin and Dom turned away from each other.

It wasn't long before Dom was fidgeting in his seat. His legs jiggled and he couldn't seem to find a place for his hands. Actions that were usually automatic were now conscious and demanding attention. He stood up and scoured the area.

'I fancy a drink. Who wants a can of something?' He stepped away before anyone had the chance to respond and he had no sooner arrived at the drinks machine than his phone rang.

'Dominic Tolen? This is Constable Blakely.'

'I'm at the hospital now.'

'Good. Is there any news on your brother?'

'None.'

'I'll be back there within the hour on another matter. Can we talk then?'

'Definitely. I have some questions too.'

Dom slid his mobile into his pocket. The lump sitting low, deep in his stomach set like concrete, turning heavier, bulkier.

II

At nine that night, Donald was still in surgery and his family were pacing and sitting and standing, waiting for news. Robin had spoken to her neighbour to check on Niamh, Lorna had called Drew three times and sent many more text messages, and Camille had called her husband twice. Dom found texting Harry with the news about Donald was a way to stop chewing his nails and to put a halt to Camille's protests that the nail biting was fraying her nerves.

Camille asked, 'What were his plans for tonight?'

Dom shrugged. 'Dunno. Tennis maybe. He's been playing it some evenings with Josh.' He stopped. 'We should tell Josh. Has anyone spoken to him?'

Camille and Robin shook their heads without looking his way.

He moved some metres away from them to make the call. They didn't need to hear the details about Donald again. He stood at an east-facing window.

The darkness shrouded the hospital. The wind, which had picked up, hurled sheets of rain, which had doubled in intensity, at the panes.

He stared at his reflection while he passed on the news to Donald's friend. Dom didn't explain why Donald was at that intersection and Josh didn't ask. Josh was quiet for so long, Dom wasn't sure if he had hung up or if he was crying away from the mouthpiece. In the reflection of the window, he watched a policewoman approach his family.

'Are you there, Josh?'

'Let me know when he's awake.' He hung up.

Dom let the call cut off but he remained fixed in his spot observing the women reflected in the glass. The police uniform was clearly visible. Constable Blakely, thought Dom. He saw Camille point over to him and his heart beat faster when the uniformed figure looked across. She seemed relaxed, not anxious, and he wanted to project that too. He pretended not to notice that she had arrived. The mobile phone still pressed to his ear, he shifted a few casual steps placing his family and the police officer directly behind him, out of sight. He took a huge breath secretly and turned to face them. The mobile went into his pocket and he headed over to them. The constable had her hands full with pen and paper, so Dom didn't offer his hand.

'What can you tell us?'

'Very little until we speak to your brother.' She jangled with items as she silenced her radio to continue the chat uninterrupted. 'People at the scene said he tried to beat the lights. He turned back and he fell.'

Robin shook her head. 'The city is so busy and the cars race by and they lose control.'

Dom said, 'Were you listening? That's not what she said.' He turned to the constable. 'How's the driver?'

'As you'd imagine, he's pretty shaken up.'

'What did he say about it?'

'He tells a similar story—your brother appeared from nowhere.' The constable passed them no more details and started questioning Dom, poised to record his responses. 'Robin thought you were meeting up with Donald. You work very close to where it happened.'

'I do.' Dom used his hands to describe how far his office was from the intersection. 'But I wasn't meeting him this evening, plus Donald knew I was going to the gym.' Constable Blakely nodded through her note taking and Dom continued. 'Donald and his wife are separated, and so he's lived with me for about a year.' Robin flushed. 'She assumed we were meeting up—she does that.'

'Do you know where Donald was going?'

'No idea. He didn't tell me. I generally find out where he's been when I get home at the end of the day, not before.'

Through sturdy glasses, Camille surveyed the constable, her inquiring eyes assessing the officer. 'Was he alone?'

'It would appear so. The witnesses said he was on his own when he was halfway across the street and nobody at the scene said they knew him.'

'Street cameras?'

'We're checking those.' The officer turned back to Dom. 'Perhaps he was coming to see you?'

'Unplanned? He couldn't guarantee I'd be there.'

'You left work to go to the gym? What time was that?'

'Let me think.' Four pairs of eyes fixed on Dom. His mind whizzed around. 'It was just before five. That's my usual hour for leaving. I'd say about then.' A rough time was safest.

Robin's scream made everyone jump. 'Oh my god, Dominic. You must've been close by when it happened. That's weird—like twin weird. You were at the scene.'

'Incredible.' His head bounced as though he was absorbing her observation. 'To think, I was blocks away.' Panic swept over him at seeing the police officer scribbling in her note pad.

'Would he have visited a bar?'

'No way.' They rejected the idea unanimously.

'How was his health? How was he when he left for work this morning?'

Everyone glared at him waiting for an answer—even Lorna looked up from her mobile.

Dom started stammering and crying. 'It's boiling in here. Is anyone else hot?' His forearm wiped his tears away. 'Do those windows open?'

'My god, Dominic. You're shaking.'

'Sit down here.' Camille patted the spot next to her.

He sat. 'I'm good.'

'Take your time.'

Dom huffed like a marathon runner tackling an incline in the final kilometres. 'He was fine, just fine. It was a usual morning and nothing at all stands out.'

'When he's out of surgery and he's awake, we'll be having a chat to him. If you need to speak to me, you can call me on that number.' Camille took the card from the policewoman and pressed it into Dom's hand.

Dom looked up at Constable Blakely. 'He left home with a bag this morning. Where is it?'

'It's safe. We have it.'

III

Constable Blakely had left about an hour before when a nurse came to them with some news. 'He's out of surgery and he's being moved to high dependency on level five.'

'And we can see him?'

'Yes, for a bit, but he'll be sedated.' She hurried off pointing the way to the lifts.

On the fifth floor, as they moved deeper into the hospital, the corridors emptied, sounds died off and the pong of antibacterial hand wash intensified. Their steps ricocheted in a corridor so suffocatingly narrow Dom doubted hospital beds would fit through it.

They arrived at the small ward and a nurse escorted them to the room. In a hushed voice, she asked them to be quiet and quick, and told them they were allowed fifteen minutes with him.

No one wasted any of their precious time protesting the shortness of the visit.

The nurse unlocked the door. The room was small with a low ceiling and there was a bed, a cupboard, a sink in the far corner and two chairs, one under the window and one next to the bed.

Camille followed the nurse first, who manoeuvred through the tight spaces with agility. Robin guided Lorna in, her hands on her daughter's shoulders as if ready to use her as a shield. Dom trailed last.

He saw the outline of his brother's legs in the raised bed, under light blue bedclothes, thicker than usual. Casts. He moved in further. His mouth opened, but he couldn't form a sound.

Very little of Donald's face was visible from under the bandaging. Both eye sockets were swollen and purple, and the left eye was covered up with dressing. A large, messy patch of hair was gone—shaved off—and what Dom first saw as a grey parting was actually a tidy row of thick staples, contrasting with the shoddiness of the impromptu haircut.

Never had the twins looked so unidentical.

Dom inched closer to the foot of the bed, steadying himself with the bedrail, where he managed one word through trembling lips. 'Donald.' His eyes scanned the battered body, each bruise and traumatised part churning his insides.

'Dad? Can you hear us?' whispered Lorna, as if she was waking him from a siesta. She stepped away when she got no response.

'Come closer, Dominic. Speak to him.' Camille led Dom by the arm towards the head of the bed. His fingers stroked an unscratched part of Donald's hand.

'It will be all right.' He wiped away tears and sank into a chair, weak and nauseous. He lifted his head to Donald but spoke to the others. 'He's dying.'

'He's not.' Camille snapped at Dom, shielding her niece with her outstretched hand. But Lorna, who had huddled into a weathered armchair under the window, appeared not to have heard.

'Not my Donnie,' said Robin, wailing into her hands.

'I feel it.' Dom rushed to the sink and vomited. He washed and dried his face and toppled back into the low chair, placing Donald's wounds out of view. The tightness in his chest extended from shoulder to shoulder and reached down to meet the lump in his stomach, which getting sick had only fleetingly suppressed.

'Are you ok?' asked Camille. Dom nodded, eyes closed. Any respite he may have received from the darkness was short-lived when the grating sound of rustling plastic filled the claustrophobic room.

Robin had pulled a thick blue bag from under the bed and was going through it, apparently unaffected by its ear-splitting crackle. 'His clothes are in here. Oh, they're bloody and torn and—' Her nose creased. 'A suit? Donnie wears a suit to his new job?'

Dom's eyes stayed shut.

'Oh my god. Look at this.'

Without needing to look, Dom knew Robin was holding up his navy tie.

Robin was gawking at it. 'Donald hates ties.' She looked to Camille. 'He detests the things.' She whistled. 'That must be some job he's got.'

'It's mine. He borrowed it for a meeting or something.' Dom's voice worked to convey vagueness and insignificance.

Robin's eyes widened. 'Where was the meeting? Maybe that's where he was going when it happened.'

'No. I got the impression the meeting was at his office.' Dom said, inventing details as he went.

'Why didn't you tell us this sooner, Dominic?'

Lorna spoke from her chair recounting the brief phone conversation with her father over the tickets to the concert, which Drew was at. 'He told me he wasn't in his office today. We were going to meet up but he wasn't around.'

Robin looked to Dom and Camille. 'There you go. His work will tell us everything.' She let the bag fall noisily away from her and she added almost to herself, 'Donnie in a suit? Now that is strange.'

Dom got to his feet, scared and irritated. 'He can tell us himself soon enough.' He unhooked the patient notes from the foot of the bed, desperate to take his mind off the mounting discomfort. Camille stopped him.

'I've checked those already. They don't have anything on them. We need to hear from the staff.'

Dom let the clipboard slip back into its holder. 'Leave his stuff, Robin, and come with me.' The last thing he needed was her meddling. 'You're next of kin. Let's go and get more details from them.'

The door clicked shut behind them. Camille went over to Lorna and hugged her close to her belly. 'Your father's going to be ok. He'll need all our support, but he'll be fine.' Camille felt the comfort of Lorna nodding at her waist while her gaze fixed on the plastic bag that sat abandoned under the bed. Without breaking her stare, she said, 'When your father goes home, we'll need to look after him and feed him, because your uncle Dominic cannot cook.'

IV

They spotted the ward nurse who had let them in to see Donald, and once they got her attention, she stopped to speak to them.

'He's got extensive injuries—broken bones and head trauma—but the surgery went well. He's in here with us for monitoring and he should be in a general ward tomorrow.' As she spoke, her vision shifted to behind them, at her colleague ushering Camille and Lorna from Donald's room. 'Look over there. You have to leave now.'

The four regrouped and moved around on the spot almost disoriented, without purpose, as if they had just arrived on the planet.

Dom clasped Lorna's hands. 'You should all get some rest. I'm staying here.'

Robin leant in to kiss him. 'I need to pick up Niamh from next door. It's getting late.' She tugged on her daughter's arm, half expecting a fight, but Lorna broke free from Dom's hold and went with her mother.

Camille tumbled into a chair.

Dom said, 'Wait here.'

He walked back to the ward and found the nurse sitting at a monitor, working on an electronic report. He apologised for interrupting, explained who he was and pleaded to sit with his twin.

'We only got to see him briefly.'

'You can have a few minutes. Our patients have to rest.' She brushed past him, swiped her card on the door and let him go inside. Her voice changed into an accomplished whisper, hushed yet audible. 'Your brother is strong. He'll be fine.'

Once the door closed, Dom sat by Donald, relieved that his face, with all its disfiguring, was tilting in the other direction. His mind focused on Donald's breathing, low and uniform, keeping attention off his brother's injuries and off the mess he was in. His eyes caught sight of the plastic bag under the bed. He leaned over to the door and pushed on it to make sure it was shut. He knelt down and fumbled with the contents through the plastic bag, as though checking for something hard, careful to keep the noisy plastic from giving his search away. He could only feel clothing and shoes.

Without looking to the bed, he said, 'Sorry'. He slipped unseen out of the room.

V

Donald died at ten to three in the morning. Minutes before his body shut down, Dom was close by stirring in his makeshift bed. His mind was alive and the knot in his stomach was a constant reminder of the situation he was in. Removing their shoes, he and Camille had positioned themselves across chairs in a small, deserted waiting space not far from Donald's room, where a broken strip light helped darken the area. The ward smelt of disinfectant after the cleaners had passed through and the only signs of hospital staff at that time of the night were the gentle knocking together of ward doors and the squeally scuffing of shoes.

Camille appeared to be sleeping. She hardly moved and Dom wondered if she was awake. The sound of running footsteps and doors banging made her sit up. 'What's that? Any commotion around here is unnerving.'

'It's just the doctors running around. I can't sleep. Can you?'

'Dozing.' She sighed. 'Look at us. Hard to believe we're sleeping in a hospital and Donald's over there in the state he's in.' She pulled her jacket up higher. 'It's going to be a slow recovery, believe me. When Tommie's father fell off the roof, it was ages before he regained his independence.'

She stopped, pondering something. She said, 'If you two had bumped into each other this afternoon, as you left work, this might not have happened.' As an afterthought, she added, 'Perhaps.'

Dom didn't know if it was the pain of Donald's circumstances, the lack of sleep or the time of night, but huddled on hospital seats with his sister created a soothing candour Dom rarely felt with Camille. She had always been much closer to Donald, but the need to share parts of his secret, to ease pressure, was strengthening, and before he had time to think about it, he was speaking.

'I wasn't around to stop anything.'

Camille was as quiet as the night.

Dom hesitated, expecting her to whisper something at least, but she said nothing. 'I didn't want to worry you when the police were asking questions earlier, so I just—' Dom left it there. Someone from the hospital approached them.

'Are you Donald Tolen's family?'

They sat up.

Camille rummaged for her footwear.

The doctor paused while Camille slipped her feet into her shoes.

'I'm sorry to tell you, but Donald has died. He passed away a few minutes ago.'

'What?' Camille started crying. 'What?' she repeated.

Dom's knees gave way and he knocked into the chair. 'Oh my god.'

'We tried to save him. His injuries were too severe.'

Camille's scream bounced off the walls. 'Please try some more.' She plopped into the seat, her face twisted with crying.

'You can see him.' The doctor sat next to Camille.

Dom remembered little of the conversation with the doctor. Thinking back, he couldn't even recall what she looked like. Although he had shuffled in to Donald's room, with Camille and a nurse, he had no recollection of getting there. His hearing underwent transformation. Every sound was dulled. And if he wasn't looking directly at someone or something, he lost awareness of it, his periphery collapsing to the point Camille's wailing at the side of the bed went unnoticed and unheard.

A while later, with a blink, he came to, staring at a face. First, he registered it was familiar. The roundness of its features and the blonde bob as blunt as rock he knew well. The cornflower blue eyes, nursing red bags, were now raw. Then, he was able to name her. It was Robin.

Something in the reaches of his consciousness told him quite a lot of time would have passed if she'd managed to return to the hospital. For Dom, it seemed like seconds ago he had been told the tragic news. Only then did he realise he was holding someone in his arms. He pulled back to check who it was. The height, the hair, the angle of his hug all pointed to it being Lorna. His squeeze tightened and he cried into her for an interminable period.

Death had stripped Donald of shadows. His formless body lay flattened, the bruises and wounds having shrunk. The bandages appeared to have loosened on his oxygen-less limbs. The staples in his skull appeared less embedded, less severe. He wasn't as swollen and the restfulness in his posture permanent.

It was a new morning when Dom uttered his first words after Donald had died. The ward was coming to life and the sun was sending shafts of light through the curtained window. Standing over the bed, Dom stroked Donald's hair.

'Even with the bruising, he looks peaceful.'

Camille stepped up to him. 'I don't believe this.' She tidied the sheets around Donald's cooling body. 'What happened to you?'

VI

It wasn't raining when they left the hospital and a crisp wind had all but dried the roads. They bundled into Robin's car and Camille phoned Tommie to tell him they were on their way over.

Dom sat silent and every now and then, he shivered and rattled as if made of metal.

Camille mumbled the names of people they would need to call, but Dom wasn't listening, cocooned in his own world.

Outside Camille's home, four bodies climbed out of the car and ambled up the path. Inside, Camille flicked the lights and was greeted by Banner, the German shepherd, its tail brushing furiously at the sight of all the visitors.

They were ushered silently through to the warm kitchen, where Tommie interrupted preparing a pot of tea to hug each of them, while the kettle's rising crescendo broke the mournful silence.

Dom claimed the nearest chair and tapped the one next to him for Lorna. She sat quickly welcoming the comforting arm Dom wrapped around her.

Camille and Robin took the places opposite, their conversations their own.

'I can't accept it. What are we going to do?'

'I hope he didn't feel too much pain.'

'Poor Niamh. This will be very hard for her.'

'Would he have suffered much? It's too painful to think about.'

Tommy leant in with steaming drinks and thoughtless questions. 'So what's the latest? What was he doing on that corner anyway?'

Neither question got answered.

Dom stood up and headed to the bathroom, closing the kitchen door behind him. He was exhausted, each limb numb, but his racing mind wouldn't let him rest. He turned on the cold tap to refresh himself.

The icy water splashed his face, easing his painful, blotchy eyes, and he looked at himself in the mirror. Wrinkles and redness on the features he knew so well.

Yet the face he saw was not his own. It was Donald's thick eyebrows, angular jaw and darkened eyes. The vulnerability there he usually found on Donald's face.

Dom's nostrils flared as he fought to take in shallow breaths. He dried his aching face and shuffled back to the kitchen.

As he walked in, Robin looked up and yelped.

She ran to him and wrapped her arms around him, hardly able to speak. 'It's not going in.' Her grief stalled her words. 'Thank god you're here, Dominic.' She stroked his bristly jaw. 'We'll always remember Donnie.'

Camille said, 'We'll remember Donald as his own person. Remembering him for him.' Her resolute tone hung in the room, suspended in the inert air.

Oblivious, Robin continued. 'He was coming to dinner tomorrow night. Niamh doesn't understand. She's too young. We told her daddy's in heaven. What do you tell a six-year-old?' She sat down.

Tommie refilled her mug of tea from the kettle. He said, 'Sometimes it's easier to make something up.'

Dom claimed a different chair and sat looking down, hands in his lap. 'Have you told Niamh yet?'

Robin's brow creased. 'I just said that. We told her.'

Dom lifted his head and scanned the room. Everyone was looking at him. 'What?'

'You should try to sleep. Lie down upstairs.' Camille reached out for his hand. 'You're in shock.'

'I'll be ok. I'll make myself a drink.' He got up.

'Your drink's there.' Camille pointed to his tea still steaming on a place mat. 'You need to sleep.'

Dom went to reply, but he let the ring of his mobile stop him. He picked it up, dropped it and caught it. It was an unknown number. 'This will be the police,' he declared. He was right.

Constable Blakely wanted to speak to them. Dom gave her Camille's address and hung up.

'She's heard and she's coming round to speak to me'—he reached for his tea—'to us.'

VII

There wasn't an empty chair around the kitchen table. Tommie and Camille had taken their usual seats. He was facing the sink, she the back door, and their five guests were dotted around, each cradling cups.

Dom, Lorna and Robin sat on Camille's right, and Constable Blakely and her colleague were opposite them.

Constable Blakely had offered her sympathy and rapidly apologised for having to ask questions. 'We're looking into possible causes of the accident—his health, his heart—information like that.' She pulled out her pad and pen but rested it on the table, making eye contact with everyone.

Robin scrunched her face at the suggestion. 'His heart? Do you think it was a heart attack?'

'It's possible. It was quick, whatever it was that made him fall.'

Camille almost whispered her answer. 'His heart was fine. We don't have a history of heart troubles in our family.'

'Was he taking medication for anything?'

Robin spoke. 'I don't think so. He was—'

Dom interrupted. 'I doubt it's relevant but he took antidepressants for a while.'

Robin gave a yelp. 'What?' She coughed out her breath. 'When?' A motherly hand extended to stroke Lorna's arm and she turned to Dom with a distraught expression, worn out from grief. 'You have to tell me these things.' She banged the table as she spoke.

'It was around the time he came to live with me. He hadn't been working and you'd split.' Dom shifted his gaze from Robin to the policewoman. 'He needed a crutch—that's all.' His soothing tap on Robin's fist, which was ready to strike the wooden surface again, was brief.

Robin wept into her hand and covered her mouth to muffle her cries.

The officers sipped their drinks.

She lifted her head and a silent look to Camille asked if she too knew about the medication.

Almost imperceptibly, Camille nodded.

'He wasn't depressed!' shouted Robin.

Dom rubbed her back. 'We know, honey. He hardly ever used them.' He looked back to Constable Blakely. 'He'd started a new job recently, and in a field he loved—computers. He adored computing. So things were looking up for him.'

'He didn't take his own life, officer, if that's what you're thinking.' Camille stroked Banner's coat, holding her ex-sniffer dog away from the visitors.

Constable Blakely cleared her throat. 'Not at all. Nothing points to that idea.' The policewoman brushed it away with a sweeping wooden hand.

'Why are you so sure?' asked Tommie.

Constable Blakely referred to her notes. 'He went to cross the road, but he had to turn back because of the traffic. That tells us he was heading somewhere and he wasn't thinking of—of—that. But he was in a rush and maybe something distracted him.'

Dom fidgeted in his chair and picked up his tea too abruptly, spilling a drop. 'Donald wasn't worried about anything. I'm one hundred per cent certain—he was fine.'

'Of course he was.'

Tommie asked another question. 'Dominic, you were with him yesterday morning at your place. How was he then?'

'I told you all—he left for work fine.'

Robin prodded the table and looked at the police with Dom watching from the corner of his eye. 'It's his work you need to speak to. They'll tell you why he wanted Dominic's clothes and why he was on Clarence Street.'

The room fell silent and Constable Blakely, who'd been sipping her tea, brought the cup back up to her lips, happy to let the Tolen family fill the gaps.

Robin spoke first. 'Constable, Donald was wearing a suit for work yesterday, which he borrowed from Dominic, yet he normally wears casual clothes.'

The police officer looked for confirmation from Dom, who nodded.

Robin continued almost to herself. 'There was clearly something special on and we should find out what.'

The police officer jotted some notes. 'We'll speak to his employer and find out what they know. If you could pass us those work details, please.' She looked up from her pad and stared at Dom.

His heart beat faster at the thought of the next angle of questioning, for he could guess what was coming. He tried not to blink.

'So Donald went to work in your suit? Did he tell you what it was for?'

'No. Donald did not tell me what it was for.' He held the cup of tea in front of his mouth, with both elbows locked to the table to steady his twitching limbs. 'And I don't know what he was wearing when he left, because I left home first.'

Camille spoke from behind him. 'This is all so confusing and upsetting, Dominic. You need to go home and rest.'

'I'm staying. There's no confusion. What are you talking about?'

'You just said *when he left he was fine,* and now you're saying you left first.'

Dom erupted. 'What is this, Camille? Bloody hell.'

'It's all right, Dominic. It's just a question.' Robin touched his arm as she spoke, and Dom thought that was that.

'So think back. Who left first—you or him?'

Dom closed his eyes. 'I haven't slept.' He wet his lips slowly keeping everyone waiting as he prepared himself, as though about to speak in a foreign language, careful to use the correct words, an appropriate tone.

'When I said he was fine, I meant in the morning as I was getting ready to leave. I noticed nothing different whatsoever.'

He opened his eyes.

'I left before—I mean, he left befo—oh.' Dom paused. 'I'm too tired to work out what's before and what's after.'

'It's ok, Dominic. Ok?' Robin patted him more.

When he spoke again, he punctuated each word with a firm pause. 'I left first,' he lied.

'Thank you,' said Constable Blakely, scribbling it in her pad.

Robin's hand slipped from Dom's forearm and her shoulders fell. 'How sad to think he hated ties and he died in one.' She scanned the room. 'Life. So sad.'

Tommie said innocently, 'He was wearing it when he was hit, but not when he died.'

Robin's lips pursed. 'Really, Tommie?' She squinted at her brother-in-law. 'Does it seem the right time for fact checking? It's not a pub quiz.'

'Calm down.' Camille stepped forward. 'Tommie, fetch my diary please. It's upstairs somewhere.' She nudged her husband up from his seat and out of the kitchen.

The officers looked at each other.

'We should go.'

They stood up collecting hats and pocketing items. 'Dominic, let us drive you back to your place. If it's ok with you, I'd like to see where Donald lived.'

Dom fought hard to keep his face muscles relaxed.

'That's kind of you.'

VIII

Constable Blakely's colleague held the car door open for Dom, who, drained and light-headed, climbed in behind the front passenger seat. He still hadn't heard the young constable speak.

The car pulled away and finally, without turning around, the officer spoke, in a voice innocent and unpractised. 'Which number on Placer Avenue?'

Dom told him and he caught Constable Blakely's smile through the rear vision mirror as she adeptly handled the inner west traffic.

He moved in the seat to avoid catching her stare. He wasn't comfortable one bit. The plastic cover he was sitting on felt harder than steel and the roof was suffocatingly close to the top of his head. The mesh between him and the officers, which was trapping him in the back compartment, seemed near enough to scrape his nose.

Constable Blakely's colleague added, 'It looks like it's clearing up. We might have a dry one after all.'

Their stony attempts at light conversation did nothing to calm Dom as they crossed Anzac Parade towards his home. It was a struggle for him to think clearly what they might find there or what they were looking for. He debated whether to ask what they expected to see at his place, but decided against it.

They stopped at traffic lights. Keeping her hands on the steering wheel, Constable Blakely spun round to him. 'I forgot to ask you all when you were together. We have Donald's mobile, but it's locked. Do you happen to know the pin?'

Dom fixed on the constable's eyes and didn't speak, answering with a shake of the head, afraid of what his voice would reveal if he tried talking.

'Not to worry. We'll apply to get access to unlock it.'

The strain to hold his face in a relaxed expression was making Dom shiver. He brought his hands up to wipe his eyes, which granted him a moment of solitude. His sweaty fingers cupped his face until the car stopped and the side door opened. He got to his feet outside his block.

The sun was creeping over everything, warming away the previous night's chill. The police officers hovered around for Dom to lead the way up to his unit.

He looked about him, as though expecting something to have changed. 'It's the same.'

'Are you ok, Dominic?'

'Yet I feel completely different.'

Inside his unit, he moved like a visitor to a museum searching for his favourite artist's work. The darkness and stale air only added to his feelings of arriving in his home as an outsider. Everything of Donald's stood out, almost larger than usual, as though illuminated especially for the three of them. The black shoes in the hall, the tennis racquet and the bothersome stack of software had all helped mark his space.

'Come with me.' Dom walked through to the back part of the unit and pointed first at his own bedroom door. 'I'm in there. Donald's room is along here.'

The hallway came to life with sound as their six feet hit the floor boards out of harmony.

'You have a lovely place. Deceptively large.'

'It was two units joined together, years ago. Here we are.' Dom stopped, unable to go inside Donald's room. 'In there.'

Even glimpsed from the hallway, the room was easily the messiest part of the house. Without pausing, the police stepped in and Constable Blakely disappeared round the door. Her comments travelled out to Dom. 'We still don't have the address where Donald worked.'

'I don't know it exactly. It's Surry Hills somewhere,' replied Dom from the hall.

'Would you mind getting that for us while we stay here.'

Dom was stuck in his place, unable to move. On Donald's desk sat the pad they had used to list everything they needed for the prank.

'Mr Tolen?' The young officer was leaning backwards to look out at Dom. 'Your brother's work details, please.'

'Oh yes—er—yes.' Dom returned to the kitchen as instructed, stepping lightly. He heard Donald's door close.

In the kitchen, he cursed and thumped the air. 'Shit. Shit,' he said, louder than he needed to.

Without needing to google Prestons, he wrote down the Surry Hills address he had visited the day before, his hands trembling. He looked behind him towards Donald's bedroom, picturing the constables moving around, touching everything.

When the police came out soon after, Dom held up a small tub. 'Donald's medication—you might need it.'

'Thank you.' Constable Blakely read the label and passed it to her colleague. 'If you need to speak to anyone, please call us. And we'll let you know how things progress.'

IX

Dom stopped in the half-light of the windowless hall. His thoughts were not organised. A fist came up to cover his mouth and stifle his groans.

As if possessed, he darted into the kitchen and dived for his phone to read his chain of texts from the previous day. When the police got access to Donald's phone, what would these messages suggest? He tried reading them, but the water in his eyes prevented him from reading. Lost, he looked up from the screen, sniffling and slurping.

Donald's room. What had the police seen?

He dashed along the dark hall and burst in, shoving the door out of the way. The apprehension at touching and approaching Donald's things had clearly gone—he had to know what the officers had seen.

The list was there on the pad, untouched.

As though at an exhibition, hands behind his back, he angled over to study it. Could the words reveal if they had been looked at, remembered and understood?

A blink sent one of his tears splattering onto the page, smudging an item in the list. He panicked further. Now there was proof Dom had thought it important enough to look at the sheet of paper. He went to rip it off the pad, but stopped. It would have to stay where it was, prominent and suspicious.

In the middle of the room, he went back to reading their string of phone messages. If it all got out, he'd be done for—with the family, at work, everywhere.

Blubbering, he staggered to his room, slamming the door and perching on the bed. The weight of the events of the last twenty-four hours were becoming too much to cope with. He dried his eyes and looked at the time. It was nearly eleven.

Time to end it all.

His mind was chaotic, barely capable of sensible thought. He needed to write a list, but he couldn't see a pen in the room. His fingers would do. He tapped his thumb.

Phone Donald's work.

Then phone Subiaco.

Next, the hospital.

He lost count. His thumb wiggled as he tried to recall which task was first on the list.

Phone the office.

He gave up trying and his arms fell beside him, his eyes filling with tears.

Minutes later, drying his face, he straightened up, nodding to himself. No more tears. There was work to do.

He undressed in the ensuite bathroom and ran a steaming shower. He didn't bother shaving, but his teeth got a brushing and he put on deodorant. Cotton buds removed grime from his ears and a touch of wax coated his hair.

Naked, he went into the bedroom, put on a pair of white underpants and stood in front of the mirror checking his body over. His toes were so cold they were distracting him. Seconds later, socks on, he returned to studying himself, avoiding looking into his eyes, where the emotion, the grief lurked.

He was ready to go, but he needed an entry point. Like a gun, his forefinger pressed skin in the middle of his forehead. Next, he tested his right temple, the pad of his finger digging into the softest flesh. He lifted his stubbled chin to stroke and prod under his jaw. His attention turned to other areas of his body. A forefinger explored his chest next to his left nipple, searching for a position over his agitated heart. That would be the spot to aim for.

To stop his lower lip from quivering, he borrowed his tongue to stretch it out of shape.

The cool air that batted his skin jolted him from his actions. He stepped to the painting hanging near the bed. With his careful movements, the canvas came off its hooks and he propped it against the wall by his feet. After a fiddle with the door, he opened the safe.

He clicked his fingers as he recalled his other tasks.
'Prestons.'

When the word left his mouth, he stopped. It was
hard to believe he had been there only the previous day.
It seemed like an age away. Weeks ago.

The number came up on his mobile quickly. He lay
on the cool bedclothes. An energetic female voice
greeted him with tones so pleasant Dom felt a tinge of
sorrow at having to pass on upsetting news.

'My name is Dom Tolen. My brother, Donald,
works there. But there's been an ...' Three seconds
passed.

'Hello? I can't hear you. Are you there?'

Dom could only whisper. 'I—I have some news. My
brother died last night, so he won't be in today.'

The reply was delayed. 'My god. That's awful. Please
accept our condolences.'

Dom hung up. Of course Donald wasn't coming in
that day. Or ever again. He was dead.

How could he live life without his twin, his best
friend, his true other half? A life alone was unimaginable
for him. Yet that was precisely what he had been hoping
for, hunting for, in recent weeks—a life of freedom,
away from the obligations of twinship, the restraints of
looking after the two of them.

And here he was, unable to go through a future
without Donald. His mind was incapable of imagining
such loss without feeling such pain and his body
fluttered at the thought of it. Yet he had a lifetime of
memories to draw from to keep Donald alive for as long
as he needed him to be.

Too lethargic to get up, he dialled the Subiaco
reception. The familiarity of Belinda's voice lifted him
only a fraction from his sleep-deprived stupor. 'I need
HR.'

'Can I please have your name, sir.'

Dom felt lifeless, empty, as he lay on his bed, holding the phone, readying himself to speak.

'My name is Donald. Donald Tolen. I'm Dominic's brother. Donald.' Dom looked across at a photo of the two of them on the wall and as he drummed his fingers on his belly, his focus shifted and he eyed the open safe.

The overwhelming pressure in his head eased the second he uttered his twin's name as his own. How good it felt to be free from Dom's ills. How easy it was to be Donald, who was worry-free. Dom's eyes caught the painting on the floor. The two boats moored in rough seas. That was Donald's dealt hand—a vacant craft, ready to be occupied and steered to calmer waters. Why couldn't Dom sail away in the abandoned vessel?

'One moment, Mr Tolen.' Dull music kept him company while he waited in limbo, stuck, hanging, going nowhere.

'Vanessa Hawke speaking.'

Dom recognised the voice. He spoke calmly. 'I'm Dominic Tolen's brother, Donald. Dom is dead.'

Dom heard Vanessa catch her breath. When she went to reply, he butted in. 'He died in hospital last night. He was knocked over yesterday coming home from work.' He paused, unsure how much she was taking in. 'We sat with him, but his injuries were too—'

'I—I am so sorry.' She stumbled over her words. 'This is t—terrible news.' She tutted in rapid succession. 'Really, the saddest news. Poor Dom. You must be devastated.'

'We are.'

'Thank you for calling, Donald. Please call me directly on my mobile if you want to talk about anything. Do you have a pen?'

'Yes. I've got one here,' he replied, smoothing the bedspread with his free hand. 'Go ahead.'

X

The wind dragged branches across Dom's bedroom window and roused him from his slumber. He didn't think he'd been asleep long, but he had a tongue as dry as wood and he felt drained of fluid.

His head had sunk among the six airy pillows, yet his skin felt icy, lying on top of the bedding. Stone cold, he shuddered. The underpants and socks he was wearing yielded little heat.

He felt calmer and lighter than before and the pressure in his torso had eased. The weighty feeling was now external, at his skin, on his chest. His hand came up to find out what was resting there.

It was his mobile phone, exactly where he had left it.

He had to check the time twice. It was four-thirty in the afternoon. Surely the clock on his mobile was wrong. He'd been asleep for hours.

The open safe and the painting on the floor, propped against the wall, caught his eye. Thoughts came gushing back. His teeth gnawed at his bottom lip as he remembered what he had intended to do. Sleep had brought him much needed clarity.

Slipping off the bed, he closed the safe, put the picture on its hooks and got dressed. One thought kept repeating in his mind. Donald was dead.

4 | Camille

|

Two days later, Camille visited Dom, early, as they had planned. Without stepping inside, she called out, poking her head in. 'It's me, using Donald's keys. Like you said.'

Not a sound. Appearing to travel from the heart of the unit along the hall and out to her, the silent rebuke made her straighten up. The morning chill intensified. The sun that had warmed her on the journey, making the winter gusts bearable, was yet to reach inside Dom's unit. She stepped into a corridor of cold and darkness where the strong smell of carnations and lilies was unmistakeable. The sickly sweet reek of alcohol was hiding under the floral perfumes. When she reached the living area, the room burst with baskets of flowers and wreaths and the empty wine bottle on the table went part way to explaining the smell of alcohol. Clothes, plates, cups, opened and unopened mail, snack food packets and CDs littered the place. Her hand waved in front of her face for fresh air.

A light snore drew her attention to Dom cradled fully dressed in the armchair tucked in the corner. His face camouflaged by flowers, both arms were spread wide, a hand hanging over each armrest.

Camille rounded baskets of flowers and stood watching over him, hoping he would sense her glare and wake to a look of disdain. The dark room amplified his deep, uneven breaths. The lack of movement, the growling snores told Camille he would not wake easily.

'Dom.'

Stepping on the spot as loudly as she could did nothing. She huffed at him. Then she huffed at her huffing. It could take all morning to wake him. What to do? His mobile was on the table. Should she call him? Near it, sat an empty beer bottle. Her fingers twiddled on her hips as she surveyed the body in front of her.

How he looked like Donald—the tuft of hair, the line of the nose and the plump cheeks. Her eyes stung with the threat of tears. She was back in the hospital standing over bruised Donald willing his body not to lose its final heat. It was that pain keeping Camille from reaching out and touching Dom, shaking him awake.

Absently, she pushed on the bridge of her glasses as though the gesture alone would stop tears. She patted her brown, cropped hair, which was more or less the colour of Dom's, but more streaky.

She inched closer to him and peered down the far side of the chair and spotted a second discarded red wine bottle lying on its side. As she picked it up, she noticed the wine glass dangling upside down from his hand and the dark dots on the carpet. Her nose wrinkled as she plucked the glass from his abandoned clasp, contorting her face even more at the feel of the grimy stem.

'Ugh.'

She realised how stupid she must look, standing over someone sleeping in his own home. With tiptoe steps, she retreated to the kitchen area, resting the glass in the sink and adding the empty bottle to the mound of rubbish by the overflowing bin.

The paper and pen she picked up were cold. She scribbled some notes about the funeral, which was what she had come to discuss.

Dom spluttered in the corner, reminding her how much the visit had been a waste of time. A note for him would have to do. It was as she was looking around for somewhere visible to leave it that she spotted the second mobile phone on the table near the jigsaw. One of his visitors must have left it behind. As her eyes scoured the scene again, the mess—the aftermath of a late night sprawled out before her—seemed less tragic. Dom hadn't drunk all that alcohol alone, after all, she decided.

But what if …? Her mouth opened. Maybe Dom wasn't alone. For all she knew, someone was in one of the bedrooms. Was that a noise out the back? The connecting door to the rest of Dom's unit was closed. Camille's eyes darted around the room looking for someone else's shoes or a friend's jacket. Was it a woman? There were no items of women's clothing anywhere. Whoever it was had to be inside showering, would come out any minute and scream almightily if they saw her standing in the dim light.

She waited for Dom's breathing to quieten and his echoes to die down before cocking her ear and listening. She was sure she could hear running water. It was best to leave.

She flitted to the front door, not before turning to scowl at Dom, who hadn't stirred an inch. The final plans for the funeral, which was tomorrow, would have to wait, because Dom wasn't able to do anything.

Outside, she clutched the door handle with both hands and slammed the front door shut, her head lurching back with the brunt. Her shoulder banged the security screen into place and it responded with an annoying echo. Steadying herself, she dusted the arm of her jacket and marched to the stairwell.

II

The moisture on the pillow and the water on Lorna's cheeks were cooler than her body. A powerful arm was wrapped around her and the morning light was filling the room. She had woken up in Drew's single bed. Although the sounds of the house were unfamiliar to her, she was sure the distant spatter was rain. The splash from car wheels confirmed it was a wet day. She reversed into Drew and they huddled together.

'Morning. You were whimpering in your sleep,' Drew said.

Closed, Lorna's eyes filled with tears and she shook in silence, hoping to shield the stirring household from her grief. She turned so they could see each other and the pairs of lips smacked together. Their legs stayed locked under the covers, young limbs seeking out the warmth of companionship.

'You were close to your dad. It will be hard for you. I lost a grandparent, but I hardly knew her.'

'I miss him.'

Drew's hand rubbed Lorna's shoulder.

Seeing a hand move to her face to dry her eyelashes brought out more of Lorna's grief.

'Your mum won't want you to come to Melbourne with us now and my dad's arrangements are almost done.' The thick fingers stroking Lorna's face moved in smooth, rhythmic waves, caressing and tickling her pearly skin. 'She'll want you to stay close to her. We should accept that or I'll get blamed for all sorts of things.'

Lorna's head shook on the pillow. 'If I stay here, I'll be at uni and she won't see much of me anyway. It makes no difference if I go to Melbourne for a few years.' To mirror what had happened to her seconds before, Lorna touched Drew's face. Her tapered fingers steered over bushy eyebrows, paused to rub the twist of shiny metal embedded in one eyebrow, glided off hair and rested on Drew's ebony shoulder.

'A few years? I want you there with me forever.' They hugged some more. 'And I also want breakfast. I'm starving.'

III

'But you're grieving for Donald. Why the guilt?'

Dom was sitting opposite Dympna, who sat high in a swivel chair behind her desk while Dom reclined low on the sofa. He sipped water from a green glass—one of a pair that nested permanently on a tray on the table—moistening his lips, preparing to respond.

His head shook and his eyes looked down letting a wounded expression cross his face. 'I don't know. I want to be free, but I can't lift this guilt.' His arms shook in front of him. 'It's so heavy. It's there constantly. And every time I see Camille or Robin, they repeat how strange it was that he was in a suit in the city, and I feel terrible.' He punched the sofa. 'Without fail, they mention it. I spoke to Camille this afternoon and she brought it up.'

'And your guilt stems from having agreed to swap jobs? You placed Donald at the intersection?' Gallant, serene, she edged him to be honest.

Dom yelped into his hands. 'I can't forgive myself, and they'll kill me if they find out.' He let out a pained cry. 'And Lorna—how could I face her again if she found out?'

'You're feeling guilty with the secret and you'd feel guilty if you shared it.'

'Exactly.' He gulped some more water. 'Are you going to make me tell them?' His voice was childlike.

'I won't make you do anything you don't want to do. Tell me'—she finished typing her text message and dumped her mobile on her desk—'why did you agree to swap that day if you were so opposed to it?'

Dom seized his hair with both hands as though trying to scalp himself. 'I don't know why. He was so dogged.' His arms crashed on the sofa at his sides. 'I couldn't think of anything worse, mixing up our identities like that.' He winced at the memories of Donald asking to do the swap. 'I've come to speak to you so many times. I'm forever wanting my sense of self intact. Then I do something as stupid as this.'

'But you couldn't have imagined the consequences, Dominic. Many people would agree that identical twins swapping roles as a prank has a magical quality about it. Of course it has its appeal.' Dympna paused.

'Yes,' said Dom.

She continued. 'His death was an accident that had nothing to do with your prank.'

'That's true.' He looked up at her. 'I want to share this with Camille and the others, but I won't be able to handle the backlash.'

'Can you know for sure how they'll respond? Would they appreciate the honesty and the answers rather than turn on you because of the prank?'

Dom shrugged. 'I also want to protect Donald.' He fiddled with the sofa stitching while gazing at the ceiling. 'And myself, if I'm honest.' His low voice became uncertain. 'Everyone will judge him for being so juvenile, and they'll judge me for going along with it.'

'Was he juvenile to suggest the prank?' She leant forward to snatch some almonds from the bowl and waited to make eye contact with Dom, who didn't answer straight away.

'I guess so. Perhaps. Well—well—it *was* childish. And I don't want them to think badly of him. He had so much on his plate.'

Dympna's words were articulate and crisp. 'You're very protective of your brother and everyone will recognise that. And remember, they'll also know that Donald was who he was. Your brother was always so strong-minded, sometimes beyond the reasonable. The family and his friends will certainly be familiar with that side of him, if you tell them what happened.'

'That's true. He was often so stubborn. When he got an idea in his head, it was impossible to change his mind.' Childhood memories flashed through his head, but Dympna's comments steered him into the present again. 'So what are your options?' she asked, glancing at the wall clock.

'I can say nothing, protect him and carry the guilt. Or I can tell the truth about what happened and give them free reign to judge us.'

She beamed a disarming smile. 'You don't have to decide right now. Let your grief take its course.'

He nodded. 'You know ...' His head swivelled to look at her. 'I hold stuff back from you quite often.'

'That's all right. Tell me as much or as little as you like.' Her eyes locked on him. 'Our chats are informal and I enjoy catching up.' She ate more almonds. 'I wish Donald and Camille had visited me.'

Dom looked up at the ceiling. 'I've complicated things a little.' His drumming fingers set the musical score for his confession. 'Do I have time to explain?'

'Yes, quickly though. Tonight's my book club and it's in Wollstonecraft.'

'I called my office and told them I was dead.'

Dympna didn't speak. Dom took the silence as a signal to continue.

'I wasn't thinking properly. Donald had just died that night and I wanted to keep him alive. So I thought of me as the dead one. In a way, I am.'

'They're common feelings in those who lose a twin. How did you feel after the call?'

'It's weird, but I felt so free. The fear and pressure to be me without having Donald around eased. Well, it eased enough for me to fall asleep.' Dom averted his eyes. 'I—I came close to … to ending …'

Dympna stopped chewing. Her nodding head enticed Dom to go on.

'Being Donald meant I didn't have to return to normality, to let things tick over. I had an escape.'

'That's right. You wanted to apply the brakes.' Her hand came up in mime.

'Exactly. Otherwise Donald's death would have been over so quickly. In the pain, I felt him.'

'And has your employer discovered you're alive?' Easing their jackets from the coat stand, she handed Dom his. 'Your colleagues will be happy to learn the truth.'

'No one has contacted me yet.'

'They will soon enough. The company may take it seriously, so you should look into sorting it out. Promise me you'll do that for next time.'

Dom nodded. 'I'll see you tomorrow.'

IV

Forty minutes later, Dom was home. A green three was flashing on the answer machine. The first two messages were from Subiaco staff. A director wanted to express his condolences to Donald and the second caller, Maggie, her voice cheerless, was hoping to attend the funeral. Both left contact numbers, but Dom deleted the messages without recording the details. The third caller was Karen from the twin research centre. Dom didn't listen to the whole message, hitting delete early. But he got that the call was to give him a friendly reminder about participating in her study.

He collapsed deep into the sofa. His chin perched on his chest as if his jaw was the heaviest part of his body. He stayed motionless, numb and tired. With his eyes fixed on the floor, he tried to halt his mind. His posture was so still his aching limbs couldn't feel the soft fabric they were resting on. From the silence emerged his inhaling, which directed his body. He let it take in air for him and he gaped at the silent rise and fall of his chest. His body felt exhausted and Dom didn't know why. Everything throbbed—his head, his feet, his entire back.

The soft vibration of his mobile beside him interrupted his meditation. Constable Blakely was phoning. A sharpness bolted across his chest. Pulling himself upright, he took the call.

'I wanted to let you know what we've found. Your brother had no alcohol or drugs in his blood. Neither did the driver. We also have no signs of a heart attack.' She paused. 'Unfortunately, we've had no more witnesses come forward to add to what we already know. And the security cameras don't cover that spot.'

'I see.'

'This is a tragic accident. Donald fell into the path of the van. A moment's distraction is all it takes.'

'Nothing—' Dom paused. 'It's hard for me to hear that Donald got distracted and went into the road. You won't understand.'

'I'm very sorry. This is tragic for families to face— the senseless loss of a relative doing something as simple as crossing the road.' There was another pause. 'I'm just about to close this file and prepare my report for the coroner.'

'Ok. That's good to know.'

'By the way, I spoke to Donald's colleagues. I visited Prestons.'

'Oh.' Dom added nothing else and Constable Blakely stayed silent too. Dom filled the silence. 'And? They told you what?'

'Some points that I wanted to go over with you.'

'With me?'

'I'd like to chat to you and see once more where Donald lived. Is tomorrow suitable?'

Dom's heart began pounding so hard he could barely reply. He wrenched the mobile upwards away from his mouth, drawing in a huge breath to combat his narrowing airways. 'The funeral's in the morning. So would you like to come after four?' He breathed sharply. 'Do you want Camille and Robin here as well?'

'I only want to speak to you. After four is fine. I hope you have a lovely service for him.'

'It will be small. A private cremation.'

V

At five in the morning, Dom jolted awake from a nightmare. He was buying something illegal from Robin, who was standing in the shadows failing to shield her face correctly. In the dream, Dom knew who it was. The wad of tiny money he was about to hand over was catching her eye. The bank notes were the size of postage stamps and he was having trouble holding on to them.

With a shiver, he leapt out of bed to escape the images. His muscles tensed at the cold. A thick top went over his head and he scuttled to the kitchen. A light breakfast would be enough to see him through the morning. He ate at the dining table, where the waft of toast and coffee was buried under the scent of flowers.

At the other end of the table, his jigsaw sat neglected, not having seen attention for days. With breakfast eaten, he warmed his palms on the mug of coffee, wondering how the day would go. Painful, grief-stricken, guilt-ridden. If only he could sleep some more to escape it all. But his incessant thoughts and the caffeine wouldn't allow it, and there were endless nightmares to plague him. There was nothing to do so early in the morning. Camille would arrive in about four hours, so he moved closer to work on the puzzle.

After placing some pieces of branches and mosaic, his focus fell on the shade of the tree and the shadows flowing from as yet unseen figures. Together, they looked set to take up the bottom left quarter of the picture. Dom sipped coffee and adeptly placed pieces.

There was the young child with its back to the photographer, huddled, left to play alone. Dom sifted for bits of the shadow to reveal what lay in the child's surrounds. He worked quietly—his breathing dry and noisy—oblivious to the daylight filling the room.

The dark tones of the shaded lawn spread across the kitchen table enveloping Dom and the subjects in the picture. The more the shadow grew, the more the child in its centre shrank, the more each snug-fitting piece cloaked the infant in murkiness.

The doorbell woke Dom from his trance. A visitor so early needled him and he had to do a double take at the clock. It was eight thirty. He looked around the room amazed at how quickly the delicate light had arrived. It had to be Camille knocking, but she had keys.

His sister stood there dressed in a warm black dress and a dark grey overcoat, but her attire didn't include a hat and there was minimal make-up on her face—a touch of lipstick and a hint of foundation. They hugged at the front door.

'Why didn't you use the keys?'

'Like yesterday?' She stopped walking.

Dom's face twisted up, unsure what stone his sister had cast.

'I knocked in case you had company.' Camille disappeared inside. Dom followed and excused himself, heading to his room.

She flicked the switch on the kettle, placed her bag down and removed her coat. Standing in the centre of the room, hands on hips, she took in the surroundings. More flowers had arrived since the previous morning, so many that Dom had to place them along the hall. It struck her how bare the place would seem once the flowers went and that most of the things populating the room belonged to Dom. There was little sign of Donald ever having lived there, certainly in those areas. At least it looked like Dom had made an attempt to clean up. The empty wine bottles were no longer there and the rubbish was not piling up.

As though dodging freshly painted walls, Camille moved from arrangement to arrangement smelling the flowers and reading the messages, careful to avoid the orange dye from the irises. Although a couple of wreaths were anonymous, with each message read, her throat tightened as she fought back tears.

Dom's tinny voice echoed down the hall. 'I've been up since five. Didn't sleep well.'

'Neither did I.'

The chime of the doorbell startled her.

'I'll get it.' She answered the door to a deliveryman, whose badge revealed he was from Nadine's Flowers. He was holding a bouquet of yellow and white roses and a small basket of black petunias. 'More flowers,' she said weakly, updating Dom as she carried them inside.

A card with its brief message partly obscured by purple ribbon was stapled to the basket handle. She moved the strip aside and choked at the message. 'Oh dear god.'

She panicked and something made her check the bouquet too. The small envelope taped to the transparent shroud came off easily, her fingers writhing to remove the crisp white card. Her teeth gritted. 'And this one!' she sniffed. With a tut, she sprang up, yanking the paper from the basket handle and using her nail to remove the staple left behind. Footsteps sounded behind her. Dom was coming. She bent the cards and, along with the tape and the staple, crammed them into the envelope. The steps got louder. The envelope she popped into a zip pocket of her handbag and spun round. A long puff of air greeted Dom.

'Everything ok?' He stood in the doorway in a black suit, adjusting his charcoal paisley tie.

'All fine.'

'Have you seen all the flowers?' He glanced at the recent arrivals. 'Who are they from?'

'No cards on these ones. But they're lovely. How kind of whoever it was.' Camille panted with her back to Dom as she admired the petals.

'We'll leave soon.' Dom saw the steaming kettle. 'You've got time for a tea though.' He walked away.

Camille sat down. Her eyes swept the room taking in the array of floral colours, stopping at her black patent handbag perched on the kitchen surface. Absently, she nipped her lower lip.

VI

The first to arrive at the crematorium, Dom and Camille were welcomed by an over-caring celebrant and her stony assistant, and shown around the grounds and chapel. The building was small and clean and the dreary weather outside stopped excess brightness penetrating the leadlight windows. The celebrant suggested they take the first bench and they sat down at once as though standing was not allowed.

The closed coffin was in front and wreaths and floral arrangements of *dad*, *husband* and *brother* skirted it. Dom stared at the coffin, a cedar box with wooden trims and a photo of Donald resting on top.

More people arrived soon after. Robin, who looked ready to topple over, had Lorna and Niamh keeping her upright. The three made it to the front and collapsed into the pew. Josh came up, hugged Dom and Camille, sat next to Robin and put a comforting arm around her.

Outside, dense clouds muffled the noises of the day, and inside the chapel, a thick red carpet helped deaden the functions of the building. When the service began, Dom had no idea who was behind them.

The celebrant spoke about Donald as if they'd been friends forever. Dom thought of childhood memories, when decades of life lay ahead of the twins.

They were thirteen, on a summer vacation with Camille and their parents. The sun blazed for an eternity and they played in the surf with boogie boards, buried each other in sand and made friends with the two children in the next chalet. But his best mate that summer was Donald. Whatever else had happened in their lives, the boys knew their twinship took precedence, forming a secure backdrop against which other events unfolded.

The pair had also had their share of fights and shouting matches and the biggest of them was *the exam*. That's what their parents had named the occasion and referring to it would help bring the boys back in line.

'Remember what happened with the exam,' their father would say, a warning intended to kill off any ideas they may have had about playing pranks.

Whenever Dom recalled the memory, his mind would start playback at the same moment—returning to class after lunch.

He bounced towards the electric blue door of his form room, pausing to tuck his shirt into his grey shapeless trousers, for Miss Flimsil would ridicule students if they dared enter her class looking messy from playtime. As he settled his clothes, he balanced on tiptoes to peer through the tiny pane of glass. There was a nasty surprise. Donald was sitting in his chair next to Dom's friend. When Donald spotted him at the door, he shooed him away. Dom's blood boiled and he kicked the wall and swore silently to his brother through the glass, but Donald had turned away. Not fair. They had sworn never to pull a trick like this on each other. They had to agree to practical jokes, to swaps. Why was Donald in there anyway? Dom scoured the room taking care to stay out of Miss Flimsil's line of sight. He knew Donald fancied Millie, who was sitting to his right. Was that it? Or was it because Benny had his new portable stereo with him?

Donald's hand flapped some more for Dom to get the hell away from the door. Dom dared not go inside the class, but he was miming to Donald that he was going to open the door. Teachers were always confusing them and were usually suspicious of their denials of wrongdoing. To be caught out mid-prank would mean big trouble for them both.

'What are you doing, Mr Tolen? Get to class.' Dom spun around, beaming a smile. Mr Oatley, the lanky sports teacher, had his hands on his sides. 'Get that smile off your face. Where are you supposed to be?'

'I was making sure Dom was—'

'Where are you supposed to be, Donald?' Mr Oatley's voice rose.

Dom guessed where Donald should be. 'In modern history, sir. With Miss Castle.'

'Then get there. You're late.'

'Yes sir.' Dom walked to Donald's class on the eastern side of the school overlooking the sports oval and of course, he was the last student to get to the unusually quiet room. Miss Castle, who terrified students and staff alike, glared at him and without speaking twisted her head dramatically to look at the clock above her. Her flexible head turned to the front again and she was fuming.

'Sorry miss.'

She put her finger to her lips and signalled for him to take the one empty seat. Dom couldn't believe how quiet everyone was, working so soon after lunch. Once he sat down and faced the front, he saw the note on the board, which Miss Castle was kindly pointing out.

```
Module exam: essay
One hour
Silence!
Put your name on
page 1!
```

Donald had tricked him, had forced him into doing an exam. Dom flipped over the exam paper and slammed it down, making Miss Castle frown so hard she looked like she was ready to bite. Dom pulled out a pen, let his bag fall to the floor and dragged his chair into position, disrupting the others, who were looking up.

'Shhh,' said the teacher. 'Names on the front page.'

Dom read the question. He knew the topic well, but he didn't want to write an essay on it.

In the service, the celebrant called for the gathering to stand and sing. Dom clambered to his feet and began reading the hymn lyrics. He didn't sing anything, returning instead to the memories of the aftermath of Donald's history exam.

'Sit down, Mrs Tolen.' The nun pointed to one of two chairs in front of her desk. Dom watched her black habit swinging off her shoulders as she spun round efficiently to take position behind her spotless desk, one solitary document sitting on it. 'Get comfy, won't you.'

Donald rushed past Dom and took the free chair next to their mother.

'Not you! Stand up there, boy.'

Donald leapt to his feet and retreated to a spot behind his mother.

Sister Anne's voice softened. 'Do you ever mix them up? They're so similar.'

'Sometimes.' Their mother paused. 'Rarely. Why did you want to see me?'

'I want you to cut their hair differently, so my teachers can tell them apart.'

'I—I can do that. But why?' The request caught her off guard.

Sister Anne eyed the boys as she spat the words. 'That way, we won't have a repeat of the deception Miss Castle was horribly subjected to last week.' Her face flushed red-purple as she rifled the document.

Dom recognised the paper she was shaking at them and he looked to the floor. Sister Anne spoke to him. 'You did well in this exam, Donald.'

'I'm Donald.' Donald's tiny finger poked up.

Sister Anne's arctic look to Mrs Tolen was laden. She turned to Donald. 'Not when this was written. You, boy, were pretending to be him'—the exam flapped in Dom's direction—'in Miss Flimsil's geography class. You, Donald Tolen, are a liar. You both are.'

'Oh boys. I thought we agreed about this,' their mother said.

Donald persisted. 'I didn't, mum. I swear. I can explain why they think we cheated. On Monday, Miss Castle asked me what I wrote for the exam and I couldn't remember. I forgot. So they think we played a joke.' He crossed his arms feigning irritation at the injustice, unaware how see-through the lie was, and added, 'I like history.'

'Ha!' Sister Anne's cackle bounced around the office. 'Donald Tolen, do not stand there lying to your mother and me. We know Dominic wrote this essay.'

With her elbows planted on the desk, Sister Anne flicked her wrist, making the pages, dog-eared and crumpled, swing in a wide arc.

Mrs Tolen huffed, annoyed at the boys' tricks, annoyed further by the sister's antics.

Scrutinising the front page, Sister Anne repeated herself. 'We know.' She paused. 'And you, Dominic. Would you like to deny—'

'Show us,' said Mrs Tolen.

The exam stopped swinging. The nun glowered at the parent opposite her. Nothing in the office moved and everyone waited for the nun to respond.

'We know who did the exam because your idiot child wrote his own name on the paper.' She turned the exam around for them to see. The three of them leaned in and read the unmistakable name.

Dominic Tolen.

The stunned silence was broken by a slap—Dom's hand coming up to his head, public confirmation of his stuff-up.

Mrs Tolen sunk back in the chair and the large sigh that came out was the longest the twins had ever heard.

Sister Anne said, 'I know how it went, Dominic. You were so nervous about your little stunt that you had too much on your mind and you forgot you were supposed to sign your brother's name.'

'Sorry, sister.' Dom said.

'Ha!' cried the nun again. She too leaned back in her chair. 'Every wicked plan has its flaw.'

The headmistress looked at Mrs Tolen and lifted her thin, greying eyebrows. 'Will they ever learn?' She fell forward on to the desk again and gave it a pat to signal she was getting down to business. 'Mrs Tolen, it's tempting to think of this as a light joke between twins. But this is run-of-the-mill cheating. And it will be punished as that—I'm suspending them for three days.'

Mrs Tolen's face reddened. 'Is there no other way to deal with this, sister?'

'Your boys are in their first year at St Mark's. Detention is not a suitable punishment, given the severity of all this. We never had such shenanigans with Camille.'

Dom didn't know that word, but he knew to refrain from pointing out Camille didn't have a twin.

'Boys, you must behave. This isn't good for you—for *us*.' She rubbed their backs as she pleaded with them.

The hymn ended and Dom sat down along with the congregation. The celebrant called for Camille to do her reading, a short, personal extract.

Dom thought back to the days soon after the school suspension. The atmosphere at home had been unlike any other time in his childhood. Their parents never discovered that the prank was unplanned, that Donald had started it all, and that Dom had covered for him through the whole incident.

The family noticed how the twins avoided each other for weeks, yet they had always thought Donald had instigated the falling out, bitter at Dom's blunder over the name on the exam. But it was Dom who had refused to forgive Donald for tricking him.

Donald wouldn't believe that Dom had written his own name by mistake. In Donald's eyes, it was less an error and more an act of revenge. For Dom, the claims about wanting revenge, as wild as they were, were typical of Donald: poorly thought-out ideas. Why would Dom risk getting himself into trouble when he could easily, and more safely, get back at Donald elsewhere? He never told his parents how he came to be sitting in Donald's history exam. Even after days of Donald's anger, Dom didn't want to have to tell his parents how Donald had abused his trust. His parents didn't hand out any extra punishment and rarely spoke to them about the episode, least of all while they served the school suspension.

The words of Dom's mother came to him as he listened to Camille's reading. 'See, Dom, honey'—she comforted him with a stroke of his hair as she delivered her earnest caution—'sometimes things go wrong when you play these jokes.'

VII

Dom made it through the service, which he didn't speak at, and got to the wake, which was at his place. He greeted the guests as they filed in, with Lorna and Harry getting big hugs from him, which caused bottlenecks at the front door.

The next thing he did was pull Josh aside in the cramped living room, bursting with flora and people, to thank him for his eulogy. Fighting back tears, Josh had spoken of his longstanding friendship with Donald, which began at university, and the unbearable pain of losing his best friend.

'He was funny, your brother. His habit of mixing up his thoughts. Do you remember his comment at a barbeque—that Christmas Eve was on the twenty-fourth that year.'

Dom smiled, aware of the countless times he'd heard the anecdote.

His solid build packed into his new suit, Josh explained the joke through his laughs, stretching the cotton as his husky frame rocked about. 'He obviously meant to say the day of the week, not the date. But he announced it so seriously and he didn't even pick up on the mistake. Funny bugger, he was.'

They retreated to their beers and food at the same time. Dom spoke. 'What a mess though. Look at how quickly life can change.' The hand with the food waved around. 'Here we are with our day-to-day and the next minute, he's gone. Too much to accept.' His head swung from side to side.

Josh mimicked Dom, shaking his head, eyes down, chewing. He then leaned in and tilted his face to the wall behind them, talking into Dom's more sheltered ear. 'It's bad enough to lose someone. Then the police come round asking questions, and make you feel as though you've done something wrong.'

'What did they want to know?'

'All about his health and that, his job, his interests.'

'What did you tell them?'

'Basically nothing. I don't know anything.' He drank his beer. 'How are you holding up? You back at work?'

'No, can't do it yet. Not sure I'll get back there. I need a change.' The office on level sixteen, the people and the Subiaco logo danced in his mind. He appeared to forget he was talking aloud. 'It has certain memories for me that place. And with all that's gone on, I feel this overwhelming guilt. That's the worst bit—the guilt.'

Josh patted Dom's back saying, 'You'll be ok' and walked off.

Dympna came up to Dom giving him a long hug and complimenting him on the funeral service. She added, 'The chapel looked beautiful.' With her hand wrapped over the silver locket around her neck, she said, 'Today, it carries Donald's photo on one side and your mother on the other.' The jewellery jangled back into place on her tanned chest.

'That's lovely,' said Dom.

Robin approached them through the crowd just as Dympna's mobile started ringing. Dympna gave her condolences to Robin, excused herself and vanished into the hallway to take the call.

'I haven't seen her in years,' said Robin into Dom's ear, her eyes drilling into Dympna's back.

'I wonder why she keeps away.' Dom turned to catch Robin's reaction.

Robin fiddled with the white carnation protruding from her suit jacket. With a lob of her head, she indicated to where Dympna had been standing. 'That's a bit too revealing for a funeral, isn't it?' She brought her wine to her lips and held it there. 'Just because she comes from money.' The glass stayed high in the air.

'Don't worry about Dympna and don't worry about money. You and the girls will always be taken care of. I mean it. Anything they need—you ask.'

She smiled at him, her eyes opening to reveal white areas beyond the redness. 'You're the second person to tell me that today.'

Dom's interest rose. 'Who was the first?' He scanned the room wondering which of his guests had offered to support Donald's family. 'Who was it?'

Robin rested her fair hand on his forearm. 'Thanks, Dominic. You're very sweet.'

Niamh appeared and tugged Robin into the kitchen.

VIII

Dom decided against driving to Bondi Beach because he'd had several drinks with the funeral guests. Wrapped in a warm jacket, he hailed a taxi. In the back, he didn't speak to the driver except to tell her to stop at the north end of the beach.

The clouds had thinned and the wind had died down, which allowed the sun's winter heat to keep Dom warm as he strolled towards Bronte. His head needed clearing and escaping the weight of the city that sprawled to his right would help. He had hoped for a forceful wind to cleanse him and salty air to purify him, as well as a turbulent sea with rolling tides and crashing waves to remind him that life was endless motion, cycles, endings and beginnings. Instead, on his left, sat a bizarrely flat sea where safe toddlers paddled and redundant surfers bobbed. Although this too comforted him. But he felt physically uneasy in his skin. The steps and the rise towards the headland took extra effort and Dom couldn't remember how many days it had been since he last went for a jog. That was what his body would benefit from—the exhaustion of a long run.

He ruminated and walked. With Donald's death, his life had changed forever. Was a return to his old life realistic? All the events that had served to place Donald at that intersection shared a common point of origin: Dom and his job. It was hard to picture doing that work again. The messy guilt was too much.

How had Donald died? Who was to blame? Harry was partly responsible—if he hadn't wanted the drugs, Dom wouldn't have snorted that line and agreed to the swap. Phil was partly to blame—if he hadn't sold the drugs to Dom, Donald would be alive. Donald, even, was implicated—if he hadn't been so bloody persistent. But Dom knew he himself was largely responsible for Donald's death. Where to begin? If he hadn't agreed to help …

High on the cliffs, his focus went to his surroundings to stop him thinking about his role in it all. Looking around him, the path was empty. There was no one about. His mobile was in his pocket. He took it out and stared at it. To start life afresh, all it needed was a subtle toss of the handset into the ocean. New friends, new contacts, new colleagues.

A young couple rounded the curve giggling and cuddling. Dom returned the phone to his pocket and walked on.

After the inward diversion of Tamarama Beach, where the waves had picked up, he leaned on the fence and watched three surfers making the most of the renewed swell. The breeze made his nose water and the sun heated the nape of his neck. He brought a palm up to feel its heat, the warmth feeling good on his fingertips. It was time to head home. He strolled back the way he had come and left the path to head to the main road. There weren't many taxis, but a bus was approaching and he found himself near the stop. The bus pulled up. Dom jumped on and zigzagged to the back, found an empty seat.

It was some time before he became aware of a man standing extremely close. He looked up from his mobile. The man was flashing a smile and holding the rails with both hands while his hips swung madly as the bus jostled along.

'Don? Don Tolen? Remember me?'

Dom had no idea which of Donald's friends was bobbing around in front of him. The thought of pretending to be Donald crossed his mind. A white lie was easier than explaining the truth.

'I'm Dom, the brother.' He presented his hand and lifted his sunglasses.

'I'm Billy Williams. I used to work with Don. How's your brother?'

'I remember you now. Your name.' Dom inhaled deeply. 'He died—recently—in a road accident. We cremated him today.'

Billy's smile vanished. 'Gees. Sorry to hear that.' Billy looked around at the woman he was travelling with and turned back to Dom. 'I haven't seen Don in about five years.'

'He died about a week ago. He's laid near here, with our parents.'

Billy released his hold of one of the handles and with a thick, masculine hand, dug into Dom's shoulder. 'I'm sorry for mixing you up.'

'That's not a problem.'

'And he had children. How are they?'

The conversation dried up and Billy Williams dangled in front of Dom, seeming unsure whether to stay or return to his seat. The roar of the bus climbing away from the beach drowned their silence.

'Tell me'—Dom said, once the engine had quietened—'why did your parents call you William Williams? Do you know why?'

'A practical joke. They always played around.'

'This is my stop,' said Dom lying. He ran to the door. His sunglasses hid the water in his eyes. Blinking would send tears down his cheeks and he didn't want Billy Williams or anyone to see him wiping them away. So he didn't dare blink.

IX

They sat opposite each other at the dining table. Constable Blakely came alone. She had finished rifling through Donald's clothes and Dom suspected the cup of tea she had asked for was an excuse to be left on her own to go through Donald's things uninterrupted. Her full cup of tea was getting cold on the table next to her hat.

Dom was thirsty. He took regular sips of tea. His dry mouth needed enough liquid to last the interview.

'Your brother was new to the job, but as far as Prestons could tell, everything was fine. That day he had some meetings and spent lots of time at his desk, but there are some things that are odd about their information. First off, they are certain he wasn't wearing a suit.'

'That is odd.'

'And secondly, he didn't have any official meetings in another location.'

'But he told Lorna he did. That is also odd.'

'So he arrived to work in casual clothes and crossed the city and got knocked over in a suit and tie—your suit and tie.'

Dom didn't blink.

'How do we explain that?' Fierce eyes bore into him.

Dom shrugged without breaking the stare.

The police officer continued. 'Can you explain that? And he wasn't carrying a change of clothes with him.'

'Maybe he had another job.'

'Did he have another job?'

'I don't know—I'm just trying to help.' Dom sipped his tea.

'Do you have another job?'

'No. I'm trying to help.'

'Then I shall write that down in my pad.' The pen and paper appeared. 'Yes. Maybe he came home and changed and went off to a second job that nobody knows about.'

The air was charged and Dom sensed the tension mounting. The walls seemed to lean in on them. He wanted to steer the conversation away from her line of inquiry. His face flashed with understanding.

'That's why you asked to look at his clothes and his room earlier—I see.' He nodded to show it all made sense. 'To check if a set of clothes were lying around or if some clothes were missing.'

'Yes. And you told me nothing was missing.'

'That's right. I remember what I told you—it was five minutes ago.'

'This case is becoming mysterious.'

'It's a case now? Donald's dead. There's nothing mysterious.'

'I'm creating a mystery where none exists?' Her eyebrows lifted and she paused, inviting Dom to speak. She saw his lips part, but he didn't say a word.

X

Removing raindrops and leaving smudges, Camille drew a finger over her watch face. It was a few minutes before half past five. Monday was her busiest day at work, but she had hurried out to make it to Nadine's Flowers. Enough time remained. Just.

Up ahead, a young woman was moving in and out of the shop, retreating with buckets of fresh flowers and trays of pot plants that had adorned the shop front. Each of her trips inside exposed more sections of light grey pavement, the parts the vanishing showers hadn't reached.

Camille stopped to pull out the crumpled cards ripped off the flower arrangements the Friday morning before. She read them once more to be doubly sure.

```
Dominic will be in
our heart and
memories.
From the Northern
Division team.
```

The second was more intimate.

```
Donald & Camille,
my thoughts are
with you at our
time of loss.
Maggie Fraser.
```

Camille put them away and headed to the shop.

The florist's pleasant features were showing signs of tiredness. Hands full, she blew a wisp of hair from her face as she hauled a bucket of yellow roses off the street. Camille moved right behind her and followed her inside. She got the woman's attention, once she was standing inside, by stepping heavily.

The woman, in her early thirties, looked back and shouted, 'Be with you in a minute'. She returned empty handed soon after. 'How can I help?'

'I'm sorry to bother you. I hate to complain, but you delivered flowers to my brother's funeral on Friday and the name on the cards was all wrong. He's a twin and you got the names mixed up.' Camille's face scrunched as she spoke. 'I want to tell you so—you know—it doesn't happen again. For you.'

She handed the cards to the woman, who huffed an apology.

'You've written the wrong twin's name on both cards and they went to my brother's house. It's not good. He doesn't need to be reminded his brother's dead!' As she screamed out, passersby looked in. 'Luckily I saw the cards before he did. He's fragile and we're worried about him.'

The smile left the florist's face. 'Oh dear. That's unfortunate. I'm so sorry about that. Let's see what happened.' She moved to a computer squeezed to one end of a desk littered with ribbons, cards and plucked leaves. 'What was your brother's surname?' One finger entered the surname into the computer while the other hand held the cards. 'I've got here two wreaths sent for Dom Tolen. Placer Avenue.'

'That's them. But Dominic is not the brother who died. It was Donald.'

The woman's gaze stayed on the monitor as she scanned the account. She compared the note on the card to the one on the screen and grimaced at Camille. 'I'm afraid that's the message we got given on the order, which was done online.' She tutted lazily twice. 'We've copied word for word both messages.' She clicked to another screen as though checking the origin of the order. 'It's always orders placed by companies. People buying on their own never get it wrong. If we're going to get wrong info, it's forever companies that are doing it. You know how it is—the person emailing us doesn't know the person who's died and they've been told to place the order urgently. They're in a rush and look what happens. I'm very sorry about that.' She held out the cards for Camille, who didn't retrieve them.

'Do you have the name of the person and a phone number? I think I should tell them, don't you?'

'I'm awfully sorry, but we can't give that information out.' She added, as though making it up on the spot, 'Policy.'

'Well, I know which company it was. It was a firm called Prestons. But it will take me effort to find out who. You'd save me time if you told me who in Prestons sent the email.'

'This order didn't come from that firm, madam.'

'It didn't?' Camille looked mystified. Pointing to the cards the woman was trying to give back to her, Camille said, 'But the note mentions his colleagues.' She looked away in despair. 'Please.'

'I'm sorry. I can't give out that information.' She laid the cards on the desk to distance herself from Camille's difficult request. 'We had a case recently of a husband beating up someone who sent his wife flowers and so we don't give out that information now.' The woman brushed leaves from the desk and repeated, 'Policy.'

Camille groaned. She grabbed the cards, flustered and confused, and stared at the message. 'If it's not Donnie's work, where else is it?' She stood still, her face trapped in a crease. Then her eyes stretched open and her jaw widened to the size of a tulip head. She locked eyes with the florist and said the word. 'Subiaco.'

Camille received the faintest of nods. Then came a brusque denial. 'You did not hear that from us.'

5 | Vanessa

|

Niamh screamed upstairs to her mother. 'Mu-um, Lorna's looking at flights to Melbourne.'

'No, I'm not.' Lorna raised an arm to her younger sister, who flinched and scampered out of reach.

Robin's voice ricocheted down the stairs. 'Get off that computer right now.'

Lorna slammed the laptop closed, lunged for her sister on her way to the living room and launched herself on to the sofa, where she started swiping through her mobile.

Humming, Niamh got up and joined Lorna at the end of the sofa, arms straight, elbows locked, hopping from side to side. She could see the phone screen, but she stayed far enough away to escape more thumps.

Robin came clattering down the stairs, her arms full of dirty laundry. 'Don't start this, Lorna. You are not moving to Melbourne.'

'It was a return flight.'

'I don't care. Not even for a holiday. We can't afford it.'

Lorna scowled, her eyes remaining on the phone screen. 'There was no *we*. It was for me.'

In the kitchen, Robin dropped the laundry in front of the washing machine. 'Help me in here, please.'

Without either hand letting go of the phone, the teenager came to a standing position and shuffled to the kitchen, knelt down in front of the washer, and only then did her hands part to toss the clothing inside. She kicked the door closed with an almighty thud, pinched an apple from the bowl and returned to the sofa. It was floury. She pulled a face and dumped the unwanted fruit on the armrest.

Robin came out of the laundry with more clothing tucked under one arm and wagging a finger at her. 'Don't start this today. Your aunt Camille's coming over later this morning and I don't want you starting anything.'

'Aunt Camille here? What for?'

'I don't know. She wants to chat.' Robin spotted Lorna's abandoned apple. 'I need those. I'm making apple pie.'

'They're floury. Horrible.'

'They're meant to be. You're horrible.' Robin added the last pieces of clothing into the machine and started the wash. 'Are you still going for a run with uncle Dominic?'

'I guess so.'

'Yes, you are, young lady. You can get out from under my feet.' Robin stood over Lorna with her hands on her hips.

Lorna lifted the phone to block her mother from view.

'Your uncle needs your company. He's lonely since your dad passed. They were inseparable.' She exhaled, lost in thought. 'They were identical twins.'

Lorna kissed her teeth and rolled her eyes, enjoying the chance to deride her mother for stating the obvious. Neither action registered with Robin, whose thoughts were adrift. She woke from her daydream and continued where she had left off. 'So make sure you're back here in time to see your aunt.'

Niamh looked up at her mother. 'What do I do when aunt Camille arrives? Where do I go?'

Robin moved over to her daughter and paused to stroke her soft hair, which was turning as blonde as hers. 'You'll stay around, won't you, petal? You won't leave me alone with her?'

II

'Gotta go, precious. That's him knocking.' Harry headed to the front door, telling himself to stay positive and keep Dom's spirits high. They hadn't met up since the funeral about a week ago. When he opened the door his jaw absently lowered. He quickly closed his mouth.

Dom hadn't shaved or combed his hair and the smell from his clothes suggested he may not have changed them for a while. The whites of his eyes were reddened and the base of each socket was so dark they looked bruised.

Harry leant in for a pat on the back as a way to hide his reaction. 'Good to see you, mate.' The smell of alcohol and body odour was strong and Harry had to clear his throat. 'Come through. It's not raining then. You're dry.'

'There were some drops on the way over.' Dom traipsed behind Harry and slumped into an armchair.

'Thanks for coming over. I've been meaning to move this wardrobe for months.'

'You asked me to help last year, right?'

'Yep, around Melbourne Cup time.'

Dom raised his eyebrows. 'That long ago?' The news sent him off with his thoughts and he rubbed dirty fingers across his bristly cheeks. 'Let's do it.' Both hands hit the armrests, but he didn't move out of the seat.

Harry eyed his mate slouched in front of him. 'Err—it's heavy. We're taking it down to the garage, so are you sure you're up for it?'

When Dom nodded and smiled, Harry said, 'I hope you don't mind me saying, but you look like shit.'

'I didn't sleep well last night and it can make me look frazzled.' Dom's squinting eyes scoured the carpet, as though focusing was a chore.

'From where I am, it looks like more than missed sleep.' Harry made no move to start the heavy lifting. 'Have you talked to Subiaco about going back to work? When's that happening?'

Dom's weighty shoulders tensed at the mention of his employer. He gave Harry the slightest shake of his head.

'What you need is exercise to tire you out. Perhaps moving this furniture will lift you a bit.'

'How many pieces are we talking?'

'Just the one. On second thoughts, exertion will do you good.'

'That's why I didn't shower. I thought I'd be getting dirty helping you. Plus I'll be jogging with my niece. No point getting cleaned up.' Dom moved forward to rest on the edge of the seat cushion as though gearing himself to stand.

'If you want my advice, you'll shower before you see her. This way.' Harry strode off tucking his stained t-shirt into faded jeans.

In the spare bedroom, flanked by a more modern piece, the teak wardrobe with its huge single door stood majestically on squat ornate legs. Harry had cleared a path from the room and the unobstructed view of the furniture added to its imposing quality.

Dom tested its weight by pushing against it with his trunk. All it did was creak. He checked inside, hoping to remove whatever heavy item was weighing it down. It was empty. Standing on a chair, he checked the top. There was nothing adding to the burden—no dumbbells, no toolbox that Harry had failed to reach. Only a layer of dust, which he blew and that managed to settle on his friend.

'Sorry—I wasn't thinking.'

Harry stepped back. 'Don't worry. I've snorted worse.'

Sensing Dom's apprehension about the task ahead, he added, 'This will take some manoeuvring, but there's a beer afterwards.' His smile went unnoticed as Dom's eyes locked on nothing over Harry's shoulder.

Dom was murmuring to himself.

Harry raised his hand to get Dom's attention. 'Are you ok? What are you saying?'

'Nothing. Let's get on with it.'

Within minutes, they had carried the wardrobe out of the unit, past the stairwell and over to the lift doors. Dom asked if it would fit inside the lift and if Harry had measured it. No, he hadn't. When they found out it wasn't going to fit—it was about three centimetres too tall—the real work started. Back to the stairwell they went, twisting and shuffling it down the guts of the building, through to the rear of the block and down to the garage. They were puffing and sweating and Dom was visibly relieved when it came to rest at one side of the tidy garage that served as Harry's work shed.

'Fuck me—why does someone small need a wardrobe so big?' Dom plonked himself in a chair. He wiped sweat from his forehead.

Harry leaned one arm on the wardrobe and calmed his breathing. 'Fantastic, Mr Tolen. Time for a cheeky beer.'

Up in the apartment, the friends sat splayed out drinking beer while most people would be having breakfast.

Dom caught Harry looking at him. 'I'm going to be ok. Don't worry.'

Harry's lips curled. 'I'm glad you say that. I am worried.' He waited until Dom was watching him to hurl the beer cap at his head, where it connected and bounced to the carpet. 'You're still dealing with a huge loss. It takes time.'

'I'm sure with time I can cope with the part I lost. It's the bit that stayed with me that I'm finding unbearable.' Dom's eyes closed as he guzzled his beer.

Unsure of what Dom was referring to, Harry stayed silent, rubbing the beer bottle label with an idle thumb. He was sure Dom would elaborate soon enough, but Dom's next question surprised him.

'Is your conscience clear?'

A quizzed look shot across Harry's face. 'Yep,' he said, and quickly put the focus back on Dom. 'Is yours?'

Dom didn't answer straight away. He fought away tears and the beer bottle came up to his eyes, shielding his face. 'Less than it was.'

Harry took a drink, unsure whether to pry more or wait for Dom to steer the conversation.

Dom let out a primitive moan. 'It's tough. You go through life, making your way, doing your bit. Then you see your actions indirectly harm someone.' Dom swigged the beer as he shook his head, almost to himself. 'Your work, your goals, your ambition turn like that.' His wrist swung through the air like a straw in an empty glass. 'And you start being ... being ... revolted by it.'

Stuck for words, Harry ran his fingers through his jumbled mane, failing to see the connection with Subiaco. 'You're right. It must be tough. And I don't know how soon things will improve for you, Dom.'

Dom's tears were gone, but he stared at Harry with severe eyes. 'Donald and I were alike—clearly, but he was so much more opportunistic, much more impulsive. That's why I—'

Dom paused to finish his beer. When the bottle came away from his lips, he added nothing to his unfinished comment.

Admiring the empty green bottle, he looked to his friend. 'I needed that. One more please.'

III

The minute he passed through the Moore Park gates, Dom spotted Lorna waiting at their meeting point. Even with her back to him, he recognised her exercise clothes and rain jacket. She was talking on her mobile, one hand gesturing, the other held to her head.

The day had turned colder, wetter and drearier. The clouds seemed to be delivering short bursts of rain in twenty-minute intervals and the wind, which had picked up, made the showers hit at an angle. Dom ambled towards the park's ring road and waited for a flurry of cyclists to speed by before he crossed to the centre.

When Lorna saw him, she ended the call. Her head was bowed and angled as though she didn't want to catch his eye. Dom hugged her tightly.

Lorna squeezed too. 'I miss dad. You remi—' She broke off.

Dom rubbed big circles into her back until she drew away. They began stretching and twisting their bodies to warm up, looking around, deciding which direction to head in. Both routes looked busy. 'I don't fancy jogging far today,' he said, raising his foot. 'My ankle's playing up.'

'Me neither.'

Dom pointed to an internal path. 'Let's walk this way and see if it gets quieter.' Further in, away from the exercise track, they joined the raised path along the right side of the pond, where the shouts from the sports field bounced around them.

He asked her how she was holding up. Her mouth staying firmly closed, she nodded she was fine.

'I bet Drew's taking good care of you.' Without slowing down, Dom leant in and put an arm around her. 'And your mum and Niamh?'

'They're ok.' She paused. 'I guess.'

The reservation in her voice made Dom look.

'I heard mum crying the other night. Niamh was in bed and mum was clearing out a cupboard. She went all quiet. Then I heard crying. It was some photos that did it—I saw them in her room the next morning.'

'Photos of them together?'

'No. Photos of dad when he was young. And a couple of photos of both of you. You looked so similar, I couldn't tell which was which.' She added after a short pause, 'What's it like to lose a twin?'

Dom looked at her. She had no idea how difficult answering the question would be, and with Donald's death so recent. He doubted her young frame could bear the weight of his grief if he was to let her know how he truly felt. And it would hurt him too much to inflict that on her, to see her beautiful, vibrant face encumbered with more sorrow.

A swarm of cockatoos circled above threateningly, the raucous screeching coming in waves. He and Lorna continued in silence until the birds had disappeared.

'I hope your mum's looking after herself.'

Lorna shrugged. 'She's getting visitors at least. Our neighbour pops in a lot and aunt Camille is dropping by today.'

'That doesn't happen often, although I'm happy to see they're helping each other.'

Lorna didn't reply. 'What are you going to do? Mum said you're doing nothing at the moment.'

Dom shrugged an answer. 'I'll sort something out. More importantly, what are your plans for next year? What are you going to study at uni?'

'Dunno.'

'Are you still thinking of Melbourne?'

'Yes. Mum's furious about it. She wants me to stay here.' They rounded a bend in the path where the space opened up. The area seemed to invite silence and the pair obeyed. The ponds beckoned them across the internal road.

Once on the muddy path, Lorna resumed her topic. 'It's so unfair. I won't be able to focus on study if I'm here and Drew's in Melbourne.'

'And the family are all definitely moving there? Can't Drew stay here? Why do *you* have to move?'

Lorna sighed. 'Both parents expect the children to stay together and the mum's health means they all help.'

'I see,' said Dom. He stopped at the bank of the lake to admire the view. The dark water rocked and the ducks bobbed closer expecting a feed. He gave his back to the water and continued walking.

Presently, Lorna asked, 'What's Melbourne like for work?' It's easy to get a job, right?'

'No different from here.' He stopped. 'Why don't you study in Melbourne? Why does it have to be that living in Sydney means you're studying and living in Melbourne means getting a job?' Up came his hands. 'Apply to a Melbourne university.'

'You can do that?' She looked off to the side.

Dom spoke. 'You *have* to go to university, honey. We all want that. Your dad would be so proud, right?'

'I didn't know you could go to a Melbourne uni. I can check online what courses they run.'

'Or check out a degree here and shift it to Melbourne after a term or two. You might be more successful that way.'

'Really?' Lorna's face radiated joy. The injection of excitement saw her dance around him foot to foot.

'I've got to tell Drew. And I've got to go online.' She pulled out her phone and unlocked it. 'Uncle Dom, can I go please? I want to check this out.'

She leaned in, pecked him on the cheek and hugged him, and as she bounced away, the phone went to her ear. Dom guessed Drew had answered the call because seconds later, her other hand was punching the air.

IV

Robin offered Camille a second cup of tea and she said she would drink it, but she outright wouldn't take more apple pie. She sat upright at the small, round table. The room was warm from the oven and the smell of pastry and sweetened apples hung in the air.

Camille hadn't removed her jacket and her handbag rested on a chair next to her. She fiddled with it from time to time, as though for comfort, or to check it hadn't been moved by Niamh, who got banished to another room after refusing to lower the volume on her tablet game.

'Will you keep the house?' Camille's eyes wandered over the contents of the huge combined kitchen and lounge, as if searching for a reason why someone would choose to stay.

'We don't intend to move. We like it here.' Robin returned to the table, placed the mugs of tea down and sat opposite her sister-in-law. The least-cracked white mug had gone to the visitor.

Camille was now studying the rim. She swung the handle from right to left sending the minute cracks away from her.

Robin said, 'How's Tommie?'

'He's good. His brother's family is coming to stay next month so he's pleased about that. You would've met Adrian and Ellen at our place years ago.'

'With the two young boys?' asked Robin.

'Yes, except they're grown up now. The eldest is going to university next year.'

'Like Lorna.'

'What will she be studying?'

'I'm waiting for her to tell me. Our Lorna won't be rushed.'

At that moment, a head bobbed past the window as it bounded along the side of the house and seconds later, Lorna appeared at the glass doors that led to the back garden and pool. 'Hello aunt Camille,' she said with a conditioned tone. She whacked the sliding door into place behind her.

'We were just talking about you. How are you, Lorna? And your studies?'

'I've got the HSC this year. I'm going to university too.' She looked from her aunt to her mother. Robin smiled and her shoulders lowered a bit. 'Drew's moving to Melbourne, so I'm going to apply for a place there.' Lorna spoke as if everyone knew Drew.

Robin's cup returned to the tabletop. 'Oh no, you're not.'

Lorna persisted. 'But Drew will be in Melbourne. What's the use of me even—'

Robin's pounding of the table startled Camille, who instinctively reached for her bag. 'Drew—Drew—Drew. If I hear that name one more bloody time.' Robin lowered her head and exhaled. She stood up and began cutting a piece of her homemade pie.

'Here.' It was thrust at Lorna, who turned away.

'Not hungry.'

'But it's my soft apple pie. You always love it.'

Lorna snarled at Robin. 'Soft apple pie is not a technique, mother. Just because you can't do pastry properly.'

Robin put down the plate and Lorna continued her attack. 'Soft pie is an accident, not a technique, and no, I don't want any of your accident apple pie. Aunt Camille, would you like some acci—'

'Listen to me, you. There is no way in hell you are going to Melbourne.' Robin blinked to keep the tears from forming. 'Now get away from me before I do something I'll regret.' She signalled for Lorna to leave.

Lorna looked from her aunt to her mother. She stormed to her bedroom using every step to vent her frustration, each foot bearing down on the carpeted staircase. The house shook as the door banged. There was silence. She must have hurled herself on the bed.

Robin shook her head. 'See—what was I saying not ten minutes ago?' She looked up at nobody. 'Uncle Dom,' she said, the words laced with disdain. 'She meets up with him and brings back all these unworkable dreams that I have to cope with—*try* to cope with. Running off to Melbourne with a—' She gave up, cradling her forehead in her hand. 'I'm going to have to speak to him.'

Camille picked up her mug, poised to drink. 'She's growing up quickly.' She drank some tea. 'I'd be speaking to her about precautions and the pill—if you haven't done so already.'

Robin froze.

Camille carried on. 'I mean well, Robin. Let me explain. You don't want accidents getting in the way of her studies—whichever city she's in.'

Robin tilted her head to look at Camille. 'What?'

'I—I feel ...'

'Not that.' Robin waved away Camille's discomfort. 'You don't know? Donnie never told you? About ...'

'Never told me what?' In a split second, Camille's expression skipped from quizzical to hurt. Her cheeks flushed as the muscles underneath stiffened. 'I should start a list of the things Donald kept from me,' she added, accentuating her wounded posture.

Robin rubbed her forehead and went to speak, but formed instead a weak smile.

Camille waited, but Robin wasn't giving. She whispered, 'Robin. Please. What else did my brother forget to tell me?'

When at last Robin responded, the lethargy was evident. 'Some other time, Camille.'

V

On Tuesday morning, Dom woke with a dry mouth and a thrumming head. His Monday had vanished, along with his weekend. After meeting Lorna on Saturday afternoon, he had returned to his unit and stayed there. On Monday morning, he had managed to spend the whole time, still unshowered and undressed, on the phone. And by late afternoon, when he opened the first bottle of red, he hadn't really been out for two days. Although, he had been down to empty the mailbox after spying, from the warmth of his living room, the post arriving.

Alone, he had read countless times the text messages exchanged with Donald that disastrous day, which filled him with sadness and fear. It was only a question of time before the police accessed Donald's phone and read them too. When that happened, there would be even more interrogation. It didn't look good.

So the next wretched morning had arrived. His limbs were stiff from the wine, the acidity seeming to penetrate to his bones, and his muscles were sore from grief, the sluggishness slowing his movements.

It was light outside, which meant he was waking late. He opened the blinds and wintry light poured in, making him squint. His unkempt face twisted.

It was a clear day, but he wasn't intending to go out, preferring to sit around in his dressing gown watching television and drinking instant coffee. He knew he was developing a routine, one which could prove hard to break. If he left the sofa to shower and dress, it was rarely before two in the afternoon, which had been the time he used to eat lunch at Subiaco. He told himself he wasn't depressed. He had Dympna to explore any issues with, and Harry visited or phoned.

When his doorbell rang around ten, Dom didn't move from the sofa. His gaze unbroken, he kept watching the television show and thought it was a salesperson or some other undesirable. He ignored the second buzz too, so sure was he that the call wasn't intended for him.

The third ring was a surprise, making him look up from the television to the hall where the chiming had come from, to the square clock on the wall, and down at his dressing gown.

His appearance was respectable. But a quick tug on his cord belt as he hobbled to the door made sure his dressing gown would stay in place. One unwelcome visitor was enough.

Even though he had the added protection of a security screen, he hardly ever opened the door without peering through the peephole. His warm eyelashes brushed the cold edge of the viewer. Beyond the reinforced mesh of the security door stood a professional woman in her mid-thirties. She was carrying a black briefcase and a plastic bag and he was certain he had never met her.

She was definitely not the police, he told himself. Nor was she selling anything. He saw her arm lift and the bell blared above his head.

Four rings. Someone really wanted to come in.

Dom straightened up, took in air, opened the door and stared at her without saying a word. The daylight flooded in. He blinked and squinted until he could see more clearly and comfortably.

The woman stood rigid, speechless, her pale skin contrasting with her charcoal business suit and a black bun of hair. She looked apparitional, taut cheekbones and uncertain eyes greeting him. A bogus smile revealed shiny chipped teeth. 'I'm from Subiaco Insurance. May I come in? I have something for you.'

Whatever Dom had expected her to say, it hadn't been that. He stepped back instinctively. His heart pumped, easing the grogginess in his head. Somebody from his work was at the door.

Hoping the security screen had prevented her from noticing his reaction, he rubbed both hands over his face and fixed his hair. 'What's—up?'

'There's nothing wrong. I'm here to go through some formalities and return some of Dominic's belongings.' She raised the plastic bag and gave it a wiggle. 'Personal items which we felt were important to return to you.' She waited. 'You must be Dominic's brother. How are you, Donald? Holding up ok? Please can I come in? I'm Vanessa. The office said you'd be here. I called by last week, but nobody was home.'

'I go out. Sometimes.' The desolation in his voice surprised him.

'Lovely.' She moved the plastic bag to her other hand and tried the screen door, which was locked. 'May I? This stuff weighs a tonne.'

Dom didn't doubt it one bit. She was so frail it was incredible she was holding her head up. He hesitated. With a clearer head, he would probably not have opened the door. But he decided it was safe for her to come in because she clearly thought he was Donald. She obviously wanted to talk about the contents of the Subiaco parcel that had arrived the day before—or the day before that—he couldn't remember when. He unlocked the screen door and pushed it towards her. She rushed in, lowered the bag and the briefcase, and held out her hand, all cold skin and bones.

Dom ushered her to an uncluttered section of the sofa and as soon as he turned off the television with the remote control, she filled the silence, launching into a script of how the office had been deeply saddened and forever changed by the tragic news and what an asset the irreplaceable Dom had been.

He wanted to respond honestly with *bullshit. Most people will say* Dominic who? *The fact I don't have a clue who you are proves how insular the culture is there.*

Instead, he thanked her and asked if she wanted a drink. She accepted.

Shuffling to the kitchen gave him more time to think. He made the tea while Vanessa talked about the flowers the firm had arranged for the funeral. The kettle started whirring and he sourced two clean cups and pottered around. From the corner of his eye, he spotted the Subiaco envelope with the paperwork she had come to chase up. Still unopened, it jutted out from under a newspaper. Dom hid it completely and went back to making the drinks.

It was a tough task doing everything at once— preparing hot drinks, guessing which division she worked in, reminding himself he had to pretend to be Donald, and chatting. His back was to her, which helped him juggle his thoughts. 'I'm coping well. It's hard. I've lost my twin. But I'll be ok.'

She smiled. 'Forgive me, but you look so like him. It's startling. Even the mannerisms and your walk.'

Dom froze, perturbed by the stranger's comments.

She must have seen him tense up because she added, 'I'm sorry if I've hurt you.'

Dom kept his face turned away. A neutral tone blanketed his confusion. 'You knew Dom—inic?'

'Yes, we worked on the same team for ages.'

He spun round with a small tray carrying tea, spoons, milk and sugar. 'Why did they send you here then? Shouldn't it be HR coming to see me?'

'Er—I moved to Corporate Services recently. I'm sorry. It was thoughtless to compare the two of you.'

Dom waved off her apology. 'It's strange. All our lives, we had people pointing out the obvious. The fucker's dead and it's still happening.' He watched her reaction.

Vanessa's head lowered and she busied herself with her teacup.

Dom sat down on the sofa and watched her add milk. She didn't touch the sugar. Her gaze lingered unnaturally on her hand stirring the tea.

'Excuse my humour. You must be glad for it, I'd say. I don't envy you visiting families. How brave.'

She showed a cheeky smile. 'Well, I have a thing to confess. I don't normally do this, but I asked to come here to return his things.' She sipped her drink.

'Why?'

'Nothing sinister. Your brother was once my lover, and the truth is I never really got over our affair.'

Dom coughed into his cup causing some liquid to spring on to his dressing gown.

'What's so funny?' she asked, shifting in her seat.

'I'm sorry.' Dom rubbed his dressing gown dry and brought himself some thinking time by overcautiously cleaning the bottom of the cup. He settled back into his seat and smiled. 'Typical Dom. Typical of him to keep it from me.' Dom produced a look of regret and Vanessa smiled sweetly at him. 'Please go on,' he said, perplexed but eager to hear more of her lies while the subtlest pang of fear twisted in his belly.

Vanessa sat quietly, drinking slowly, as if punishing Dom with silence.

Dom coaxed her. 'So coming to my place—my brother's place—will hopefully bring you some closure? I see, Vanessa.' He aired the name, certain it wasn't her real one, to put her at ease.

'Exactly.' She put down her cup and warmed her hands in her lap. 'I collected his things from the office and I wanted to see his place again, you know.' She looked away. 'I wanted to meet you.' She breathed out deeply as if deciding right at that moment to give up a big secret.

'If you're wondering why he never mentioned me, and I can tell from your expression that you haven't heard of me, it's because I asked him to keep our relationship a secret, even after it had finished. People wouldn't have liked it at Subiaco.'

Dom looked at her, leant back in the seat and covered his eyes with his hands. It was too much. He was too hung over to make sense of this charade. His thoughts were foggy and his eyeballs ached. His head rattled from side to side. 'For heaven's sake,' he whispered to a quiet flat. Was he hallucinating or dreaming?

He spoke to himself with his hands still over his face. 'This is not happening. It can't be real. When I open my eyes, she'll be gone and I can go inside, get dressed and go for a jog. The drinking has got to stop.' Two short breaths calmed him enough to want to look out.

His hands parted like centre doors opening to a theatrical extravaganza. The doors came to a halt. Dom opened his eyes. Vanessa was gone. The sofa was empty. 'Thank god for that.' He patted his chest to comfort his erratic heart.

'For what?'

His body locked still.

'Thank god for what? Are you ok?' asked a voice behind him.

He looked around in horror.

Vanessa was at the window opening the blinds with hushed, graceful twitches. 'Let's get some more light in here, shall we?'

Dom stared at her.

She caught his expression. She said, 'What's up?'

The only thing he could do to respond was wobble his head.

VI

At the quiet end of Glebe Point Road, with the last passenger out and the engine switched off, Harry deleted an unsent message, put away his phone and read the newspaper fished from the side of the driver seat. He tried to get Dom out of his head by focusing on a league write-up.

His instinct was sound. Not sending the text was the right thing to do. It would be pushing the boundaries of the friendship to expect Dom to do it. Dom was having a difficult time with Donald's death and it would be heartless to even ask him to spare it a thought.

The paper crinkled as he moved to the next page while he avoided eye contact with the people who had congregated at the bus stop metres ahead.

Harry next told himself that life went on—Dom was still functioning and all he wanted from his friend was a phone number, which he knew Dom had. It couldn't hurt to ask and Dom was free to say no.

How would Dom react to being asked to pass on the dealer's number? Dom might blast him for being selfish and pleasure-seeking while he was mourning.

If that happened, Harry would take it and he would apologise.

If Dom reacted like that.

Hell, he knew Dom well enough and sure he might not like Harry's request at such a bad time, but he'd give a straight answer either way.

Out came his mobile.

His inky fingers typed the message for the third time as he rested his lean body on the steering wheel.

```
        Hi mate. Thanks
        for your help the
        other day. Sorry
        to trouble you,
```

but can I get the
number of that
dude you visited?
Jeff and I are out
partying next week
and we'd like
something. No
worries if you
can't. Let's catch
up soon.

The phone confirmed the message had left and Harry started the bus.

VII

'I'll be honest, Donald. I really wanted to meet you. I wanted to be the one to give you Dominic's belongings.' She came back from behind Dom carrying her two bags.

'Did he bring you here often?' The ridiculousness of the question dawned on him. He knew full well he had never brought her to the unit.

'Not much. My place was closer to work and he so loved his privacy. Ours was a brief passionate affair, ended mutually to preserve work relations. Yet the brain can want one thing, and the heart the opposite.'

'You're right about Dom cherishing his privacy. Clearly, you knew him well.'

Vanessa grinned and nodded as her hand dipped into the plastic bag. 'Ready?'

The strangeness of the question didn't escape him and he watched the next part of her show in silence. He was the skeptical viewer and she the apprentice pulling unloved rabbits from a musty top hat.

When the first item appeared, Dom's confusion intensified. His tongue was outside his mouth. Rather than drawing out unfamiliar objects as part of her network of baffling lies, she tendered his own effects, with her thin lips locked in a smile, eyes fixed on him.

It was his desk calendar. She gave it a jiggle and put it down on the table between the two of them.

Next came a tightly twisted pouch, which Dom knew would contain his gym trainers and deodorant. She paused as though giving Dom a chance to respond.

He sat upright on the sofa, arms out to the sides to steady himself, and closed his mouth again to keep the emotion off his face. The urge to cry was enormous. He fought the tears. Even though he had only seen those items a couple of weeks ago, they belonged to another time, a different Dom.

Vanessa dipped in to the bag and removed the final object. It was his portable music system. He hadn't realised it wasn't in the unit and this shocked him more. A cry leapt from him.

'I can see this is upsetting you,' she said, waving a petite hand over the collection as if promoting a product range. 'I get quite emotional when I see these too.'

Dom stared at his things, catatonic. It dawned on him that she knew somebody within Subiaco. But who had passed her his stuff? And why?

She cupped her tea and drank with greed, and she hardly blinked as she dissected Dom's reaction. Her hand smoothed her hair and fixed up the plastic comb that held everything in place. 'As difficult as this must be, it's just the first step, Donald. HR will be in contact soon with all the final paperwork.'

He held up his palms. 'Let's be honest with each other. You're here mainly for personal reasons. I get it.'

Her mouth opened to feign a dramatic protest, but she closed it without verbalising resistance.

'I reckon this is an unofficial visit. And that's ok with me,' said Dom, going along with the sham.

'Thank you,' she said. 'You're right. I just had to come again. I loved this place—even though I only came here a handful of times.' Although her eyes danced around the living area, they returned to the closed door that led to the rest of the unit. One of her bony fingers tapped at her lips. 'I wonder if you could do me a favour.'

Dom wobbled in his seat. 'Yes?'

Her request was interrupted by the ring of the house phone. Dom let the machine take it and they looked at each other as the recorded message played loudly. After the pause, a crotchety female voice started speaking.

'Mr Tolen, this is Rita from Brain Food, the puzzle shop. I'm calling to let you know we have a slight problem with your next jigsaw delivery, the one due in September.'

Dom's stomach flipped, fearful something incriminating could be said. He drew Vanessa's gaze to the puzzle on the dining table and pointed at it silently while the caller continued.

'We're so sorry and we'll call again once we have more information. But just to confirm, your September delivery will be delayed. Thank you and goodbye.'

When the machine stopped and the room was silent, Dom continued his charade. 'He loved his puzzles.'

'Oh dear, you'll have to tell them he's gone.' Coldly, Vanessa gestured to the jigsaw Dom was working on. 'I saw that there. What will you do with it?'

'I don't know. I do it at times.'

'You could get it framed, incomplete, in memory of your amazing brother.'

'That's an idea. Getting back to this favour.'

'Mmm. I'd like to see his bedroom once more and say my goodbyes properly. We were all told your family wanted a small service, so we sent some flowers but otherwise we kept away. It was hard for us at the office.' She waited for him to respond, but he was motionless, glued in place.

'Donald?'

Dom sat still.

'Donald, are you all right?'

Dom answered after a pause. 'What was it you wanted?'

'To see Dominic's room one last time.'

'Er—er—I don't—er …'

She repeated her comments on missing the funeral.

Dom heard them this time. 'That was my decision. Dom wouldn't have wanted a huge service.' He stood up and re-tightened his dressing gown belt. 'Follow me.'

He led her past his bedroom, where the door was ajar. They walked down the hall almost side by side, his bare feet drowned out by the snapping of her heels. The few strides to the bedroom lasted an eternity.

Clack. Clack. Clack. Clack.

Shadows enveloped them as they left behind the light of the living room, moving deeper into the darkness. Her footsteps filled the hall.

It may have been her fear or Dom's poor balance, but in the dark, they rubbed against each other. He was unsure if it was her searching out his hand or him taking hers, but fingers found fingers and they walked hand in hand to Donald's room.

Dom pushed on the door and the flood of light that greeted them shook him from his momentary trance. His hand snatched away, the motion launching Vanessa into the bedroom. She scuttled into the middle and turned full circle.

Dom stepped inside and watched her eagerly.

She drummed her mouth as she scanned the furniture, the cluttered floor space and the overflowing shelving. 'Just as I remember it,' she lied. The desk with Donald's papers spread across interested her and she turned her back on it to look at Dom.

Subtle, he told himself. He pointed to the bed. 'Comfy, isn't it? Or did you guys use the floor?'

'Not as much as I would've liked,' she said, sitting on it. Her eyes closed as she pretended to reminisce. After a moment, the pale eyelids flapped up and her eyes opened to a stretch. She sat absolutely still, staring—almost glaring—at Dom as though he were intruding on *her* space. So strong was the feeling, he retreated to the doorway.

'Would you mind if I had a moment on my own?'

'Erm … I don't think that's appropriate. I don't know you and you know how he loved his privacy.'

'Please, Donald. It would mean so much to me.' She had one hand on her chest and the other resting on his forearm.

Just as Vanessa had done, Dom scoured the room, taking it all in, the shelving, the bed, the floor, the walls and the desk. What was she after?

He assessed the situation. She had shammed her way into his home to find out something about him. She would, of course, find nothing of interest in Donald's room. If there was one room she could roam unattended, it was this one, because Donald had no connection to Subiaco.

'Ok. Five minutes won't hurt. Say your goodbyes and I'll be out there.' Watching her watching him, he closed Donald's bedroom door and he returned to the living room, pulling his own bedroom door shut as he passed.

He moved straight to her briefcase and, listening out for her heels, knowing they would make a racket on his floorboards, he slowly opened it. His breath was raspy and uneven. His cold fingers worked awkwardly. To see inside, he had to undo a tricky buckle and free a flap of black leather. Before he prised the bag open, he peeked into the hall. No sign of her. She was still in the bedroom. He pulled back the flap and peered inside. It contained a small umbrella and nothing else. His fingers searched the interior compartments hungrily while he kept his eyes on the door. The only thing he felt was the lining of the bag. There was nothing. All her personal items had to be stashed in her jacket pockets.

He let go of the bag and sank into the sofa with the reality dawning on him. A bolt of icy electricity torpedoed through him. A stranger, a liar, was alone in Donald's room. What the hell was going on?

VIII

Ten minutes later, Vanessa came back ashen and forlorn.

Dom was at the end of the kitchen table back to drinking coffee, and her cup, which he had refilled and placed opposite his, sat waiting.

With deliberate movements, she sat, pulled her suit jacket to her body and drank her tea. For two minutes, neither of them said a word.

'I hope you found what you were looking for,' said Dom.

'What?' Her hands held the teacup steady a centimetre above the table.

'Finality. Isn't that what you wanted?'

Her body relaxed and the fake smile returned. 'Yes, I found a certain comfort and I said a prayer. I have some peace and I'm so grateful to you for that.'

'Good for you. Nice tea?'

'Just right. Now, before I go, I promise to check to see if there's anything else of Dominic's at the office. You know, in case something else turns up.' Her eyes widened and she clicked her fingers. 'Come to think of it, has Dominic got anything here belonging to Subiaco? I could take it back to the office now, if so. It would be easier.'

A stranger was sitting in his house claiming to be his ex-lover and this was his unit and he knew there was nothing of Subiaco's here. 'Good idea, but I'll need to check first. When we came back from the hospital, a relative took all his belongings.'

'Who?' As though realising her curiosity was out of place, she looked away.

'And the police have his mobile.' Dom was talking to himself. Would he ever get it back?

'The p—' She sat up with a burst of renewed energy and reached for her bag. 'It's so tragic when someone falls into traffic. You wish you could change the speed limit or something, don't you? If cars slowed down, when people trip over and fall by accident, it wouldn't be so dangerous. Let me give you my card. Whatever you find, you can call me straight away.'

She went to leave it on the table, hesitated and retrieved it.

In a fraction of a second, Dom spotted the logo adorning the card. She was about to hand him a genuine business card from Subiaco. The thoroughness of her charade made his breathing quicken.

'Best I give you my *new* mobile number.' The pen clicked loudly and she crossed out the printed digits and jotted down a number.

More lies. Dom gritted his teeth.

'There you go.' The card rested on the table. 'Would love to hear from you.' On her feet, she finished her tea, checked she hadn't left anything behind and moved closer to the hallway. When she joined Dom at the front door, she squeezed by. 'Thank you, Donald.'

Dom watched her leaving his unit. Her saunter to the stairwell didn't seem phony.

He slammed the front door and hurried to Donald's room. What had she done? He shuffled papers, checked cupboards and drawers, and sat on the bed. There was no way of knowing what she had touched or removed or added. He was at a loss to explain what he had witnessed. His head plopped into his hands.

Back out in the front area, he kicked the chair she had stopped in and plonked himself down. When he saw whose business card was on the table—Vanessa Hawke's—his hands clenched in fury.

'That was not Vanessa Hawke. You fucking liar,' he shouted.

Staring into space, he snorted deep breaths and banged his fists on the table so hard both cups rattled and a teaspoon clattered to the floor.

'Fuck! Fuck! Fuck!' His fists came down again.

Bang. Bang. Bang.

6 | Maggie

|

In his open plan kitchen, Dom made himself another cup of coffee, glancing over his shoulder and fiddling with his dressing gown cord. His belongings sat in a row on the table where she had left them, and each time he turned to look, with a scowl across his face, he half expected them to have disappeared. He stirred his coffee for almost a minute, letting his thoughts drift to the rhythmic scraping of the bottom of the mug. With a toss, the spoon clanked into the sink and Dom returned to the sofa, sitting opposite her wall of souvenirs. Several times, he made a move to pick them up but stopped, a surge of fear pushing him back in the seat. The calendar was showing Monday the fourteenth of July—the day of the swap. It was Donald who had ripped off the previous slip of paper.

After a moment, he slammed the mug on the table and, snatching up the desk calendar, said aloud, 'This is ridiculous.' It gyrated at his touch as though he needed more proof it was definitely his. Thumbing through to a day in August, there he saw a reminder in black pen in his scribble—the webinar he was booked on. It was his calendar for sure, and the gym clothes were definitely his, as was the music player.

The memory of her dramatic display splashed across his mind. Her eyes had fixed on his as she pulled out each piece, her words clearly meant to draw a reaction. She had presented her gifts and she was hoping to receive something. He had no idea what she wanted from him, or from Donald, or from his home. Perhaps Donald's bedroom held the answer.

Again, he trotted through to the room and sat where she had. The small crease in the beige bedcover told him where she had placed herself minutes before. He scanned the room, his face crumpled in bewilderment, his eyes dragging with suspicion. Everything looked in its place with no sign she'd even been there. Did she search the place? Did she find something? It was impossible to know.

Dom looked around at the walls, the bed, under the bed, in the wardrobe. If she'd opened drawers and cupboards, he wouldn't have heard from out there. Did she leave something behind—a listening device perhaps? Preposterous. None of it made sense.

Even a scan of his room was ineffective. His unmade bed, the furniture, the walk-in wardrobe and the ensuite offered no clues to the reason for her visit. Surely she had come to see his room, not Donald's. Yet it was just his bedroom, where he slept. He stood still breathing slowly, waiting for the room to explain her visit. But he couldn't see any connection it would ever have with Subiaco. And there was no way she had the slightest idea the bedroom contained a safe tucked behind a painting. Only he knew that existed. Only he knew what it contained.

He left the room. Running his hands against the walls of the dark hall to steady himself, he went to the living room, slumped onto the sofa and made a call.

'Police,' he said to the person on the other end, his mind a wash of confusion. After a short pause, a second more commanding voice told him he was through to the right area.

'Go ahead, please,' said the operator.

Dom struggled to put into words what had just happened. His mouth opened, but words didn't form. 'Err—erm—I—'

Looking at the three items she had left behind muddled him further and gluing his eyes shut didn't help. 'A woman—er. She lied about—erm and she brought my things from the office.'

'Sir, do you wish to report a crime?'

He wasn't sure.

The voice repeated the question. 'Are you reporting a crime?'

'I don't know,' he whispered.

Dom ended the call and sat peering. After a moment, his eyes opened. He dialled another number.

II

'Thanks for this.'

'Cassandra must like you. She never lets people squeeze in to see me between—'

The unfinished sentence caught Dom's attention. He turned.

Dympna's mouth sat open and her hand pointed to a chair. She could sense something was troubling him.

Dom beat his chest. 'I can't sit down. I'm too wired.' The suite lacked the striding space Dom's legs demanded, and he paused next to the comfy chair he would usually sit in. His hand rested on the cushioned back. 'I don't know what to do. Something extraordinary has happened.' His feet were soon moving again, small dancey steps going back on themselves.

'Are you ok? I've never seen you so agitated'—she looked him over once more—'or scruffy.'

It was Tuesday afternoon and Dom had spent the last few hours replaying the events of the morning in his mind. With relentless thoughts, he felt as if he had done a full day's work. He hadn't shaved or combed his hair, but he had showered.

'The weirdest thing—and I mean the weirdest thing—happened this morning. I had a visit from a woman I've never met in my life. She was claiming to be my colleague—' He was interrupted by his own incredulous laugh. 'And apparently she's my ex.'

'How strange. Where would you like to sit while you tell me about it?'

Dom missed the glint in Dympna's eye.

'Here.' He made himself comfortable in the chair. 'She thought I was Donald.'

Dympna listened as Dom recounted the morning's inexplicable events, telling her about being surprised, then unsettled, by each of her lies. The whites in Dympna's eyes glistened when she heard about the woman removing the objects from her bag and willing Dom to burst into tears. Her thin lips parted when Dom talked about the imposter's request to see the bedroom and to be left alone. But Dympna didn't interrupt him. She noted his rage at being betrayed in his own home and his confusion over the web of lies the visitor had concocted. Each time the panic seized him, he would flee it by getting out of the chair.

For most of the time, he spurted chaotic chatter and hardly looked at Dympna. It was as though he were alone. He finally flopped back into the chair and made eye contact.

'I feel like I'm going crazy. I can't make sense of Donald's death and I didn't help things by pretending to be dead.' The leather armrest received a sluggish thump. 'And now this woman comes along and she's not who she says she is. I'm scared.'

'Scared?'

'It's this huge unknown that threatens my tranquil life. Something big is about to blow up—I can feel it. There has to be something. People don't come to your house pretending to know you, do they?'

Her soothing voice calmed him. 'It's certainly puzzling, Dominic, and it's clearly affecting you.'

Without interrupting, Dom nodded. He wanted Dympna to tell him about it. When she spoke, big problems shrank. She would make it less bamboozling.

'Perhaps you won't see her again.'

'I doubt that. She begged me to stay in contact and besides'—he reached into his shirt breast pocket for the card she had left and he pounced across to Dympna—'you must see this.'

Dympna read it. 'She left this with you?'

'Yep. She's not Vanessa Hawke.' Dom's index finger wagged furiously at the business card while Dympna examined the number and handwriting. 'And she made a point of casually giving me her mobile number—the crossing out and the handwritten number there—all of it an act, of course. She did that right in front of me. Completely planned, but made to look spontaneous.'

'And you let her have time in Donald's room alone?'

His shoulders lifted with exasperation. 'Hello—what was she gonna find? Plus, I didn't want to let on that I knew something was up. If someone comes to your house claiming to know your dead brother, most people would let them sit alone in a room to say their goodbyes.' He stopped. 'Wouldn't they?'

'Most people would have done the same.'

'At least now I have a chance to meet her again and perhaps get to the bottom of it.'

'It? Is that so wise, Dominic?' A hint of worry crept into her voice. 'You've been unsettled by one visit from Vanessa. Do you want to go through that again?'

Dom shrugged his indifference until it registered what name Dympna had used. 'I'm not calling her Vanessa,' he snapped, his anger directed more at the stranger. 'She's not Vanessa. She's a bloody imposter and I'm going to find out what she was doing in my fucking house.'

Dympna brought the conversation round to Donald's death, her focused eyes trying to trap Dom's gaze. 'It's a big loss, losing a family member. How would you describe that change?'

Dom couldn't answer straight away, an immobile squint locked on his face.

'I don't know. I—I feel more isolated. More lonely and vulnerable. There's a hole now and I guess I need to re-adjust.'

Dympna agreed with a soothing hum.

Dom covered his lips with a hand as he got ready to still the tremble that would begin. His voice was about to break. 'I miss him.' He shook his head in disbelief and dried his closed eyes with each hand. 'It just feels too hard. I'm trying to get over the death. And this comes so soon after it and I don't know what it means. It's just all screwed up. I didn't ask for any of this. I'm not a bad guy—I don't try to cause problems. I just want my life to mark itself off all easy and simple.'

'Who says you cause problems?'

'Nobody.' Dom's eyes, which had started to open, closed again. 'What I mean is why did she choose me?

It's so beyond sense. I've spent weeks feeling guilty for Donald's death and now this immense confusion comes.' He corrected himself. 'It's not immense—it's blinding.' He leaned back in his chair, arms by his sides, eyes closed.

Dympna scribbled notes and looked up. 'I'm going to suggest you—'

'She was clearly there pretending to pay her respects.' Dom opened his eyes and in doing so, silenced Dympna. 'Yet she never mentioned the funeral really, or the accident. She didn't talk *about Donald*, you know? Only to prattle about road safety and falling into traffic.'

'That was less than tactful of her, I'd suggest.'

Dom's eyes widened. 'Do you think they're connected?'

'What do you mean?'

'Do you think they're connected?' he repeated. 'Oh god.' Horror swept over his face. He rocked back and forth and his breathing became erratic and noisy. His hands twisted awkwardly in the air. 'They could be connected.'

'What could be connected?'

'His accident—her visit. It's possible. This—this—' A puzzled look contorted his face to the point it was almost unrecognisable. Dom froze.

They stared at one another.

He asked, 'Was he pushed?'

Dympna shrieked. 'What?'

'He was pushed.' It turned from a question to a statement.

'Dominic!' She shifted awkwardly in her chair.

'Donald was pushed. He didn't fall. And she wanted to find something. She was at my place because she killed him.'

'I don't see the connection. This is—Dominic, what's the connec—'

'Oh my god. This woman killed Donald. I need to find out what he did that day, what he saw.' His private conversation went out to the room.

'If you think that, you must go to the police with this information. Something is very wrong.' Dympna lowered her pad and sat forward. 'Do you hear me?'

Dom looked at her as though he was surprised to see her in the office. His hands patted together marking out his logic. 'He's overheard something at Subiaco. Something someone would kill for.'

'Dominic, please go to the police.' Dympna paused. 'This is a matter for the police. They'll find out what your brother did that day. They will clear things up. It's getting too complicated.' She raised her voice. 'Dominic?'

'No one knows about the swap. Only you and me. I don't want that getting out.'

Dympna tried reasoning with him and pointed to the business card. They had some physical proof. Dom snatched it back from her desk. 'I can't. It'll be awful for Donald's memory and for the family. Not to mention the trouble I'll be in.' A shake of his head told her there would be no going to the police.

'Listen to me.' Her voice rose further, losing its usual soothe. 'If you're right, whoever they are, they think they've killed you. You mustn't let people at Subiaco know you're alive—it'll place you in danger.'

Dom looked through her. 'But why me?'

Admitting defeat, Dympna leant back in her chair, which swivelled as Dom carried on articulating his jumbled thoughts and ignoring her comments.

'I don't know anything that would bring someone snooping to my place. I don't.'

Dympna fiddled with her pen.

'I want to know what happened the day of the swap.'

Her head came up. 'You've got no way of getting that information safely. I urge you to use the police.'

'I'll think of a way.' He stood up and went to leave.

'Tell me your plans. I want—' She made a move to stand, but he was too quick.

'The less you know, the better.' The door closed. He was gone.

Dympna retrieved her pad. She jotted down some notes and underlined the final words.

Vanessa Hawke doesn't exist.

III

Maggie passed some final instructions to the division secretary and left. Although Subiaco Insurance was her focus during the day, switching off was easy, as was avoiding the lure of taking work home, apart from an occasional article to read on the bus.

The winter evening rushed to greet her as she stepped outside. Habitually leaving the office late, a quiet commute to her modern inner-west flat was a fixture of her evening routine. In winter, that meant travelling in the dark, where people were watery figures brushing in front of one another. She navigated her way to the bus stop, dodging a homeless woman asking for a coin, and nestled herself at the bus shelter, ignorant of the person loitering a few metres behind. Her bus soon arrived and she took the first seat she came to. Her follower passed her, keeping his face hidden.

The handful of commuters were oblivious to his interest in Maggie and he hid himself reading the free newspaper abandoned on a seat. When Maggie left by the front exit, he got off through the back doors, approaching her when nobody else was around and the roaring engine of the departing bus had softened.

He called her name. She glanced, but didn't stop.

'It's me—Dom.'

She carried on for a few steps, stopped and turned.

'Donald? Is that you? How are you?'

Dom stepped closer to her, open palms at his sides. 'Maggie. It's me, Dominic. I'm h—here.' He had been pondering all day which words to use. He couldn't say he was alive because he hadn't died. 'I have to explain. I need your help. It's serious, but can we talk upstairs?' He gestured to a top floor of the building they were outside, where she lived.

She looked around her and turned side on as though ready to defend herself. 'You said *Dominic.* Are you ok?'

Dom inched closer.

Maggie stared intently waiting for the shadows to give up more detail of the twin's features. 'It's great to see you. I've been worried.' She leaned in to pat his forearm. 'How are you?' Under the streetlight, tears were visible. 'I still can't believe he's gone.'

'I'm not Donald—I'm Dom.'

Maggie brushed her cheeks dry with cold knuckles while her body relaxed when his hand came up to squeeze her shoulder. 'But—'

'I'm Dominic. Donald died—he was murdered.'

She recoiled and her quizzical expression looked like it would never leave her face.

'December, two years ago—where were we?'

Dom didn't blink. 'Strahan. Four days at the something-something manor. I can't remember. But it's me. I wanted to go along the east coast, but you'd been there, so we went to the west.'

'Close enough,' she said, stepping in to hug him. His arms wrapped her tightly. He could feel her trembling in his hug as the emotion overtook her. It felt great to hug her and he cried with her.

After a while, she lifted her head an inch. 'Is it really you? What about the funeral? We sent flowers—' She rested her head on his chest again.

'I'll explain upstairs.' Dom rubbed her back in comforting strokes.

'Dom?' In his arms, her weight shifted to one side.

'Yes?'

Without warning, he felt a powerful impact against his groin. His yelp was automatic, before he felt any pain, and it echoed away in the dark street.

With her knee lowered, Maggie let Dom fall away and she cried into her hands. 'How could you?'

When the pain arrived and spread throughout his lower body, Dom was already on his knees, his legs too weak to sustain him. Cradling himself, he groaned and writhed on the pavement.

Maggie's bawling sent her head bouncing around. 'I thought I'd l—lost y—you. This is the worst thing I—' Her wails drowned her speech and threatened to collapse her, but she steadied herself on a nearby bench.

Still without the breath needed to form words, Dom looked up with pleading eyes. 'I'm—'

Her fight returned. 'You didn't even let me come to the funeral. You're a cruel bastard. Why didn't you return my—' She screamed into the street. 'I said goodbye to you all b—by myself.' She scurried away and left him wriggling where he had dropped.

He hobbled to the bench to recover some more. Staying on the ground would draw more attention from passersby. The pain was not getting worse, but he was too weak to follow her just yet. When he pulled out his mobile—a poor attempt to escape the pain—he saw a text from Camille asking him to call. Dom popped the phone away, choosing to control his breathing and massage his groin instead. Minutes later, he had the strength to take the lift to Maggie's unit.

He rang the bell and its shrill streamed through his body making his aching crotch pulsate.

IV

Minutes passed before sounds appeared from within the unit. The door opened a few centimetres. Enough to release the lock. It sat ajar as Maggie, unseen, retreated from the entrance.

Dom nudged the door inwards checking it was safe to enter. He crept in, the familiarity soothing him. He had forgotten about the hall walls covered with pieces of her own artwork—tapestries and paintings of varying sizes. A hint of incense—detectable only if he let it drift up his nostrils, vanishing if he breathed in—brought back memories of good times, evening chats and hours of intimacy.

Several short paces took him to the open living area, where Maggie joined him, shuffling out of a room, blowing her nose.

'Sit down. I need answers.' She waited until Dom had taken a chair before she sat. She tapped her thigh and from nowhere, Jasper, her oversized ginger cat, appeared. Maggie gave him a squeeze and he stayed curled on her lap. She began stroking him and, through red eyes, finally looked at Dom. 'That's a cruel trick to play. It feels like a wall has crushed me. I'm so hurt I can't look at you.'

'I'm sorry. I couldn't deal with—I'm not thinking—' He gave up speaking. Not a word was uttered by either of them for five minutes.

An occasional wince helped Maggie hold off the tears. She drummed the table from time to time and immediately after, her face heavy with sorrow, she would lean in to Jasper for a comforting hug.

Each time, she grabbed a fresh tissue. The box, handy in the middle of the empty table, looked like it had been positioned there in preparation for their chat. 'What's going on?' she asked, after blowing her nose. The noise bothered Jasper, who pounced down and walked to the sofa.

Dom's gloomy eyes, darkened further by his stubbly face, twitched as he started his story. 'It was Donald who died.'

'We were told it happened near the office. Were you with him at the time?' She wiped tear-dampened strands of hair from her face.

Dom shook his head. He widened his chest as he took in a huge breath, as if preparing to lift something heavy. 'There's so much to tell you.' He put his palm out across the table, gesturing to her. They squeezed hands.

He launched into the events of the last few weeks that had derailed his life, from the day they switched roles and the call to go to the hospital, to the funeral and the visit that morning from the woman pretending to be their colleague.

'Vanessa?' Maggie was astounded. 'She's not even in the country. She's in New Zealand.'

He knew the woman wasn't Vanessa Hawke, but the independent confirmation settled him.

As Dom was recounting his story, Maggie fetched two wine glasses and an unopened bottle of cabernet merlot.

'So what have you stumbled across?'

'I know so little. That's why I'm here. I wanted to ask you what happened the day Donald was at Subiaco.'

Maggie went quiet. 'Nothing out of the ordinary. He definitely didn't seem troubled or scared.'

'You didn't see anything suspicious?'

Maggie shook her head. 'We had lunch. We went back to the office and I didn't see him again. I went into a meeting with Ian and Patricia about some plan changes, and that's it really.' She brushed away any significance of the events with a hand.

'I do remember a meeting with Wayne before lunch that day and now it's so obvious. You didn't know a thing and Wayne was getting pissed off—really pissed off. I remember thinking you seemed different somehow. But it was you, you know? Nobody knew it wasn't you.'

'Ok, that's good to hear—that nothing odd stands out. If we can narrow it down to a specific period, I have a better chance of finding out what happened, I guess.' He said, 'How are you feeling? Better?'

'I'm annoyed. And hurt and betrayed and feeling for you. All mashed up together.'

Dom's eyes fell.

Maggie carried on. 'What I don't understand is why you told them you were the one who had been killed.' She reached for a clean tissue and dried her eyes.

'I had a meltdown that morning. I had just told his work he was de—dead and it was crushing. I couldn't think straight. I had this flash of an idea of living on as him, stupid I know. But it was as if I could go to a new job as Donald, and I wasn't up to telling people for the rest of my life that Donald was gone.' His hands cupped his eyes. 'That's what will happen. I will have to tell people forever that he's—' He wriggled in his seat. 'It's so painful. Ugh.'

'That will ease. You'll make this more difficult if you take on the burden of worrying about the rest of your life as well as now. One stage at a time.'

He nodded.

'But why did you agree to swap in the first place?'

'I'd been drinking and he was asking constantly. He just wouldn't leave it. And he'd been so down and fragile—for the last year really—with work and his marriage breaking up and having to move into my spare room.' He paused. 'Does the name Karen Bush sound familiar?'

Maggie shook her head.

'She's the specialist for the twin research we do. That's always been there, right in my bloody face and as I saw Donald get more and more down, I remember thinking great, me next. That's the one thing that research has shown—if it happens to him, it'll happen to me. So I thought the best thing was to get him to cheer up. Or I had it coming too.'

Maggie rubbed his arm.

Dom continued. 'He presented this idea as if this one little prank would make him so happy. And I feel so guilty about his death because he was only at that bloody crossing because I agreed to his stupid game. And the reason I agreed was because, if I'm really honest, I wanted my depressed brother better and out of my life. And on top of that, I end up hurting you.'

With a lift of her eyebrows and a slow nod, Maggie agreed. She took a sip of wine and left the glass aside.

'I understand your guilt. But what you did is just a small part of all this. You're not to blame for what happened. Where did he get the idea to swap anyway?'

'He never told me, but we hadn't done it for years.'

'And no one else knows about it?'

'No one. He swore to me he wouldn't tell a soul. It had to be a secret. Part embarrassment and part job safety—it's a huge security breach. If it got out that strangers had access to our system ...'

'Did he have any other enemies or troubles?'

'No, I don't think so.'

'Is his ex seeing someone else?'

Dom's eyes bounced at the unbelievable—Robin with a new partner. 'Nope. There's no angry new boyfriend who wanted to do something bad to Donald, as far as I'm aware. Subiaco—it's got to do with that place.'

'How are you so sure?'

'The visit. Bringing me my things. Vanessa's card.'

'Maybe all this predates the swap day. You could be the intended target. It might not have anything to do with Donald's actions.'

Dom blinked at her, content to hear her guesses, not wanting to fuel her theories.

She jiggled in her chair, a shiver spanning across her shoulders and up into her head.

'You're cold?' he asked.

'Spooked by the thought someone in our office is a killer. Someone who is so determined and so confident they're willing to show up at yours to snoop around.' The goose bumps eased when she rubbed her arms. 'What is going on?' she said almost to herself. 'What's at the office that's so important?'

Dom squeezed her hand. 'That's what I want to know. I'd like your help. We need to see what Subiaco can tell us Donald touched that day. Maybe he did something on the system. If so, it'll be against my profile. I want to give you my logon and you see what comes up. But you need to be careful, Maggie. Really careful.'

Maggie reached for a pen and paper for Dom to jot down his logon details.

He handed her the paper. 'At least it's just confined to one day. If it's not the fourteenth, ignore it.'

She looked directly at him. 'What are you expecting to find?'

Dom's face was expressionless.

'Be honest.' Her voice was close to cracking.

'I am—I have no idea. He was a genius with technology. He's probably picked up an anomaly and gone exploring or something. Lord knows.'

Together, locked on each other, their eyes widened. Their gazes answered her question. An insurance company, dealing with payouts and huge transactions, relied on the sound morals of its employees so that, most of the time, a calculated mix of good conscience, strong management and security controls meant temptation stayed away. But that precarious blend would prove ineffective if staff chose to cross a line.

'He's either heard something he wasn't supposed to or he's stumbled across something in the system.'

'Or seen something on a printer,' said Dom.

'Who?' Maggie was astounded. 'Who would do that?'

Dom's mobile buzzed loudly and they jumped. He batted it closer to him without picking it up. It was a second text from Camille, this one demanding a response. He nudged the phone away and looked up at Maggie, who was waiting, poised to ask more questions. Dom massaged his forehead.

'This woman claiming to be Vanessa—how did she get the business card? Or rather—how did a colleague of ours get Vanessa's card and pass it to this woman?'

Dom stopped his massage. 'That's easy to do. Go past her desk. She's away, you say? Perfect chance. And sometimes our cards are kept at reception for when we speak to visitors in the meeting rooms there.'

'And you're sure she asked you for physical things?'

Dom pictured the woman creaking about his home. 'Definitely. She was after an object—something.' His fingers nipped the air. His eyes hunted for a clue. 'She gave me some things and she was hoping I'd pass her a *thing*.'

'Let's hope it turns up. Have you eaten?' Maggie emptied the last of the wine into their glasses and moved to the fridge.

As they prepared dinner, the conversation turned to lighter topics. Dom praised her art. She explained it had been one of the positives to come from their break up.

'Would another break up help further?' His eyes twinkled.

They sat close and ate chicken pasta.

With her plate almost empty, Maggie asked, 'Did you take a photo of her?'

'No. I didn't get a chance. But that will be useful for the police later on.'

'What do you mean?' Maggie began clearing the table and decided not to use the dishwasher. They could stand close as they washed and dried the plates.

Without answering the question, Dom stood to help, slipping into the customary role of dish dryer. The tartan tea towel looked clean, and he began folding and unfolding it as he waited for Maggie to hand across dripping items.

Dom raised his voice over the noise of the sink filing with hot water. 'I don't plan to report anything about her yet—that's what I mean.'

Maggie looked up from the plate she was submerging and made a face at him.

Dom defended his actions. 'I want to see what I can find out first. It's just circumstantial really.'

'That's an understatement. Your brother ge—' She started afresh. 'We lose Donald in unusual circumstances and then a woman—' She stopped talking and washed some pieces in silence, leaving a plate in the rack. 'You need to go to the police,' she added, watching him pick it up.

'I want to be …' Dom searched for a way to explain why he had chosen not to pass on his knowledge.

'The hero.' Maggie butted in with her characteristic directness. She thrust the next plate straight at him. 'Don't make that face at me. This tragic situation is presenting itself to you as a great way to redeem yourself with Camille, I would guess. Yes, everyone will find out you agreed to the swap, but you'll be off the hook because you will have single-handedly found the criminals.'

'Kick me while I'm down, why don't you? And you're wrong. Yes, I feel guilty and helping uncover what actually happened could alleviate that. But there's something else. We have an advantage in that the killer thinks I'm dead. We've got a chance to look into things freely. The minute I go to the police, that advantage ends. The police will charge in to Subiaco asking questions, trying to sniff out what happened.'

Maggie locked eyes with Dom, readying her hand to tug on the chain of the plug. Like a hawk, she watched his hand come up and caress her shoulder. The same old Dom. When his words didn't work, he'd try to win her round with intimacy or by playing with the cat. And he was at it again. She pulled the plug out of the sink, letting the dirty squelch of the water do her talking.

Dom's hand withdrew. He discarded the tea towel and went in search of Jasper.

Maggie came over shortly after. 'It's late.'

'Can I stay the night?'

'Sure.' She left the room and returned with sheets and pillows, which she dumped on an armchair. Dom didn't move. When she appeared with a thick blanket, she asked, 'When were you going to let me know you were alive?'

'Soon. Sorry. I have papers from HR at home and I was planning to call you but all this came up.'

'That's a lie,' she said, matter-of-factly. 'And my flowers? I phoned your landline god knows how many times. I take it you got those messages.'

He said sheepishly, 'All of them.'

She shook her head and pointed behind her to the hall, off which sat her bedroom. 'I'm sleeping in there. You have a choice. Out here or in there with me.'

Dom looked from the sofa to the bundle of sheets he would need to convert into his bedding. 'In there, please.'

'You're brave—I kneed you in the balls a few hours ago.' She left the room. 'Turn down your phone. I don't want to be disturbed until seven.'

V

Dom woke up alone in Maggie's bed, which was bathed in weak daylight. There were no sounds coming from within the unit, and he had the faint recollection of a door shutting. Perhaps she'd just left. He clambered out of her bed, dressed immediately to warm himself against the cold morning and, as her scrappy note in the kitchen commanded, prepared himself breakfast.

While the kettle boiled, Dom checked his phone. Texts and missed calls from Camille—not one revealing why she wanted to speak to him—added to the headache brought on by the red wine. He committed to calling her once outside Maggie's.

Groaning his way through a full stretch, he released the tension that was building up. The bones in his shoulders and back cracked as he twisted around. With his knee up on a chair, he bit skin from a nail inattentively and buttered his toast.

He clicked his fingers. He had nearly forgotten. Harry was after the dealer's contact details. His short reply warned Harry not to get too hopeful because Phil had said he wasn't doing random deals anymore.

After breakfast, Dom stepped out to a cold and blustery day, the sun being kept away by thick, light-grey clouds, and while it didn't look like it would rain, it wasn't the morning for strolling. He hurried by the bench he had rested on the night before, tilting his head away from it, not wanting to be reminded of that crushing pain, and caught a warm bus to the centre.

His attempts to resist the pounding urge to contact Maggie failed. She had her work to do, but a quick message wouldn't hurt. After typing a few words of thanks for her support, he ended with a request to call him as soon as she had something.

When a short time later, he felt his phone silently vibrating, he yanked it out of his pocket as if it was burning his skin. Energy jolted through him. But it wasn't Maggie. His shoulders sank.

'Hi.'

Camille was wondering where the hell he'd been and why he hadn't answered any of her messages. Dom said he had been tied up with a meeting and hadn't been able to call or respond. She wanted to see him today after work. She had some questions.

Questions? He was to come to hers for dinner this evening without fail. She asked him if he understood. That sounded lovely to him. Another night without having to cook, he said. Did he need to bring anything? A cake perhaps? No, of course not—since when did he turn up to hers with dessert? He was to be there at six and Tommie would let him in.

VI

His finger hovered inches from the bell. The day was over but the porch light gave him a soft yellow glow. Dom paused at Camille's front door getting his account in order. The swap never happened and Donald was in the city that day for some unknown, unimportant reason. She didn't need to know about his visitor from the previous day because it would complicate things too much.

'What are you loitering for? Are you rehearsing?'

Dom brought his hand down as naturally as he could and turned around to see Camille approaching. He smiled. 'You're early,' he pointed out.

'That's impossible. It's my home.' With seamless precision, she nudged him away, put the key in the door, and stepped inside the cosy terrace.

Classical music was playing.

Camille ordered her brother through to the kitchen and Banner escorted him there, getting pats on the back in exchange.

Dom greeted Tommie and sat down ready for the torrent of questions and accusations.

But the ordeal didn't start. Where was this morning's urgency? Camille and Tommie instead opted for small talk, more interested in the news—a political scandal developing in Canberra, a whistleblower of a public transport swindle killed in his home, arrests over a drug haul.

Tommie served dinner of a huge portion of pasta and spicy sauce, which Dom weakened with a blanket of grated cheese. 'Delicious.'

Tommie replied, 'I'm doing a cooking course.' His eyes only lifted from Dom's plate of food when he reached for the cooking manual. He turned back intent on detailing what Dom was eating.

The beep of Dom's phone made Dom smile and Tommie frown. The cook wasn't ready to change the subject, but when Dom kissed radiant fingers off pursed lips, Tommie yielded.

As Dom fished out his phone, he commented how lucky Camille was to get the benefit of the lessons.

The message was from Maggie. It had one word.

Bingo

Dom became fidgety. 'What did you want to talk about? It sounded urgent.'

'I just had some questions. About flowers and things.' Camille circled the table and Tommie retreated clutching at his cookbook.

'Oh yeah?'

'The day of the funeral, flowers arrived but the cards were written to Donald about *your* passing. They'd mixed up the names.'

'Happens all the time. Dom—Don.'

Camille's words formed slowly. 'But two wreaths came, both with condolences about *you*. I want to know what's going on.'

'Going on? Nothing's going on. It's just a mistake, Camille. What's it got to do with me? And what's it got to do with you?' Dom thrust the plate away and leant back in the chair. 'What are you getting at?'

Camille stayed quiet.

Dom pressed her for more information. 'I didn't see these wreath cards. Where are they?'

'I hid them from you. I thought you'd find it too distressing. Which it was. And so I went to the florist to complain and I showed—'

'You did what?' Dom's jaw opened.

'I wanted to tell them they had the wrong name. And thank god I'd seen the card before you had.'

Dom raised his eyebrows in disbelief.

'I did—I did. But they checked and this is the odd thing.' She fiddled with her knife and fork, repositioning them on the empty plate. 'The flowers came from people at your work. They were from Subiaco.'

Dom looked from her to Tommie. 'What's going on here? You're spying on me?'

Camille's fingertips rested on the base of her cutlery. 'So my question is this—why do your colleagues think you're dead?'

Dom's breathing became ferocious, his huffing and puffing audible over the music. In. Out. In. Out.

Camille and Tommie stared at his nose.

'It's just a mistake I suppose. What do I say here?'

'Someone thinks you're dead. Why? How? Doesn't that bother you?' Her voice escalated.

'Drop it.'

'How does someone you work with think you've passed away? Help me understand. What's going on?'

'Leave it, Camille. I mean it.'

'She's got a right to know.' Tommie warmed Camille's shoulder. 'What have you been up to?'

'Piss off.'

'Enough, Dominic.' Camille stood up and took her plate and cutlery to the sink. 'If you won't tell me, I'll ask the very people who ordered the flowers.'

Dom bucked up, his arms straight out. 'Do not speak to anyone at my work.'

The pitch of his scream made Camille's eyes widen with fright. Tommie rested his cookbook on the side.

'Do not contact my fucking office. Is that clear?'

Camille buckled against the cold steel of the sink. 'Tell me what's going on. I want to know.' Her face was angled away from her brother, as though to protect herself.

Dom could see her chin wobble. Her next words were almost inaudible. 'What have you done?'

'Have you contacted my work?' He moved round the table and stood behind her.

Sobbing, she ignored him. 'What have you done?'

Dom turned to his brother-in-law. 'Tommie?'

Tommie's lips stayed sealed. He looked to Camille.

'Have you contacted my fucking office?' Dom's voice reached a climax and his finger prodded the air.

Camille spun round. 'Stop that talk!' She batted away his hand. '*You* answer *me*.' Her face contorted as she held back tears. 'What have you done?'

'I've done nothing,' he screamed, his spit landing on her jumper.

Without his eyes leaving hers, the angle of his head invited Camille to speak.

She only sniffled.

'Answer me. Have you contacted my office?'

'Keep your voice down. No, I haven't.'

'You mustn't call them. It's a misunderstanding. That's all. I'll explain to you when I know more.'

Tommie guided Camille to her seat, where she sat, watery eyes pleading.

Dom thudded the air, palms open, fingers rigid. 'Just promise me.'

'Ok. Ok. I won't call them. But you need to tell us what's going on.'

Dom calmed himself and poured a glass of water. 'I left work. I haven't been back since Donald died, but I told them it was me who died. They keep mailing me paperwork to fill in. I don't know how long I can keep it up for.' From their faces, Dom saw his explanation wasn't helping. 'It's strange, but it's part of losing him. We react to grief in our own way. I can't put it in words, but that's the truth.'

Neither Camille nor Tommie spoke, but Camille's expression softened.

Dom continued. 'I had this weird feeling, the day Donald died, the day I phoned in to the office. I made out I was Donald calling to tell them I was dead, that Dom was dead. It meant I didn't have to be me, but somehow I could still be me.' He finished his water and played with the empty tumbler. 'I'm expecting it all to blow up in my face any day now. And that's why I don't want anyone calling Subiaco.'

'Oh,' said Camille.

Tommie gave a huff of disdain and Camille's reaction to it was so vigorous, it sent him heading for the exit.

She glared at her husband until the kitchen door closed with him and Banner on the other side. Only then did she turn back to her brother.

'Have you been to see your therapist friend? She'll help.'

VII

Out in the street, Dom's excitement bubbled. He waited until Camille's house slipped out of sight before he called Maggie. While the phone was connecting, he cranked up the speaker volume and covered his other ear to block out any interference. She answered straight away.

'What's the bingo?' he demanded.

'I've spent the afternoon searching against your name. Your profile doesn't show up anymore, so HR has done something to it.'

Dom's body sank. 'Where does that leave us?'

'It means I had to go in through my profile and search for activity against your name for the day Donald was here.' Maggie's tone was upbeat.

'And? What do we have?'

'Well, this is the odd part.' The phone went quiet.

Dom crushed his ear with his hand to hear her over the street sounds. 'What is it, Maggie?'

'It turns out you ordered some reports and you modified two accounts.'

He repeated her exact words to her. 'Are you sure? Modified accounts? Did you check the activity date? You're sure that's right?'

'There's nothing to double check. You know how simple these pages are. The record is there. I'll take screen shots and email them to you and I'll keep digging. But it looks like I've found all there is to find.'

'And no one saw you do this? Nobody came up to you? You've got to be careful, Maggie.'

'All safe. Don't worry.'

'Look around, Maggie. Stay alert.'

'Yeah, yeah. With the reports, you ran'—she paused—'well, I mean Donald ran a pending report for the Cypress accounts with privileges.'

'What the—' Dom laughed and snorted into the phone. 'Donald did that? Gees. He knew his way around a system.' He whistled. 'Go on.'

'He made name changes to two accounts and he sent insurance proposals for our suite of products to each address, both in this state.'

'What? The little shit. I knew he'd be bored, but I didn't think he'd go to the trouble of amending records. These accounts he amended—who created them?'

'You.'

'Me?'

'That was in March this year. The system would've sent out the information packages by now, of course. I don't suppose you want the account names?'

'Sure. Why not?'

Maggie rattled them off. 'The surnames are Bauer and Drake.'

Dom's face lit up. 'What was that? Bauer?' His heart began a steady bop and he walked out small circles on the pavement. 'What's the address for that one?'

'Hold on a sec. Is it familiar?'

'Very.' Dom waited while Maggie pulled up the details.

'Gipps Road in Kingsgrove.'

'Number ten Gipps Road?'

'Yes. You know who it is then?'

'I don't believe it.' His thumb ended the call as forcefully as possible. 'The little shit.'

7 | Josh

The peak hour traffic that Dom streamed through seemed never ending. Flipping the windscreen wipers once or twice to clear specks of rain, Dom leaned forward in his seat, more than usual, and eyed the roads eagerly. He had to confront Donald's—he was unsure what to call him—accomplice. So many questions needed answering.

The tough rubber of the steering wheel vibrated under his thump. The police hadn't returned Donald's mobile. He was willing to bet some revealing texts were sitting on it—ones where Donald organised whatever he had organised. If only Dom could access those ones. Hard evidence of another person's involvement in whatever plans Donald had would be helpful. With his shoe clamping the accelerator, lurching the car forward, he couldn't wait for that proof.

The car swung into Gipps Road, a short street of well-kept bungalows, and pulled up at number ten, where the buzz of machinery could be heard. The car engine went quiet and the wail of an electric saw monopolised the night, tearing through the darkness. The garage roller door was open with the car outside, angled on the driveway. Deep in the garage, Josh was hunched over a bench controlling the cutting tool, his wide back to the street.

As Dom walked up the drive, he felt like he was watching a nativity scene—the dark exterior of the house, the inner lighting of the single-car garage with all the pieces skillfully arranged for the viewer.

The roar intensified as Dom approached. He stepped inside the garage, still unseen by the machinist, and he waited. A library of tools adorned the entire right wall. Running the length of the garage from waist height to high above his head, each implement hung from its own hook or rested securely on nails. Someone—it could well have been Josh, but Dom doubted it—had drawn an outline of each piece in thick black marker as a handy reminder of where each tool should go once it had done its work.

The fading border of an axe at head level caught Dom's eye. It was the only large tool that wasn't in its place and he wondered where it was. Maybe Josh had been chopping firewood in the garden. Dom looked around the garage for it and found it standing head down in the front corner.

The screeching stopped and Josh put down the tool. As he removed his protective goggles and rubbed his jaw with a knuckle, he caught sight of Dom. His pinched face managed a slight smile and his dusty hand extended out. 'How long have you been there?'

'Seconds. You knew about the swap,' Dom blurted.

Josh drew away. He straightened up, placed his hands on his lower back and leant backwards to ease his spine, without taking his bleary eyes off Dom. Bones cracked more than middle-aged bones should. Josh shuffled around the workbench and removed from their hanging spaces a gleaming chisel and a worn black mallet, leaving their inky frames to stand out, like the chalky outlines of crime show victims. He started cutting grooves into the untreated pine riveted in his workbench, which allowed him to turn away from Dom.

'Yeah.' The mallet came down on the chisel slicing out white chocolate curls of wood. He blew them away. His steely blue eyes drilled into Dom, who had moved around to face him. 'How did you find that out?' he asked.

Thud. The mallet embedded the chisel into the flesh of the pine. Each dull nick splintered the wood effortlessly and Josh's coarse fingers came in to wipe the section clean.

Dom ignored the question. 'Why didn't you say anything to me about it when Donald died?'

'No point. That was the end of it.'

Thud. Thud. Nick.

Josh glanced at Dom for an instant. 'Why didn't you say anything to Camille? I bet you still haven't told her.' He turned back to the hammering in time to drive the chisel home.

Again, Dom ignored the question. 'The day he was there, he created a false account in your name. Why did you ask him to do that?'

Josh stopped chiselling and lowered his arms. 'You don't know shit. It was his idea. I was doing him a favour—a very small favour.' Josh glowered at Dom. 'Of course it wasn't my idea. How would I ever get access to your systems?'

'Access for *what*? Tell me what you two had going on.'

'I told you—it was all his idea.' The irritation made Josh's voice deepen.

'Who do you know at Subiaco?'

'What are you talking about? I don't know anyone there except you. You were the only connection Donald needed.'

'You're lying.'

The chisel and mallet swung by Josh's sides. 'And you're in denial. You clearly know shit about it.'

Dom shouted, 'So tell me what you know.'

Josh circled the mallet above his head and whacked the work surface with killer potency, making the garage vibrate. 'Fuck!' His hanging army of tools sprang to life.

'What's going on?'

Josh ditched the tools and picked up his beer, which had been tucked away on a narrow window shelf. 'I don't want to be the one to tell you.' He swigged.

'What? Tell me what?'

Josh drew a long breath. 'He had a plan to create fake accounts and pay out false claims. He needed real addresses from people he could trust, so he asked if he could use here. I agreed. And I gave him the address of my parents' place up in Springwood. That's all of it.' He went for his beer.

Dom struggled to speak. 'Wha—' He spluttered his disbelief. His mind swirled. 'Fraud? At my firm? From my—my logon details?'

Josh nodded, giving the beer in the bottle a swish.

'No—no—no.' Dom stamped around, the scale of the swindle making him dizzy. His head shook wildly as though his hair was on fire. He swung round to Josh, whose stony expression kept any sympathy for Dom well away. 'You mean Donald's prank to swap was all set up to help him steal money? There was never any of this needing to cheer up. This boredom to get over was all—'

Josh looked Dom up and down, letting the twin work things out for himself.

Dom thought back to those evenings of Donald catching up with Josh to play tennis, having had Lorna fish out his racquet and bring it over. 'And the tennis the two of you played? Lies?' Dom's eyebrows knitted together. 'You weren't playing sport—Donald never came home puffed out. You were planning it all. Gees.'

'We played tennis a lot.' Josh's flat response vanished into the beer bottle.

The horror hit Dom in waves and his body swayed as the cruel tide lashed him. He braced himself ready to challenge Josh again. 'Like that would work. He would need to go there a few times. What else do you know, Josh? Come on.'

'He said he had a way to cover his tracks, so you wouldn't get brought into it. He was trying to keep you out of it. He wasn't a total bastard.'

'And I guess he was planning to swap again? But I'd never agree to it. So? Tell me.' Dom shook his hands high.

Josh paused. He returned the beer to his lips and mumbled.

'What was that? I didn't hear,' said Dom.

Josh huffed. 'The swap you did wasn't the first time he had been to your office pretending to be you.'

Dom was a statue gawking at Josh. Mute, astounded, Dom waved open hands at him, imploring him for more information.

Josh sprayed his story in detail. 'In March, he went to your office on a Friday night. You weren't in Sydney and he took your access card. His thinking was hardly anyone would be there and it turned out he was right. He got to your workstation, logged a call with the helpdesk, told them you were locked out and they reset the password on the spot. He created some accounts that day.' Josh's neutral tone downplayed the significance of Donald's actions.

Dom was blown away. He swore at the top of his voice. He remembered what Maggie had told him earlier on the phone. On the day of the swap, Donald had *amended* accounts that had already existed, ones that Dom had previously set up. Well, it hadn't been Dom.

He thought back to where he was in March. China. A business trip. And he had a sketchy memory of returning to work and finding himself locked out of his machine, and needing to call IT for help. He glared at Josh. 'How many other times did he pretend to be me?'

'No others—as far as I know. The first time was to create the accounts, he told me. And the second was to change the addresses. He said it was safer to proceed in stages. Each time he wanted to wait and see if anything was uncovered.'

Dom shook his head. 'Wait. How did he know where I sat?'

Josh didn't hesitate as he rattled off Donald's plans. 'You sent him a picture of the view from your office. Or he managed to get it through Lorna.'

Dom recalled swapping photos with his niece ages ago. 'Yep, yep,' he said, eyes closed. He opened them again. 'And the third time was going to be when? He knew I wouldn't agree to another swap.'

'Right. He planned to go in again very early or at night while you were away or off sick. You call in sick and he goes in saying he feels better.'

'The fucking bastard. And you let him make this plan. You cunt.'

'Whoa. Like I said—all his idea. He knew you worked in large claims. It was his idea to do the swap. He needed that second day with your permission to get to know the layout and the systems. He was a whizz. He had the accounts amended by nine thirty that day. He texted me to say he'd done it.'

Dom shouted and crouched to the floor, his legs unable to maintain him. Josh looked out at his neighbours' houses and pushed a button on the wall. The roller door came down with a screech trapping the two of them inside. Dom looked up at Donald's co-conspirator. 'So he was going to wait until I was ill to rock up in my place?' The craziness of it was baffling. 'He could've been waiting ages. I never chuck sickies.'

Josh turned away. He picked up the mallet and chisel and held them at chest level like a shield. 'He told me he'd found something on the net that could guarantee you'd be too sick for work. He'd add a bit to your dinner and—'

'What?' You're fucking kidding me.' Dom brought his hands to his head, locking his knees to steady himself. He closed his eyes and coughed his words. 'He was going to poison me to get me out of the way. And steal from my employer? That is the worst thing he has ever fucking done.' He stood up. 'Donald! Aargh! How cou—that is fucking low.' Dom thumped the air with both hands. 'Let me get this straight. He was going to pay the premiums, then get back into the system while I was ill and authorise large payouts of bogus claims?'

'Something like that.' Josh shrugged. 'He wasn't himself since the split with Robin. He was desperate for money and he wanted to improve things. That's all he thought about. He wasn't always thinking well.'

Dom pointed at Josh. 'And you thought you'd help clarify his thinking by supplying him with addresses? Wonderful Josh. You're both fuckwits.'

'Piss off. You didn't want to help. At least I listened to him.'

'Listened to him? He didn't need your ears'—Dom tapped his head—'he needed a fucking brain.' Spit flew from Dom's lips and he wiped his mouth with a clout. 'I did fucking help him. I gave him a home. Fuck you—I did help him.'

The timbre in Josh's voice calmed. 'Donald was convinced you'd already done it yourself. Fiddled with work accounts. How else would you have all your money? That's what he used to say to me.'

Incensed, growling, Dom charged at his accuser. As Josh stepped back, Dom raised his fist and smacked it into his cheek. Josh howled, but reacted quickly, his big arm hurtling the chisel around him in a defensive arc. Its sharp, angled blade dragged on Dom's t-shirt, exposed through his open jacket, and sliced into his abdomen.

Josh stepped back brandishing the tool. 'Don't you blame me. You keep away from me.' As quickly as their fight flared up, the men settled down.

Dom moved back nursing the hand he had punched with. Josh pointed to the blood showing through Dom's t-shirt just as Dom was starting to notice the burn and pain of his bleeding stomach. Dom lifted his clothing to reveal a thin slice of a wound, long but superficial, across his hairy belly.

'I'm not fighting you, Dom. I get that you're angry and everything, but this mess is not my work.' He hesitated as though waiting to see if Dom would accept his explanation. 'I was just helping out a friend. He wouldn't take help any other way.' Josh touched his cheek and checked his hand for blood. Dom's punch hadn't torn skin.

Dom nursed his own wound, patting and cupping his belly. 'I have *never* defrauded Subiaco.'

'Ok. I believe you.'

Still dabbing at the blood, Dom asked if Josh had tried talking Donald out of it.

'Of course I tried. Loads of times. But he was your twin. You must know how well that would have worked. He wouldn't let it go.' Josh's explanation was met with a nod from Dom.

'What other contact did you two have that day?'

'Texts on progress—not much else. He called me in the afternoon but I missed it. Like I said, it wasn't a joint plan between us. He merely wanted two addresses. Perhaps his call was to let me know things were going fine. Towards the end of the day, I sent him a text for an update, but I didn't get a reply. And that was the last contact I had. I—' Josh rubbed his cheek, which had reddened. 'I guess you and I are the only two people who know what went down that day. I take it you haven't told the others?' Dom shook his head. He hadn't said a word to Camille and Robin.

Josh pleaded. 'Think of them—how comforting it would be if they knew why he was in the city, and that he probably slipped because he wasn't paying attention, that he was thinking of some bigger thing he'd just pulled off.'

Keeping one hand under his t-shirt, Dom backed to a wall. 'At first I thought that too. I kept picturing Donald with all these thoughts racing around stepping into the traffic preoccupied.' He inhaled. 'But yesterday, all that changed. He was pushed.'

Josh swigged his beer. His impassive look made Dom snap.

'He was killed by someone at Subiaco. Someone who, I'm guessing, was doing exactly what you two were trying to do. He was murdered, Josh. He died because of your stupid fucking plan.' Dom's pointing finger shook high.

'No way.' Josh's head smacked from side to side. 'You're lying to me.'

'It's true. Now someone at my work thinks I've got something of value. I want to know what that thing is. And whatever Donald did that day, he must've come to the attention of someone who had something big to protect. Someone silenced him. I'm sure of it.'

Horror froze Josh's features. 'Gees, Dom. I can't believe it. Are you sure?' A hand shot up to cover his mouth.

'I need to know what he took from my office. Someone's after it.' Dom watched Josh's hand drop and his mouth open. Nothing else of Josh moved. Not even his eyelids.

'What did he take from Subiaco?'

Josh woke from his stupor. 'I'm so sorry, Dom. We didn't mean—'

'Josh!'

'What?'

'What do these people want from you? They're after something.'

'*Something?* We never talked about taking things from the office. What thing?' Josh fell against the workbench, the bewilderment creasing his face. 'He wasn't murdered. Impossible. By who?'

'I don't know yet. But it means they're very dangerous and because they think I'm dead, I'm safe. But you could be in serious danger too. They've killed him. I know they have. And if they know what Donald did that day, they know where you live.'

Josh groaned and swivelled to look for his beer. 'And where my parents live. Donald used their address for the second account.'

'You could be in real danger.'

The menace permeating Dom's words struck at Josh. He calmly drank his beer, scanning the garage as he drained the bottle. There was about a two-metre stretch to the switch that operated the roller door and close by was an array of tools. He pulled the plug out of the socket on the electric saw he had been using and wound the cord. 'Am I in *immediate* danger, do you think?'

Dom's eyes were glued on him. 'They're desperate to preserve whatever it was Donald stumbled across.'

II

Dom opened his car boot, laid the axe inside and sped away from Gipps Road without looking back. Ten minutes later, having calmed enough to think more clearly, he pondered his next step. With the car stopped at traffic lights on the Princes Highway, he glanced at his mobile in its dashboard dock. The screen was blacked out. A tap woke it up and he called Maggie. He asked her to print a report—any report—and a cover page with Subiaco branding. It had to look genuine.

Maggie told him she had seen nothing else on the Subiaco system to suggest anything out of the ordinary and Dom explained he had news but he would fill her in when she came over with the dummy document. She promised to be there the next day after work.

As his car wound through the suburbs cloaked in darkness, he thought back to any comments Donald had made in the days before the swap searching for a hint of his true motives. His was a fantastic plan that meant abusing the trust Dom had shown him. He was struggling to fathom that Donald would do that and place Dom's job at risk along the way. With his mind less on the road and more on taking in Josh's news, he approached a roundabout too fast and screeched to a halt in time to avoid ploughing into the car in front.

The wheels sang out. His body hurtled forward against the seat belt. The car seat cushioned him as he jerked back and he exhaled with relief when he finally stopped moving. He took another couple of deep breaths and accelerated.

His mind went back to Subiaco, picturing Donald carrying out his plan. How far would Donald have gone to get access to the office? Drug him and steal his swipe card? Then what? Go to his desk and do whatever he needed to do?

An audit would easily pick that up, but possibly not for years. Times when Donald had insisted he go away without applying for leave crossed his mind. *I can go in for you*, Donald would say. So casual, so devious.

Dom's thoughts turned to what Donald had found online that could make people ill. The absurdity of it made him laugh and snort. Donald's plan alone was turning Dom's stomach, no poison required.

His sedan swung into its car space and he winced as he twisted his torso to get out. The cool night air nipped at his face as he collected the axe from the boot. Up in the unit, he rested it against the wall head down, like a hockey player might with a stick.

His wound needed a clean. He removed his t-shirt as painlessly as he could and dressed the cut. The bleeding hadn't stopped, but he didn't think stitches were necessary. Padding and a bandage would do.

He pulled on a shirt, which was less painful than pulling something over his head. He rolled up his sleeves. A friendly rat-tat-tat at the screen door could mean only one person.

'I was just passing by. I can't stay long,' Harry said when the door opened. Wobbling a six-pack of beer was meant to tantalise Dom.

Dom waved him inside. 'No—you can't stay long.'

Harry stepped in and paused. 'You don't look so good. Just as well I came by.' He elbowed his friend and carried on.

'Careful.' Dom brought a hand up to protect his stomach. Not in the place a minute and Harry was already disrupting things.

Harry made a face, clueless as to what Dom was referring to.

In the living room, Dom waited until Harry had found a seat before he began his warning. 'Mate, this shit will take a while to explain. And talking about it *will* make me angry.' Dom welcomed the icy cold beer and sat opposite his friend. He trapped the twist cap in his fist while he guzzled the drink.

'You've got two beers of time left,' said Harry, holding up his first empty bottle. 'And what's an axe doing in here?' He frowned at it as he uncapped his second.

'I'm waiting for the right moment. I want to destroy some things.'

'Yeah? Speak.'

Dom lifted his shirt, flashed his bandaged stomach and watched Harry's eyes bulge. 'I just found out Donald had a plan to defraud Subiaco using my employee details, IT expert that he was.' While this was far from the full story, Dom reasoned it was enough for Harry, who sat still gazing at him. Only his arm moved to bring the bottle up.

'He tricked me into letting him'—Dom waved his head, showing the caution behind his words as he glossed over the details of the prank—'go to my work to set up this fraud.' He dug the folded beer cap, which now resembled an oyster, into the arm of the seat. 'And a friend of Donald's, who you would have met at the funeral, knew all about it.' He cut lines in the fabric one after the other with the sharper end of the cap. 'It's the worst thing he's ever done. I've never felt so betrayed.' With his voice resolute, the cap tore at the sofa until the sturdy material came close to ripping. 'And all of that while he was living here.'

Harry swigged his drink and grunted how astonished he was, which allowed Dom's outpourings to go on.

Dom stabbed the sofa with his miniature metal oyster, his gaze to the floor. 'To make things even worse, it looks like he had plans to—' He stopped, unable to bring himself to put in words how far Donald had been prepared to go to extract money from Subiaco. A quick look to his friend was Harry's invitation to comment.

'That explains why you look like that,' he said. 'And this friend, he did that to you?' He was pointing at Dom's stomach.

Dom nodded. 'Admittedly, in self-defence.'

'Ooh,' said Harry with interest. 'And who's got the worst injury?'

Dom paused. 'Me.'

Harry laughed strong and loud. 'That's tough. It looks like it can't get any worse for you.'

Already tetchy, Dom found Harry's attempt to lighten the atmosphere nothing short of irritating. He didn't trouble himself to respond, but went back to belting the sofa with the cap.

'Well, I have some good news,' said Harry after a moment.

Dom put down his drink and latched his arms across his chest.

With the best of intentions, Harry delivered it. 'Your dealer contact came through, thank you very much.' His face lit up as he spoke, his youthful grin showing his teeth. 'I went round to his place today at lunchtime. All sorted.'

Dom hurled the cap onto the floor, and Harry watched it bounce away without breaking his flow of conversation. 'He whinged about not passing out his number, that I was his last ever drop-in—risky, risky, risky, moan, moan, moan. But after that, he gave me everything I asked—' He stopped. 'Dom?'

Dom's features twisted into a mask of fury. 'I don't fucking believe it.' Dom stood up and walked behind Harry, stooping for the axe. It swung high above his head. Harry turned and caught sight of the blade moving through the air. He gasped and vaulted from his seat as Dom powered into the back rooms.

His beer still in his hand, Harry hovered on the spot, unsure what was happening or what to do. He heard Dom kick open a door at the very back of the unit. An almighty racket followed.

The crack of wood, muffled thuds, items and furniture crashing to the floor, plastic splitting and more wood splintering seemed to tumble from the back room. The short pauses in the demolition must have come from the head of the axe trapped in thick wood because the din would start again. Harry positioned himself closer to the front door. Dom's huffs and growls travelled out to him, along with the jarring percussion of metal contorting and twisting as the frenzied trashing of the room played out.

Harry jigged from foot to foot and peered down the dark hall. He looked behind him. The front door was metres away. His head jerked in all directions, unsure if his body should stay or go.

The commotion ended. Harry stopped swaying. The only noise in the unit was his dry panting and he seemed to stay like that for minutes. Then footsteps—calm, regular steps—sounded. Dom was coming.

Harry's breathing picked up. Dom appeared, empty-handed. His face revealed none of the fury that had fuelled the assault. But his cheeks were rosy, his forehead sweaty, and the only clue to the destruction that had gone on was a splinter of wood the size of a paper clip wedged into his hair.

Dom tucked in his shirt. Over the cotton, he patted his bandage into place and dried his forehead. He spotted Harry standing immobile away from the seats, as if leaving, his beer bottle locked in both hands.

'What are you doing?' Dom asked, moving into the kitchen.

Harry stared after him noticing the huge wet patch on the back of his shirt.

'Have you eaten yet?' Dom turned back to look at his friend when he got no reply. 'Harry?' Harry didn't respond. 'Sit down—I'll make us dinner.'

Harry moved to a different seat, this time with his back to the wall, where he could see everything Dom did. The homely clattering of pans and utensils contrasted with the furore he had just witnessed. And even though Dom hummed calmly as he tossed oil into a pan, Harry's eyes were fearful and his breathing shallow. With lips wet with beer, he tried to speak. 'Was that Donald's room you just tore up?'

'I can't stand liars—liars who think nothing of complicating my life.' Dom took steak from the fridge.

Harry stared at the coffee table, afraid to catch Dom's eye. He stole the odd glance when Dom's back was turned.

The meat sizzled as it browned in the pan, with Dom talking over it. 'You have to be able to trust people. My big problem is I'm too trusting.'

Some oil spat on to his bare forearm, which recoiled.

'Ouch. That hurt.'

III

The next day was windless and cloudy. The windows were open and cool air was refreshing each room. Dom was at the dining table, cradling a coffee in one hand and clutching a jigsaw piece in the other. He scratched his stubble and belly non-stop.

The call he'd been putting off had to be made. Josh's comments from the night before nipped at his conscience—Camille and Robin deserved to know why Donald had been in the city.

Camille answered her house phone after two rings.

'I have more—er—information for you about the day Donald died. Some things I found out recently. Other things, Donald and I organised weeks ago.'

'What things?'

Dom detected a touch of fear in her question but couldn't think what she would be afraid of. His voice took on a matter-of-fact tone, as if surrendering to an interrogator, and relief swept through him as he shared the story. 'I went to his office and he went to mine. That's what he was doing near my work.'

A tiny gasp travelled down the phone.

'He had begged and begged me to do it. I found out yesterday why. He was planning to—' His pumping heart interrupted his breathing. Sitting up straight allowed him to fill his lungs, catch the rhythm of his breath and start over. 'He was planning to defraud Subiaco using my profile.' He paused. 'Are you there Camille?'

'Yes.'

'I've been feeling so guilty about his death. If I hadn't agreed to the prank, he wouldn't have been on that street crossing the road when he did.'

'That's right.'

'I'm so sorry.' Dom's difficulty speaking dragged on and he was sure she could hear his struggle for air. 'I have some other news, but it's too painful.'

'Tell me.'

'His death wasn't an accident—he was killed.'

Her pant sounded like a newborn's hiccup.

Dom lowered his head and spluttered more words. 'This guilt has been eating me. I've wanted to tell you, but the shame got the better of me.'

'That's a horrible thing to say, Dominic. Stop it. I'm hanging up.'

'Listen, Camille. Our Donald was murdered.'

'What's got into you?' Her words boiled. 'This is nonsense. Who would want to do that to him?'

'Someone at my work and a woman who came to visit me the other day. She thought I was Donald and she was pretending to be someone from my office. They're in it together and she asked if Donald had anything on him belonging to Subiaco when he died. She thinks he has something valuable and I'm trying to find out what it is.'

'Oh Dom'—the compassion flooding her voice buried her anger momentarily— 'you need to speak to someone.'

'No, we can't involve the police yet,' he said. 'This woman—she searched Donald's room looking for things and I think—'

'I don't mean the police!'

He angled the mobile from his ear to avoid her roar.

'You need to speak to a specialist. You're not well.'

'I'm fine. You think I'm making this up?' Dejected, he waited.

There was silence from his sister's end too. 'Why didn't you tell me all this sooner? What else are you keeping from me?'

'Please stop screaming. I didn't say anything because I—I—I couldn't handle any more blame.'

'Who else blames you?'

'No one. It's just the crap I've been putting myself through. Last night's news about Donald's plan to embezzle was the tipping point. I had to share this with you.'

'Stop it! Camille was crying.

Dom heard Tommie speaking in the background and Banner yapping too.

'You're not well, and you can't see it. And you're to stop saying those things about Donald.'

'This is why I don't share things with you—'

'You need help. You're—you're—grieving. And you're hallucinating. There was no woman and nobody killed Donald. He slipped.'

'He was pushed into the road to stop him revealing what he discovered.'

'I don't want to hear any more talk of killing. It was an accident.'

'He was murdered. I'm grieving, but I can still think clearly. You have to trust me.'

Camille bit back in a flash, emphasising each syllable. 'I don't *trust* you one bit—you are not *worthy of my trust*—you are *untrustworthy.*' There was another pause. 'We're all worried for you. You told your work you were dead, you don't go to work, this talk of swapping with Donald and he was murdered. Not true.'

Dom protested and Camille went silent. He imagined her perched on the armchair in her hallway massaging her graying temples.

Half a minute passed before her voice returned.

'You say you swapped roles the day he died—that would explain why he was wearing an expensive suit. Have you told the police?'

'No. I want to find out first what these people want from Donald.'

'You haven't mentioned any of this to that constable? How could you even think of keeping this to yourself?'

'I need more proof. I only found out last night that Donald had a hidden motive for going into my office, and that was exactly the thing I was afraid would come out. I've been protecting him. I had to know what Donald had planned. That's why I didn't want you to contact Subiaco. This is dangerous, Camille.'

'Proof,' she said. 'What proof do you have this strange woman visited you?'

'She gave me a false business card.'

It lay on the table, the handwritten mobile number drawing Dom's eye. If Camille saw it, would she think the scribble was his? Some of the numbering looked quite similar to his handwriting—the squared *five*, the droopy *nine*.

The tutting at the other end ripped him from his thoughts.

'Camille, you have to believe me. Donald and I switched and Donald was killed. She visited me two days ago and I'm meeting her again. I'll work out what's going on. Donald created false accounts while he was at my desk and was planning to defraud Subiaco for tonnes of money. Josh confirmed all this to me last night—to my face.'

Camille's protests eased and Dom persisted. 'Yep, Josh was in on Donald's little trick to screw me over.'

'Josh said that to you? Well, I'll speak to him myself. Give me his address.'

'He's not there. He's gone. I sent him away for a few days until all this blows over. That's how much danger he could be in.'

'You did what? Who are you to send him away? I can call him then. Give me his number.'

'He won't answer.'

'Why not? What have you done?'

'I told you, Camille. He's gone away.' Dom spat the words.

'Where is he? Tell me he hasn't come to harm.'

Last night's altercation with Josh flashed in his mind but he thought it best not to mention. 'He's fine. Don't worry about him. I told him to hide, but he'll be back soon.'

'This is preposterous. I want to check for myself. I don't trust you, Dominic.'

IV

Camille arrived at Josh's house in a taxi. She asked the driver to wait because she was expecting to be there briefly, and she had rung her workplace, a small independent publisher, to let them know she would be in a little later.

Pulling her jacket flaps together, but not bothering to pull the zipper, she walked up the driveway. Josh's car was nowhere in sight. Three rings of the doorbell and calling his name out as loudly and comfortably as she could several times spawned nothing but stillness. There was no answer when she tried Josh's mobile from the front porch.

At the right side of the house, a small lawn cut off by a white gate also yielded no sign of him. Camille retraced her way to the front and, after nodding to the waiting driver, she investigated the pathway on the house's left side, which ran the length of the garage. Nothing. She pulled on the garage roller door, which didn't budge. There appeared to be no access to the back of the house that way so she stood on her tiptoes to see through the garage window. Just like the garden, it was empty.

The only signs of activity were some tools and a bottle of beer dotted around the workbench.

'Josh! Are you in there?' She strained to hear for movement from inside.

With one hand on her hip, the other shielding her eyes from the glare of the clouds, she surveyed the neighbouring properties. Her avenues for tracing Josh were limited.

Dom, shifty and untrustworthy as he was, was not helping her. An idea occurred to her. Robin could be of some use. Returning to the front door, she knocked and called out a few more times, then hurried back to the taxi.

When the driver asked Camille if everything was ok, he was met with cold silence.

V

Lorna closed her laptop. Enough of checking sites about Melbourne. Up went the volume of her music just before she bounced on to the bed, causing the schoolbooks and notes she should have been reading to flap about. There was much more study to do, but a knock at the door interrupted her.

It was Robin, who motioned to the schoolwork covering the bed. 'How's it going?'

'Not bad. Lots to get through. What's up?'

'Can I come in? I've been doing some thinking.' Before Lorna could reply, Robin slipped in to the room and softly closed the door. She turned the music down and moved books to sit close to Lorna, resting a hand on her shoulder. 'What if you and—and Drew went to Melbourne for a few days? You could see if you like it. You've never been.'

Lorna squealed. 'Are you serious? When?'

'Why not this weekend? Or tomorrow. Take a couple of days off school and get to experience the city, visit the universities. It's a beautiful part of the country. Did you know your father always wanted to live there?'

'Oh mum. Thank you.'

They hugged and Robin caught the scent of her daughter's sweet-smelling moisturiser.

'Pack your books though, honey—do some study while you're there.'

Lorna leaned away and Robin rubbed the soft skin on Lorna's cheek.

'Ok. A bit. I'll need to tell uncle Dom. We were going to catch up for a run this weekend. Oh and I'll have to tell Cassie too. She wanted some help with study.'

'Don't worry about your uncle, love. Give him some space please.' She tidied Lorna's hair off her shoulders. 'He's not well. Your aunt says he's not feeling so good. Promise me you'll leave him be for a few days. You two slip away to Melbourne and see what you think of the place.' Robin nodded encouragingly to Lorna. 'See how it feels to forget Sydney and show me you can do it.'

'Fine,' said Lorna stretching for the laptop. 'The flights are so cheap, mum. And we can stay with Drew's cousin. It's gonna be awesome.'

'And I'll take you to the airport,' Robin said, standing from the bed. 'When I speak to your uncle again, I'll tell him you're away exploring Melbourne. You can tell Cassie yourself that you won't be around.'

VI

Later the same day, the woman pretending to be Vanessa was in her cluttered living room wearing only her underwear, painting her toe nails purple. She looked about her. 'Are you sitting on my cigarettes? Up, lazybones.'

Lazybones, in underwear too, raised a bum cheek off the sofa and like a diver collecting pearls, pretend Vanessa hunted for the pack of cigarettes with the lighter inside.

When she mumbled, 'Got 'em', Lazybones rolled back and carried on watching television, absently rubbing pretend Vanessa's back.

Using a free hand, Lazybones bit into lukewarm pizza. The half-eaten slice was hurled into the box. 'Yuk. Malaysian food has to be better than this shit.'

'Of course it will be.' Vanessa blew smoke up to the ceiling, away from the food. Her chirpy mobile ringtone drew her attention from the television. As Lazybones reached to kill the volume, she stretched for her phone. 'It's him,' she whispered. Her index finger came up to eye level. 'Not a word.' The conversation played out on loudspeaker. 'This is Vanessa.'

'Hello. This is Donald Tolen, Dom's brother.' The couple locked eyes while the voice floated up from the mobile resting on the brown velour cushion between them.

'How are you, Donald? Thanks for calling. I have something of your brother's, which someone at the office passed to me.'

'Thoughtful,' said Dom.

Vanessa hunched her shoulders and raised upturned palms as the phone stayed quiet.

'I have some things for you too,' Dom added finally. 'They belong to Subiaco—that's why I'm calling. I spoke to my sister and she found these things in the bag Dom had with him that day.'

'Wonderful. I'd be happy to collect them tomorrow.'

'Tomorrow? I'll be in the city sorting some of Dom's papers, so I'll come to the office, you know, to save you the trip to mine. Shall I come up to level—'

'No. How about we meet in a café close by? It will save you coming up. I'd like to hear how you're doing. How does that sound?'

'Like the perfect compromise. I'll get to a café near you guys and text you when I'm there. Say nine thirty?'

'Let me check my diary.' With puckered lips, she delivered an unvoiced kiss to her partner. 'That suits me very well. See you then, Donald.'

After double checking the call had ended, she paced around the room, blowing smoke everywhere. 'I wonder what he's got.' She stubbed out her cigarette in a brimming ashtray. 'You heard him—*a café near you guys*. Plural. Do you think that means something? Does he know?'

'Do you mind? I'm watching the news.'

'Do you mind? I have to meet the dead twin's twin. It's all right for you. Your bit's done.'

Lazybones waited until Vanessa's spindly body flitted by again, caught her wrist and yanked her down to the sofa.

'Mind my nails. They're still drying,' she said in a whinge.

'You're worrying over absolutely nothing. It'll be all right for you, too. Whatever he has for us is useless now—it can't get in the way.'

Draped over Lazybones, Vanessa lay still. Having her hair stroked settled her thoughts, but the vexed look on her face remained. 'Leave me alone, pizza breath. Your fingers'd better not be greasy. I've just washed it.'

'Enjoy the hot running water while you can. The first village we're going to won't have these mod cons.' Vanessa got her forehead kissed twice. 'Listen to me, darling'—continued Lazybones—'the transfers have gone through and the last one clears tomorrow. We're fine. Whatever he has for you is nothing. It can't incriminate us. We don't need it and he won't understand its use. It's meaningless to him.'

The small nod she gave was unconvincing.

Lazybones trapped Vanessa's fingers to stop the varnish bottle from twiddling and squeezed her chin to lift her face. 'What are you so worried about? Nothing can go wrong.'

Vanessa opened her mouth to protest, but her companion's finger pressed her lips closed.

'Just play along and have a coffee with him.' Lazybones patted her bum with each word. 'Give him the book, thank him for the stuff he gives you, don't draw attention to yourself and don't look too eager about what he hands over.'

Vanessa nodded again.

'Then we can head off quietly next week—easy.'

Vanessa pulled herself up. 'Like I said, it's ok for you.' She went to get up. 'I've got to sit with him again. And have those eyes staring right at me.'

The living room door was thudded out of her way with the bottle of varnish.

'I'll be worrying about this all night now. It would've been better if he'd called in the morning.'

'Take one of your pills,' shouted Lazybones. 'I can't have you tossing all night. Big day tomorrow.'

As an afterthought, Lazybones said, 'For both of us.'

VII

No sooner had he ended his call with her than he checked his phone had recorded the conversation correctly.

'This is Vanessa,' his handset sang.

The whole exchange was there and a small part of him relaxed, knowing Maggie would get to hear it later.

Listening for a second time shed no light on what it was the woman would be handing him the next day. An image of his desk took form as he tried to recall what he could have left behind at the office. But his ability to picture the interior of Subiaco was fading by the day.

Whatever it was, Dom had a hunch she had withheld it from their first meeting as a way to compel a second. Which hadn't been necessary for her, as he had got in first.

His left hand dialled Maggie's number. His right held the misappropriated Subiaco business card with the handwritten number. If the meeting tomorrow went nowhere, the mobile number would lead him to her.

Maggie's message bank activated, but Dom didn't leave a voicemail.

Sitting back in the chair, hands interlocked behind his head and elbows wide, he imagined how the meet-up would go. He would pass her a blank disc and the dummy report. Together, the two items would look more authentic. They'd chat for a short while and once they parted, he would follow her.

Of course, it might be more difficult tailing her in daylight. Where would she likely go afterwards? Obviously not to Subiaco. Another office, maybe. Another office *tower* would be a fail. Hanging around the entrance to a skyscraper for hours waiting for her to reappear was out of the question.

If Dom was lucky, she would lead him to where she lived. And if exceptional luck came his way, she shared a home with her contact, Dom's colleague, and that would lead to his next step. Which he didn't have completely clear yet.

Dom's phone came to life. It was Maggie.

'Sorry, I didn't hear your call. The phone was in my bag. I'm in the car now heading over to you and I'll be about twenty minutes.' He told her there was no rush, she was to watch the roads and he would start cooking.

Only when he ended the call did his nervousness become apparent, its source at first unclear. What he understood to be anxiety about the pending meeting with the imposter was something else, something more positive.

It dawned on him—Maggie was coming to his unit and she hadn't been there since they'd broken up.

A quick check in the mirror confirmed he looked decent enough, and after a five-minute spring clean, so did his home.

They embraced warmly at the front door and Dom stepped aside waving her ahead, watching keenly for any reaction.

In the living room, she stayed standing, jacket on, looking around her, hugging herself as though for protection. Her head nodded with every portion of space she recognised and her alluring smile made Dom beam. As the memories bounded around, she reached out for another hug and the pair came together in the centre.

The jigsaw in progress on the table caught her eye and she moved over it.

Dom said, 'A present. From Donald. I'll finish it soon. When I'm less—' His words didn't come.

It was time to turn down the heat on the food.

'Go through to the end room and see what I've done—what I've become.'

Maggie cast him an inquiring look, pulled the report from her bag and left it on the table, and stepped through to the rear part of the unit. Dom only got to leaf through a few pages of the fake report, which looked ideal, before Maggie came out again, her fawn gabardine hanging off her arm.

'You're going to have to explain that to me.' Her coat was plonked over a chair. 'The only things intact are the walls.' Her comments, layered with warmth and intimacy, reverberated around the room.

Dom stopped chopping the coriander. How good it felt to hear her plummy voice in his living room, her crisp, commanding tones filling his vast, vacant home. A smile coated his face.

When he detailed Josh's version of events and the major plan Donald had to defraud Subiaco, Maggie pulled faces like never before. At the end, a scaling whistle summed up her amazement.

'Ok, now the mess in that bedroom makes more sense.'

Dom played the taped conversation on his mobile and they listened to the illusory dialogue together. The last thing they heard was Dom saying goodbye.

'That's a weird conversation. You're not Donald and she's not Vanessa.' Her nose crumpled. 'I don't recognise the voice.'

'I didn't think you would.' Dom rested his hand on the document. 'I'll hand this over with a blank CD and see what comes of it. And printing this didn't attract any attention at the office?' A concerned hand smoothed her arm as he went back to the cooking.

'No. It's nothing but output stats anyone in the office could get hold of. For someone in our division, it's unimportant data. To an outsider, it will look like important text. But you should dog-ear it to make it look like it's been carried around. What are you hoping to get from tomorrow's rendezvous anyway?'

Standing up afforded Maggie a better view of Dom at the oven. 'I must say, I don't think this is the best way forward. I've got a bad feeling about it all. You're not one hundred per cent yourself—I can tell. You're grieving.'

'There's no time for grief now.' Dom projected his voice over the sizzle of food. 'They still don't know it's me, so she may accidentally let something out.'

'I can't see that happening.'

'I want firm evidence. I'll follow her out of the café. I can get an address, take a photo or two—all covert, of course.'

'Be careful, Dom.' She pressed her palms. 'I don't know if this is such a wise move. In fact, it's more than unwise—it's bloody dangerous. I can see it going wrong. I—' Her hands danced in front of her face batting away the worrying image.

'It'll be fine, Maggie. She has no idea who I am, so she'll be totally at ease. You should've seen her the day she was here.' The wooden spoon spun in the air as he gesticulated. 'She walked around like it was her place.'

'You're going about this all wrong. You want firm evidence that Donald was murdered before you go to the police? Why wait? I don't get it.' Her eyes bore into the back of his head. 'Unless it's revenge you want, not evidence. And are you honestly going to get that in a café?'

Maggie's voice proved no match for the clack of the spoon hitting the plate as Dom served dinner. 'Open some wine, please.'

The drawer with the bottle opener was to Dom's left. As he pointed it out, Maggie swung behind him, hanging off his shoulder for stability. Moments later, two glasses of merlot sat waiting on the table.

'Whatever comes from tomorrow you should be taking to the police. I know you don't want to involve them, but it's getting to the point where they would want to know about all this. Why play detective?' She tutted. 'Here you go again never fully sharing information, keeping something to yourself.' Her fingertips rubbed together as she couldn't quite pin down what it was Dom was doing, her expression both crestfallen and reconciled. 'Are you listening to me?'

Dom marched towards her with their steaming plates of food.

'Let's eat.'

The Swap

8 | Dympna

|

It wasn't even six and with a start Dom woke to a gale howling round the building and a palm frond punching his window. A door was banging somewhere in the unit as well. Rubbing his eyes and staring into the dark, not feeling the slightest bit refreshed, Dom realised he had slept poorly. The grief, the alcohol and the worry of the day ahead were bubbling inside.

The events of the day played out in his head again. His meeting with the woman would end with him following her. How would he stay hidden? Sunglasses would be useful. A lazy hand parted the curtains. It looked like rain, so sunglasses were out. Could he follow her in a taxi? It wasn't impossible. A train would be easier. Hopefully she used trains. He pictured her weak frame—she didn't look like a walker.

Too worn out to properly plan, he flopped off the bed out of the room. Donald's bedroom door was the one that was making noise. The darkness encased him as he crossed the hall and before he could reach for the handle, the door banged once more. His body shook with fright in the dark corridor. He reached for the handle, but the draft sucked the door from his clutch. It drifted open, the blackness inviting him inside.

With the light turned on and the door held open, he waited for his eyes to adjust to the glare. Even then, he was hesitant to look at the wreckage that filled Donald's room, with its telltale waft of splintered wood.

The weapon lay flat on the carpet at his feet like an obedient hound. From the corner of his eye, he saw it, but he didn't look square at it.

The room was obliterated. Not one item was undamaged and the carpet was strewn with fragments of wood, plastic and paper. The chair, the wardrobe, the shelving were smashed beyond repair. The desk was in ugly halves. Even Donald's computer was chopped up, the monitor split, the hard drive ripped open, its guts hanging out. Whatever clues it may have housed about Donald's plans were irretrievable. He cursed his stupidity for wrecking the place.

Barefoot, he stepped carefully over the mess and shut the window, hit the switch and closed the door tight.

Soon the smell of toast and coffee were filling the front of the unit. He ate standing up, pacing around the dining room table and retracing his steps, going over the possibilities of where she might lead him once they parted ways in the café.

The jigsaw, which was nearly finished, beckoned. The huge tree was now taking up the centre of the image. The remaining sections were of a cloudless sky and the intricate mosaic. Dom sat, confident he could finish the puzzle in one sitting and forty minutes later, the final eight pieces were scattered near his elbow. Yet it looked like he had nine spaces.

He completed what he could and sat back. There was one missing piece—part of the mosaic. He got up and searched the area, under the table, around the sofa, but he couldn't find it. Turning on all the available lights didn't help. The piece was missing.

He decided a hot shower was in order and it was while he was hiding in the steam that he thought about going for a short run. His breakfast had gone down and he wouldn't push hard. Jogging would ease some tension and energy. Under the steaming jet of water, which lashed at his skin turning it blotchy, he stretched.

When he stepped on to Placer Avenue, the daylight was just arriving and he felt warmed enough from the shower to jog once around the park at a comfortable pace. The sky was covered in a racing grey-white sheet, which frustrated sunrise and let the night chill linger. A powerful wind carried him to the park. In the twenty-eight minutes he spent jogging, three light showers covered him. His waterproof jacket kept him dry and the musical scrunch of the tough material calmed his mind. Dom used to think jogging was about running away from problems, not dealing with them, until a fellow jogger had corrected him explaining running was a way to process, to move on and leave the past where it was. That was why he avoided doubling back. Loops on loops were fine, but never running to a point and turning around. What good did retracing steps do?

As he completed the track and turned into the wind, the gusts became strong enough to slow him down and he battled his way home. His body felt invigorated. The physical stresses of the last days eased while the howling wind rattled the trees and the clouds bubbled and blackened.

The second hot shower soothed more deeply than the first with his muscles warmed and stretched. He dressed in trousers, a thick shirt and casual shoes.

Slurping milky coffee, he stared at the puzzle of nine hundred and ninety-nine pieces. The garden was done, but one of the rings in the mosaic was incomplete. Still, it was a lovely jigsaw. But would he have started it if he'd known it had a piece missing? No way.

His lip biting started when his attention shifted to the meeting. Dom went through a list of things to do and say as his teeth kneaded the flesh of his bottom lip. He unravelled a finger for each item.

Find a suitable café, one that wasn't so noisy, where they could talk easily, freely, and not too close to the office.

Sit facing out with the best view of the street.

Text her the location.

Hand over the items.

Ask for her colleagues' names.

Leave together and go to walk the opposite way.

Who was the woman's contact in Subiaco? He had to find out today. And he wasn't to let his nerves get the better of him. He shook out his hands, anxious energy buzzing through each finger.

Half past eight was slow to arrive. On went his black jacket and with pocketfuls of belongings and one hand carrying the bag of sham Subiaco files, he went to leave. He stopped. There was something making him look behind him. He scoured the place as if going away for a year. It wasn't a final check for everything, because he was doubly certain he hadn't left anything behind. He was being compelled to take a look at everything he had achieved, being invited to value his private space with its luxury furniture, even the marred puzzle that would never be complete.

Glancing at a photo of Donald and him pegged to the fridge with a frothy beer magnet, aloud, he said, 'Keep an eye on me, buddy.'

II

Battling the weather, he fought his way to the corner shop, a route he had taken thousand of times. Yet the street seemed unfamiliar, the day felt different and he felt different. It was as if the wind, pushing him around, making him fight for composure, had transformed this common street with its ordinary features.

He ducked into the corner shop for a bus ticket and a paper, which would double as an umbrella.

'Good morning, Dominic'—the owner, who now knew his name, greeted him with a smile—'better to stay home. A storm is coming.'

The bus ticket looked foreign in his clasp. It seemed like ages ago he had used one of them. Dom had loved the routine of the bus trip to and from the city each day, some journeys spent looking out of the window listening to music, others with his eyes in a book. Its simplicity and normality would calm him. He craved that trip now.

With the ticket buried safely in a pocket, and gripping the newspaper, he braced himself against the growing storm.

A bus arrived. So did more rain. Cold and wet commuters squeezed on with Dom, who found standing space towards the back under the glare of harsh lighting, as bright as a theatre stage, while outside the city grew darker. Too agitated to sit, he went over his to-do list, struggling to keep his feet in one spot.

The bus chugged into the centre. Dom looked out to the streets as if on a new route. How quickly the open spaces of his suburb vanished, replaced with looming buildings capped by threatening clouds. With each lurch of the bus to one of its stops, annoyed commuters jostled their way on and surly travellers elbowed their way off. The poorly lit streets were hostile and unwelcoming like never before. Windswept trees joined in the city's ominous display listing menacingly and returning tall only to collapse again as though ready to pounce.

Off the bus, he fought with the crowds along blustery streets and over breezy intersections. Umbrellas made the pavements seem impossibly crowded and his newspaper protected his eyes from the rough handling of passersby. It wasn't raining, but the wind was scattering water from the trees. Soaked leaves tattooed the ground. To avoid the threat to his footing, he sidestepped as many of them as he could. The plastic bag flapped by his side, the sharp edge of the disc hacking into his thigh.

He got to Sussex Street, where his first choice of café had a perfect seat facing outside. Unobstructed, he could watch her arrive and leave, if he couldn't leave with her. But it was too busy, too noisy. It was just after nine and the café was still heaving.

His second choice was Four-Calendar Café, which was on Clarence Street and quieter and emptier, but closer to Subiaco than he wanted. He spotted a table inside that afforded him a partial street view and, with its elevated flooring, would allow him to watch her arrive and leave. The shop sign above the entrance displayed the street number and before Dom could shield himself, two massive spots of cold rain hit his face.

He stepped inside on to the slippery tiles, treading carefully past the bucket used for dripping umbrellas. Two black ones and a red one were jutting out.

His coffee ordered and paid for, Dom sat looking out. A shiver travelled up his spine as he sat still. The hard tile flooring and dark wooden panelling of the walls, as stylish as they were, did little to warm the place.

Everything about the place was cold. He wanted the damn coffee to come.

He sent the imposter a text message with the café's name and address. Moving the stumpy menu stand and the cup of sugar sachets around the table failed to ease his growing agitation.

A young waiter with a trendy hairstyle crept over to him. Not much faster than slow motion, his delivery yielded a large, unspilt cup of coffee, which Dom raised with both hands. It tasted delicious.

His nerves were building. He wiped sweat from his brow with the back of a twitchy hand and dried himself with a napkin. He pulled out the report and saw instantly that the clean pages didn't look right—they were too tidy. Maggie had suggested he make it look old but he'd forgotten. The report was supposed to have been carried home and passed between people. Checking around him, he dog-eared some of the edges and crimped the entire report. The dissecting crease protruded like freshly scarred skin. A loud whack made Dom jump in his chilly seat. The wind had banged the café door. His heart pumped that bit faster.

The waiter strolled to refasten the door and Dom checked the time on his mobile, which was on the table right under his nose. She wouldn't be much longer. Two wobbly hands brought the large cup to his lips. Then he sat back and watched the passersby, all the while fiddling with his mobile.

He drew a second mobile phone from his jacket and sent a brief text. After checking the volume was down, Dom popped it back into the concealed pocket, where it was to stay unseen and unheard.

A memory from his conversation with Josh two days before appeared from nowhere. Josh confirmed he had received messages from Donald on the day of the swap. Who else had Donald texted that day? Was there something revealing in the ones that Dom had received from Donald, something he was missing? He picked up his other phone and pulled up Donald's texts, some of his brother's lasts messages. He scrolled through them casually.

They had been read many times, but nothing stood out. Donald had always kept texts very simple. It was unlikely they contained a hint as to who in Subiaco was working with pretend Vanessa. He scoured each text noting Donald's characteristic style of almost no punctuation or capitals. A glance to the door every so often confirmed she wasn't around. With the coffee in one hand and his mobile on the metal table, a finger swiped the texts.

His finger stopped. His mouth dropped wide open as he re-read one of the messages. That was a name. It looked like an ordinary word, but bloody hell, that was a name! How had he missed it so many times before?

The name stood out on the small mobile screen as though it alone was lit up by a thousand stage lights. He read the text four more times.

Rather than diminishing, Dom's gape grew. He placed his coffee down but misjudged where, and it slipped from the table onto the floor, smashing to pieces sending brown liquid everywhere. Too engrossed to care, he let the staff do the cleaning up. The waiter waltzed over with a mop and a dustpan and brush.

Here was a text from Donald that day which explained who was acting corruptly in his office, who was defrauding the company, and—for sure—who the killer was. He had the name of Vanessa's accomplice!

Dom leant back to let his chest open. His lungs couldn't fill quickly enough. The enormity of his discovery made his mind explode.

He sat still. He couldn't believe the name he had in the message, nor could he believe that person was stealing money.

The café clock showed nine thirty. He had to call Maggie. While his heart hammered in his chest as though breaking out of its cavity, he dialled her number. Slow to connect, the phone rattled in his impatient clasp.

Sitting upright sent a shaft of cold air up his back. A scan of the street showed the woman was not close by. Maggie's phone was still ringing.

Then he saw her.

He ended the call and laid the phone on the table.

Adrenalin roared through him and he exhaled in long puffs to calm his breathing. It didn't work.

He wanted to kill the person named in the text. The effort to unclench his fists was herculean.

He was frantic—she had to be at ease when she sat with him.

His shoulders came down and without believing for a second he appeared relaxed, he pushed his forearms onto the table.

Harassed by the rain, dragged by the wind, Vanessa danced along the road.

It was as though she was being carried to the meeting against her will.

III

Camille sat facing forward on the ferry as it bobbed its way to Circular Quay. She was inside, clutching her bag and fighting to ignore the schoolgirls opposite her whose music was blasting from tiny headphones they shared, each with a headphone in one ear. Their two heads bounced in harmony and they looked liked conjoined twins, the earphone cord taut between them.

The music was too loud for Camille to even concentrate.

When the songs ended, the pair replaced the racket with chatting and giggles.

Camille felt her bag vibrate and her mobile sounded low but clear. She pulled out her phone and glasses. Finally a message from Josh. She sat upright and for a moment, the nearby distractions drifted into the background.

```
Hello. I'm fine.
No need to worry.
I'll call you
soon. Josh
```

Camille sent a short reply.

```
I must speak to
you now. Please
call me urgently.
```

She cradled the handset desperate not to miss his call. But the phone didn't ring. She looked up and caught her travelling companions sniggering.

One was mimicking her, cupping her own phone in her lap. The other was writhing in her seat giggling.

Camille's blood boiled. She dialled Josh's number and his voice message, which she could now recite word for word, jacked her anger beyond control. She fought back the emotion.

'Josh, this is Camille. Again. I just got your text message. You have to call me. I need to speak to you about Donald. And Dom. Why won't you—'

When her tears came out, she cut the call and covered her face with her free hand. The phone stayed pressed to her ear, shielding her face from the other passengers. The nearby giggling stopped.

Camille removed her hand from her eyes and caught their pained expressions as the schoolgirls suppressed smiles.

'Fuck off, you two,' she said, wiping her eyes.

IV

Tufts of dark hair swooped around despite her one-handed attempts to trap them down. Choosing not to leave her umbrella at the entrance, she shook it and stepped inside, undoing the black overcoat, which hung off her like a bin liner.

Dom signalled to her and noticed she had on the same two-piece as the first time they met.

She went over to him, tiptoeing through the damp patch where the waiter had cleaned.

'Can you believe this weather? Hello Donald.' Dom stood up and shook her fingertips, which were freezing. She must have been outside for ages—she had travelled some way to be there.

She stayed standing. Her eyes, once shameless and determined, were weary and secretive. 'I'm over this weather and we are so busy. I need a holiday. Let me get a drink but I can't stay long—we're hectic upstairs.'

She returned in a flash rattling a bottle of sparkling water and a straw and sat down, her skeletal frame as rigid as a method.

Dom sensed she was more reserved than their first meeting and he put it down to her reading his body language, watching the fury toss him around. He drew back his cheeks, stretching his hard lips into a hollow smile. His throat scraped. He was angry with himself for not realising sooner the significance of Donald's text. His mind was flooded with images from Subiaco over the last two years, images of his colleague. He had to focus on the woman in front of him. All his grief, torment and frustration from these recent weeks came to the surface, ready to pour onto this guilty party.

'You sound like you need a holiday.' His words quavered.

'I'm going away real soon.' She popped her straw into the bottle and started drinking.

'Where?'

'I want beach and sun and cocktails. We have a few options.' She smiled. 'How are things for you, Donald? You look better than the last time we met.'

'What do you mean by that?' His jaw clenched making his teeth jar.

'You must be sleeping better', she said. Dark red lips pulled eagerly at the lime straw. She seemed to be bobbing her head to the tune on the radio, which ricocheted around the cold café.

Dom shrugged. 'My brother died not far from here.'

Her eye contact was fleeting.

'We miss him so much,' she said, all whiny. 'You have some things for me,' came her attempt to switch topic.

Dom presented his gifts. 'I spoke to my sister after we met. She had a look around. Turns out these were with his things.' He catapulted them across the table.

The disc was labelled *Green accounts third quarter* in thick, black marker—Dom's crude attempt to make it look authentic.

'Great. That's what the team was looking for. John mentioned the—those accounts and this report.' Her fingers flicked the pages as if the action would help her recall the contents. 'We should file it.'

'John who?'

She snatched up her drink, dragging on the straw, locking eyes with Dom. With the green tube jettisoned, she said, 'John—Brown.' More calmly, she added, 'He's a nice guy.'

She rummaged in her bag, talking into it. 'It's as if we swap presents whenever we meet and I have this for you.' The medium-sized paperback, held high, jiggled slightly in her nervous grip. Before he could take it, she lowered it to the table and pushed it across to him. Her feeble hand drew back.

'I recognise this. Dom read it a few times. You probably saw him walking around the office with it.' He waited for her to respond, but she said nothing. 'Who gave it to you?' he demanded. 'John again?'

'Look, I don't remember, Donald.'

The tutting and mumbling that emanated from Dom as his head lowered sheepishly sparked her curiosity. Her left side twisted in to him. 'Stop *what*? Stop calling you *Donald*?'

She sat back with her drink held up masking her awkwardness, shielding herself. 'Are you—feeling ok?' A phone sounded from in her bag and she snatched it up. For privacy, or comfort or safety, her body turned almost ninety degrees. 'Yes, this is Vanessa ... yes ... yes.'

There was no doubt who she was talking to, given her one-word answers. Dom felt like ripping the phone from her hand and confirming the caller's identity. Enough of her games and lies.

His head raised a tad. Her eyes were fixed on the wall with the chalked specials.

Dom activated the camera on his mobile and pretended to read the screen. A quick tilt of the handset gave him the angle he needed and he pressed the screen. He fiddled with the phone some more and tried to get another shot.

'We're almost done. I'll be back at the off—' Her face froze. 'You just took a photo of me,' she said to Dom. 'He's just taken a photo of me,' she repeated, to the caller. Her icy glare as she lowered the phone made Dom react.

'I fucking didn't. I'm reading a text.' Hiding the phone in a pocket, he watched her with dark, monstrous eyes.

'I'm going. Like I said—very busy.' She shoved her mobile into her coat and went to gather her things.

Dom pinned her scrawny arm to the table and a look of horror came over her. The wrestling between them sent her water bottle spinning across the smooth surface and smashing to the floor, echoing through the café.

'Sit down.' The words leapt across at her. 'I want to know how things are at the office.' Dom's right hand tensely corrected the sugar bowl.

Vanessa looked around the café, then at her arm trapped by Dom's hand. Her fear quickly turned to disgust.

'What is it with you two?' She jerked her arm free and wrenched to her feet. 'You're fucking weirdos.'

'What do you mean?' Dom's eyes pleaded with her.

Vanessa didn't move, frozen in her place.

'What did my brother ever do to you?' The question, painted with anger and hurt, went unanswered.

Vanessa cried out, fear plastering her face once more. She lost only a second getting to the exit, squeezing her thin body out the door.

Dom hopped up. As he pushed back his chair, he picked up the book but slipped on the wet floor and collided with the waiter who had arrived to clear up the latest spill. They both crashed to the ground where Dom howled and wriggled while customers cried out and went to help.

Dom was first to stand up, leaving the waiter to come to his feet with the help of customers. His ankle had twisted in the fall, but before anyone reached him, with a shake of his leg to test its strength, he limped out to the street.

V

People, umbrellas and rain hampered his view but she was hurrying in the direction she had come from as she roughed her way along the road. She looked behind her and saw him and he stayed on his tiptoes to make sure she did. He didn't care now. He wasn't thinking clearly and his rage, overwhelming as it was, propelled him towards her. When she saw him coming, she ran, crossing the street in a crowd and speeding ahead.

The road was safer for him to cross once the cars and buses banked up. The rain and gales were making his task more challenging, drowning out the street sounds. He dived through the lanes only to be narrowly missed by a motorcyclist with the same idea of squeezing between the stopped traffic. The abrupt halt put pressure on his weakened ankle and pain tore up his leg to his knee.

The motorbike rider swore at Dom, who darted off the road and focused on looking for his prey. She had almost reached the next intersection. He had to catch up if he had any hope of staying with her, yet his ankle, burning from the fall, wouldn't hold out much longer. A twist on wet pavement and the chase was over.

Dom guessed she might turn left and head towards busier George Street. But before reaching the corner, she crossed to the right, awkwardly clutching her belongings to her chest, her black jacket and hair flapping in the wind. Dom crossed too and sped up. She stopped only metres before the corner and looked over her right shoulder, her face red from running and her features stiff with panic. He ducked into a glass doorway, which allowed him to see out while keeping hidden.

Her face darted around searching for him. Good. She would now think she had got rid of him. Her frail shape disappeared around the corner and Dom hobbled out of his hiding spot to the intersection. At the junction he stopped, his breathing rough, exertion feeding rage, rage feeding exertion. He inched his head around the brick wall just as the wind blew a gale. A shaft of wind came behind him and upwards and flapped his jacket nearly over his head. He beat the material off in a fury and stepped into the middle of the footpath.

There was no sign of her. Presumably, she had turned left or right at a cross street, or she was hiding in a building. If she had turned right again, Dom thought, she was doing a loop in a poor attempt to lose him.

He ran to the next corner and looked north along Kent Street. Nothing. He turned to look south. The rain was easing giving him a clearer view. Still nothing.

He looked back again and saw her scurrying along on the far side. She turned her head and Dom skulked out of view, waited a few seconds, taking long breaths and wiggling his ankle, which was weak. He poked his head back around. She was gone again. Darting across the road, he determined to catch up to her, as he was sure she would be thinking she had lost him.

Had she ducked into a small arcade? Or was she sticking with the freedom of the streets? He reached the next corner of cross streets and stood on tiptoes for a better look. Then he spotted her again. She was back on

Clarence Street, where the elevation of the road made her position stand out.

The traffic lights sat about thirty metres ahead, and there she was waiting, hiding, trying to fit it with the pedestrians. Dom advanced.

'Shit.' His ankle couldn't take this much longer, the burn travelling down into his foot and up into his calf. Trees lining the road helped conceal him. This was his last chance—he couldn't afford to chase her again. His ankle was about to pack up.

Dom's anger was boiling over. He cursed the people that were crossing against them, blocking his view of her. He moved closer, taking his time. The lights were still red. Only a few metres separated them. If she turned now, she would see him. He could make out the fresh spots of rain splatting on her shoulders.

A quick look sideways and he saw the traffic entering the intersection. Long bendy buses and vans whizzed by. His breathing was rapid, his limbs tense. His cold eyes darted around. He looked straight ahead and moved his eyes to her, to the lights, to the traffic and back to her.

Hurting her badly was all he wanted to do. Donald's text messages were enough evidence to get his colleague, so Dom didn't need to follow her. He didn't need her anymore—she was useless to him.

The lights turned amber and a taxi accelerated to pass through. If he timed it well, it would work. His sore ankle would be fine for the short distance.

He burst towards her with an open palm cocked.

Five metres.

His approach went unseen as he dodged people.

Two metres.

A gust blew her hair over her face and as she turned sideways raising a hand to uncover her eyes, Dom saw it wasn't her. It wasn't Vanessa. But it was too late.

With a smack, his body propelled hers into the taxi's path. The unknown woman, her face locked in a grimace, launched into the road, with her handbag and an umbrella being hurled across the intersection.

The taxi screeched. She headbutted the window and skimmed along the side of the car, crumpling onto the bitumen. Bystanders screamed and Dom stood still, trying to prevent himself from falling forward, hands outstretched to guard equilibrium. He choked. With him staggering away from the edge of the pavement, his back came in contact with a building. He spilled to the wet ground and covered his face. His book lay discarded close by.

Sounds of chaos filled the intersection. Horns blew. People's footsteps clattered around him. Concerned voices fired off questions. All of it carried to him by a turbulent wind.

He could hear someone crying and he hoped it was the woman. Crying meant she wasn't dead. What if that wasn't her crying? That could be an onlooker. What if she was dead? He couldn't look.

A tide of panic passed over him as the atrocity reverberated in his mind. He had to find out the extent of the harm he had caused. Whimpering, he raised his head. A ring of people blocked her from his view, as if shielding her from further wrongdoing. He could see she was lying down.

The taxi was empty, a front and back door open, and the driver was one of half a dozen people tending to her.

A man was standing near him taking a photo of the scene with his mobile. He swung round and snapped Dom, who was sitting with his mouth open, catatonic.

'Are you ok, mate? Is she with you?'

Another young man squatted and rested a cautious hand on Dom's shoulder.

Dom shook his head ever so slightly. 'I didn't mean to,' he said to nobody. 'What have I done?'

Had people seen him push her? Did Vanessa see?

The police would come soon. He had to act. He staggered to his feet.

The young man offered his hand saying, 'You should sit there. Don't move—we've called an ambulance.'

Dom cantered away from him and was accosted by another passerby.

'What happened? Did you fall against her?' She pointed at the woman. 'She's badly injured.'

Dom wriggled his ankle and his audience looked down. 'My ankle. It was an accident. I—' He scanned around deciding which street to take.

The taxi driver retrieved something from his car and walked towards the small group encircling Dom. His thick accent conveyed disbelief.

'What were you thinking?'

Dom pushed himself off from the wall and ran.

The shouting rose above the traffic and the gale, and Dom didn't turn to see if anyone was following.

VI

'Read me your one again.' Camille stepped behind her sister-in-law to sit close, moving papers from the kitchen table for elbow space.

Robin put on a cheery voice as she read from her mobile and waved her free hand, punctuating each point.

'Hello Robin. I'm fine. Just away for a few days. I'll call you when I get back to Sydney. Josh.' She looked at Camille. 'It sounds fine to me. Except ...'

'Except we must've called him thirty times between us,' Camille said, verbalising Robin's concern. 'There's something odd about it. And what makes it more frustrating is Dominic saying there's nothing wrong. But he's being his usual evasive self.' She wiggled her head in disdain.

Robin began cleaning her phone screen with her jumper. 'Why won't he answer our calls?'

'I'll tell you why.' She prodded the table with a steel-like finger. 'It's not him sending those texts. I bet it's someone else.'

A jet of air blasted from Robin. 'That's—no. No!'

'Something's seriously wrong. He sends texts to say he's ok. He won't ring us or answer our calls. Who's to say it's him sending these messages? Someone else has his phone.'

'Why would they do that to us?' Robin stared at Camille in bewilderment. 'If it isn't him, who is it? Who's sending the texts? Why do they have his phone?'

Camille lifted her shoulders, which were buried under cashmere. She didn't know the answer. 'We must go to the police. If it's nothing and we're over-worrying, that will be good news. And if something's up, they should know about it.'

'We have to tell Dominic.'

'Oh no, we don't. Number one rule—we don't trust Dominic. That man will say whatever he fancies saying to help him through a situation. Not two days ago he sat right there and told me I couldn't call his office. And now he's saying everything with Josh is ok? And we can't get hold of him?' The theatrical look she wore brought her questions to life. 'He's making wild claims about Donald's death and the one person who can corroborate it all won't return our calls.'

'I agree he's not handling things well'—Robin broke off to ponder her next comment—'but he won't be

236

happy when he finds out the police got involved.' Her bob shook as her head turned side to side.

Camille collected her handbag, her phone and a jacket, and grabbed her set of house keys from a hook near the door. 'Who gives a damn what he thinks? I'm going to the police and you're coming with me.'

VII

'I still love him.' Bawling, the woman flopped into her lap, the shame of her plight too much to deal with.

Dympna saw her client's bald spot. She looked away before the woman's head came up and her focus returned to listening to the tale of infidelity.

A commotion was happening at reception and Cassandra was shouting, which was rare. 'You can't go in there.'

Something thudded against the other side of her office door with enormous force. It flew open and in ran Dom. He looked from Dympna to the woman sitting opposite her and back to Dympna.

A puffy, wet face lifted from a damp lap, with eyes and mouth open wide.

Dom cried, 'You have to help me—something awful has happened.'

Cassandra's quick steps, impeded by her tight skirt and heels, sounded on the carpet outside. Her sharp succession of tuts made her sound like someone doing an impression of a train. 'Come out of there, Mr Tolen. Right now. Nobody goes—'

Crash.

Dom slammed the door and locked the three of them inside. His edgy voice competed with Cassandra's raps on the door, the desperation in his eyes not having the impact he was hoping for. 'It's serious. I don't know what to do.'

Dympna spoke calmly. 'I'm with Gwen now.' She looked at her client, who was now standing. Dympna flapped her hand lightly at the woman. 'We'll keep going, Gwen.'

Gwen zipped her coat, blew her nose and pocketed the tissue. Through teary eyes, she scowled at them.

Dom insisted. 'I have to talk to you now.'

'I'm so sorry, Gwen. Bear with me.' Dympna opened the door to a small room connected to her office, a door Dom had always believed gave on to a cupboard. 'Wait in here, Dominic.' She went over to her client. 'Don't worry, Gwen. It's soundproof.'

'He can stay. I'm leaving,' said Gwen. 'This is—'

'I'm so sorry. Please reschedule. Cassandra won't charge for this session.'

'Just try it.' Gwen scoffed and walked out, dodging Cassandra standing guard.

It was Dympna's turn to lock Cassandra outside. With the door closed, she gave him her attention. He was busying himself at the window. The back of his trousers and jacket were wet and his shirt was out. When he turned back from scouring the street, Dympna noticed how different he looked. Darting eyes, body hunched down, he looked terrified.

Dympna calmed herself before speaking. 'You are a special friend, but what you ju—'

'I pushed someone into the street and a car hit her. People stopped and I ran off.'

Dympna's tranquility vanished. 'Oh my god.' She squinted at him. 'On—purpose? Is she—ok?'

'I don't know.' He slapped his hands to his cheeks. 'It complicates everything. The poor woman.'

He recounted the morning's events, punching his own palm as he explained how angry he had become at Vanessa.

'When the taxi driver came over, I jumped up and ran.' He bounced back to the window. 'I came straight here. I didn't know what else to do.'

'You're all wet.'

'I fell over. Or I tripped.'

'You'll need to go to the police'—Dympna tapped her desk—'before they come to you.'

'It was an accident. I—I—I thought she was the killer.'

'Then it was no accident, Dominic. You tried to seriously hurt someone.' There was a pause. 'The police may think you wanted to kill her.'

He moved to another window and cocked his neck to see as much of the street as possible. 'I'm going to be charged with attempted murder. What am I going to do? I'll have to run. Shit.'

Dympna watched him do circles and punch the air.

'Is that wise? Come away from the window—I don't think the police will have located you so soon.'

Dom stepped to the centre of the room, but didn't sit.

Dympna straightened her spine and tugged at her jacket with both hands. 'How did you get here?'

'Taxi. I sat in the back but he kept his eyes on me the whole time. He could see me getting upset.'

'The state you're in will catch people's attention.'

Dom checked himself over. When he looked back up at Dympna, her hand was out. 'The book. You said this Vanessa woman returned your book. Where is it?'

Dom looked around him. It wasn't there. 'I must've lost it when I push—when I fell. Oh bugger.'

'Did you have it in the taxi?'

Dom threw his hands up, unsure.

'You said earlier you were planning to follow her quietly. What changed?'

'Why are you asking me that? Don't you believe me?'

'What changed?'

Dom wagged his head. He would struggle to explain it. 'Things went bad in the café and I got so angry. Then she said something about the two of us.' His face scrunched up. 'Her face had this look of—of—of revulsion. I just wanted to kill her.' His gaze drifted to the floor. 'My god, what have I done?'

'I want to see the photo you took of her.' Dympna's hand was out again, as if demanding a child give up its toy.

Dom fumbled in his pocket and he left her to inspect the photo while he paced the room some more.

Although blurred, the image was clear enough. It was of a strikingly thin woman with long dark hair, her face to the side. She had a mobile to her ear and the camera angle was low.

'You've met her how many times?'

Dom marched around.

'Dominic?'

'What?'

'How many times have you met her?'

'Twice'—he did a detour behind the chairs and passed the windows—'and one phone call.'

'The police will struggle to believe that in daylight you mistook someone for her.'

'Their clothing was identical and I was all confused.' He screamed at Dympna as the panic overwhelmed him, pointing at the photo she was still examining. 'I can't tell the police about her. If they find out about Vanessa, that's it—I'm dead. Because if the woman dies, that's a murder charge. And it gets worse. Vanessa may have seen the whole thing.' His arms flapped as he strode around. 'I've completely ruined everything. Fuck!'

'This is very serious. You knocked someone into the road and you fled the scene. The police will be very suspicious of your story.'

'I'll tell them I tripped and slipped—it was windy.' He waved her away with a dismissive hand. 'You're supposed to be helping.'

'You'll need to find this woman and your book. You need a credible story that you think she's a killer.'

'No way.' His hand cut through the air. 'If I tell the police I met up with a woman I think is Don's killer, they'll make the connection that I deliberately pushed this other woman, and they'll charge me.'

'Of course they will. You've just done an extremely dangerous thing.'

'That's why I'm here.' He charged at her. 'Help me. You'll think of something. I know you will.'

Dympna leant back into her chair, its high back nestling her regal head. After some moments, a nod confirmed her commitment. Her shapely frame coasted efficiently around the room.

'We've got to be quick.' Cupboards got snapped open and items were gathered on to a small metal tray.

'Remove your jacket and lift up your sleeve.'

'I don't understand.'

'And you don't have much time, so do as I say.'

Dom obeyed, watching her prepare a hypodermic of medication.

A small square sachet was thrust at him. 'Open that and clean your inner elbow. We need a vein.'

Soon the addictive smell of alcohol filled his nostrils and the wet pad was cooling his skin, awakening the pores and readying them for the metal.

Her face was serious and her eyes fixed on her task.

'When your mother died, she told me to take good care of you all.' Syringe in the air, she stopped. 'But I didn't think it would extend to this. Look away.' The therapist found a vein instantly and Dom barely had time to tense before the syringe pierced his skin. Dympna pumped it in at top speed.

'What are you giving me?'

'This will calm you down. I need you clear-headed so we can get your story straight.' She put cotton wool on the puncture and gestured for him to hold it in place as she stood upright pausing over him.

He looked up at her quizzically.

'What's in that? I didn't know you were a—' The need to speak left him. He looked at nothing as his attention went inwards. 'Ooh'—he hummed—'nice.'

'Our little secret.'

She tidied up her tray of equipment, stashing it in a deep drawer that glided silently back into place.

'Mmm, lovely. The knot in my stomach's gone. I haven't felt this good in ages.'

'Good. Mind you, we don't want you too relaxed. You're going to the police, not the cinema.' She passed him a band-aid.

'You're funny.' He looked at her with big bouncing eyes.

Dympna rested her hand on his shoulder.

'Here's what you tell them.'

VIII

Absently, Maggie returned the phone to its holder and slumped back on her chair, taking in what Dom had just relayed. Not only had he told her who the killer was, he had the name in a text that had been sitting on his mobile for weeks. Their colleague was clearly implicated in stealing from Subiaco.

At her workstation, she shielded her eyes with a jittery hand as if Dom's news was written on her face for all to see.

Dom hadn't given much away when he had called from the street, insistent but relaxed, saying he needed her help to trap the killer.

Somehow she had to get their colleague's home address.

Dom suspected they didn't have much time. He mentioned having had a horrible morning and he was expecting to have a tough next few hours with the police. What was that about? He had promised to call her as soon as he could and he would go into more detail then.

Her lips were dry. She drank the rest of her coffee in one gulp. What Donald had uncovered at her work was terrifying. Shutting her eyes helped her head clear and the ideas flow.

Dom's instructions had been simple.

Be quick. Be discreet. Be careful.

She doubted that was how to quickly get an address.

The Swap

9 | Harry

I

Climbing the steps was tricky while the wind forced him back and sidelong. With his arms out, Dom felt as though the world had lost its gravity and he was walking weightless into the building. Without the basics, like a clear head and down being down, he doubted his ability to deal with his predicament. He was way too woozy.

There was a recent memory of steadying himself against the enormous column at the bottom of the steps, but he might have imagined it. He hoped so. It wasn't the ideal way to enter a police station to confess.

Big muffled paces failed to carry him as far as he was expecting but eventually he reached the entrance, where it took him time to realise the dreamy hand reaching out and pushing open the door was his own. He stopped. He turned around to look at the view, the chaotic sky and the drenched buildings. Familiar George Street sprawled away from the steps—the quiet church, the empty town hall, the silent buses, all whipped by bursts of wind. Yet the scene had taken on an unrecognisable tinge with the mid-morning crowds avoiding his gaze, pretending to dawdle, all the while lingering and plotting.

Content to leave the world of conspiracy behind him, he moved inside and let the door swing away. If it made a sound behind him, he didn't notice. Sheltered now from the gale's relentless tugging and propelling, an eerie silence greeted him. His lumber to the front counter dragged on and, using the smooth wood for balance, he looked around.

There were no screaming children, no worried tourists and no talkative drinkers. Neither were there officers herding resistant perpetrators. Indeed, there were no officers. Dom was alone. Time was standing still for him, no motion, no sound. The only sign of life had been his sleepy arrival.

He wondered what to do. Sure he could go back to the door, peer outside and check he had used the correct entrance. But the wooden door with its small glass windows seemed so far away and each step plagued his body as if he was waltzing in quicksand.

The clack of footsteps behind him made him turn. On the other side of the counter arrived a colossal policeman, as tall as he was serious, with a uniform stretching over bundles of muscle. Dom squinted for a better look at the tiny object he was holding. A pen.

Dom looked up as the officer was mouthing some words and he thought he recognised *how* and *help*. Licking dry lips to prepare for speech, he caught the officer following his tongue as it peeked out of his parched mouth.

Hopefully, the correct words would come forward and float up, yet Dom felt disembodied, his mind incapable of responding adequately to the endless questions that could blast him.

The officer's peaceful nodding meant Dom's mouth had already started explaining why he had come.

The policeman's tiny black pen communicated with Dom. It hovered in the air and it told him to sit in the row of plastic chairs, disordered and damaged, under the windows.

The policeman moved away inside the station offices and Dom floated to the nearest seat, which he landed in with one smooth unbroken motion, his lower body navigating the rest of him into place flawlessly. He found himself happy to sit and wait.

There was no way of knowing how long he'd been there, but a police officer appeared and asked him to follow her. It felt like he had only just sat down, but he couldn't be sure. She led him down a hallway, dark and carpeted and Dom was thankful she was walking at a pace he could manage.

What few sounds there were—material rubbing on limbs, metal jangling on metal—became muffled and another layer of silence cradled Dom as he moved deeper into the police station.

They rounded a corner and ahead of them, Dom could make out two people approaching and he strained to see if they were in uniform. He stepped behind the policewoman so they could walk in single file and let the approaching pair pass.

Dom lowered his head and stepped on but the figures didn't approach. As he got closer, their shapes became clearer. They were two life-sized cardboard cut outs—a chirpy thief with a sit-com smile and a stern-looking Indigenous policeman with handcuffs at the ready. Before he could read the accompanying caption—difficult in the low light—the policeman and the thief trotted off.

A set of languid steps later, the corridor widened and they came to a small vestibule containing three chairs in better condition than the ones in the front waiting area.

Just what he needed—a sit-down.

The policewoman motioned for Dom to wait and his bum touched the seat while she was still signalling a chair.

It felt good to rest his legs, which became lighter again, and miraculously his ankle was improving. His surroundings were alien. He was waiting outside what were most likely interview rooms. They were going to take a statement from him. How did he feel about that? It was hard to say—it was hard to feel.

He watched the policewoman go back the way they had come, disappearing into the shadowy hallway, her stature distorted as though she were waddling to the back of an Ames room.

Dom rubbed his eyes and focused on the wall opposite. The fuzziness in his thoughts had to go. He needed a clear head if he had any chance of convincing his interviewer this morning's incident was not deliberate. The police were skilled at interviewing people, he told himself, and they had ways of checking if a story was genuine.

It dawned on him again how quiet the station was. The front counter area had been empty, but this section was deathly silent. Where was everyone? He glanced up and down the corridor wondering how long before he would be interviewed and how long it would last. The chair he was in was comfortable. His tired head rested against a cold wall and the chill was a welcome surprise. He moved his head around cooling his crown, and when voices sounded, he sat still.

'Heading there now. It's got forfeit written all over it.' The booming masculine voice travelled well. Two plain-clothes officers rounded the corner.

'Anderson says they're doing some pruning. I—'

They spotted Dom and passed him in silence. The mumbles started up as they went through a far door.

Dom went back to rubbing his head against the wall and he recalled the police officer's remark.

Pruning.

Someone was pruning.

A big smile spread over his face, his mind started wandering and without a hint of resistance, he let it take him.

The scene came swiftly.

The sun was belting down, scorching his skin as he stood working at a low hedge, clipping the troublesome branches. The garden shears swung through the humid air, branches tumbling to his bare feet, torn leaves dancing off the blades. Taking two steps back allowed him to assess his work. Neat angles. He looked to the left and the right. About fifty metres away, there was Donald, also gardening. Dom raised a slow hand. Donald waved back. It made Dom smile.

Then gardener Dom realised the other gardener wasn't Donald. Dom was watching a reflection.

Dom's face cooked under the intense midday glare, but he kept his eyes open wide locked on his image. The shears kept working. *Trim. Snip. Snip.* Only the brush of petals against his foot made him reluctantly take his eyes off his reflection. He saw a freshly chopped pink rose by his untanned heel.

Further along the hedge, his reflection worked feverishly. But now he didn't recognise the gardener's face. Whoever it was worked the shears like an expert, unaware of the advancing shadow that was growing behind him. The dark shape transformed into a police officer, who crossed the tendered lawn stepping lightly, his gleaming handcuffs swinging noiselessly by his side. The officer had come to arrest the unknown gardener and he raised his free hand to tap him on the back.

'Run!'

Dom screamed in the dark corridor. He shook himself from the hallucination and hitched himself up, huffing oxygen into his lungs and leaning back to rest. He stilled his head against the cold wall and wiped beads of sweat from his forehead. Only then did he spot the security cameras, which he prayed weren't on.

II

Maggie stuck her head around the door of the human resources group of offices and was glad to see it empty except for the casual worker readying mounds of physical files for archive.

'James, is Vanessa still in Auckland?'

Without looking up, he gave her a short, informative response. 'It's Jamie. She'll be here next Monday.' He clarified the timeframe as though Maggie were new to time keeping. 'She's not in this Monday. She comes back a week later.'

'Jamie, I have something to add to my personal file. How can I get access to it?' Flapping a sealed envelope at him caught his attention and he looked up.

The irritation in his voice was evident. 'It's locked. Like I said, she's back next Monday. Wait 'til then.'

As Maggie moved into the office and brushed past him, she tapped the desk surface in front of him with the envelope. 'You're looking for permanent work, aren't you?'

He didn't reply straight away.

'Guess so.'

She tried the door to the interior, darkened office and peered through the blinds glimpsing a row of filing cabinets along the far wall. The drawers didn't carry labels and she had no idea which of them would contain staff details. The door got another twist and this time, she pushed against it as she twiddled the handle.

'Who has the key?'

'No idea.' Jamie shrugged and went back to his filing. 'Her boss. I don't remember his name.'

Maggie didn't fancy explaining to an executive director why she needed the key to Vanessa's office. 'You're right—best I wait until she comes back.'

'Exactly.' Jamie retrieved one of two discarded earpieces resting on his shoulders. He bumped it in his ear and after a light tap on his device, the beats started.

Maggie stood over him planning how to get him out of the way. She raised her voice. 'What time are you going to lunch?'

'Soon.'

'I need something hand-delivered to a client on Macquarie Street. Do up your top button, put on a tie and be at my desk in ten minutes.'

She walked away, leaving him reaching for his shirt collar, checking his appearance.

III

When the operator answered the call, she couldn't finish her jovial welcome because of the panic-stricken voice that interrupted her. The woman who had pretended to be Vanessa Hawke belted out her request.

'I have tickets booked for Tuesday. My name is Ruth Arthur and I need to—to—oh. I have the booking number here. But we must leave Sydney today. We *have* to leave today—oh.'

Ruth's frantic tone didn't faze the travel agent. 'Wonderful, madam. We'll see what we can do. So you'd like to bring forward your travel date? Certainly. Can we start with your booking reference please?'

Ruth stumbled over the letters.

The operator worked to repeat them. 'Checking, I have g-w-b-l-s-o.'

'Without the *o*!' Ruth rattled the phone. 'It ends in *s*. Oh, hurry!'

'Madam, you keep adding *o* to the end and I can't tell what the reference code is. I'll repeat it.'

Seconds later, she announced Ruth's details were on the screen. 'You're flying on Tuesday evening. Two tickets. These are under our SunAsia promotion. Unfortunately, you can't change the booking. I'm so sorry.'

Ruth cursed into the phone. 'Get me two tickets to Kuala Lumpur for today. A new booking.' She clutched her free hand to her chest and struggled to breathe deeply. 'Oh, please tell me you have something.'

'Let's see what we can do for you.' The line went quiet for a few seconds. 'You're in luck, madam. I have two tickets leaving today at five thirty.'

'Shit—that's too early. The other person won't be ready by then.' Ruth knew there wouldn't be time for him to return home and pack. 'Do you have anything later on?'

'I'll need to look into this. I suggest I call you back.' She checked the contact number on file was correct, sounding happy to be ending the call.

'Please.' Ruth begged down the phone and fought back tears as the call ended. With the mobile on the bed, she cradled her face. She had had a shocking morning, but they could be escaping within hours. They would soon be out of the country, safe, far away from everything going on in Sydney. In fact, far away from everything.

She needed to update him. When she had rung earlier to tell him what had happened at the café, he had been with someone and had told her texting was safer. He'd managed to soothe her a bit over the phone, but she was left to calm herself after he hung up.

The wardrobe's full-length mirror prevented her from escaping inspection. She sat up. Studying her face, its wrinkles and blotches, it dawned on her she looked too exhausted to travel, too scared to make it through customs. They couldn't bring attention to themselves when they checked in.

Her note to him was short.

```
They're looking
for seats for
tonight. Will call
with news. Love
you.
```

IV

'You're here to make a statement about the incident on the corner of Clarence and King this morning. A woman was knocked into traffic.'

Dom nodded, his eyes drawn to the camera mounted high on the wall. 'Yes, I am.' The officer opposite him, who had introduced himself as Sergeant Collins, was tall and stocky, and impeccably dressed, and his shirt and stationery looked new. His head was shaved to within a millimetre of bald, the starkness of his skull contrasting with his saucer-eyed face.

'She's going to be all right, isn't she?' Dom knew little about her condition. On his phone, he'd seen a news report about an accident in the city where a woman had severe injuries. Maybe that was her.

The officer attended to paperwork and checked his wristwatch.

'Oh god—you have to tell me. Is she dead?' Later on, looking back, Dom would think his tone was over-exaggerated. The tug of war going on between his nerves and the drugs, the stress and the calm, was distorting his speech. He wanted to know what happened to her and he needed to play innocent. Despite his misgivings, his performance had the desired effect. The sergeant answered.

'No, Mr Tolen. She's breathing, in hospital. She will recover. Tell me what happened.'

Dom took what felt like the longest breath he had ever drawn. He doubted the windowless interview room contained enough oxygen for him to breathe or enough space to collapse comfortably if he passed out.

The table, three chairs, the officer and him occupied most of the floor space. On the walls below the camera, perched a clock that gave the time as twenty to two and a poster on citizen obligations to cooperate with the police.

If he stretched out both arms, his hands would be only centimetres from each wall, he guessed.

'It was all just a horrible accident. I am so sorry. It's my entire fault and I feel devastated that I've put someone in hospital.'

'What happened?'

'I was trying to move forward to be first across the road once the lights changed, and I bumped her.'

The officer scribbled in his notebook. 'Why the rush?' He quizzed Dom without making eye contact.

'I had errands to run and I got impatient. People are always dawdling, you know. I ran forward and she moved to the side and that's when I knocked her.'

The pen stopped moving. 'She moved to the side? So it was her fault?' A disbelieving look darkened the officer's face.

Dom's arms madly waved. 'Oh no—I didn't mean that. I take that back. It was definitely my fault. I meant to say I was thinking I could squeeze past her and I misjudged, and I fell against her and I couldn't stop myself.'

Dom's grimace was genuine as he pictured her colliding against the taxi and crumpling to the rainy ground. Her black jacket flapping along the white body of the car was engraved in his memory. The account he gave of his contact with the woman and her fall was as accurate and detailed as he remembered it.

'I couldn't believe it. I thought she was dead. Life flashed before me.'

'I'm sure it did.'

Dom went quiet. 'What's going to happen to me?'

'Let's get your statement first. You must've been running incredibly fast. That's quite dangerous in such a busy space. And all because you're impatient?'

'Yes.'

'Then what happened?'

Dom blew out a puff of air. 'It's a blur from there.' He wagged his head in confusion. 'I remember coming to.'

'You were knocked out?'

'I mean I seemed to wake from a daze. I was sitting on the pavement and people were asking if I was ok. Then I ran. I'm sorry to say I ran as fast as I could. I freaked out and I ran. I—'

'You've said people were helping you. So why did you run?'

The officer wasn't looking up, but Dom stared at him, willing him to lift his head. He said, 'I lost my twin recently and I'm not myself. It's no excuse, but I'm not myself. That's all I can say. And he was struck by a car. When I saw her hitting the road, all I could think of was—my brother—my brother's injur—'

Dom rocked in his seat to escape the image of Donald in the hospital bed. He tried to change the subject. 'What's going to happen to me?'

'Where did you run to?'

'Home. I paced around and around and then I came here.' He rubbed both cheeks vigorously. 'God, that feels so much better talking about it. I feel terrible for her, but a weight has lifted—if I'm to be honest.'

He placed both palms on the table to signal the interview would be going to a deeper level of frankness.

'I am here to face whatever you dish up. I came here without a lawyer and I've got nothing to hide. Use whatever you want against me.'

'What made you come here?'

'I knew I'd made a mistake leaving the accident and I wanted to correct it.'

'Have you ever been in trouble with the police before?'

'Never.' He wanted to shake his head for emphasis, but something held it steady. A prolonged silence sat between them. Dom felt it awkward, but the policeman's expression was neutral while he wrote his notes. The longing to ask again what would happen to him was burning his insides, but he held off.

As if reading Dom's mind, the policeman answered his question. 'We still need to interview the woman. We also need to assess her injuries. If they are very serious, you'll be charged with reckless behaviour. In fact, you probably will be. Rushing through city streets clearly brings its dangers. We may also charge you with leaving the scene of a traffic accident, even though you weren't in a vehicle.'

Dom worked to stop a smile forming. Minor charges really, he told himself.

'And if her condition gets worse, we'll consider further charges, more serious ones. You made some poor choices today …' Seeing Dom's eyes glaze over, the policeman paused, allowing Dom time to bring his attention back. 'Mr Tolen?'

Dom sat up and looked at the officer.

'My book—did anybody hand in a book? I dropped it there.'

'No.' The policeman's throat cleared in two sharp hacks. 'I'd say people were focusing on more important things.'

Chastised, Dom nodded, his hands drawing together in his lap to regain self-control.

The officer continued. 'When we get to speak with her, we'll explain to her she can look at suing you for compensation. Undoubtedly, her lawyer will tell her the same thing.'

'I hope she goes through with it. That will certainly ease my guilt.' Dom's voice trailed off and the policeman's face showed nothing close to sympathy.

'And you're sure you don't know her?'

'I'm almost certain. I saw her face for a split second. I'd be amazed to find out we know each other. Truly.' In a soothing rub, his scheming hands comforted one another.

'You're free to go. Come with me.'

Dom's face radiated, then he pulled back a little and his mouth straightened. 'Thank you, sir.'

The sergeant stepped into the corridor.

Dom said, 'The grief over my brother is too recent. That's why I ran away. Too overwhelmed by the physical pain of everything.'

'Mr Tolen'—the officer turned around to face him and from his tone, it sounded like he was going to tell

Dom to shut up—'you've had a major shock. Don't be alone this evening. Go see family or friends.'

Three minutes later, Dom was on the street.

The blanket of cloud was breaking up, helping patches of blue peak through. The ground was drying out and the wind had started settling.

Dom felt like sitting quietly for a time and Hyde Park was close. He found a dry seat on a café terrace and with Elizabeth Street extending in front of him, small and unnoticed, he assessed what he had done.

Things had gone terribly bad. He'd lost the imposter and caused an accident, and now the police had his name. It was not a good time to get police attention. Being caught up in something and not having full control unsettled him.

Had the sergeant believed him? Dom thought so. The policeman had been upfront with him about the possible consequences of his actions, and he had also thanked Dom for coming in voluntarily. He hadn't pushed too hard with his questions on Dom running to the lights. But that could easily change, he warned himself.

And the poor woman he had pushed into the road! It hurt him physically to think about what he had done, and her injuries and Donald's mixed in his mind. Her bruised face became Donald's wounded head. Her lacerated hands turned into Donald's broken limbs.

There was Dympna to worry about too. She had helped him think things through and act quickly enough to avoid a worse situation. He was lucky to have her in his life. But she had crossed a line. He had almost killed someone today and she had helped him cover his tracks. If the woman died, Dympna's help was all the more serious. It would affect her professional status. An altered version of her business card appeared in his mind. *Accessory after the fact* wouldn't look good.

Dom was struck at how easily she had set herself on to the task, efficient in her devotion and motherly in her loyalty. What would it be like meeting her next time? Would he feel embarrassed? Would she? Would she ask him to promise to keep her misdeed a secret? And what had she put in his veins?

A grimy ibis strutted by pulling Dom from his disquieting thoughts.

The streets were pumping. How freely people scuttled between the cars and trucks, pausing on painted lines as if the white strip granted immunity.

He remembered he had turned off his phone. When it came on, he saw a missed call from Harry. The policeman's advice echoed in his mind, so he dialled his friend's number.

'Come over. Just bring you. I'll cook us something.'

Dom agreed. He pushed himself off the bench, brushed the back of his jacket and trousers, and hailed a taxi. When one stopped, he peered inside. Luckily, it was a different driver to the one who had earlier taken him to Dympna's.

V

The ping of the email lifted Maggie high in her chair with fright. She was on edge anyway doing the thing Dom had warned her against—searching the database for any sign of her colleague having rorted the system.

The message was from Wayne Thomson advising her he wouldn't make it to the two-thirty meeting.

Maggie cursed and quit the accounts database. She marched round to the west side of the building, chin up as she passed partitions and plants. At Wayne's office, she inhaled and leaned in. He was eating at his desk.

'Please come. I really need you there. Sylvie is going to push for those changes.'

'No she won't—she's not going either.' He rested his sandwich on the wrapping nestled between him and the keyboard.

Maggie sighed. 'Well, I still need you there. Ian will push Sylvie's case for her.'

'Mags, I'm snowed under and I'm not around next week. I could really do with—'

His mobile beeped and before he had time to speak, it beeped again. Another message arrived.

He gestured to it. 'See what I mean? I can—'

'Please.' She hoped her cutting in would reveal more her desperation, less so rudeness.

Wayne ran his eye over the pile of papers on his desk and looked at her. 'We've got to keep it quick.'

Maggie smiled at him. 'I'll let Ian know you're coming. See you in a while.' She returned to her desk taking a small detour by Ian's office.

He had his back to her, facing the window. His shoulders tensed as she spoke, but he made no movement to face her. 'Ian? Wayne's coming to the meeting after all—just letting you know.'

'Thanks,' he mumbled.

'See you soon.' Maggie slipped away.

VI

Dom rang the doorbell with a free finger, careful not to let the weight of the Thai food burst through the bag. The hot food warmed his hands while he waited for Harry to let him in.

'I told you I'd cook something. Is that Thai?' Still in his work uniform minus the shoes, Harry batted Dom inside.

'A late lunch, early dinner. Call it what you like.'

'I wanted to cook. It gets rid of stress.'

'Not for those eating it. Serve please.'

Dom rested the food on top of a magazine on the dining table, removed his jacket and dropped on the sofa. 'I've had an awful day, mate. Awful.'

'Were you really in a police station? I thought you were kidding.' Harry disappeared and came back with plates and cutlery.

The food was still steaming when he handed it to Dom, who took the plate but not the beer. Harry drank from the can.

'I'm not up for telling you everything—way too painful. But I caused an accident and pushed a woman into the road and a car knocked into her.'

Harry had begun eating the fishcake starter and his eyeballs seemed to take on its circumference. 'You're kidding me.' He saw Dom's weary face. 'You're not kidding me. Oh shit.'

Dom repeated everything he had learned from the police about the accident. Dympna was the only other person who knew the real reason he had been running towards the woman. It was best it stayed that way, for the moment.

With his usual insensitivity, Harry asked, 'Have you checked to see if you're on the tele?'

The television lit up and Harry found a news channel. Perched on a stool at the end of the sofa, Harry wolfed down his dinner and drank his beer, eyeing the box.

Dom picked at his food, looking up only to give a scowl to the screen. 'Can I have some water, please? It won't make the news—there's no footage of it and she didn't die. People must get grazed by cars all the time.'

'Grazed? You're evil, Tolen.'

Harry leaned over and hit his friend on the arm. 'If it doesn't come on now, I'll check it again later and in the morning. Get it yourself.'

Dom stepped away for a glass of water and moments later came to stand behind his friend.

Harry muted the television, ready to hear more about Dom's day. 'Go on then. Tell me more.' Harry launched his commands over one shoulder, a raised bushy eyebrow capping an eager eye.

'Not much more to say.'

'Bullshit. You've told me nothing.'

Dom shrugged and ate his food in peace, as Harry didn't press for details.

With one leg twisted up on to the sofa to relax and get Harry's attention, Dom said, 'I'll tell you what led to me being in the city this morning. I have a lot of evidence that suggests Donald was—'

'Fucking hell, Dom. Look!'

Harry swooped on the remote control for the volume.

Dom spun round half-expecting to see footage of him hurling himself into the poor woman. But the swarm of police cars on a residential street told him a different scene was playing out, a scene that brought him immense relief.

'It's Phil,' shouted Harry. The surprise made his voice go so high it was almost unrecognisable.

'Who?'

'The dealer. The bloody dealer you know—Phil!'

A female reporter's voice burst from the television as they watched house-proud Phil being led out of his terrace shirtless and handcuffed.

'Dramatic scenes in Sydney's eastern suburbs this afternoon, when a suspected cocaine and heroin dealer was arrested and charged with numerous offences over the sale of the illicit substances. The alleged dealer, Phillip Scotland, claims to have been set up by police.'

The reporter's voice was replaced by the events on the suburban street. Bare-chested Phil spoke outside his mansion.

'It's a set-up.'

One word flashed across Dom's mind.

Pruning.

On the screen, Phil was spitting at the cameras. As officers guided his head inside the police car, Phil leant back and raised both feet on to the car body to prevent the police bundling him inside. All of it captured on camera, Phil used powerful legs to push himself back, and the three men stumbled away coming to rest on the ground. Phil head butted the officer closest to him as they staggered to their feet in a wild dance.

Harry and Dom exchanged a look of amazement, which made Harry appear younger and Dom older. They turned back to the television.

The second officer pounced on Phil from behind and a third officer joined in, dragging the dealer down. Seconds later, Phil was flattened into the back of the car, his shouts reduced to muffles as the car doors, one by one, closed around him.

When the next bulletin started, Dom and Harry's eyes met. A finger pointing at the television and a grin formed Dom's question.

Harry reacted. 'Don't look at me like that—I didn't dob him in.'

With Dom's arms lifting to ask for calm, Harry turned back to the screen. The perplexed and fearful expression lingered on his youthful face. Frowning, he looked at Dom, but turned away before Dom could see.

'There goes your party line.' Dom avoided Harry's gaze as he delivered the blow. 'That was close. You could have been there at the time buying something.'

Harry nodded in shocked agreement, his head bobbing up and down thoughtfully.

Dom gulped. 'Your number's in his phone.'

'Yours too. The police will call us, won't they?' Harry crossed his arms high on his chest.

'Don't worry. So we rang him a couple of times. It means nothing.'

'I'll say he was a friend.'

'That's worse. The police will be after his supplier, not his one-off customers. How many times did you visit him? Be honest.'

'Once. Just once.' Harry stared absently at the screen, which he had muted again. He shrugged at nothing, at the arrest. 'He was all right. A bit annoying.'

'Annoying? He was an arsehole. You can find another one.'

Harry drank his beer. 'It's a risky business, I tell ya. Who'd do it, eh?' He stood to tidy his plate.

'They get paid very well for their risks, I'm sure,' Dom said, holding out his empty cup for a refill. 'I guess they get greedy or careless. We love to complicate life, don't we? The trick is to keep things simple.'

'Which one was Phil then—greedy or careless?' Harry eyed Dom as if his response was critical.

Dom shrugged to show he didn't care enough about Phil to answer. His mind was somewhere else. Dom's eyes, glassy and distant, held disdain, and this made his face droop. 'I wish I could go back in time to a few weeks ago. I wish I could have done one or two things differently.'

Harry didn't ask Dom to explain. Dom's look told him he had no intention of clarifying the comment.

VII

Maggie, Wayne and Ian were huddled around a circular table in what could have doubled for a broom cupboard, where they were analysing the division plan they were to submit in the coming days. Like a metronome marking their meeting, Wayne's phone beeped them through the agenda.

On top of that, Ian had told them to expect interruptions as he had a sick relative in need of attention and he could receive a call or two. The vacant look he wore, when Wayne and Maggie spoke of parts of the document he hadn't contributed to, went unchallenged.

It was when Wayne was questioning Ian about his sections that Ian's phone lit up and a Pink Floyd ringtone filled the room. Ian excused himself and was outside in a flash.

Without a hint of irritation, Wayne huffed, more at the challenges of the task than the interruptions. 'I hope it's no too serious. He seems rattled.'

'Yes.' Maggie pretended to read a section of text.

Wayne's look lingered on her. 'Are you all right? You seem preoccupied.'

'Me? I think we all are. Everyone's—'

She was cut short by Ian bursting in. 'Sorry, gotta go.' He swept up his things. 'We'll continue this next week.' He was too quick to notice the irritation on Wayne's face.

Wayne said, 'I don't need this now, Maggie. Why we didn't cancel—I don't know.' He flipped forward a page on his copy of the draft plan. 'I'm away next week. The risk analysis needs some work. Viv won't approve it unless it brings in the Ipso project. So why don't you get her team to comment on that.'

When he looked over at Maggie, he noticed her steely eyes transfixed on nothing. 'Maggie?'

She stood up and squeezed her way to the door. Wayne went to speak but he was silenced with a hand. 'Wait here. I'll be back in a sec.'

He lowered his pen and sat back. The door closed leaving him alone in the meeting room. He occupied himself with his phone messages. 'I'm only here because of you.' Maggie wouldn't have heard him.

Out in the corridor, she moved quickly. She raced around to the north side of the building and stopped abruptly but quietly. Unseen, she watched Ian on his feet at his workstation as he filled a briefcase with personal items. He ripped the one photo from the wall and tossed it in the case. In went the tablet. He checked for anything else around him. That was when he spotted her.

He stopped moving, but only for a second. They stared at each other and neither spoke. Realising she was there to watch, not to intervene, he carried on gathering his things.

He looked up again and Maggie's eyes were still on him. She hadn't moved. His briefcase clicked shut under his grasp. He grabbed for his jacket and headed calmly to the exit.

Maggie trailed him keeping a safe eight metres or so behind. When he called the lift, she hovered at a distance, ignoring Belinda's greeting from the front desk on her left.

Ian looked down to the carpet, as though her gaze could harm him. Even the ping of the lift arriving didn't break her stare.

When he stepped inside the lift, she moved forward to stand in front of the doors.

Head down, his back hit the wall.

She could see his chest moving from the pounding of his heart.

In his final moments in Subiaco, Ian lifted his eyes and returned Maggie's gaze. They glared at each other until the lift doors closed between them.

Maggie sprung into action and sped round to the meeting room, almost cracking open the door. The rattle of glass walls shook Wayne from his messaging but Maggie's grunting made him freeze. He knew to stay out of the way.

She snatched her phone off the desk. 'Meeting's over,' she said in a puff and vanished again.

Wayne uttered something in response, but the slamming door drowned it out.

She dashed to a quiet area near a service lift and called Dom.

VIII

He stepped out of Harry's flat and as he turned to say farewell, his phone sounded. Quietly, Harry waved him off and closed the front door, leaving Dom in the stairwell to speak privately. The tiled walls had the opposite effect, amplifying his words, bouncing them around the building's interior, making it sound as though two of him were talking.

'Where are you?' Maggie cried. 'He's leaving. Ian's running away. I've just seen him packing everything up. He's going, Dom.'

She blurted out what she had just witnessed. 'He knows I know—I could tell. We've got to go to the police. He's got to be stopped.'

'Screw that. The fucker's mine.' Dom bounded down the stairs and crashed through the foyer doors, his ankle not as strong as he needed it to be, despite the relief brought on by Dympna's secret hit.

The evening was cold and starry. The earlier gales had blown away the clouds to reveal a twinkling canvas under which the night's events would unfold.

Dom sprinted as fast as he could across the road to hail a cab still speaking to Maggie.

'And his address?'

'But—'

'Did you get his address? I don't want advice on getting the police involved.'

'I can't get into the office.' She told him of her several attempts to access Vanessa's room, of trying the locked door, of getting Jamie out of the way, of hunts for a key. No luck.

'Break in—there's no time to lose.'

'I know he's in the northern beaches somewhere. Dee Why or Brookvale.'

'That sounds about right, but break in. I'll go that way now. You try for the address while I'm heading there.' He paused. Where he was expecting assent, all Maggie gave was silence.

The urgency in Dom's voice intensified. 'I need that address, Maggie. Please. You're right—he's leaving the country.' Dom's mind went back to the morning's meeting in the café, the comments about getting away. 'In the café, she told me she was going on holiday.' The certainty rang out in his voice. 'It's today.' Standing on a corner, he scoured for an empty taxi.

'I'll see what I can find.'

A burst of energy swept through him at hearing her promise of help. An approaching taxi responded to his wave, and he yanked the door open and spoke before he was inside. 'I'm making a quick stop at Centennial Park. Then Brookvale.' After checking for the second time that day, Dom was relieved not to recognise the driver.

The car sped off. They soon stopped outside Dom's block, where the car's headlights bathed the driveway in yellow-white light. As a dark shape, Dom leapt out. 'Don't move.'

'You owe me money. I'm going nowhere.'

Dom tore up the steps to his unit. His heart pounded and his dry throat ached. He turned light after light on as he zoomed through the place, coming to an abrupt halt in the hallway and smacking his hands to his head. 'Think.'

The green flicking light on the answer machine caught his eye. It could be important. He stretched over to play the message, cranked up the volume and carried on into the back area. The speed at which he darted into his bedroom saw him slamming into the wall, his face just in line with the painting that hid his safe. With a caring toss, the canvas landed on the bed.

The machine sang out and he recognised the voice immediately.

'This is a message for Dominic. This is Rita from Brain Food. We have good news about your September delivery. Your puzzle will be on time after all. I just thought I'd let you know. See you then, Mr Tolen.' The machine went quiet.

'One less thing to worry about,' he said, spinning the dial of the wall safe. It opened without a sound. The second-hand gun was on the top shelf, with a box of bullets next to it. Trembling, he checked the chamber was full. The cold gun throbbed in his warm hands. He drove it down the back of his trousers. The stark difference in temperature between his skin and the weapon told him exactly where it sat. If the piece shifted, he would feel it.

A long breath helped him collect his thoughts. After locking the safe, he returned the painting to its hook. He stepped away admiring the pretence.

In the front room, he marched around. Biting adrenalin soared through his veins, making his movements jerky and unnatural. He had to go through with it.

A glance at his watch revealed it was quarter past five. He stormed to the front door, turning the last light off.

The door received the strongest of yanks and cool air rushed in. Dom was taken back.

Two men were standing there lit by a dirty balcony strip light. They surely heard the noise of complete surprise that had escaped from Dom's mouth. One of the men was reaching for the bell but stopped when he saw Dom in the shadows.

'Good evening Mr Tolen. I'm Detective Inspector Nyugen and this is Constable Porter.' The two men stood right outside blocking his way.

Dom squinted to get a better look without turning on any lights and fought hard not to shift on the spot, agitated and impatient. The desire to slam the door closed and lock the gun in the safe was colossal.

'We'd like to come in for a quick chat. May we?'

Dom cursed under his breath and made a point of looking at his watch. His hand went up to dry his sweaty forehead.

The detective smiled when he pulled on the security screen and it opened for him. 'Ah good.' He peered round the mesh frame into the unit. 'This looks cosy.'

From the darkness, Dom saw the detective turn and grin at his colleague.

10 | Ruth

|

Maggie stormed into Vanessa's office area and was greeted by Jamie's miserable expression. As she skidded to a halt, he lowered his mobile and it slipped into the rucksack protruding from under his desk. Sitting upright and with both hands free—a rarity—he took the chance to fix his fringe.

'Get up,' gnarled Maggie. 'I need your help.'

'What now?' Jamie clambered to his feet.

The sound of Maggie's quickening footsteps made him lift his head. Without hair or hands to obscure his view, he saw Maggie launch herself against the locked door she had tried opening earlier.

There was a loud crack. The lock giving way slightly made Maggie bounce back from the frame and Jamie's rigid jaw plummet.

Maggie retreated and pointed at the door. 'Your turn.' Without moving, Jamie stared at her. His body moved back and forth on the spot as if debating whether to freeze or help out.

'Hurry.' Maggie's scream spurred the youngster to act.

Jamie converted his hesitant rocking into momentum and stepped round the desk. His face adopted an aggressive slant as he shouldered the door three times in succession, brushing Maggie to the side. After a spray of splinters, he stumbled sideways into Vanessa's office.

'Bravo.' Maggie moved into the office and nudged him. 'I need an address. Where are the surnames starting with R?'

'How the fuck do I know?' He sang a screech of hysteria.

Maggie spun in a circle looking for a likely place where Vanessa stored the employee files. The personal files had to be in one of the filing cabinets on the far wall. She wagged a finger at them. 'One of these, right?'

Jamie shrugged and stepped forward with her to start pulling at the drawers. 'I haven't used these cabinets yet. I don't know what's in them.'

They tried all the drawers and met each other in the middle of the row. They were all locked and they would need a crowbar to work them open.

'Shit.' She wiped her forehead. 'We need the keys.' She looked at her watch. It was five thirty.

'We've got to move quickly.' She guessed that alphabetical files would place the R surnames a few drawers in. She pointed to the second filing cabinet. 'Let's get this one open.'

'How?'

'We'll just pull at the drawers until they give and chuck something in the mechanism to break it.' She began tugging at the cabinet and the little movement she caused suggested the cabinets were packed.

They yanked at the second drawer together and bit by bit, it lost its taut shape. After a minute of tugging, they could see inside to the hanging folders, and soon after, the folders and documents in the hanging folders were visible. They carried on yanking a few seconds more. Maggie pulled on the buckled drawer while Jamie squinted inside.

'What's the name on the file?'

'Watson,' he said after a moment's hesitation.

Maggie released the drawer and stepped back. 'Good. That means it's that one or that one.'

They both wiped their foreheads.

'Let's try this top one. It should be easier now that we've weakened the other. They're all connected.'

They dived into the task, drawing on their remaining energy. Minutes later, the top drawer squealed open when Maggie pulled on it with reddened hands.

Jamie moved aside while Maggie's ringing fingers flicked through the files. They had the right drawer. She skimmed the nametags of the hanging folders.

Radcliffe. Ram. Read.

I Read.

'Got it.' She clutched the file and yanked with the last of her might. As she pulled back, the adjoining files spilled out on to the carpet. She smiled at Jamie.

'Good work. Can you get this back to some sort of normality before you go?' She moved to the outer office and turned to him. 'Remove your fingerprints too.'

Horrified, Jamie looked up from clearing the papers off the floor. 'What? But you—'

'Just kidding. Thanks for helping. I'll deal with all this.' She ran off.

Jamie surveyed the ransacked office. He had some work to do, but first things first. He retrieved his phone and earphones from his bag under the desk and photographed the mess he had helped make. The phone's music kicked in and he started humming while he shared the photos online.

With a caption posted about how enjoyable the smash up had been, and after misspelling *destruction*, he cranked up the volume and cheerfully started cleaning up, knowing that by the time he finished he'd have a handful of comments and likes to check on.

II

Dom sucked air through his teeth, mimicking a shonky seller facing a demanding customer.

'It's not the best time, to be honest. I'm on my way out. Can I come to the station later where we can chat uninterrupted?' Dom blocked the entrance to his flat hindering the inspector's advance. 'I need to see a work mate before he flies out.'

Dom realised that was the second time that day he had explained to a police officer he had been hurrying. That could work in his favour—he usually rushed around on errands and that morning had been no different.

'This won't take long.' The policeman knocked Dom backwards into the unit and stepped inside with his colleague trailing. 'I'm sure you're keen to know more about the woman you almost killed.'

An intense heat swept through Dom and a clenched jaw stopped him from saying something inflammatory. The cold steel at his lower back reminded him now was not the time to get arrested. If they found the gun, he could forget about seeing Ian any time soon.

Dom shuffled backwards into his flat, talking as he moved. 'Two minutes—that's all. I mean it.' He looked out the window at the taxi below and back to the detective. 'That's mine waiting.'

'We won't keep you,' said the inspector, glancing around.

The three of them stopped in the centre of the room. Dom didn't point to chairs and neither policeman made a move to sit.

Inspector Nyugen took out a card, wiped it clean and handed it to Dom, who threw it down without looking at it. But he was too hasty and the card skated across the lacquered surface and dropped to the floor, where it had to stay. He couldn't retrieve it without risking the gun protruding under his clothes. Leaving it where it was, he turned back to the inspector in time to see his face change. The cocky friendliness had gone. In its place were folded arms and a surly expression.

'We only wanted to check how you are after today's incident. You've bounced back obviously, but the woman is still in hospital.'

'I feel terrible about it. I told your colleague.'

'And you're sure you don't know her.'

'That's what I said. I didn't get a good look at her, but it was an accident.' The anxiety the police saw plastered on Dom's face was less from his mistake that morning and more from the urgency to get to Ian.

A car horn sounded two long beeps confirming Dom's unpaid taxi was still there. He hoped the driver wouldn't leave. His heart thundered. He couldn't lose time flagging another taxi.

'Let's go over what happened this morning.' The inspector searched himself for his pad and the constable stood at the ready to take notes. He was about to clarify what he wanted when Dom launched into an efficient account of the incident, blurted out in small bites.

'I was in the city. On some errands. I was rushing around …'

After twenty seconds, he had explained everything and he finished off with his rehearsed phrase.

'And I freaked out and I just ran.'

His flat hand cutting the air symbolised him fleeing the scene. The message was clear—he had covered everything and they should go.

Inspector Nyugen lunged at him and, instinctively, Dom jerked back in defence, banging his shoulders against the wall. The inspector grabbed Dom's shirt and paused, half-expecting—almost wanting—Dom to wrench himself free.

'We want the truth about this, Mr Tolen. Did you know her?'

'I've told you—not that I know of.'

Inspector Nyugen's face was inches from Dom's chin and dry mouth. If he made a wrong move, the lunatic might seize him and find the gun.

'What's her name? You haven't told me her name yet.' Dom kept the inspector occupied by asking a question, hoping that would stop from assault.

'Salthouse. Susan Salthouse.' The inspector fixed his gaze on Dom's eyes, as if waiting to catch a subtle reaction or flicker of recognition. 'Was she a girlfriend you wanted to get rid of?' His grip relaxed and Dom's shirt left his fingers.

'No.' Dom slid along the wall away from the inspector. 'I don't know anyone by that name.'

'It turns out her husband is a police officer. He's based in the shire.'

'You're joking me.'

He wagged a finger and again moved towards Dom, who retreated. 'If you were having an affair with her, we will find out. Your account of all this is unconvincing and we'll keep digging to see what comes up.'

'I understand. Please go now.' His words came out cautiously, but he raised his arms, palms out and digits flapping, motioning for them to go.

Nyugen spun around in search of a place to sit. He settled himself into the centre of the sofa and while he stretched his arms along its crest, he missed Dom tutting. 'Your name keeps coming up.' He ran his hand over the cushion as if admiring the fabric.

'Your brother died recently.' His colleague spoke for the first time, his voice shaky but loud. 'A traffic accident on an intersection in the city.'

'That's right.' Dom's forehead creased with irritation. 'Are you here to arrest me?' An image of Ian in a plane taking off flashed through his mind.

'Today you caused a traffic accident on an intersection in the city,' said Nyugen.

'I was nowhere near the city when my brother was hit. That's an awful thing to suggest. And when this Salthouse woman wakes up, she'll confirm what I've just told you.'

'Her family said she doesn't know you.'

'Well, there you go. Some evidence for you.' Dom pointed towards the front door.

'We've spoken to your family too. We got the same story—you don't know one another.'

'What?' Dom's eyes bulged. He didn't register the long beep coming from his waiting taxi. 'What did Camille tell you?'

The policemen shot a glance at each other.

'For god's sake, what did she say?' The irritation evident in his voice surprised the three of them.

The inspector motioned to Dom's forehead. 'Are you nervous? You're sweating.'

Dom wiped away the signs of nerves and inspected his damp fingertips. 'More annoyed than anything.'

'Your sister told us she's never heard of the woman. So at the moment, we can't see a connection between you and your victim.' Inspector Nyugen pushed himself off the sofa and stood up. 'Are you okay if we use that word—victim?'

'I don't know her and I wasn't trying to hurt her. But use whatever word you like.' Dom creased his face. 'Why did you go to my sister? I don't unde—'

'We didn't—she came to us. As I said, your name keeps coming up.'

Camille! She'd gone to the police after all. He was desperate to know what she had told them, but he couldn't appear worried. And his impatience was growing—he had to leave now. He paced around the room keeping at least an arm's reach from the two policemen.

'It's such an odd coincidence. You will agree, Dominic. About a hundred pedestrians a year are involved in traffic accidents in the centre. These accidents almost never concern pedestrians on the pavement *falling* in front of a car'—his hand swivelled in front of him to signify a body collapsing—'yet two take place in the space of weeks, and you're connected to both of them?' He shook his head with exaggerated amazement.

'Wherever this is heading, can't we do it tomorrow?'

'Your sister tells us you think your brother was pushed.'

'I told my sister lots of things and I thought she'd understand I was not coping with Donald's death.' Dom lowered his head. A fuzzy mix of emotions swirled around—anger with Camille for sharing his suspicions, frustration towards Nyugen for starting another line of questioning, and shame at needing to deny what he knew to be true.

'Just me grieving for him. Coming to terms with it all.' He waved it away. 'It seems so ridiculous now.'

Dom's mobile started ringing in his back pocket and he pulled it out carefully. Maggie.

'Police are here. I'll get to you as soon as I can. They're going now.' He ended the call and laid the phone on the table.

Nyugen pointed to the doorway leading to the other wing of the unit. 'Which one is Donald's room?' He stepped forward. Dom made a slight move to block him but thought better of it.

'Last door on the left. It's in a bit of a state.' Dom calmed himself as the inspector's steps echoed along the hall. It's no crime to smash up your own home, he told himself. It meant nothing.

He listened for a profanity or a rush of footsteps while he eyed the constable waiting obediently by the table. Only the swing of Donald's bedroom door suggested anyone was in that part of the unit.

Heavy deliberate footsteps sounded after a short while. When he reappeared, the inspector was staring into his pad, which he didn't look up from.

'Renovating?'

'You're funny.'

'What happened?'

'I got really pissed off and took it out on Donald. Well, Donald's things. Smashed the place to bits, I did.' Dom chuckled nervously. 'That was my therapy. I was pissed with Donald for getting hit and dying. If only he'd not fallen into the road.'

'Quite a temper that.'

'Have you lost a twin?' Dom's question hung in the room unanswered. He pressed the inspector some more. 'I'm over here. I asked if you've lost a twin.'

Nyugen nodded to his constable but spoke to Dom. 'Some good news and some bad news.'

Dom took this as a sign they were heading off.

'The good news is I'm going to look into your brother's death.'

'Thank you.'

'The bad news is I'll be making you a suspect.'

Dom kissed his teeth. 'That's not news, is it?'

Nyugen repeated his comment. 'I'm making you a suspect.'

Dom waved his hands in frustration. 'What more can I say? I have nothing to hide.'

'Yes, you keep telling us that, so often it looks like you do have something to hide.'

As Nyugen asked his next question about the axe, the taxi horn rose up to the flat.

Dom ran to the window and screamed out. 'Don't go. One minute.' Dom's manners deserted him and his voice exuded rudeness. 'I got it from a friend. His name's Josh. And yes, I borrowed it for the sole purpose of smashing that room to bits. You need to go right now.'

The inspector's face lit up. 'Josh Bauer?'

'Ye—es.'

'Your sister has reported him missing. She says you were the last person to have contact with him. Where is he?'

'For god's sake.'

Dom tore round the table to gently pick up the inspector's card from the floor, cupping the small of his back as though nursing lumbar pain. Upright, he snatched for his mobile, dialled with one hand and held the card up. His spoke into the voicemail system fast.

'Josh, it's Dom. The police think your dead. I'm sure they think I killed you. So I need you to call Inspector Nyugen straight away. Identify yourself and tell him you're not dead.' He looked up from the inspector as he finished the message. 'Thanks for the axe. It came in handy.'

He boomed the inspector's mobile number into the phone and hung up. The policemen received their last command. 'Now get out.'

As they moved to go, he followed and still with some distance between them stopped to watch them leave the unit. The tension in his body eased when the customary clunk of the front door sounded behind them. The door was locked.

He spun round whipping the gun from its hiding place under his clothing. He thumped the air and, through clenched teeth, swore repeatedly, the muffled profanities almost inaudible.

Another beep from the taxi below spurned him forward.

He bolted to the safe and sent the painting into the air and landing on the bed, and he unlocked the small steel door. He had no choice but to return the gun to the safe, to leave unarmed. Shooting Ian was out of the question now. He whacked the wall next to the safe.

If he was going to beat the hell out of him, it would need to be with something he got hold of at Ian's.

Dom returned the gun, dampened by his sweat, to the top shelf and closed the door. He caught sight of the compact parcel pushed to the back of the lower shelf, partially concealed by the shadow of the interior ledge. He waivered.

The door hovered open less than a centimetre. He toyed with what to do with the contents. An idea formed. It was risky, incredibly risky, but if successful, it would blow Ian's plans apart.

He yanked the tiny door open and the stone cold safe swallowed his arm.

III

Dom had to get rid of the taxi. The inspector would have noted its registration and he couldn't risk being followed. Not now. He'd take it part of the way, then get another.

'Thanks for waiting,' he said jumping in.

A promise of a large tip seemed to appease the driver but when he pulled away, he growled, his eyes on the dark road. 'Put your seatbelt on this time. You're trouble.'

Dom obeyed and excused himself to make a call. He activated the last dialled number and waited for the line to connect. Josh's voice mail came on again.

'Josh, the police have left my place. They're keen to speak to you, but I haven't told them anything about Donald being at my office and his plan.'

His hand caressed his forehead. 'Erm, if you can think of a way of not mentioning that just yet, that would be good. I need the police to leave me alone for a while. And while you're at it, why not give Camille and Robin a call? I'm quite sure it's safe for you now—after what I found out today. These guys aren't coming after you. And no doubt, Camille and Robin would like to hear from you. Don't go into any explanations—just hellos.'

Dom disconnected and straight away called Maggie.

She picked up after one ring. 'What did the police want?'

'Complications. Thinking I was involved in Donald's mess.' His deliberate use of vague language would keep the taxi driver in the dark. 'Two of them turned up, one of them a total arsehole, pushing me around and talking shit.'

'Are you okay?'

'Yep. Tell me you have the address. Give me some good news.'

'I have the address—I'm giving you good news.'

'Yes! Where would I be without you?' The surface of the road and the adrenalin rocketing through his veins sent Dom bouncing in his seat.

Maggie continued. 'The office is wrecked, but I'll deal with that. Where are you?'

'In a taxi, about to cross the bridge. I fucking hope I'm in time.'

Dom noticed Maggie didn't respond. She was less keen for him to catch Ian. 'Are you there?' he asked, without needing to.

She told him the address and confirmed she had sent it to him in a text too. 'How long will it take you to get there?'

'At this time of day, ages.'

'And what will you do when you get there? You can't knock on the door.'

The ludicrousness in her voice irritated him. 'Why not?'

'Because they'll kill you, Dom.'

'Ian didn't try to silence you today.'

'That's different—I didn't try to stop him going. I merely watched him leaving. If he thinks you're there to get in the way, he'll kill you. We know that, Dom.' The phone went quiet. 'You ought to call the police.'

Dom assessed where things were at for him. In the darkened taxi, splashed by the throw of lights from cars and streetlamps dancing past, honesty found him.

He admitted he had stepped along a path that could not involve the police. Ian—he was sure—was about to leave the country, having siphoned off huge amounts of Subiaco money. He had to act quickly to stop him and he could make him pay dearly for what he had done to Donald. 'There's no time. Ian's not coming back.'

'Listen to me, Dom—for once. You're blinded by revenge. Let it go. You can still stop him leaving.'

Dom huffed loudly into the phone. 'I'll call you back in five.' He squirrelled the phone away and asked the driver to pull over.

Military Road was full of angry, erratic traffic.

With the fare paid, including the promised hefty tip, he leapt onto the pavement. A minute later, he was in another taxi. 'Fern Park Road, Brookvale. As fast as you can.'

The driver motioned to the lanes ahead. 'You're joking, right?' In his rear view mirror, he checked out Dom, who moved his eyes out of the reach of the reflection.

Dom called Maggie, who dived straight into a question. 'So what was in the text message?'

Dom was glad not to be fighting with her about his plans.

'I'd read it loads of times before. I'll send it to you now.' He pulled up the message and forwarded it to her.

'Got it.'

He continued. 'So I got that message after lunch that day. Donald never used punctuation and if you capitalise the letters, it takes on a whole new meaning.'

He read out the text.

```
Been checking out
yr system u know
me i read varied
cypress accounts
whats going on
there
```

'I read varied Cypress accounts. With proper capitals, it could mean *I Read varied the Cypress accounts.* Ian varied the accounts!'

Maggie said, 'Bloody hell, Dom. Donald wasn't commenting on what he'd done. He was telling you what Ian had been doing.'

'Donald was a genius with technology. It wouldn't have taken him long.' Dom's mind filled with images of Donald carrying out the entire plan months ahead, premiums being paid, false claims going through and large amounts of money landing in the same accounts.

One day for sure, Donald's transactions would have ended up on an audit report and Dom would have had to answer for them. It was too painful and he pushed from his mind a future that would never arrive.

'Then he asks you what it all means.'

'Yes, and I thought he was asking me what was happening at his work, how it was going for me. Completely misinterpreted it, I did.'

'But it's not proof of murder.'

'No, but it's totally dodgy. Ian's got no need to change his access. I bet he's been increasing his privileges on the system and manipulating the accounts. Then he changes his access back to normal and no one suspects a thing. If Donald found it odd in a day, imagine what an investigation would uncover.'

'So what do you think happened, Dom? Did Ian find Donald snooping? Donald wouldn't have gone up to him and confronted him about it, would he?'

'I don't know. That's what I'm going to ask him.'

Dom looked out of the window watching the suburbs shoot by. He ended the call with Maggie, but not before adding that if things went wrong for him, the police should access Donald's mobile phone messages to get the message that incriminated Ian.

Maggie had urged him to take care. 'I love you, Dom. Please be careful.'

'I love you too.'

Dom passed the rest of the trip without speaking, impatient to arrive, glad to have the night around him, cloaking him, concealing him.

The driver was looking at him more than necessary. Yet he didn't think he had done anything to draw attention to himself. Perhaps he had seen Dom get out of the other taxi. Dom nodded to himself absently. It was vital not to do anything out of the ordinary once they arrived in Brookvale.

At last, the taxi was purring along Ian's road. The muscles in Dom's chest tightened, making his breathing laboured. He willed the house not to be in darkness. Ian had to be home.

The driver didn't speak, waiting for Dom to tell him which house. The last thing Dom was going to share with the driver was the street number he was after.

'Where?'

'I'm trying to see if I recognise the place.' Dom looked around, pretending to hunt for something familiar.

The road was quiet and tree-lined and Dom could see from the letterboxes that they had arrived at the low end of the numbers.

He counted the houses as they moved along and he almost stopped breathing when they came to Ian's house. Sitting rigid, careful to keep his face secreted in the taxi's murky shadows, should Ian or his accomplice be outside, his emotionless eyes cruised over Ian's house.

There it was, number twenty-three, with lights on throughout, upstairs and down, and a sedan in the driveway that had been reversed in, ready for a swift departure. The empty car was in darkness.

Dom let the taxi carry him to the cross street, where he handed over cash and got out quietly and calmly.

IV

'I've been sick with worry, Josh. I really have. You don't know how much this has knocked me. On top of everything else. My world is changing and I want my old life back.' Camille's croaky voice wailed through the phone. She was crying. 'I called the police and everything.'

'Yeah, I'm sorry for not calling back.' Josh lost count of the times he had apologised to her in the minute or two they'd been speaking, but it was enough for him to notice he was doing it too much. Yet he didn't know what else to add. 'Thanks Camille. That's okay.'

As he spoke, agitated, he ambled around the tendered lawn of his parents' garden. Far from the glow of the city lights, the crescent moon was strong enough to brighten the yard, which was empty except for the black poodle playing at his feet.

He almost stepped on its paw, so he shooed it away with a light kick, sending it scurrying inside to join his parents in the lounge at the front of the property.

'What's going on, Josh?' she asked again.

He didn't want to be the one to tell her what had really happened, nor did he want to draw out her pain. Ignoring her phone calls had been bad enough. But phoning to tell her he was fine, and saying little else, felt even worse.

When he worked through the truth to himself, it sounded ludicrous and he didn't expect to be confessing it to anyone soon—Donald decided to rip off Dom's employer and he helped out. When he found out Donald had been murdered in the middle of all of it, Dom suggested he hide away for his own safety and not speak to anyone. He went to check on his parents because he used their address along with a fake name as part of the swindle. But Dom tells him he's safe now—all of it was as mind-boggling as it was embarrassing.

His words groaned down the phone. 'Oh—er—well—er, if I'm honest, Camille, I think Dom should be the one to explain this. I wanted to call you to tell you not to worry, that I'm all right.'

He toed the soft grass, wondering if Camille giving him grief over the phone was the worst it was going to get. A criminal plot had gone wrong, leading to the death of his friend. What information would the police press him for and how would they respond? Dom would help him out, he reasoned. But was he set to experience the wrath of Subiaco *and* the police *and* the entire Tolen family? Camille pressing him for answers was the easier part of the mess he was in, he reckoned. In the far banks of his mind, he knew it was going to get a lot worse.

He came back to the conversation with Camille waiting patiently and sobbing on the other end. A hungry silence sat there waiting to be filled. Whatever he said was going to sound pathetic. He deliberated further. His silence lasted so long that for a brief moment, he thought she had given up her battle and would abandon the inquisition.

But she wasn't finished. Her pitch climbed.

'What you did was cruel, really cruel. Texting me back, letting me call and call and not answering. Who would do that?' Each word—delivered with such bewilderment—made Josh cringe.

'I had to lie low. It was risky—er—we think Donald may have been killed because of ...' He left the explanation incomplete and he couldn't bring himself to share with her that he had dragged his parents, both in their eighties, into the situation. 'It's best you hear this from Dom because—'

'Dom?'

Josh felt relieved at being interrupted.

Camille sniffed a mix of moisture and derision. 'I don't know what to think there.'

'Dom knows more than me and you'll hear from him—er—soon. I just wanted to say I'm ok and I'm sorry.' Another apology.

'He's saying Donald planned to do something wrong. Is that true?'

Stop with the questions, he thought.

'All I know for sure is Donald worried about the girls and he really wanted them to have the best in life and so—er—that's, you know—'

'We all want the best for the girls, Josh. We all worry for them now they've lost their father. And Robin knows Tommie and I will help out wherever we can.'

'That goes for me too. I've told Robin she can rely on me for anything. I love the girls like my own.'

Josh recalled the day of the funeral, promising Robin any help she needed. Alone in the back garden, he pictured a cross-section of a house and in it were him and Robin and Lorna and Niamh.

V

Lorna and Drew sat close, angled inwards to each other, in a café on a Melbourne terrace. The aroma of coffee and the smell of recent rain cocooned them, and the splashing of water from passersby and cars made them huddle together, limbs twisted on limbs.

Only the buzz of Lorna's mobile was powerful enough to tear them from the rapture. Drew reached for the phone.

'It's your mum.'

'Don't answer it,' said Lorna.

The phone was cast aside, less with loathing and more with indifference. Everything they needed was at the table. A beep told them Robin had left a message.

With a nod from Drew, Lorna freed a devoting hand from her companion's flesh and accessed the message bank. She placed the phone on the table and activated the loud speaker, stealing a kiss before Robin's voice reverberated from the handset. They parted to catch better sight of one another as they listened.

'Lorna honey, it's mummy. I hope you're both having a lovely time. Is Drew taking care of you?'

This brought smiles to their faces. Robin listed bits and pieces she had been doing—Niamh had another loose tooth—something had arrived in the post from a university. This was followed by a pause so lengthy they thought the call had ended. Robin's voice appeared again.

'Mummy loves you, sweetheart.'

Lorna instinctively straightened her spine and leaned further back in her chair.

'Daddy would be so proud of you. We want the best for you.'

Lorna's expression hardened, even as she fixed her eyes on Drew.

The message kept going.

'Call me and let me know everything is working out.'

Lorna recognised her mother's tone. Robin would end the message as she always did, so Lorna mouthed to Drew the words her mother spoke.

'I love you, sweetie.'

The message ended.

The pair giggled through another embrace.

VI

Dom stopped on the footpath and looked around to familiarise himself with the road. Apart from a shadow moving at the far end, which looked like someone walking a dog, none of Ian's neighbours were out. The rumble of distant traffic added an unnerving pounding to the deserted street.

Without taking his eyes off the surrounding properties, he placed his phone on silent and kept hold of it. A sliver of a moon poking through clouds added no light to the road and street lamps at full blast washed the scene in a dirty yellow.

As he neared the house, the sound of an engine caught his attention and he turned to see a bus coming towards him, flashing an indicator. It was heading to the bus stop two houses from Ian's.

It stopped. The doors opened and Dom heard the steps of only one person getting off. She walked in the same direction as the bus, past Ian's house, and vanished into a laneway. When the bus turned off and the road was quiet once more, Dom walked a bit further and stopped opposite Ian's.

He was struck by how familiar the house looked. It reminded him of his parents' place, the red brick house he had spent his first twelve years in. Dom was transfixed. He had never seen a house that looked so much like the one he grew up in. Never had a property had this effect on him.

Every feature was recognisable—the cement driveway on the right with a strip of grass marking its centre, the raised undercover porch accessed by three steps, and even the distribution of bay windows over two levels, crowned by a steep brick roof and central chimney stack.

Images flooded his mind and his skinned tingled hot against the cooling night. He didn't find it too large a leap to picture his parents standing side by side on Ian's lawn. Close by were three young children—Camille, Donald and him—enjoying a childhood that skipped by. His mother craned her neck behind his father, keen to watch over her young ones. With her entire face a smile, her frame, under a loose-fitting dress, revealed nothing of the disease that would take her from the family.

Dom's lips wobbled. He wiped some tears away and with them, the mirage.

An upstairs light went out. Time to move.

He scooted across the road, approached the car from the far side, and crouched down between a wooden fence and the car's passenger side. He waited for signs he may have been spotted by Ian or a neighbour. Nothing happened.

A peek inside the car informed him there was no luggage anywhere. That was a good sign. They might still be packing inside. He tried both doors, but they were locked and thankfully, not alarmed.

Then he inched his way around to the other side and checked the doors. They were locked too. There was no luck with the boot either.

Making himself as small as he could, he returned to his shady hiding space sandwiched between the fence and the car.

His mind raced over all the actions that had brought him to this place outside Ian's house, all the hard work that had led to this, and he didn't know what move to make next.

From his spot, he could see most of the house lights that were on, but he couldn't see inside. He stepped silently to the base of the porch stairs and stopped, looking around, listening. At least no neighbours were outside watching him.

The sounds of people moving randomly through the rooms of number twenty-three travelled out to Dom, but he would need to get closer to hear voices and conversations.

Stooping, he crept up the stairs. The porch he entered was tiled, affording him the stealth he needed. Light steps got him to one of the windows, which had frosted lower halves, but he would need to stand up for any chance of glimpsing the occupants.

He pushed off from a pot plant to get the momentum to stand up. As he did so, the porch light flicked on. The security sensor had triggered.

Dom jerked around in shock as if the light harmed his skin. Like a stage dancer pirouetting through a scene, he scurried back to his hiding space and waited.

The front door opened. A tall figure carrying a large suitcase came out jerking towards the car under the uneven weight. Ian's lanky frame and grey head of hair were instantly identifiable.

Dom froze by the fence with nowhere to escape and banked on Ian not needing to access the left side of the car. His mouth closed in the vain hope of muffling his beating heart. Dom heard the jingle of keys and the boot opening, and Ian loading the suitcase into the car. In the quiet street, the boot door closed and Ian sneaked into the house.

Dom came from out behind the car and tried the boot. It was locked. He kicked at one of the tyres and turned to face the house. There was no choice but to go in.

Just when he thought his heart had hit top speed, it raced that bit more. Inhaling deeply, he walked to the porch and stopped. He turned and bounded back to the car, placing his hands on the boot lid and the bumper, the prints he left barely visible.

With his eyes fixed on the front door, he knew he had to knock. If he entered the house innocently and through the way visitors usually did, Dom reasoned they wouldn't kill him.

The tension in his back eased as he stretched himself tall and confident. He walked up to the front door. He reached for the bell, not only pressing it with his index finger, but smearing the black rectangular unit with his other digits, to leave prints wherever he could.

That might be the last thing he ever did—ringing someone's doorbell. An image of Inspector Nyugen wearing white forensic overalls dusting Ian's porch brushed across his mind.

When he pressed the bell, the screech made him start. It was loud enough to bring everyone out of their homes. The sounds inside the house stopped. Dom counted the seconds before the door opened. Forty. They must have been watching him.

The rasp of the shifting lock came first. Then the door floated open. The woman who he knew as Vanessa stood with the doorframe protecting her. He thought she could have aged twenty years since the morning.

Behind her strained smile and wild eyes sat muscles shot with panic. She was dressed in light beige trousers and a thick woollen jumper. Only her left hand was visible and it was empty. She smiled at him as if she'd known him all her life.

'Hello again, Donald. You found us.'

'I'm here to speak to Ian.'

'Then you'd better come in. He'll be down shortly.' She shouted over her shoulder into the house while keeping an eye on Dom. 'Honey, it's for you.' Her body swung backwards into the hall and as Dom crossed the threshold, he caught sight of a large red suitcase, its lid open and sides overflowing with women's clothing.

She turned to see what Dom was looking at.

'My luggage.'

'I don't want any trouble. I just want to talk.'

'This is a nice surprise,' she said. 'We're about to head out, but we can spare some time.'

Dom saw her eyes dart from his face to behind him, beyond his right shoulder. His thoughts moved much quicker than his body. *Ian behind me. Brace—*

Before Dom had time to swivel to defend himself, he took a ferocious knock to the head that sent him collapsing on the carpet at her feet, where he formed a neat bundle inside twenty-three Fern Park Road.

The Swap

296

11 | Luis

I

Dom felt a cracking ache at the back of his head and he realised he was lying on carpet. He had been knocked out and the commotion going on behind him was in fact happening *to* him. He wanted to nurse his head with his hands, but he was being tied up and each pull of whatever cord they were using made him jiggle and wobble.

Stretching out his legs would help him orient himself once he opened his eyes. But he couldn't extend them at all. For sure, his captors were tying his ankles to his wrists, which were behind his back. He opened his eyes and cocked his head to focus on the couple working on him. He hadn't been out for long.

'You came to attack us. We had to tie you up.' Shoes passed close to his head. Ian leant down in front of him, steadying himself against Dom's body.

'Fuck you. You killed my brother. I wanna know why.' Dom hardly recognised his own voice, slurred from dizziness and the angle of his neck.

Ian slapped him across the face and yanked on a tuft of hair to lift his head. 'You Tolens are crazy. First, my colleague turns on me and starts acting like a clown. Then the brother chases poor Ruth through the streets. Next, he turns up at my house stalking me. We had to take the law into our own hands just then, Mr Tolen. Ruth was in danger and I had to protect her.' He twisted Dom's head. 'God, you look alike.'

'Why? I just want to know why.'

Ian averted his eyes. 'We didn't kill your brother, mate. I liked Dominic. We got on well.'

Patting Dom on the shoulder, Ian pushed off from him to stand up.

The action made Dom's sore skull boom harder. His head slumped on to the carpet and he closed his eyes until the ache eased a fraction. While they pottered around, he lay there thinking.

At least he had his mobile—he was sure that's what was in his pocket digging into his side. And during the seconds he had lost consciousness, they couldn't have checked his wallet because they were still calling him Donald. He swore at himself for being so stupid as to carry it with him. But the day had been one bizarre turn after the next and his rush to get to Ian's had stopped him double checking his plans.

So he had got into Ian's place after all and there he was tied up on their carpet. How was he going to get out of this? Maybe speaking with them was sensible. He could only see Ian, who was plugging a drive into a laptop.

'He stumbled on to something you're doing at work and you killed him.' Dom patted the small of his back as he spoke.

'First part's true. We've taken some money that's not ours and we're going to a nice, warm country to spend it.' Ian ripped a shirt off a chair, rolled it up and jammed it into the open suitcase. 'But we didn't kill anyone. So you stay calm and don't get in our way. I don't know how you know all that and I'd love to find out, but we don't have time.' Ian looked behind him up a narrow carpeted staircase and belted out, 'Come on, Ruth. There's nothing up there.' He turned back to Dom with a smirk on his face. 'Look on the positive side. The two of you will never be mixed up again.'

Dom shook his restraints. He raised his head to look around, but his muscles tired instantly and he laid his head on the carpet, staring at the bottom of the stairs, aware he didn't have much time.

Ruth—he finally knew her name—came rushing down the stairs with a garment swinging in her hand, which she bundled into the suitcase. She ignored Dom, who watched her turn right and disappear into another room. From her steps, she was crossing lino. She was in the kitchen. A drawer was yanked open and Dom heard utensils being shuffled around. The drawer banged shut and she rounded the corner speeding towards him in a ball of fury clutching a carving knife.

She kneeled down and stroked the cold blade into his cheek. Dom winced and clamped his eyes shut while his chin moved instinctively to his chest to protect his vulnerable sweaty throat. The fear of being sliced made him tense to the point of breaking.

'See this?' She pulled the knife away and his scratched cheek bounced back out. She paused, waiting for his eyes to open.

When he looked, she was waving it in front of him and his eyes scattered to focus on the reflective metal. 'You do anything to slow us down and I'll cut your throat.' She glared at Ian as she went back to packing her suitcase. 'What did I tell you?' She spat her words at him.

The two of them darted around colliding with each other as they finished their packing. They were out of Dom's line of sight, but he could hear them talking and disagreeing.

'We can't leave him here. I think she'll notice him even if we stuff him in a cupboard.' Ian's head appeared from behind a wall to check on the hostage. He lowered his voice. It was too faint to hear what he was saying, but Dom could see a hand pointing at him and signalling away at a distance.

The anger in Ruth's voice made her volume rise. 'It's too dangerous. What if we get stopped? What if he gets away?'

As Dom listened, he collected saliva in his mouth. He twisted and writhed his jaw and when it felt voluminous, he leaked it out onto the carpet. If they killed him, he could at least help seal their convictions. They continued debating what to do with him. Ian spoke. 'He's not a crazed psycho—he's a fucking nobody. You're overreacting.'

'How will we get him past the fucking neighbours?' Ruth appeared. She looked over in mid-sentence and spotted Dom dribbling. She screamed. 'He's leaving traces.' She dashed for him picking the knife up along the way.

Dom shouted out. 'No! No! No! Please!' He couldn't speak anymore. He had to compress his neck to hide his throat. Drawing his shoulders to his earlobes was his best attempt at self-defence.

Ruth dropped to her knees in front of the wriggling Dom and brought the knife to his throat. She tried spooning it under his jaw but his clamp was too powerful for her weedy grip. She jerked the knife away and started stabbing clumsily at his stomach.

Desperate to keep her away from his throat, with his chin locked to his chest, he yelped and shuddered. The pain at having Josh's recent wound pounded brought water to his eyes, Ruth's anger giving her the power she needed to wield a knife.

She brought her arm back and high above her head ready to plunge it deep into his belly, ready to kill him.

Dom's eyes widened in horror as he stiffened at the metal that was about to ram into his abdomen. He loosened his jaw as he went to scream for breath.

'Stop!' shouted Ian. Ruth let the knife linger in the air while Ian spoke. 'She's coming to clean up tomorrow.' He flashed a finger at her. 'No sign of violence.'

Dom didn't know who they were referring to, but he was thankful to her. He guessed that their hasty exit from the country had messed up their plans and they were now leaving before the cleaner had been. Ian tugging the mat by the front door and thrusting it under his head pulled Dom from his speculation.

'Kick him instead. Do not get blood on you. It'll look suspicious.'

Ruth stood up and before Dom could react, she swung her foot into his trunk. She stepped back and repeated the kick more. Each time, she became more frantic, more hysterical. Dom yelped in pain and coughed and spluttered over the carpet, wriggling and stretching out as much as his ties would let him, rope and limbs rising off the carpet.

'You cunt—you fucking cunt! Leave us alone.'

She kicked and kicked while Dom's wrists wriggled and his fingers fanned out instinctively, helplessly behind him.

'No more, please,' he cried, writhing and coughing. 'Please don't hurt me. I just want to know'—he paused to catch his breath—'why. What happened that day?'

Ian pulled Ruth off him and snatched the knife from her hand. 'Enough. Where are your pills?' He elbowed her away. While Ruth fished around in her hand luggage on the sofa close to where Dom was lying panting, Ian zipped up the red suitcase and disappeared outside with it.

'We have got to leave tonight, Ian. We *cannot* miss this flight.' She rushed past Dom and pelted a blister pack at his face. It hit him on the forehead and fell to the carpet in front of him. He fidgeted backwards to get a better look at what he was about to be force-fed. He couldn't make out the product name but he was relieved to see it was prescription. It was legal.

When Ian came back inside, Ruth yelled at him pointing at the tablets on the carpet. 'Ram four of those down his throat. That will knock him out until we take off.'

'Four?' Ian stopped.

Dom lifted his head. 'What are they?'

'Move it, Ian,' screamed Ruth. 'We've got to go now.'

'What are they?'

'Shut the fuck up, you.'

Ian lunged at Dom. 'You're coming with us and if you make any trouble, you're dead. Understand?'

'In the boot?' Dom asked with feigned horror.

'No, upfront. You can drive us there.' Ian paused as if expecting Dom to join in the humour.

Ruth came up behind Ian with a glass of water. 'Get him up. Get the tablets.'

'Kneel up,' said Ian, helping Dom come up onto his knees.

With his vision corrected, Dom saw his surroundings better but also felt his injuries more. His head was sore and his stomach felt bruised from the kicking and knifing. He looked at his belly. There was some bleeding, but they didn't need to worry about bloodstains. Choking for air, he tried to speak. 'Let me breathe first. I need—' He inhaled and exhaled in starts. 'I need to breathe.'

Ian popped a few tablets from their casing.

'What are they?' Dom tried reading the name on the foil.

'Sleeping pills. Open. Wider.'

Dom stretched his mouth obediently. Ian moved his fingers close to Dom's lips.

'No biting.' He glared at Dom.

Dom nodded. When Ian's fingers were close enough, he popped his tongue out. They looked at each other, both unsure what the other was about to do.

Like a matron watching staff medicate a troublesome patient, hand on hip, Ruth watched them.

Ian pinged four pills into Dom's mouth as if going for a prize at a fair ground. Most hit the mark but one bounced away. Ian retrieved it.

Dom gagged. Ian packed the fourth into Dom's mouth, keeping his fingertips away from his teeth.

Dom felt disgust at the warmth of Ian's fingers on his lips.

Ruth stepped in with a glass of water. 'If they come back up, you're dead,' she hissed.

Dom sipped the water.

'Lift up your tongue.'

Dom exposed as much of the underneath of his tongue as he could. He had swallowed them all.

'More water.' Dom opened his mouth.

Ruth stepped in.

Dom thought he must look like a fallen walker, and Ian and Ruth a pair of Samaritans. He hoped this wasn't their final good-natured deed knowing it would be the last time they would see him alive.

II

The television remote control didn't end up where Maggie had expected it would. Her pitch from the sofa had been too powerful, so it sailed off the coffee table and fell to the carpet, where it stayed.

Jasper, who was lounging out on the balcony, hopped off the ledge, came in and sniffed the remote. He pounced on the sofa. He settled himself on Maggie's stomach, where he was sure to invite a stroking.

Maggie obliged. Her warm fingers ran over his velvety fur, yet Jasper's young face carried a scowl. Maggie tried stroking it away.

'What's up with you?'

Perhaps he could see she was ready to head out—she did have her jacket and shoes on. Or maybe he could sense the unease in the frantic beating of her heart inches from his. Whatever it was, he wasn't prepared to stay there for long. He stretched himself out and pranced off. He minced to his bed and curled up, giving Maggie his back.

She was geared up to leave the unit in a split second—a signal from Dom and she would drive to his aid.

Her mobile was by her side, its ringtone at full volume. The television was on mute, unnecessarily, to hear a text or call.

She flapped her feet like a pair of windscreen wipers, her body eager to expend nervous energy. Her twiddling fingers nabbed the mobile and she checked if a message had arrived. It hadn't.

It was half past seven. That meant she had spoken to Dom way over an hour ago. She was sure he was fine, but that was a long time not to be contacting her.

Once more she checked her mobile. The coverage was good and the battery almost fully charged. She sent herself a text just to be one hundred per cent certain that everything was working fine.

Test

It arrived in a second.

She cursed her situation. Why hadn't she got Dom to agree to stay in contact frequently? The not-knowing was debilitating. She rested her phone in the spot Jasper had vacated.

The flickering television drew her eye. She stared at the large black unit, but without volume, the screen couldn't hold her attention.

From her phone, she googled Ian's address, which she scorched into her memory. The maps section had a photo of it. In blazing daylight, the picture gave the house a nondescript quality. The home of a killer.

She checked how long it would take to drive there.

III

Ian was loosening Dom's feet. 'We're going out the front door and you're going to slip into the boot. 'This'—he shook the rope cradled in his hands—'is going over your head. Any funny moves and I'll snap your neck. Got it?'

Dom nodded.

'The choice is yours. Walk out with me and live. Or make a noise and die. Outside the door, you don't speak.' Ian's finger jabbed him in the chest. 'Got it?'

Towering above them, Ian looked at Ruth. His brow hardened but his eyes flickered.

Dom spotted a hint of apprehension. Whether it was fear for Ruth or fear of him, he couldn't make out.

'You ready? Open the boot.' Ruth scampered outside as the rope plopped effortlessly around Dom's neck. Ian pulled it tight.

'Please let me breath. You're too tall—' Dom flinched in agony.

Ruth came back inside and turned off the lights. 'It's open and the street's clear. We've gotta go now.'

She opened the front door wider and the three walked out together, Ruth leading. They guided Dom down the stairs.

Hands still behind his back, he shuffled down each step taking care not to stray too far from Ian, who tugged on the rope thoughtlessly every time he moved his head as he checked to see no one was around.

But the street was empty and only they were making noise. A few garden lights and the street lamps lit the scene. The cool air bit at Dom's face and he liked it. His skin felt overheated from the two attacks he had received.

Dom sped up to the open boot and turned around ready to fall in.

'Not so fast.' Ruth slapped him.

Dom jerked away and Ian pulled him back with a flick. 'Get in.'

Dom tried to hop in from several angles but he couldn't get in unaided with his hands tied.

Ian pulled his feet up and Dom tumbled backwards, his head thudding against what was clearly Ian's luggage.

His legs hung outside the car, protruding like a ventriloquist dummy, until Ian gathered them up and tucked them inside, almost dotingly. The size of the boot meant Dom ended up lying in the fetal position, his white face standing out against the darkness of the space.

'Go to sleep. When we come back for the luggage, if you're awake, I'll slit your throat because we've got a flight to get.'

Dom nodded swiftly. Ian caught the movement. He looked into Dom's eyes, the little he could see.

'Good night, Jim Bob'.

The boot door came down with a wallop, with Ian's palms muffling the echo. The darkness encased Dom.

The car was old and the fumes of oil and tyre rubber were overpowering—the spare wheel had to be right under his nose. As well as the smells of the car, he picked up the musky tang of Ian's travel bag. Even though he couldn't see a thing, Dom's eyes stretched open with delight.

He needed to act quickly to free his hands. He'd swallowed four tasteless pills and he hoped they were nothing more than sleeping tablets. To stop the drugs working, it crossed his mind to vomit them up. But the two of them would see the sick or smell it and they would kill him.

He had to free himself but be asleep when they arrived at the airport. Dom knew one thing—if they sensed that he wanted to disrupt their departure, he was done for.

Feeling his way around the binding on his wrists, he decided it was safer to start undoing the knots once the car was moving. Why weren't they going? What were they doing up the front?

His right forearm was lodged under his body, which helped steady his right wrist, and this allowed him to use his left hand to feel the workings in the ropes. His fingers touched every bit of cord. In the dark, he could picture all the twists and turns of the rope. There were three large knots and Dom doubted they would take too much time to undo.

'Fuck it,' he mumbled, no longer able to wait, and started untying the first knot. He was pulling at the rope when the light footsteps, probably Ruth's, came running close to him.

There were keys jingling and a car door opening and closing with a slam. Its vibration travelled through the body of the car and reached Dom's weary head, sparking more pain. Then Dom heard voices. He stopped moving.

'No, Ben.' It was a short sharp command to a dog.

Ian spoke. 'He can smell our luggage.'

'You guys going away? Where to?'

'Thailand,' said Ian.

'Vietnam,' said Ruth.

'Stopping off in Vietnam, then on to Thailand.' Ian explained away the contradiction.

The man commented on how lucky they were. 'Come away, Ben. What are you sniffing at?'

With his heart in his throat, Dom willed him to piss off and stop slowing them down.

They said their goodbyes to Ben's owner and Ian called out that they would be back in a fortnight.

The engine chugged to life, drowning out whatever else Ian was saying. The car was moving. Dom began jostling around against the luggage. Every uneven part of the road made itself noticed, each bump and hole magnified in the uncushioned boot.

He hurried to free his hands. The first knot came undone easily. The left indicator came on and as the car moved over, which must have been them turning off Ian's road, they stopped.

With no way of combating the strength of the braking, Dom's face sank into the tough material of Ian's luggage. The driver's door opened and someone ran to the back of the car.

Panicking, Dom tried tightening the loosened knot with his bound fingers. Luckily his hands were behind him pointing inwards to the reaches of the boot.

The door rose and streetlight lit Ian from above, an angelic aura framing his head of wild locks. He reached in and began feeling Dom's body. A swift look around told Ian it was safe to speak. 'Phone.'

Dom moved the left side of his body up towards Ian, as much as this pained him, his abdomen sore from Ruth's beating. Ian bent over into the boot and the two collaborated well together. 'This one,' whispered Dom.

Ian ran his hands over the outside area first, verifying Dom's instructions. It was the right pocket. The zip buzzed and Ian whipped out the phone.

Dom was sure Ian would have also felt the wallet, but that was no use to them. As if reading his thoughts, Ian tapped the wallet through the material. 'You keep that. Get a taxi home tomorrow morning. Password for this?' he said, shoving the phone in Dom's face.

Dom rattled off the code.

Ian typed it in and the light from the screen lit up his jacket, including the logo and brand name.

Snowtrap.

Dom's lips creased into a smile before he could stop himself. Quickly, he returned his line of vision to the boot's gloomy interior.

'What's the joke, dickhead?' Ian stood erect and looked around him.

Dom closed his eyes and said nothing.

Ian looked at the mobile screen but spoke to Dom. 'Step three—divest troublemaker of all mobile devices. Step four—spit on troublemaker.' Ian collected a mouthful of saliva and spat at Dom's face, where it sat on his cheek and eyelashes. 'Step five—slam car boot.'

The boot door snapped shut and Ian sped to the front. They started moving again.

Dom twisted his neck and dried the saliva from his face with the bag, the motion of the car making his task more difficult.

The knots!

Dom needed to get back to work.

The pitch black of his prison brought on feelings of drowsiness. The pills were working. Within seconds, his head felt like it had doubled its weight and he sensed a loss of control in his limbs. They were watery. He swore and shook his head to combat the looming fatigue, and he wiggled his fingers to wake them up ready to work on freeing his hands.

IV

Dom's phone rang out again. Maggie's despair and irritation mounted as she heard his recorded voice. It needed a mountainous effort to cool herself enough to leave a polite message asking him to call as soon as possible. She instantly followed it up with a text.

> Are you ok? How
> did it go? I'm
> worried. Call me.

With the highest volume checked again, she rested the phone on the kitchen work counter. What to do? She was too anxious to paint and too worried to sit. The pangs in her stomach strengthened into a nauseous mix of nerves and hunger. The thought of eating was off-putting, yet something light would set her up for anything that happened later.

She gathered the ingredients for a small salad and added a can of red salmon. With her mind on Dom's whereabouts, she drowned it in olive oil, added balsamic vinegar and salt, and picked at the lot keeping one eye on her mobile, which sat in front of her near her bowl.

Her phone sprang to life and so did Maggie. But her heart sank. It was a friend phoning. She let the call ring out, and mechanically chewed her food, which lacked taste despite all the condiments. Jacintha was probably calling to finalise their weekend plans to catch an exhibition that was about to close. But Maggie couldn't think beyond the evening.

When her mobile sounded that she had a missed call and a message, she swiped the screen clear ready to receive Dom's updates. Jacintha's message could wait. Dom might call at that moment. The silence returned to her home and she laboured through the meal.

The next text message arrived when she was at the sink dumping her bowl. The tension in her body eased even before she knew who it was from. When she saw it was Dom, her mouth opened into a gaping smile and her chest muscles relaxed.

> Nothing to worry
> about, Maggie. Got
> a fresh lead. He's
> heading to the
> Blue Mountains.
> I'll call you when
> I get to WF.

Maggie frowned. 'Don't call me when you get there. Do it on the way.' She guessed the *he* was Ian. But the final two letters had her puzzled. 'WF?' Was that an area or a venue? Then it dawned on her.

Wentworth Falls.

Ian was heading to the suburb in the Blue Mountains. She comforted herself knowing at least Dom was alive. The short return text she tapped out revealed her relief, frustration and worry.

V

Ian cruised through the car park. They were in a desperate rush but he couldn't afford to cause a scene. Their trip across the city had been uneventful and he wanted the check-in to be equally ordinary. The airport car park ticket lay crumpled at his feet, where it had landed after he snatched it from the machine.

Ruth checked the time on her mobile phone again and muttered under her breath for him to hurry up and pull over.

He ignored her, focusing instead on finding a quiet place to park. The car park was nowhere near full and theirs was the only car rolling around finding a spot.

It was five to nine and they had left it tight for an international flight. But then, they had been slowed down by the unexpected arrival of Donald Tolen.

Ian couldn't believe he had shown up to confront them and he looked in the rear view mirror as though expecting the boot to pop open and the twin to jump out. But his look behind showed nothing out of place. The boot lid was closed.

He was comforted by not having heard a sound from the boot for the whole trip. Ruth had wanted to blast the radio, but Ian had insisted they travel in silence to listen out for any trouble and to give Donald a chance to fall asleep.

Ian had to stay focused on the road. He hadn't wanted to wake the guy up and he had watched for uneven surfaces, and had braked and accelerated as gently as he could. Ruth's sleeping pills had obviously worked.

He steered the car to a far corner. It was an ideal spot—far from the ticket booth and close to a busy road, where cries from the boot were least likely to go unheard.

The car stopped.

The pair exchanged glances but didn't speak. They looked around to check no other cars were approaching and when they listened out for movement from the boot, they couldn't hear a thing.

Ruth flashed her knife to Ian and prodded her wrist to remind him they had to be quick.

He nodded and they got out quietly.

Without saying a word, Ian watched Ruth collect her bag from the seat behind her. He spotted the mobile phone she had tossed in the back after sending the text message to Maggie, a message he had dictated. He leant in and knocked it off the seat to the car floor, where it was less likely to tempt opportunistic thieves. He wasn't taking chances.

Ian had been surprised that Maggie was in contact with Dom's brother, but he was getting a sense of how everything had connected up.

Maggie and Donald had found out somehow, and although Ian didn't know exactly how they knew what they knew, it meant Ruth and he needed to leave the country straight away.

He moved to the rear.

Ruth and her luggage were clear of the car.

Ian scanned the car park and unlocked the boot door.

Ruth came to Ian's right, concealing the knife by her side, ready to pounce. Ian waited a moment before letting the door spring up to complete its arc. They stepped back.

Their prisoner didn't stir. He was breathing deeply and the car park lamps lit his statue face.

Ian lowered the boot to shield Dom's eyes from the powerful light.

They noticed Dom's hands were untied. The rope sat scrunched around his one visible wrist. The other arm was outstretched into the back of the boot. His lungs and throat rhythmically signalled he was sleeping deeply.

Ian murmured to Ruth keeping his eyes on the sleeper. 'He's dead to the world, but we should cover him. We don't want the cold to wake him.'

Ruth turned to look at him.

'What are you whispering for?'

She whacked him playfully on the arm and let the knife hit the ground—it was no longer needed.

The pair sniggered at how deep his sleep must be, clawing at each other as they fell about.

Ian got the giggles. An image of the man kneeling as the pills went down his throat, arms behind his back made Ian crack up even more. He steadied himself on the rim of the boot and stayed like that half-suppressing the laugh.

His snorting settled down and he turned to Ruth, but she wasn't there.

Through the darkness and fuzzy car park light, he caught her heading to the terminal, hauling her luggage by her side, weaving among the cars.

'Wait.'

Ian leant in to the boot, his head close enough to hear the raspy breathing of someone deep in sleep. He lifted out his luggage without it touching the person sleeping. He lowered it to the floor behind him and turned back to face the car.

The boot door closed. Stepping back, Ian's foot found something—their knife. Cursing Ruth for being so careless, he kicked it like a football making it skim several car spaces away.

A final tug of the handle confirmed the car was locked, and he ran to catch up with her.

VI

About ten hours after Ian and Ruth had parked their car, a ute snailed its way through the same area with its driver singing along to the radio in a Spanish accent. Puffy-eyed and tired, Luis parked next to the rockery he had been scheduled to work on and cut the engine. He checked himself in the mirror. The scruffy woollen hat warming his head—already covered in coarse grey-black hair—got another adjustment and he left the cabin, stepping out to a chilly start with a perfect-blue dawn sky.

His chunky frame, warmed by a padded jacket, shuffled round the edge of the tray looking for his work gloves. He would need those on before he'd even think about touching his toolbox, which would be icy cold. The gloves lay on the passenger side and he sidestepped round to them, where an object on the ground caught his eye. It was near the rock garden, a part of the outer edge of the airport car park, beyond which sat the motorway, dashed with morning traffic.

It looked like a knife. Slipping on the gloves, he walked over to it. It was indeed a knife. No sooner had he crouched down to pick it up than he thought he heard shouting. Without touching it, he straightened up and looked around, saw no one and heard nothing except the passing cars. He waited a few seconds because he was sure he had heard a voice.

He knelt down again and picked up the large kitchen knife, which looked clean. The shouting returned while he was still squatting, and gripping the handle, he shot upright listening and watching like a meerkat.

A man's voice, which sounded trapped and enclosed, was bellowing. Luis studied the blade and spoke to the invisible man.

'Hello? Where are you?' He waited and scanned the cars close by.

'Help me. Do you work at the airport? I'm trapped in a car boot.'

'Yes. I work here.' Luis lobbed the knife into his ute tray and moved towards the voice. 'Which one? The Holden or the Merc?'

'The Holden. In the boot.'

'*Joder macho!* How did you get in there?'

'I was beaten up and dumped in here. Can you see a man and a woman around? Are you alone?'

Luis checked. 'It's dark still but there's nobody. Just cars. I think I found their knife.' Luis bent over, moving his ear to the body of the car, taking care not to touch it. He could hear the man inside moving. 'Is the alarm on?' Luis asked.

'I don't know. I doubt it.'

Luis tried the boot. It was locked and no alarm sounded. He tried the four side doors but they were locked too. Then he cupped his hands around his face and peered in through each window. There was no hint of keys but he spotted a mobile phone at the back on the floor, jutting out from under the driver seat, glinting up at him. He reported the closed doors to the man in the boot and he asked for his name.

'My name's David. You've gotta get me out. I'm freezing.'

'Ok David. I'm Luis. How long have you been in there?'

'Since last night. Help me get out. Do you have a crowbar?'

'*Cómo?*' Luis's face twisted up. 'A what?' He turned his ear to the boot to better hear and his eyes swooped upwards catching the sky turning from blue to orange.

'Something to break the lock. Quick. I have to get out. I can't breathe.'

Luis fancied that wasn't true, that there was plenty of air in a car boot, but he guessed David was panicking. 'You will have enough air, sir. You will. Don't worry. Panicking makes it worse.' The Iberian tones softened the edges of his English words. 'You can pull on a wire and the boot will unlock.'

'I can't see a thing. Please help me. There's nothing.' Luis heard David patting down the interior of the boot, double checking he couldn't free himself from inside. 'Hello?' said David.

'I'm going to my ute to get my tools. I'll get you out ASAP.' He strode to his open truck and stopped. He took three steps back to David and called out. 'Shall I phone the police?'

'No! I've already done it. Help get me out.'

'You have a mobile? The police are coming?'

'I called the police. *Then* they stole it from me. The police know I'm in a boot somewhere. They'll locate us soon. Do you have the tools? Hello? Are you there, Luis? What time is it?'

'*Uf. Qué pesado.*' Luis had sympathy for anyone trapped in a boot, but David was rather demanding. 'A minute,' Luis called as he went for his tools. 'It's after seven.'

The shovel was in easy reach, but he had something more powerful. A brutal flap of his tarpaulin revealed what lay underneath. The varnished handle of the pickaxe caught his eye and soon he was back near David plonking both tools on the ground.

'Hurry,' came the muffled command.

Luis flapped his arms like a swimmer warming up, gripped the pickaxe and rested it on the car's bumper. One final question came for David. 'Mate, are you the good guy or the bad guy?'

'The good guy, of course.'

'*Mierda.*' He swore at the dilemma—whether to wait for the police or save the guy now. He studied the body of the car, which was far from new. It would be fine to smash. 'Ok. Move to the back of the boot. I start now.'

'Go,' came one more order from inside the car.

For five minutes, Luis worked the lock and the boot lip, ignoring David's requests for updates and his running commentary once light had pierced the interior. Metal screeched against metal and Luis huffed and, with a quick pop, the boot lid finally bounced up.

Luis looked down on a man awkwardly hunched into the pit of the boot, his squinting eyes blinking and watering.

Still without having seen his rescuer, Dom smiled towards the sky. 'Thank you, Luis. You've saved my life.'

'No worries. Is it your car?' He extended a hand to Dom, who was shuffling forward.

Dom's head shook. 'It's theirs. Bastards. They've left the country.'

'*Dios.*' He guided Dom out of the boot patting the twisted metal. 'Watch the lock here—it's sharp. Come out this side.'

As Dom came up on his knees, he peered around. They were in an almost deserted section of the airport. In one hit, he got the blare of the passing traffic and the crispness of the day's weather. He filled his lungs with fresh air and coughed from the abdominal pain that stopped him taking in more.

Luis held out his hand for him.

'I got drugged and bundled in here.' He clambered out, slipping down the car's body, stumbling to the ground, his legs, weakened by the hours of cramped confinement, not ready to sustain him. He managed to right himself. 'Ah, that feels good.'

Luis returned his tools to the ute tray and he walked back to Dom smiling and pointing at the boot. 'The leg room's worse than the plane, no?'

'I can't move my left arm. I must have slept on it all night.' Dom jiggled his limp limb.

With eyes wide and a guarded angle to his stance, Luis watched on as Dom soothed each part of his body that Ruth and Ian had brutalised the night before. His stomach was the most tender, but he didn't think anything was broken or punctured. The lump on his head felt like a hill under his hair and any blood had long dried up. His throat and neck, grazed and welted from Ruth's failed go at slicing it, were losing their heat.

'Is that your phone at the back?' Luis squeezed in between Ian's car and the Mercedes, and pointed inside.

Dom moved around and peered through the glass. It definitely looked like his. 'I need to break the window. Can I use your—'

'Here.' Luis had picked up a boulder from the rockery. When he saw Dom still massaging his numb arm, Luis stepped forward and obliged, lifting the rock high. He brought it down, but released it too late and it missed its target.

The bodywork took the brunt of the blow, the window cracked and the boulder bounced off the metal into the Mercedes parked alongside Ian's Holden. A piercing alarm started and both men cowered.

Luis said, '*Torpe*. I'm clumsy. Again. Wait.'

He picked up the rock and rehearsed the trajectory of his shot. It plunged into the glass and disappeared inside the car. He leant in, flicked the lock and held the door open for Dom, who swept up his mobile like an eagle collecting its prey.

It was definitely his mobile and it was low on battery. He popped it away, looked around them and motioned over to Luis's ute, away from the din of the alarm.

Luis turned and walked ahead.

'I hope I don't get in trouble for the damage I've done.'

When he turned round, waiting for David to arrive at his side, he was surprised to discover he was alone. The car with its mangled boot raised was unattended. David wasn't there either. Luis stood tall and did a sweep of the car park.

Some way off, darting between the cars, David was heading to the terminal.

'David! Wait!'

VII

An hour later, Luis was making a statement at the airport police station. The officers received a thorough account of everything that happened from when Luis arrived in the car park as well as a decent description of the mysterious, bashed-up David he helped free from the car.

He described forcing the door of the boot with his tools the minute David told him he couldn't breathe. As he spoke, Luis's hands slammed against his chest with indignation and his eyes rolled at David's vanishing act. More than once, he patted his red face to display how cheeky David had been.

When the police questioned the damage to the Mercedes, Luis's expression or voice didn't change. He described watching David clumsily smash his way through the window to retrieve a mobile from the back. David had missed and hit the Mercedes too. Once he had the phone, he shot away.

12 | Dom

|

After strolling in the sun, Dom and Maggie found a salt-dusted bench in a quiet park in Little Bay. Cauliflower clouds shuffled across the sky. Dom had taken Maggie to see Donald's plaque in the nearby cemetery. Both hidden behind sunglasses, they faced the sun admiring the green. Dom played ping-pong with the ball of rubbish he had fashioned from his café snack wrapping and Maggie clutched a festival brochure she had collected along the way. Dom locked the paper ball in one hand and turned to her.

'What I don't understand is—if Jamie's there to back up your version of events, why have they made you take leave?'

'Because it's a load of crap. At the meeting, any time they could, they kept referring to it as my disciplinary hearing to try to intimidate me. Even Vanessa called it that. They said it would be best if I took some time off. They gave me the choice of either being sent on leave or taking indefinite leave myself. They would rather I wasn't around while they looked into things and decided my penalty for the damage I caused.'

'So who was at the meeting?'

'Vanessa—she had just returned from her NZ trip—and three more directors, and my lawyer.' She chuckled. 'You should've seen Vanessa's face when I explained how we trashed her office. She was tutting and moaning so loudly the others couldn't hear me.'

Her brow creased. 'I don't think they doubt my explanation. They're annoyed with how it all unfolded. You know—that I knew about your switch and passed on information to you and didn't report anything.' She scrunched up the brochure until it stretched her palms.

Dom watched her hands working eagerly. 'Are you worried about it?'

When Maggie shook her head, Dom laid a hand on her upper arm. 'I've caused you an enormous headache, and for nothing—they got away.'

She patted his hand and said, 'It's not that bad. You were still an employee when I passed you that info. And once they uncover how much Ian stole from them, they'll go easy on me.' Her voice was sad.

'But?' said Dom.

She let out a long sigh. 'Now that I've wrecked one of the director's offices, their image of me has forever changed, I'd say. And when word gets around …'

Her head rocked lightly.

'At the meeting, they hardly looked at me and not one of them shook my hand.' She sighed. 'I should find out in a few days what they've decided. It's two weeks today that I smashed the place up—where has that time gone?'

She looked at Dom, still fiddling with his paper ball. 'And how are you? How are the wounds? Each time we meet, you look like you're getting back to your normal self.'

'I'm getting there. No major damage to my head or stomach, the hospital said. Just bruising and small punctures. It's only in the last couple of days that my head feels one hundred per cent'—his hand went up to rub where Ian had socked him—'but the mobility in my torso is fine now.'

They were silent. Maggie asked the question she was itching to ask every time they caught up. 'Any update on where they are?'

'Ian and Ruth? None. I'm still trying to find out. I'm quite sure they took their flight. I don't think they're in the country lying low—but you never know.'

'It's impossible to confirm, isn't it? Even the police would have a task confirming that. Speaking of which, have you heard from them yet?'

Dom fidgeted. 'Not a thing. I guess it's just a question of time before they find out it was me in the boot. I'll let them come to me.'

'How? Through Ian and Subiaco?'

'Yes. Once Subiaco looks into the scale of things and puts the police on to Ian, everything else will sort itself out. I hope, anyway. The quicker the fraud comes out, the safer for me. The police won't want to know about me—or Donald for that matter—once Subiaco reports Ian's crimes.'

'They'll come to you as a witness rather than a suspect.' It was a statement to Dom, not a question.

His awkward nod betrayed his sentiments.

'And your family? How are they coping? Your dear nieces.' She squeezed his hand.

'The girls are very sad. So is Camille—apparently.'

Maggie turned to him. 'Apparently?'

'She still isn't speaking to me. I'm hearing everything through Robin, who also isn't interested in wild stories about murder. It was an accident as far as they're concerned. They're all keeping their distance.' Dom's head lowered. 'I need to give it time there. When the police get on to Ian, it will sort itself out.'

Maggie moved in closer and wrapped her arm under Dom's and massaged his hand resting on his lap. Minutes passed before they spoke again. He propped himself up and moved an arm around her. She squeezed his thigh to get his attention. 'So what's next for you? Thought any more about work?'

'I want to make some changes. Maybe move interstate—Perth or Hobart perhaps—for a year or two. Get away from Sydney for a time.'

'Understandable, that.'

'I miss Donald every day. I think about him constantly. And I had my perfectly balanced life and now it's all messed up. I've lost a huge part of it and what remains is all wrong.'

Maggie nodded and said, 'Uh-huh', though she could only guess what he meant. 'Go to Perth.' She tapped him with the bunched-up pamphlet. 'I don't know anyone there.'

II

Dom insisted on driving Maggie home, despite her protesting. On the return, he wound his way to Centennial Park via Anzac Bridge. The traffic was light and within the hour, he was swinging his car into his underground parking space. The noisy yawn and stretch he made before getting out confirmed he needed a nap before lunch. He remembered to check if any post had arrived—he hadn't looked in days and he walked back the way he had come to stop at the mailboxes. The smallest key of the bunch revealed the contents. With the junk mail separated from the envelopes, he climbed the stairs.

Once inside, he chucked the post onto the workspace, where it fanned out like a deck of cards. Only then did he see the overseas envelope, which was from Malaysia and addressed to Donald, not him. He examined it first before opening it.

The envelope was handwritten on cheap paper. It was noticeably thin under the massage of his coarse thumb. At a guess, it contained just one leaf of paper. A quizzical look covered his face.

Donald didn't know anyone in Kuala Lumpur. Come to think of it, he'd never been there—as far as Dom knew.

His chest constricted. What did the letter contain? Was it another of Donald's secrets about to surface? With his curiosity at breaking point, Dom marched into the living room with the letter, stopping at the fridge for a can of beer. He sank into the sofa cushion and tore the envelope open, tremulous fingers unfolding the paper.

It did contain just one sheet and it had to be read. He placed it down beside him and opened his beer. His lips smacked together to savour the taste of cold alcohol.

He paused. This needed thinking through. It was worth asking if he was truly ready for the contents, for the message—however weighty—the thin paper was about to convey.

Dom gave himself a potent nod and put down his beer.

He picked up the sheet of paper and flapped it open.

Donald

Please forgive me for writing to you, but I am desperate. Today is 3 August and I don't have much time. My life is about to end but I have a chance to live if you help. I choose my words wisely to not get anyone in trouble. God, I hope you get this letter.

If you do, I'm begging you. Please help. I'm quite sure I know what happened the night Ruth and I left Sydney. I deserved it. It serves me right, for what we did. They arrested me as soon as we landed. When we got our bags, they dived on us. Ruth almost had a heart attack. I've been in custody ever since but I've seen her a fair amount.

Now I'm facing the death penalty. They say it was a large quantity and the penalty for trafficking is serious here.

I am so sorry for what I've done. I want to go home to Australia to serve time for killing your brother. I confess. I killed Dominic. But I need your help. I know that puts you in an awkward position, but it's my only hope. I know you probably want to see me dead, but I'm asking you to save me so you can get proper justice for your brother.

I don't have much time. Please. I'm begging. You can go to the authorities or the Malay consulate there and tell them what happened.

I have my first court date in the last week of September and I'm sure your evidence could help get me deported back to Sydney. I can then confess to everything. I'll plead guilty. No trial.

Please help.
Ian

Dom doubled the single sheet trying to keep the grief from deforming his face. So there it was—a confession.

He read the fourth paragraph another three times and seeing Ian's admission spelled out allowed a weight to lift from him. That lightness and headiness brought the emotion to the surface. His tears ran and he wiped them away, holding the page at arm's length to keep it dry. He collapsed into the seat and howled for the part of him he had lost, for the twin he could not live normally without.

When his eyes dried, he read the letter again, and again. And he cried again. With his other hand gripping the armrest, as though preventing him from falling to the floor, he belted out his cries of grief and anger. He pitched back in the seat and looked around through watery eyes. The letter, now creased and blotchy wet with tears, loosened in his hand.

Mechanically, he looked at what his right hand was doing. His tunnelling forefinger had found a break, an imperfection in the material and his nail had disappeared into the interior of the sofa.

He remembered how the hole had appeared—the fork he had rammed into it, furious at Donald's relentlessness to do the swap. That plunging of metal into the sofa had signalled the start of so much brutality, so much violence—Donald dying, his fight with Josh, pushing the woman into the road, and Ian and Ruth's attacks on him. And now a final act—Ian's execution.

Dom stared transfixed at the hole, his finger having opened it further. It resembled a flesh wound with the entrails exposed. His hand jerked away.

He flattened the letter and sipped the beer. So his plan that night had worked. He pictured himself in the boot of Ian's car, bouncing around as his captors sped to the airport. In the dark, he had set to work untying himself before her bloody sleeping pills kicked in. He remembered the joy at finding an unlocked zipper compartment in the bag and pulling the parcel of cocaine from the back of his trousers.

A huge smile dominated the damp, red face that had minutes before been distorted with crying. He cherished the intense satisfaction that had swept over him at finally delivering the parcel he had been hell bent on planting on Ian.

And now the person who had forever changed Dom's life, who had taken Donald's, was asking Dom to save his.

III

'*Tamu!*' The enormous guard shouted only one word and Ian looked up from the grubby book he was reading, scratched what looked like food off the page and stuck his garnished finger in his mouth. Tasteless.

On the other side of the bars, the low-ranking officer growled at having to tell the prisoner a visitor had come.

Ian understood the one-word message. But he had no reason to expect it was for him because Ruth had been to see him two days before. In a tone exclusive to the English-speaking inmates of Pudo prison, Ian discharged the tiresome guard.

'No. She came the day before yesterday.' He fanned himself with the book and wiped his head dry.

The part of the prison he was in had no air conditioning and the unbearable heat in the tiny cell, which he had to himself, saw him needing to take deep breaths to feel like he was getting even a hint of oxygen. Yet when he did inhale, the smells that the heat sent into his nose were rancid—so rancid he couldn't bring himself to breathe through his mouth for fear of puking. The stench of the stalest body odour and the freshest human shit clung to his nostrils. It had to be days since the men holed up next to him had touched running water.

'Up.' The guard signalled with a baton. 'Guest for you.'

Ian, who was shaking his shirt to cool himself down, let the book flop to his messy bed. He stepped to the door. It opened and he was directed out. As he padded along, the baton landed between his shoulder blades once he moved too far ahead of the guard, and the wham he got as negative reinforcement was enough to dislodge a rib.

Whenever he was being taken through the corridors, the second he hesitated in which direction to walk, the baton came down on to the corresponding shoulder of the direction he was meant to turn.

To minimise the work his shoulders received, he learnt to listen carefully for directions. But the pain he would suffer made remembering the left and right turns of the corridors difficult. The fact the location of his visits changed every time—he had last seen Ruth in another visitor area—made his task near impossible. He tried following the fresh air.

Shuffling along, he leaned left and the baton bit into his right shoulder. Ian lurched forward to the right and tripped, too weak to steady himself against the force of the beating.

A tirade of Malay rang out and after a couple of uncoordinated whacks, Ian was given time to get to his feet and walk unaided along a less stinky corridor to a solid steel door that led to the administration building.

The door wheeled open and the guard used his baton to launch Ian through a doorway to the right.

Inside there were two people. The prison guard, half-blocking the entrance into the dilapidated room, ignored Ian. The other person didn't. Ian recoiled in shock and he saw the Tolen twin do the same.

The howl Ian let out made both guards start. His uncontrollable yelling bounced off the brick walls and instinctively he pulled at the long hair his shaved head no longer sported. His legs couldn't move. A split second before they buckled, he crept to the table in the centre of the room, roaring tears, and found the vacant chair.

The first guard left closing the door behind him.

Dom sat still. He had been directed to stay on the other side of the warping table with its plastic surface dotted with thousands of cuts and slices, short lines that crisscrossed in every direction.

Ian's eyes couldn't meet Dom's burning glare. 'Thank you,' he repeated, making futile attempts to tidy himself. 'I'm sorry for what I've done.' His voice escalated into a whisper. 'I can't say it, but I'm sorry.'

'We don't have much time.'

'I'm so glad to see you.' He sniffed and wiped his nose with his forearm, leaving snot resting on his hairs.

'What happened the day you killed my brother?'

'They're pushing for the death penalty. They say it was a huge quantity. You must know how it got—'

'You will tell me what happened.' Dom's frustration was barely under control. 'You killed him—how? Why?'

Ian lifted his head, but his eyes stayed low. 'He had somehow discovered what I was doing, and it was so close to the payments going through, I just had to'—his eyes met Dom's for a split second—'stop him.' The concrete floor got his attention once again.

'I followed him outside. I was planning to trail him home and talk to him there, but he got stopped by the traffic lights. And I—pushed—' A couple of Ian's fingers twitched as though he was demonstrating the action. 'But I want to come back to Sydney to sort it out.'

'Why?' said Dom. The guard looked over at him. Dom leaned forward with a fake smile and spoke more softly. 'Why did you kill him? What happened in the office?'

'I saw that he was snooping around our large accounts—'

'The Cypress accounts.'

'Ye—es.' Ian paused, surprised at the detail the twin knew. 'He had printed off a report, which I found, and when I asked him about it at the office, he turned on me. He knew everything. I don't know how, but he knew.'

'And you killed him for that? You're vile.'

'Everything I'd done, he was jeopardising. He was odd. He scared me, his bravado about it all. We were days away from six huge payouts.' He looked down at his sweaty hands. 'Do you know about the—the money we—'

'The reason you thought he was acting strange was because it wasn't Dom. I'm Dom. That was my twin, Donald.'

Dom paused, thinking of ways to prove it. He lifted a hand.

'I worked with you on the Bells upgrade and we helped with the regional strategy after the second merger.'

'My god. How do you know that?' Ian's gaunt face was a stretch of surprise.

'Ian, I am Dominic, the guy you worked with for almost two years.' Dom took a deep breath for strength. 'The person you murdered was my twin.'

Ian's forehead creased. 'Impossible. How? I don't understand. I was with him. I watched him leave the office. I—I followed you.'

'It was him.'

Ian was like a statue in the chair, reviewing that afternoon, the day of the murder. His lips hardly budged as he spoke. 'You're Dominic?'

Dom nodded but Ian's confusion didn't ease.

'So I killed your brother?'

'Moron. Next question. What—'

Ian leant forward and cried into filthy hands, which clenched into fists as his tears of distress turned into moans of frustration. 'No!' he yelped, as though electricity was burning his insides. He curled himself up to the smallest Dom had ever seen him.

Dom carried on when Ian's cries had died down. 'What was Ruth doing at my house that day?'

Ian went to answer and cradled his stomach in agony. 'I'm not well.' He groaned.

'Hurry up.'

'Out on Clarence Street, in the—commotion, I was hoping to get his bag. The report had to be in there, but the bag was under—under him. So I walked away. We thought Ruth might get hold of it at your house and we had nothing to lose by following it up. I knew your brother lived there too and—'

Ian nodded to himself as the revelation sank in. A fragile finger pointed at Dom. 'So when she turned up, you knew instantly she was lying?'

'And you gave her one of Vanessa's business cards.'

'Fucking hell.'

'Where is she now?'

'She's here in KL. She'll be happy you're here. She visits every few days.'

'Where's she staying?'

'The Hilton. We're happy to pay you for your help. She can show you where my lawyer's office is.' Ian spluttered. 'I can't believe you're here. What a miracle. This place'—he looked over to the guard—'is hell.'

Dom lowered his voice and spoke without betraying his anger. 'I didn't come to help you. I'm here for some answers and I have them. I should be going.'

'Wait. What? I've just helped you.' The horror returned to Ian's face. 'Please. You can get your revenge back home. You'll see me pay in court.' He was leaning so far forward in the chair, its back legs came off the ground. 'You didn't come all this way just to—'

The muscles in Dom's face set and the humanity drained from his eyes.

Ian looked bewildered. 'Did you?' His eyes reddened and he started crying.

'Why would I help you? You're a trafficker.' Dom smiled the faintest smile ever. 'I can't confess to the package for you. That would cause me a much bigger headache legally. And besides, what makes you think I had anything to do with this?'

Ian whispered, 'I know it was you.' He shifted in the chair as though afraid to continue. 'I do.'

'How do you know?' Dom leaned in.

Ian looked at the guard, who was looking down.

'Tell me.'

'I know they were your drugs.'

'How can you be sure?'

'You were in the car boot.' Ian's eye shot to the guard.

'And?'

'When I came to get your phone, you saw the logo on my jacket and you laughed. It was *Snowtrap*. And you had set a trap for me with snow.' He pointed at Dom. 'It was your *snow*.'

Dom laughed aloud and leant back in the chair. 'I would love to see you giving that as evidence in a trial to save your neck. How desperate would you look? Unfortunately, I won't be here for all that. I'm going home.'

Ian's hand went up. 'Dom, I've got money.' He waited a moment to let Dom absorb his words. 'We have *millions*. Ruth has access to the lot. I'll give—'

'If I came to your place that night to plant something, I would've expected you to get stopped on the way out of Australia. It would never occur to me that you would evade customs as you left Sydney.' Dom relished the devastation that was drawing Ian's body closer to the ground.

'To find you facing the death penalty—that's a bonus. I wish I was that strong a soul not to enjoy your predicament, Ian. But I'm not.'

'Dominic, please. I know it won't look good for you. It'll mean a charge of possession, but you can save a life, and you'll never have to work again.'

'I don't have to work. I choose to lead an ordinary life. It's a good cover. I don't need your money. You have nothing for me.'

Ian looked confused. 'Cover?' He hunted for reasons to persuade Dom to act. 'Won't the guilt eat you up?'

Dom laughed again, which caused the guard to get up and circle them. Ian massaged his stomach and rocked forward. 'I guess not.' He started whimpering, and lowered his head to his forearm. 'Take it from me—having someone's death on your conscience is not somethi—'

'It's hardly the same. I won't be the one killing you. The Malaysian government will take care of that for me. But we're getting ahead of ourselves. It's not certain that you're going to die.' Dom smiled. 'Do they automatically kill drug traffickers? What did your lawyer say?' Dom laughed some more.

Ian closed his eyes as he tried to contain his despair. 'I can't live here forever. It's so oppressive. The building, the guards, the weather, the vicious thugs.' He sat back to open his airways, his chest jerking outwards so hard it looked as if something was knocking its way out. He lowered his sweat-beaded head to his forearm. There was no battle left in him.

They sat in silence. Dom guessed this would be his last look at Ian. He noticed his stark face, made all the more severe by the shaved head, the lines over his cheeks and the sunken eyes. Were they the effects of worry, when it becomes clear death is imminent?

Dom looked to the guard, who stood and grabbed Ian to help him up.

With a final burst of energy, Ian launched forward. 'Please Dominic. If you're worried about the charge and the police and all, we can pay someone off. You don't have a record, right? As a first offence, you won't even go to jail. It'll just be possession, won't it?'

As he was being pushed towards the door, Ian backed to the wall, sliding low, where he twisted his head to look beyond the guard, coming to meet Dom's cool stare.

'Be reasonable. What's the harm in the authorities knowing you're a user? You can save my life.'

Keeping his hands in his trouser pockets, Dom rounded the table and put his face as close to Ian's as he could without touching him. All three men were huddled near the doorway and Dom could hear the guard's raspy breathing and smell his tobacco breath.

'I don't take drugs. I value my health.'

Confused, Ian tried to hold Dom's gaze, but the guard shuffled him away.

'But you had all that—how—wh—what are you then?' He dared not blink, as he had to know. 'A seller? Or—or someone higher up?'

Ian caught the flicker in Dom's eyes. In shock, he coughed the words.

'You're a supplier.'

'This can't come out—you've got to sort it yourself.'

'No!' Ian crumbled at the guard's feet sobbing, the significance of what Dom had said demolishing him.

Dom could never own up to his part in placing the drugs in Ian's luggage. Ian alone would have to convince the Malay authorities of his innocence. His wails died out fast as he was escorted to his cell.

IV

The motorbike purring to a stop caught Dom's ear. He was pacing around his unit, having returned from Malaysia the day before. The afternoon was cold yet his brow glistened with sweat, even in the low lighting. A staff member from Brain Food, Dom's favoured jigsaw shop, had phoned not thirty minutes ago. The caller had said the puzzle would be arriving within the hour by courier, as Dom had asked. He didn't fancy collecting it from the shop this time.

The bell rang. Dom stole to the front door and peered through the spy hole. The shop's courier was dancing around fretfully. With lightning speed, Dom yanked open the front door, kicked the screen outwards—the young man stepped backwards—and Dom snatched the parcel from his gloved hand.

'Rita's pissed off with you. Like big time,' said the courier, holding out a black handset and its stylus for Dom to sign for the delivery.

'Fuck off, you piece of shit.' Dom made himself taller as though readying himself to kick the delivery unit over the balcony railing. The young man pulled it away but stood his ground.

Dom slammed the front door. From the other side, he heard the courier's parting comments. 'Rita wants you to phone her right now. You'd better call.'

Dom swore again. In the kitchen, he ripped open the packaging and pulled out the cellophane-wrapped jigsaw.

Down in the street, the courier's motorbike roared, as angry as its driver, and spun off in the direction of the shop.

Dom carried his delivery through to the bedroom and did what he always did. He sat on the bed, gave the box a light rattle, removed the cellophane and admired the cover photo. For sure, he would enjoy doing the puzzle soon enough. A deep calming breath stretched his lungs open and he removed the lid of the box and lifted out the contents.

As usual, inside were two bags. One was transparent, filled with a thousand green-backed jigsaw pieces and a smattering of green dust. After a light wobble in his palm, it was placed gently on the bed.

The other, brown and opaque, he handled even more carefully. It contained small bags of cocaine, which, over the next few days, would pass to Dom's network of dealers. Their job of sampling was critical to the quality of his supply business.

He sniffed the bag, checked it wasn't leaking and locked it away on the lower shelf of the safe.

The box he crushed, ready to dispose of. Along with the wrapping and the jigsaw, he took it through to the kitchen. He binned the packaging and dumped the puzzle on a side table.

He scratched his head in protest at the call he was about to make. The courier had verified Dom's concerns—Dom had done something to annoy Rita, the co-owner of Brain Food. She was not the type of person he wanted as an enemy.

Dom used his landline to call her. 'It's arrived,' he barked.

'Glad to hear it. Now what the hell is all this about a missing parcel? There's nothing missing, buster. You picked it up from here yourself.'

Gone was the usual sweetness that marked her voice machine messages. Now her voice boomed, accusatory.

'Something came up. I needed it elsewhere.' A picture of Ian's car boot flittered into his head.

'And payment for it? When can I expect that? I've got a shop to run.'

'You'll get it,' Dom snarled. 'When am I ever late? And your smartarse courier needs to watch his mouth.' Dom cut the air with a scissor hand. 'Rita, he is *way* too cocky. You've spoilt him and that is a danger. It means he doesn't know his boundaries.'

There was a pause where Rita should have spoken, which Dom tried to fill. 'Y—'

'What's this about you handing Phil to the police? He wasn't your dealer to give up. If you wanna talk boundaries, buster, let's talk.'

'So that's what this is about?'

Dom prodded his forehead. Weeks before, he had visited Phil's place on the pretence of buying drugs for Harry. In reality, he was tasked with checking if Phil would sell to a stranger—a favour for a friend.

'That moron is a fucking liability. He sold to whoever called him. He did walk-ins, for fuck sake. I've seen clothes shops with stricter policies.' Dom punched the air as he relived the anger that swept over him the night Harry had told him even he had managed to buy cocaine from Phil with nothing more than a phone call. Harry's disclosure had spurred Dom to take the axe to Donald's room.

No mistake—Phil was a danger.

A weed that needed pruning. *Pruning.*

Rita's huff down the phone pulled Dom from his thoughts. She said, 'From where I am, *you're* starting to look like a liability yourself, buster'—Rita liked that name for people—'so what should I do, huh?' There was silence for a couple of seconds as her threat hung between them. 'Huh?' she repeated, launching it down the phone line like a missile.

'Let me make a suggestion,' said Dom calmly. 'You sit tight and remember how fucking good I've been to you for the last few years, how loyal and how reliable. Correct—Phil wasn't mine to give away, but you don't get to hear everything I do at this end. And he was a major liability and he had to go—' He stopped.

Rita had hung up.

Dom kicked the table. 'Shithead.'

V

'He didn't *hit* me—he *walloped* me. I came to, tied up on the floor. I was terrified.'

Dom was about to continue when Cassandra knocked and entered Dympna's office. She handed the file to her boss and left, making every effort to ignore Dom.

It was the first time in a long while he found himself sitting in Dympna's suite and she commented on it when he had arrived.

'I notice you've been leaving it longer between visits.'

Dom was familiar with her questioning style. She could tease so much from someone without asking questions, just by offering an astute observation, innocently delivered, one that invited response.

Dom shrugged and attempted to match Dympna's style. 'You sound worried about that.'

'Of course, I am, Dominic. I worry whether you're doing well after everything that's gone on, and I enjoy seeing you anyway.'

Dom continued explaining the events of the night he tried to stop Ian and Ruth leaving Australia. The small lines in Dympna's forehead creased a bit more with each shocking scene Dom relayed.

She wanted to know why he hadn't gone to the police.

Dom shrugged and they let the talk dry up as they chewed almonds together, a sign their get-together was coming to an end.

She reached into a drawer.

Dom watched her take out a business card and do nothing with it except let it loiter in her fingertips as though it belonged there. He stared at it and her.

'You're tiring of the research. We both know it. And you've been like that for quite a while now.'

'That's an understatement. I'm absolutely fed up with it. The fun's gone out of it completely.' He pointed at the business card. 'If that's more research—twinless twin research or something—forget it.'

'Of course not. But you're aware of the label. Twinless twin. How does it sound?'

'It is what it is. I am what I am. I'm getting there.'

Dympna looked at the matt purple card.

'Well?' said Dom.

'They're a group for the surviving identical twin. You would benefit from their support and shared experiences.' She pushed the card midway across the desk and leaned back in her chair, allowing the computer to steal her attention. Clicking randomly at the screen, she played with her mouse.

The armchair Dom was in creaked from his wriggling. Then he inched a bit closer to the desk and raised a slow arm. With only a forefinger, he dragged the card, which was good quality, towards him until it came to the edge of the desk. Once he'd read the text, he sat back.

'They're out in the suburbs. That's an inconvenience.' His eyes locked with Dympna's.

'Those are merely the contact details written there. They meet all over Sydney, moving from house to house.' Dympna had clearly prepared for their chat.

Dom made a move to speak. Dympna cut in. 'I know what you're going to ask and no, you wouldn't have to. Not unless you wanted to.'

'My place wouldn't be right to host a meeting.'

'You wouldn't be hosting meetings straight away. You may not even like the group. Just test it out. Plus, you don't know how many people go to their get-togethers.'

'I bet you do.'

Dympna nodded and smiled. 'About a dozen and they meet monthly.' Bending forward, with a strong, polished nail, she rapped the desk. 'Take it with you and keep it in mind. Go to the website.'

He moved the card into his jacket pocket.

'Are you working again?'

Dom nodded. 'Not yet. And I'm feeling it.' His head fell into his hands and he massaged his scalp. 'I miss my job at Subiaco. I had a stable life, which Donald was a big part of. The role was easy. It was comfortable.' Dom gnawed at his bottom lip. 'It provided the counter balance to my shadow.'

Dympna's eyes widened. 'Ah, your shadow. Tell me about that.'

Dom raised his head. 'They're the parts of me I like less. Without Donald and without the Subiaco job, those darker parts are overwhelming. That's all I'm saying. I don't want to talk about it now.'

'What can you do to reintroduce symmetry in your life?'

Dom puffed out. 'Perhaps a move is what I need. Interstate or international. Asia.'

Dympna's mouth curved down. 'Interstate—I can handle, Dominic. But an international move would be too sad for me. And besides, it's too dangerous overseas for Australians.' She tapped the newspaper by her side. 'Another Australian woman found dead in her hotel.'

'Where?'

'Malaysia, I think. Or Singapore.'

'Don't worry. It's likely to be interstate, if it happens. Although, a move overseas would mean I could better hide from Ian Read. His lawyers are still bugging me to help their case.'

'How?'

'Apparently, my testimony can weaken the prosecution by suggesting there was plenty of time for someone to tamper with his bag. I've had phone calls and letters.'

'That sounds very suspicious. Please steer clear of all that. One minute, you're helping someone and the next, they'll be pinning it on you.'

'The nerve of some people,' said Dom, shaking his head.

'Total desperation, I suppose,' said Dympna.

Dom's head bobbed up and down with measure as he agreed. 'Believe me, you could certainly understand that desperation. It was an awful place that prison. And Ian, I barely recognised. He looked shocking.'

'And would you sell your beautiful home?'

'No. I'll keep it empty while I decide what to do, whether to stay away from Sydney for the long term.'

'It's enormous for one person. Fill it with a family. Or get something smaller.' Dympna glanced at her wall clock. 'My next appointment will be here soon, and I'd rather you didn't see her. Or rather, that she didn't see you.'

'What?'

'It's the client you burst in on that day. She returned after all.' She saw the surprise on Dom's face. 'Yes, I'm that good.'

He smacked his thighs. 'Well, there's some good news at least—the client coming back to you.'

Dympna strode to the door collecting a tan bolero from a coat stand. With a moisturised hand on the door, she paused to free hair from her collar while Dom stood up.

'What do you know about the woman you almost killed?' Her voice was neutral, but Dom's eyes squinted at the mention.

He shook his head. 'I was thinking of sending her flowers or something.'

She swung open her door and peeked outside. 'Any sign of Gwen yet, Cassandra?'

Sitting upright at reception, her assistant shook her head without removing her eyes from the gigantic screen.

Dympna turned round to face Dom and lowered her voice. 'Or you could send her some surgical staples for her jaw.' She waved him out. 'Go.'

Dom went to protest but changed his mind when he saw her sharp eyebrows arch, almost daring him to reprimand her. He trudged by pausing for a goodbye kiss on the cheek.

VI

Two days after catching up with Dympna, Dom was still unsure of his plans—whether to stay in Sydney or escape to another capital.

The morning had been overcast so he had settled onto the sofa, unshowered and undressed, to google the cities he was considering, Hobart and Perth. A cool breeze flooded the unit, shaking the plants.

When his search reminded him Perth had a suburb called Subiaco, he fixed on Hobart. Forty minutes later, he was still keen on going there, especially after finding out it was the only Australian capital with snowfall. He had been once years ago. It was time to revisit Tasmania. Harry had family there, so Dom was sure he would approve.

Through the window, he glimpsed the sky was clearing and the street was filled with soft sunlight. He would miss this area. But he would be back.

He picked up his business mobile phone and began deleting numbers one at a time. He scrolled, he debated what to do with each number, he deleted or kept it, and he scrolled some more.

This clean-up was interrupted by his personal mobile ringing, with Robin reporting she would be at his within ten minutes. Dom tottered to his room to hide his second phone and when he returned, he pulled cans of soft drink from the fridge.

Robin arrived with a salad of plastic bags. Casually dressed, she bustled in and deposited everything on the table and carried on a conversation she'd been having in her own head while Dom handed her a drink. 'I've accepted the fact Lorna will be studying in Melbourne. But she'll be with Drew and I'm ok with that too.'

Dom walked to her with his eyes stretched as wide as possible, only blinking once Robin caught his expression. They tipped cans.

'That's a change. It's great, but it's still a big change.'

Robin nodded. 'There's been too much loss recently, way too much fighting.'

Dom locked her in his arms. 'Good for you. Drew's a lovely girl. Lorna will be very happy with her.'

Robin wagged her head against his chest. 'Donald never told Camille that Lorna had come out. She still doesn't know. I'll tell her soon.'

'Didn't he? I thought she knew.'

'And you?' she asked. 'Have you spoken to her yet?'

'She's avoiding me. I think once the police close Donald's case with Ian, we'll chat. Until then, I'll leave her alone.' Dom pointed at Robin's bags. 'What's this?'

Robin fiddled with them. 'It's sports clothes for Niamh in there—she's getting into her athletics—and this is a cake. For you. I thought you could use a treat.'

Dom thanked her and peeked inside the plastic tub. Chocolate. His favourite.

Robin opened her handbag and took out something small. 'This is yours. I think Niamh picked it up by mistake.'

Dom held out a hand. It was a jigsaw piece showing part of a mosaic, one he recognised straight away.

'The little devil,' he said grasping it tight, casting his mind back to when his niece had been there. He changed topic. 'I'm thinking of moving to Hobart for a while.' A swig of drink kept him busy while he waited for Robin's response to the news.

'The traveller travels again.' She amassed her bags. 'Hobart? You'll be close to the girls in Melbourne—you can visit them.'

Dom smiled. 'That's what I was thinking.'

Six weeks earlier

In the open-plan kitchen, Donald filled a water bottle. He leaned back against the counter, as though taking a breather after a tough day of work. He looked out to Dom's workspace, to Dom's colleagues whose heads appeared over the partitions. He wondered when he would be there again or if he would even make it back. Perhaps his plan was too grandiose.

The only visible clock was hiding right above his head. It was twenty-five to five. Almost time to leave.

Footsteps approached.

'There you are, Dominic. Can we have a quick chat?'

A tall man in a suit, who Donald hadn't seen before, had stopped on the carpet close to him. He had a worried look on his flushed face and he was carrying a document, which he clasped to his thigh as if shielding its contents. 'This way.'

'What's up?' Donald didn't move.

'What have you been doing in the Cypress accounts? I thought we agreed you'd pass that on to me.' He wiped his forehead. 'W—we agreed.'

Donald guessed this could be the guy he had texted Dom about.

Ian. He must have been monitoring access to those accounts. And all of the day's work had flashed up somewhere. Shit.

'Oh that. I went in to check some figures'—he plucked details from nowhere—'one of the managers asked me to. It turns out I was in the wrong place.'

Donald stepped back to signal the chat was over but Ian hooked his sleeve, shaking the report at him.

'So why do I find this on your desk?' He looked around nervously and choked out the words. 'You printed this *today*. What's going on?' Ian passed a dry tongue over drier lips.

Donald snatched the report from him. His neck stretched to look at him directly. 'Did you hear me? One of the managers—'

'Bullshit,' said Ian. 'Who? No one goes into these accounts. No one.' He lunged at the document but Donald held it high behind him, as if aggravating a younger sibling. 'You've been very busy, haven't you?'

'What are you insinuating?' Ian's hands went to his hips and he nodded grey hair off his face.

'Nothing. But this will *all* have to wait until tomorrow. I have to go now.'

Donald shifted his body sideways to brush past Ian. He picked up the pace as he returned to Dom's desk.

When he turned around, Ian wasn't there. Donald decided it was best if he left Subiaco right then. He worked swiftly, closing down the computer, bagging his things and putting on his jacket, and guarding the report that had rattled Ian so.

A detour to the printing area was in order. He searched for the equipment he had seen that morning, keeping an eye out for Ian as he all but tiptoed about. A film of paper dust covered the shredder, which sat next to the printer that had churned out the blasted report glued to his hand.

The top left corner where the staple pinched the sheets came off easily and he rammed the pages into the mouth of the machine. The teeth started grinding automatically. Donald kept watch as the shredder ate. He let out a huff of relief. One less piece of evidence.

With Dom's bag hanging from his shoulder, he headed for the safety of Clarence Street.

The end